VANISHED
TIDES OF DESTINY

MORGAN VELA

CONTENTS

Preface   xv

1. Tactics of War and Love   1
2. The Fates   22
3. Nightshade   45
4. Serfier   66
5. Calm Before the Storm   91
6. Tempting the Odds   115
7. Stowing Chaos   150
8. Battle of the Euresians   170
9. Darkness Ascending   181
10. Into the Deep   186
11. Rise of the Tides   222
12. Alliances   251
13. Treading Fire   274
14. A Rising Star   305
15. Whispers of the Past   333
16. The Darkest Tempest   363
17. Ties that Bind   404
Becoming Chaos   411

Acknowledgments   431
About the Author   433
Also by Morgan Vela   435
Stay Connected   437

"I'm trying..."

"I'm trying to fight this madness—this consuming desire to have you."

"I can't explain this irrational need to drown myself in you. I can't stand to see you pull away every time, fighting against the tide. Wanting to be with him..."

*"I'm trying to stow the storm, believe me, but I am desperately
fighting not to drown in the process."*

UPHERYA
HESTIAN CLAN
The Windless Cliffs
Aviscal Fjord
Planes Of Ishtar
Hills Of Tirsia
EURESIAN CLAN
ASTREAN CLAN
BOREAN CLAN
OUTER LANDS
Falls Of Whispers
Bay Of Turdia
Mountains Of Volten
Hereter Isles
Burning Forests
Dalgamur Seafront
TEMPLE OF THE ELDERS
DRULESKA

ABRYAS
THE FOUR REALMS
Graveyard Of The Gods
Grettos Cave
Shores Of Galnora
Shores Of Galnora
Shores Of Galnora
III
RUINS OF THE LOST
Sea Of Varenver
GLACIER PEAKS
Zodrox
SERFIER
N
W
E
S

PREFACE

Beyond my knowledge will be your gifts but know that only in death will you discover your truest self.

Bonded through blood, water, and soul, together as one we shall be...

Isabel Adams Cromwell

I

TACTICS OF WAR AND LOVE

A S AN IMMORTAL, I NEVER FEARED TIME AND THE *ABSENCE OF SUCH WORRY* was liberating. No fears, no expectations, but that peace was a whisper of the past, and that tranquility had long since vanished. The instant Callix disappeared through that portal with her, he robbed me of my sanity—my reasoning, which was now gone. Adrift under the Sea of Varenver. Deep into the depths of the Water Realm.

Nothing really mattered anymore. Not without her by my side. Not while I was deprived of knowing if she was alive or dead or if I would ever see her again.

Slowly, the hours turned to days, days which pooled into weeks and then months. And still, there was no news. No word from Callix...

I often placated the desperation, reminding myself that no news was better than the alternative...learning that she was gone, and that we had both failed to save her. But just as often, different thoughts entered my mind—darker, vile thoughts that only taunted the monster clawing inside of me. Callix's provoking words and images of the two of them succumbing to their desires.

I paced about the leaders' meeting room and then out onto the open deck overlooking the fogged city below, sleeping still beneath the morning mountain mist. Getting the warriors to agree on something was hard enough with a clear head, even less so with my judgment lost to darker thoughts.

"Drake..." Euros called, marching into the hall. He poured himself a cup of wine, extending the decanter in my direction. I declined with a firm nod.

"I think we all need a clear head," I said as the warrior drowned the liquid in one draw and then slumped into his chair, running his hands across his face. Although sleep wasn't required for immortals, unlike the fire people, the air realm adapted to the old customs, and it appeared the lack of sleep was beginning to affect them. Although, that wasn't the only reason for their despair. They had watched the darkness shred apart their Realm and slaughter their people. They must feel helpless, a feeling I shared, too.

"Will Link be joining us? How is he holding up?" I asked. Euros braced his forearms on the tabletop, where their clan names were intricately carved into the stone.

"Nothing will keep Link from fighting. Though he is the youngest of us all, he is perhaps the wisest. I don't know if I could accept the loss of my clan like he has. Thinking about it just..."

"We will defeat Dagasti." I spat the words clipped one by

one from my lips like knives. Euros glanced at me, and for the first time since arriving in Upherya, the warrior looked defeated.

"There was a time when I thought we could, but seeing my world shrivel under darkness, watching that monster's creation clear our valleys and take our people... I don't know if I believe victory is possible. Not for us."

Euros only dared admit this to me, not his brothers. The warrior I had come to know would never show weakness or defeat, not with Link and Phoenix looking up to him. Even though they made decisions as a group, it didn't take me long to realize whose trust I had to earn when I first arrived here.

I took the wine bottle and refilled his cup. He certainly needed it. Once I returned the bottle to its place, I stared at Euros with a firm gaze.

"This war is not lost. Not as long as we breathe or have the strength to fight. Giving up now and claiming defeat will not give your people back what they have lost. So, you will drink that cup and pull yourself together. Especially for your brothers. If you give up now, then everything will be lost indeed."

The man drowned the wine in one draw and struck the cup against the table with resolution.

"Who would have thought I'd be listening to you when it was your mate who placed us all in this predicament to begin with?"

My fists clenched at my sides.

"If you truly blamed us, you would have never allowed me and my people to fight by your side. If you truly thought I was your enemy, you wouldn't be here admitting your darkest fears to me. Belynda did what she did to save me, even against my advice and her better judgment. But I cannot blame her. I would have done the same for her, no matter the cost. I would have unleashed this army if the alternative was I could save her."

Euros stood, his chair scraping across the stone floor. He strolled across the room and came to stand before me.

"I must admit, I did blame you at the beginning, but I don't know that I would have done anything differently if I were faced with the same choice. If it were one of my own and their life was in my hands..."

I nodded. That was as much of an apology as I could expect from him. I cared little about whether he believed us innocent, but it did make our stay here—and our formed alliance easier—if we managed to trust each other.

He walked to the open promenade, and I followed. Fueled by magic, the mountain range rose like a wall, emerging after the rising sun.

"Do you truly believe Dagasti's army won't attempt to cross the mountains?" I asked, glancing at Euros.

"I would bet my life on it. The Hills of Tirsia are protected by ancient powers—magic we can't even begin to understand. We've seen the Darklings turn from their borders. If we could yield whatever power shields our mountains, we could use it to guard the borders... but luck is not on our side. That is why we've sent our women and children there for safety, but it is Phoenix's clan I'm worried about. Dagasti's only move is to march his army to the East. The only things standing between the darkness and us are those mountains and Phoenix's clan."

"Why not move all of your people to the mountains then?" I asked.

Euros' brow furrowed as he glanced at me.

"We will not offer this Realm to Dagasti freely. We will fight to protect it until the end. It's like you said, not as long as we breathe and have the strength."

I offered him my hand. "Till death," I vowed.

"Till death." Euros declared, firmly shaking my hand.

"What did we miss?" asked Phoenix, entering the round chamber. Link followed like a silent shadow, and I didn't have to read his mind to know he fought an internal battle now plagued by guilt. These warriors were trained to fight to the death, not to cower or run in fear. Link could not forgive himself for surviving when so many of his men had died, with the others taken by the darkness. If Phoenix had not knocked him out cold and ordered me to fly him out of the West Valley battle, he wouldn't be standing here now.

"Nothing. We were waiting for you, actually." Euros fortified himself, donning the face of armor he so often wore in the presence of the other leaders.

"Shall we?" Euros took his chair, and Phoenix and Link followed. I didn't dare take the last empty chair. It was an honor reserved for clan leaders and clan leaders only. The empty seat honored the memory of the Borean leader. Their lost brother.

I brought the map and flattened it before them. Resting my fists against the stone table, I stared at the warriors.

"I scouted the trail of the valleys a few hours ago. The army is divided." I pointed to the lower lands of Upherya. "Dagasti has ordered half of the Darklings back to the South towards the borderlines. I'm afraid the rest continues to march East." I glanced at Phoenix, for we knew their aim: to overtake the Euresians.

"What reason would Dagasti have to separate his army? It makes no sense?" asked Link. I regarded the young warrior with respect. Few could bear witness to the loss of their people and still find the strength to stand here, keeping a cool head.

"That's what we need to figure out. Perhaps Dagasti's plan is to return to Druleska to grow his army."

"I feel like that is precisely what he intends," muttered Euros, "but not by going to Druleska. He means to cross the Fjord."

"Why would he risk separating his army now when he knows Herod has prevented the Darklings from breaking the magic barriers across his shores?" I paced around the table, trying to understand the reasonings behind the monster's cunning mind.

"Perhaps he's found a way to breach Abryas," Phoenix offered, but it made no sense. Even if Dagasti had figured out a way to cross the barriers, why would he want to rush into Abryas with half of his army?

"We know Dagasti will not be satisfied with Upherya, so yes. It is a given he intends to cross into Abryas. His first attempt to breach it didn't stand, so we can assume he plans to try again. But the question is, why now? His aim has always been to sweep across Upherya, so what are we failing to see?"

"Let's think like Dagasti for a moment. What has driven him from the start?" asked Link.

"Power. He wants to take over all the realms," said Phoenix.

"Precisely!" I said. "And if our army had succeeded thus

far, claiming both the Southern and Western territories, why would we split our men when the strategic move would be to claim the East, border the mountains, and take the North?"

A deep frown settled within Phoenix and Euro's brows.

"Perhaps Dagasti has grown too confident. He must think claiming the East won't be a challenge," added Phoenix.

"I wouldn't doubt it, and if that's the case, his oversight might earn us some advantage."

Everyone nodded. This could tilt the scale in our favor for once.

"If that's the case, let's not make the same mistake Dagasti has. We must focus on what we don't know..." said Euros. "We need to follow the army that marches to the borderlines as figuring out Dagasti's plan is just as vital as guarding our borders. We cannot afford any surprises." The warrior's agreement was unanimous. Euros was right. We couldn't afford to weaken our guard. Dagasti was no fool, and not knowing what he was up to made my skin prickle.

"I will patrol tonight and report back. It looks like you could all use some sleep," I said.

"I will accompany you," said Euros. I accepted with a firm nod. There was no point in protesting; he wouldn't change his mind, or take the time to sleep, at least not until we discovered Dagasti's plan.

EUROS

The village had yet to wake, but I knew Amirth was up. I recognized the sound of metal clashing in the distance; it could be no other. The girl was relentless—a truly worthy adversary, though I would never dare to admit it, at least not to her. She was as skilled as she was infuriating. A true child of the Earth, which was perhaps why we often disagreed.

I tried to pass the training Forge unnoticed, but I knew I was unsuccessful the second the echoes of clashing metal stopped.

"What's got your panties in a notch? Didn't get laid last night?"

I rocked on my heel and bit my tongue before turning to face the demon girl.

"If you must know, I had the pleasure of two last night. Perhaps you should try it; it might help improve your aim." I jabbed, smiling. I was pleased to watch her anger flourish, but I braced myself, knowing her tongue was as poisonous as a snake's.

A dagger flew, landing inches from my ear. I balked, plucking the silver blade from the wooden post behind me and turning with narrowed eyes to face her.

Her eyes widened to the size of saucers as I strolled towards her with determination. The sword fell from her hands as I secured her wrists against the wall above her head, trapping her body with mine.

"Do you have a death wish, woman?" I whispered, anger seeping from every pore in my body. She had clearly lost her mind, and I was not in the mood to be trifled with.

Amirth pushed against me, and I eased away before releasing her hands.

"I was merely stating a point," she stated, her eyes burning into me.

"And what point was that exactly?" I hovered above the earth demon, who was set on claiming my soul if I allowed it.

"That there's absolutely nothing wrong with my aim," she declared, and I could not keep from laughing.

"You missed, so it seems you proved *my* point. Don't you agree?" I grinned, and Amirth's scowl deepened. "You better sharpen that aim. Here." I pulled her dagger from my back pocket and returned it to her. "Keep at it. Practice makes perfect." With a wink, I strolled out of the Forge before she could bite back—or worse. If I stayed a second longer, I had no doubt she'd make me eat my words. I grinned to myself, and with a start, I realized it was the first time I had smiled in weeks.

"You're in better spirits, I see." Drake materialized, as if appearing from thin air. I scowled; he knew I detested the stealthy way in which he travelled, but he had never once tried to alter his habit for my benefit. In the short time we had fought side by side, I had come to know the Dragon Prince, and one thing I had learned was his character was as sharp and unbending as the steel of his Dragon claws. Something I had come to respect and appreciate on the battlefield.

"Perhaps your keen eyes are failing you."

"You forget it's not just my eyes that are sharp, but my ears, too."

"Yes, how could I ever forget..."

"If Amirth is becoming a problem, you must tell me," said Drake. "I am responsible for the girl."

"I don't think she would appreciate hearing you say that," I added, having witnessed her temper. Drake grinned.

"Be that as it may." Drake peered across the dusk-painted

skies with a frown. "I know they can take care of themselves, but I still feel responsible for bringing them here. Even if it was their choice."

"I understand, but I promise she is no problem. She's just a thorn in my side at times."

"Good. But if I might offer my opinion..." I turned to the Dragon Prince, bemused. "Don't tease her. While I might feel responsible for her, I won't be held accountable if next time she does draw blood to prove her point."

I laughed.

"Thank you. I will heed your warning, although I feel I would welcome the challenge..." I confessed, and Drake frowned.

"That's exactly what I'm afraid of..."

We marched through the now-sleeping city towards the edge of the mountains.

"How are you holding up?" I dared to ask, knowing how private Drake was.

"I'm existing. Breathing. Waiting..." His pain didn't surprise me—it was the one thing he could not hide—but the honesty with which he shared his darkest emotions did. It meant he trusted me, and that was a privilege not easily earned.

"I don't presume to know how the Fates work, but magic can be a complex affair, especially when interfering with the balance of life and death. Such an endeavor might take time. Besides, you know the flow of time is different in Serfier."

"Yes, that is all I have to hang on to for now. Hope."

"That *is* all we have." I conceded. Hope was precisely what every son and daughter of Upherya clung to now.

"Has your mother sent word? Or said when she's expected to return?" asked Euros.

"She will remain in Abryas for now. She thinks the invitation of the Queen to stay in Abryas will work to our advantage."

"Your mother is a wise woman. I trust her judgment. But I hold my reservations where Herod is concerned. This is a truce neither side would have chosen."

"Indeed, but the unification of the Realms is necessary. Retrieving his ships and his men from your shores was an act of good faith, and I believe he will make good on his promises."

"I hope so. For all our sakes. Now, let's track some Darklings."

DRAKE

I envied the ease with which Euros wielded his element. One draw from the Winds of Tirsia, and his golden feathers materialized, glinting off the warrior's back. He sprung into the night sky as I removed the last vestiges of my clothing before allowing the fire to claim me.

We flew, side by side, soaring across the hills and the upper lands of the East clan, trying to avoid the Windless Cliffs. No amount of magic could enable a single person to fly over that domain.

We were forced to dive close to the water's surface as we reached the Fjord and left Upherya's guarded territory. I trailed behind Euros, lost in the shadows of our reflections in the water. Belynda invaded my thoughts, and I fought against the need to divert our mission across the bay and plunge into Callix's territory. I resisted, but only because I knew that was a battle I could never win. Not against the ocean.

Our plan was to veer West before reaching the bay and cross between the outer lands and what remained of the southern region, but when I spotted the army in the far distance, I took a sharp dive, and Euros followed.

While we expected to find the broken branch of Dagasti's army approaching the borderlands, we thought they'd be much closer to the West. We had clearly underestimated their advance.

Euros glided above my right flank, and I noticed his resolve. He dove. Plunging towards the trees behind the valley, Euros headed to where the Darklings marched. He had a death wish, but regardless, I followed. He touched the ground, and I eased my landing. Euros tucked his wings behind his back, but I didn't change. It was too risky.

I growled, and he turned to face me.

"I know. Stay here," he said, but I extended my left wing, blocking his path. He glared at me.

"Seriously? Remove yourself. That is an order." He was a bigger fool than I thought if he expected me to step back, allowing him to risk everything we had fought for. His brothers would never forgive me if I did—a part of me wouldn't forgive myself, either. I didn't move. As a warning, the monster bared its teeth, wrapping the warrior in a breath of smoke.

"Fine. Let's use the cover of the cloud banks. We will trail from a distance." Euros stepped back, uncurling his wings as he disappeared between the foliage.

It didn't take us long to figure out what the Darkling soldiers were up to. They laid most of the trees of the bordering forests to waste. The army worked resiliently to build a fleet. Euros was right. They planned to cross the Fjord. We had to warn Herod. Dagasti would only pursue such lengths if he had a way to breach Abryas' defenses.

We reached the Hills of Tirsia, still under the blanket of night. Euros didn't stop, zooming straight through the mountains' mist to the round chamber. He was furious, but he would get over it. He could thank me later. Slipping on my clothes, I streaked through the sleeping town and up the hills to the mountain peak, where the clan leaders gathered. Euros was already there, standing at the edge of the open terrace, a cup of wine in his hand. I entered and marched to his side, but he didn't turn.

"We have welcomed you. We have entrusted you with our lives, but by no means are you bound to remain here if you do not wish to. However, you will not defy my command again. Do you understand?" He turned to face me. "Do you understand?"

I marched to the very edge of the polished floors and paused at the precipice, which ended in an abysmal plunge into darkness. I took a deep breath, inviting the purest air into my lungs before turning to the warrior.

"Perhaps my benevolence has made you forget who you're speaking to," I said with premeditated ease. "I am not your subject to command. You will show *me* the respect I deserve." Darkness seeped from my mouth with each word. "I have come to trust you and your people. I even glimpsed the beginnings of a friendship between us, but I will not bow down to anyone. You viewed my actions tonight as defiance when it was a mere extension of kindness. I could have allowed you to place yourself in danger, but instead, I chose to stop you for the sake of your brothers and your people—for your own sake, too. Believe me, the monster wouldn't hesitate. So, next time you think to come at me, I suggest you think twice, for I am not your enemy."

I strolled past him and into the room's shelter.

"Thank you." Euros' subtle apology made me pause. "You're right, and I don't often admit that." He conceded. I paused, turning to stare at the warrior.

"I think we should leave for Abryas at first light," I suggested.

"Yes. I will speak with Link and Phoenix."

I acknowledged Euros with a firm nod, and he returned the gesture. It appeared we had both said enough for one day. As I streaked through the mountain mist, only one thing was for certain. Euros would never underestimate me again.

MORNING BROKE over the horizon as Link, Phoenix, Euros, and I flew across the Shores of Galnora. We landed near the bordering woods that neighbored Grettos Cave, where the Elvin posted closest to the castle protected the borders. They would send news of our arrival to Herod and allow us passage.

The woods appeared endless before us, and though the magic shields were invisible, I knew they were there. They were poisonous to Darklings, humans, and immortal creatures alike.

I lifted my head, breathing in the winds coming from the North.

"They've detected us. The golden army is approaching."

Phoenix picked a small stone from the ground and tossed it to the distant forest line. As expected, the stone flew through the invisible shield, but the poisonous magic hissed in ripples where the rock hit the invisible barrier.

Phoenix retrieved another stone, but I held his arm before he could throw it.

"Don't forget that we are uninvited visitors here. Let's behave."

Phoenix smiled and reluctantly dropped the stone.

"We are doing them a favor by coming," said Phoenix, motioning with his head to where the line of Elven soldiers emerged from behind me beneath the shade of the trees. Their golden armor glinted under the filtering rays of the morning sun.

"Who are you? Speak your business."

"You raided our borders and shores long enough to know damn well who we are!" Phoenix retorted. Euros glared at him, a warning to keep his mouth shut.

The golden regiment assumed a defensive stance, and the warriors beside me reacted.

"Stand down!" I stared directly at Euros, for I knew his brothers would follow his lead.

"State your names and your business in Abryas!" demanded the leader of the golden company. His eyes glowed, and by his side, he flexed his fingers—a subtle gesture, if not for the gentle ripples across the ground. They were pushing the barriers of the field towards us.

"Stop," I said, and the Elven leader dropped his hands, and with it, the movement of the barrier ceased. "We came on urgent business to see King Herod. These are the clan leaders of Upherya."

"We are not aware of an invitation." The Elvin commander raised his hands, and once again, the wall moved inch by inch to where we stood.

"There is no time. My mother is a guest of Queen Leiwen! Just have your men send a whisper, and your King will receive us." The barriers stopped advancing once more, and the commander turned and instructed two of his men. They disappeared into the forest, hopefully to deliver the message. The Elvin relied on the magic of the trees to communicate their messages; they called them whispers.

"We await the castle's orders," said the commander.

"Remind me why we're doing this again?" Phoenix muttered, but no one said a word. He needed no encouragement.

One of the guards returned twenty minutes later with an answer. The commander turned towards the invisible wall, and as he parted his hands, the barrier opened like a giant curtain.

"You may enter," said the Commander, who looked no more than twenty. But I knew that was an illusion of the Elvin people. They emulated *youth*. Most chose to never age, but as the boy held a senior position, he must have been much older than his peers. Perhaps as old as me.

The poisonous mist closed behind us, and the Elvin commander bowed his head.

"My apologies. We must always be careful. I have orders to accompany you to the castle gates, where King Herod will receive you."

WE WERE NOT ALLOWED to shift. The barriers erected around and above Abryas formed a protective dome that forbade such transformations. We rode fast to the north without much rest. It took two days until the lush green hills surrounding the Elvin city and castle came into view.

The ornate golden gates into the city limits opened at the commander's request, and we rode through until reaching the heart of the city to the castle gates.

As we dismounted from the horses, the young commander stiffened.

"My Queen," said the soldier, who fell to his knees before Leiwen.

"Thank you, commander." Leiwen offered kindly.

"It is an honor, my lady."

Rising, the young soldier gathered the horses.

"Welcome. We are honored to have you," said the young Queen, beholding me and the three-clan leaders with a smile. "Your mother will join us momentarily. I'm afraid Herod is occupied, but he will receive you soon."

"Thank you for taking us in without notice. We wouldn't be here if we didn't think it was urgent," I said.

"Of course. You are always welcome in Abryas." Leiwen offered, though I wasn't sure if the King would agree with such an invitation. He seemed to be the one with reservations about forming alliances with Upherya. Leiwen, on the other hand, was their champion.

"Thank you," said Euros.

I was sure the warriors had noticed, too. It appeared she was the only Elvin in this kingdom whom they respected.

"Come. You must be tired." The warriors followed Queen Leiwen, but I stayed behind as my mother descended the stairs.

"My son," she said warmly, kissing my cheek. "I've missed you."

"So, have I." I smiled, pleased to see her. "I received your message. How long will you remain here?"

"For as long as the invitation stands. I'm safe here."

"Yes, I know. I wouldn't allow you to remain if you were not."

"What has happened to you?" She noted. I pulled her hand from my cheek and kissed her knuckles. I offered a smile to try and ease her worried expression.

"I'm fine. I promise."

"You can lie to others; you can even lie to yourself, but you cannot fool your own mother."

I sighed, and, arm in arm, we began walking through the gardens. "I take it there has been no news?" she asked as we reached the fountains.

"Nothing but silence. I swear if I had Callix before me now, I would strangle him with my bare hands." Mother placed her hand over my clenched fists.

"Just because Serfier is connected to the Fates, it doesn't mean they do Callix's bidding."

"I know." I paced about the spring, and my mother followed.

"I have faith that Belynda will be alright. We would have heard from him by now if it wasn't so. I'm sure of it."

"It doesn't make it any easier." I stared, losing myself in the falling water. "I should have never kept that promise to her. If I hadn't, she would be here now."

"But *you* wouldn't!"

"I much prefer that alternative."

She gripped my shoulder.

"Never say that. I couldn't bear it. Without your help, Upherya would have been lost long ago."

"You think I care about Upherya or Abryas?"

"You should!" she admonished. "If the Realms fall under darkness—if Dagasti wins—there will be no place for her or you. It will no longer matter if she lives or dies."

I cringed at the truth in my mother's words.

"Please. I need to be alone, mother."

I stared at the waters, yet all I saw was Callix. Taunting me. The monster took the bait and lines of black sand danced around my fists.

"Drake... this isn't you," my mother whispered before squeezing my shoulder and walking away.

I flexed my hands, easing the darkness on my skin, but the monster craved retribution.

It will no longer matter if she lives or dies... My mother's words bit into my soul.

If you insist... I will take her. I rammed my fist into one of the stone statues as Callix's words echoed in my head.

"You made me promise! Now fight, damn you! Why won't

you come back?" I stared at my reflection on the water's surface and prayed to the Fates or to any God listening. "I will give anything to have her back. My life, my soul. Just take it."

CALLIX

I will give anything to have her back. My life, my soul. Just take it.

I moved my fingers across the still water of the large basin in my chamber, and with every ripple, Drake's haunted image morphed and changed.

"You and I both…" I sighed, resting my hands against the marble basin.

"Sire. You called?" I glanced at the nymph who entered.

"How is she?"

"No change, Sire." I clenched my fists. Belynda should have awoken by now. It shouldn't have taken this long.

My footsteps thundered against the marble floors as my mind stormed. These crystal halls had lost its light in recent months, and it was something the nymphs had noticed, too. They thought I failed to notice when they darted at the sight of me, though I didn't blame them. The silence engulfing the castle was haunting. It was almost like it had been placed under some spell, yet it was all because of her, and because of me. Because of the storm everyone felt brewing inside of me.

I descended the stone steps into the caves, where its iridescent walls illuminated the faces of the sea witches, who stopped their prayers and left the chamber at my command.

Step by step, I plunged into the stone-carved well where her body rested, floating above the water like a sleeping goddess, the tendrils of her golden hair glowing.

The blue radiant water moved around my waist as I reached hesitantly to stroke the moist skin of her cheek. I glanced at her pale lips and withdrew my hand. I allowed myself only that much without disturbing the process. However long that might be.

2

THE FATES

MY BODY DRIFTED, DRAPED IN AN ENDLESS BLANKET OF DARKNESS. I floated within the water, surrendering to its soothing lullaby. Nothing else existed. Only stillness. Death welcomed me, and I surrendered to its calling.

The shimmering light probed my senses. *Belynda...* my mother's voice whispered in my mind. *Belynda...* my name echoed again, except this time it was Isabel who murmured my name.

I'm dead. That's all I could think, and as the soothing darkness lifted, the light reached for me. I raised my hands to it, fighting against its blinding radiance while allowing my eyes to adjust.

A stream flowed gently beneath my ankles. Wildflowers danced on the riverbanks, rustled by the subtle gusts of wind. I was in heaven, and the angels smiled down upon me.

Atop a great pillar of rock, where water cascaded, three

women sat in dresses, their long tendrils of braided hair resting upon their shimmering skin.

They sang in unison a soulful tune. A siren's call.

"Beautiful…" I whispered, opening my eyes as the song ended.

"I sing of the things that were…" sung the youngest.

"I sing of the things that are," whispered the woman in the middle.

"I sing of the things that are to be," added the oldest of the angels with long silver hair.

"Who are you? Am I dead?"

The woman in the middle said, "Too many questions, child." The younger smiled while the eldest stared, but it was she who offered the answers I sought.

"We are the Moirai. You, my dear, know us as the Fates. You are not dead; you are merely transitioning." The Fates. The ones responsible for this mess. "That is Lachesis." She gestured to the youngest. "This is Clotho." The woman in the center lowered her head. "And I am Atropos."

I glanced between the women perched on the stone pedestal before me, and suddenly, everything they said unraveled in my mind. *I sing of the things that were, I sing of the things that are, I sing of the things that are to be…* Lachesis represented the Past, Clotho the Present, and Atropos… the Future.

"I wouldn't be here if it wasn't for you," I said, unable to contain my anger.

"You are here because this moment is weaved into your destiny," corrected Clotho.

"So, what you mean is, you controlled my life just like you manipulated everyone else's. That's what you do." Atropos glared at Lachesis but didn't say anything. Instead, she turned her attention back to me.

"We do not manipulate anyone's life, child. We simply weave the tapestries of fate. Life is a delicate balance of choices and consequences, and every thread we add must fit seamlessly into the grand design. We do not take joy in your suffering, but sometimes, sacrifices must be made for the greater good."

I glanced away, unsure of what to say. While I wanted to be angry at them, the more reasonable side of me understood my life was unimportant compared to the grand purpose. The Fates had put me in danger but saved me, too, and made it possible for Drake to come back.

"Why me?" I whispered. "Why was I chosen for this path?"

"There are forces at work beyond your understanding, child," Clotho replied. "But know this: we chose you because you possess something essential for the upcoming war, a quality that is instrumental in determining the outcome."

"What quality?" I pressed, curiosity weakening my anger.

"That, my dear, is something you will discover in time," Atropos answered cryptically.

I looked between the three Fates, feeling a mix of awe and fear. They held the threads of my future in their hands, and I was helpless to do anything but follow where they led me.

"How do I know you are speaking the truth?" I asked, glancing between them. "What's going to happen to me?"

"My sister always speaks the truth, even if it's not what you want to hear. You are here to ascend." I realized then that nothing they said would ever be easy to understand.

"What does that mean?"

"You must undergo a transformation," said Lachesis. "Your mortal body cannot withstand the dangers that lie ahead. We must make you stronger, immune to the threats that seek to claim you."

"And what are those threats?" I asked, a sense of foreboding creeping over me.

Atropos leaned closer, her voice low and ominous.

"The army of darkness is gathering strength. They seek to overthrow the balance of the Realms and plunge everything into chaos and destruction. You are the only one who can stop them, but you *must* be prepared."

It was ironic that I was responsible for releasing the darkness, while also the one destined to end it.

"How do I stop Dagasti and his army?" I asked, confused as to what was required of me.

"Immortality," said Lachesis. "Your human life force must transition."

"How?"

"You must die and be reborn." Atropos spoke, as if that explained everything. I needed to see Drake. I didn't care how.

"As long as I get back to Drake, then fine. Do what you must."

The echo of Clotho's laughter chilled my dead soul.

"The Dragon... yes. We understand the fascination, but love has many forms."

I didn't like the sound of that.

"No more riddles, please."

"You will return to the Dragon. However, you must know that immortality comes at a price. His life force will be lost to the flames when your fight comes."

"No! I refuse. I don't want immortality. No more sacrifices."

"You cannot refuse. If you do, the darkness will consume all there is, including your Dragon," said Atropos.

"I don't believe you. There has to be another way."

"Do you think you can avoid what is written, child?" The older woman's eyes narrowed on me.

"No, but you can. You are the Fates. The Weavers of Destiny."

"Not even we can change what is written," said Clotho.

It was Lachesis who spoke next, and the Fate's words were my lifeline. "Perhaps she might."

"Lachesis, no!" chastised Atropos.

"Let her speak." I said, "You want my help, yet you refuse to help me."

"Trust me, we have interfered enough," Clotho confessed. "This, we cannot alter."

"But there could be a way... You think there's a way I could change things?" I turned to the younger Fate, desperate. "Tell me how."

Lachesis hesitated but eventually answered.

"There is one possibility. The threads of fate are not set in stone. They can be influenced and nudged in different directions, but that comes with great risk. If you choose this path, you may alter the course of destiny and alter the outcome of all the realms."

"And what does it entail?" I asked. Damn the risks, especially if it meant saving Drake.

"You must walk the Threads of Possibility," Lachesis said, her voice low and serious. "It is a dangerous path, one that few have attempted. You must navigate many possibilities and choose the right one. If you fail, you could alter everything. For better or worse."

"But you said this is all just a possibility. What if I can't?"

No one spoke this time, and I was thankful for the honesty of their silence. "No. My answer is still no." I couldn't gamble. Not with Drake's life.

"Child, you don't understand. If you don't ascend—if you do not join this fight—all will be lost regardless. If you don't choose to continue your path, there is no future, and the darkness will claim him. He will be lost along with everything and everyone you hold dear." Atropos stared back at me. The future beckoned me to defy its plan. If even the Fates believed in a possibility, why couldn't I?

Yet choice was merely an illusion. When the only options were to fight to live or die without trying, one's path was clear.

"And if I do this, there is a way that maybe..." My voice trailed off, knowing what my answer would be.

"Your future has many paths. Your choices determine your fate, but remember, nothing is ever as it seems. Sometimes what is meant to be is not what comes to be, and other times what comes to be is not what is meant to be."

I shook my head, refusing to listen. I was done with the riddles. I had no way out of this unless I accepted their offer. As always, they would play their games and spin their wheel, so I made my decision with finality.

"How can I transition?"

"You already have..."

A dark and endless abyss seized me and sucked me into its vortex as their voices dissipated far in the distance.

"Tell me!" I called out, but only darkness answered, and suddenly, I was floating again.

"Wake up..." Their voices whispered.

"What do I do?" I asked the shadows.

"Wake up..."

"How do I transition?" I could no longer see the Fates. Endless darkness engulfed me, and I was once again suspended in space, except this time, my body felt different. Heavier. More resilient. It was as if the threads of fate had shifted and changed around me. A myriad of possibilities. I sensed the weight of my newfound immortality and a new sense of hope. This was the beginning of my journey, and I knew that the Threads of Possibility held the key to saving Drake and all the realms.

"Wake up," said the darkness.

I tried to do as it asked, but my eyes were heavy.

"Wake up!" The voice called again, louder this time until the darkness dissipated.

CALLIX

Her pale face glinted against the glow of the cave's stone walls, her long lashes quivering.

"That's it. Come back to me..." I probed into the stillness of her mind. *"Wake up."* Her fingers jerked above the water. *"Wake up."* I urged softly, slipping my thoughts into her mind. Her lips parted, and as she took a breath, I reached for her waist, holding her in my arms above the water.

"Wake up," I whispered gently against her cold cheeks, and

as her eyes fluttered open, the tension surrounding the castle ebbed like remnants of a passing storm.

She regarded me with confusion, and I smiled warmly.

"Welcome back."

BELYNDA

Everything around me glowed in a shimmering hue of blue, and I was surprised to find a set of Cerulean crystal clear eyes welcoming me into the world of the living.

I tried to speak, but my voice failed me.

"That's normal," said Callix. "Your body and voice will return to normal soon, but for now, just rest." I felt the strength of his arms as he lifted me out of the water.

I wanted to ask where I was and how I had gotten here, but the words wouldn't come.

"You're in my home. Serfier. I will explain everything in due time." He replied as if he could read my thoughts. I realized then that perhaps he could.

There was so much I wanted to say, but whatever transformation my body had undergone had taken its toll. The last thing I saw before my eyes closed was Callix's worried face peering down at me and the crystalized walls behind him.

"*Sleep now.*" His voice echoed in my head.

I DREAMED I WAS WATER, Wind, Earth, and Fire. I dreamed I was light. A whirl of golden-woven strings surrounded me, plucked one by one by a slithering shadow. The shadow crawled over my feet and up my body, and I couldn't move. It closed around my neck and covered my mouth, drowning me.

I SCREAMED , jolting from the bed. I fought with the sheets tucked around my body, desperately trying to escape the darkness, which still felt all too real.

"It's alright. You're safe," said a familiar voice, and my eyes trailed to the doorway, where Callix leaned casually against the threshold.

"What am I doing here? Where is Drake?" I placed a hand against my throat, startled. My voice sounded strange—smoother and melodic. Callix smiled and pushed away from the door. He strolled into the room and walked to a small vanity, where he poured a glass of water before strolling to my bedside and handing me the cup.

"Here. This will help." I took the glass and had a small sip. He was right; I felt better. I gulped down the water, and when I was done, I felt his eyes studying me.

He took the empty glass from my hands and placed it on the small night table.

"Thank you," I said, testing my voice again.

"My pleasure." He took a few steps back until he stood at the foot of the bed.

"Are you going to tell me how I got here?" I asked him.

Callix leaned against the bed canopy, crossing his arms. I didn't miss the way his biceps strained against the white fabric of his shirt.

"You died," he said matter-of-factly, but I had deduced that much.

"I remember we were in Druleska. The forest was burning and Dagasti..." I glanced at my stomach and trailed my hands across the skin he had pierced. It felt normal. "Drake?" I glanced at Callix, noting the rigid set of his jaw at the mention of his name.

"He kept his promise, if that's what you're asking." I relaxed into the bed at his confirmation.

"Then what happened? How did I end up here?"

"Bringing you here was the only chance you had."

"And Drake allowed this?" Callix failed at hiding his smile.

"He had no choice," was his response, though I knew Drake would have permitted anything if it meant saving my life. By the look on Callix's face, it seemed like it wasn't an easy decision.

"Where is he now? I want to see him."

"I'm afraid that won't be possible. Not now, at least. He has been helping the clans in Upherya. The darkness has claimed the Southern and Western territories. Presently, he is in Abryas forming alliances with the King."

I stared at Callix, confused.

"How long have I been here?"

"A few weeks."

"Weeks?" It felt like days to me. I moved the sheets from my legs, but as my feet hit the floor, the walls spun.

"Easy there." I didn't hear Callix approach, yet he held my arm, guiding me back to bed. "I know you want to see him, but there are more important things you must worry about. You need time to adjust to your immortal body. You will only stand in his way and be another thing for him to worry about. But I promise if you stay, if you are *patient*, I will make it worth your while.”

If I could glare at him, I would have, but I was afraid to open my eyes to find the room spinning again. His laughter shook the bed.

“I never claimed to be a gentleman or good, but I would never take advantage of you. I’m no monster.”

Was he in my head? He couldn’t be… I opened my eyes slowly, and the room was still. Raising my hand, I noticed the woven bracelet my mother and I had made together remained secure around my wrist. I turned to the side of the bed where he stood, narrowing my eyes in his direction.

“You told me you would never lie to me…”

“And I meant it.”

“Then tell me the truth. How do you always know what I’m thinking? Can you read my thoughts?”

Callix ran his thumb over his lower lip, then reached to touch the woven bracelet on my wrist.

“Some bonds can’t be broken, not even with all the magic in the world.” His eyes found mine, and he smiled. “Don’t worry. It works both ways. You can see into mine as well.”

I suddenly felt nauseous, though I wasn’t sure if it was due to my recovery or that revelation.

“When I said I would make it worthwhile, I only meant that if you stayed, I could teach you to use your new powers.”

I pondered his offer, yet I couldn’t help but feel like a terrible person. I was alive because of Callix, and I hadn’t even offered a thank you. Even worse, I mistook his kind offer as an insinuation. I was the worst kind of person.

He was still smiling when I looked at him.

"Really, there's no need to apologize. And if I were you, I wouldn't disregard the insinuation altogether..." He amended, and I glared.

"Seriously, that is the first thing we need to work on. I need some boundaries. Some *privacy*. You can't just pry into my head whenever you please."

Callix at least tried to show some contrition by covering his laughter, but he did a poor job.

"I'm sorry. I can't help myself when your thoughts are screaming at me."

Callix, get out of my head NOW! I internally screamed, and the echo of his laughter resonated throughout the room, and I was sure down the halls, too. He was impossible. His laughter died, and his blue eyes held mine.

"I promise I'll try to behave. Rest, and tomorrow, we will have your first lesson."

I stared after his retreating form with a sinking feeling in my stomach. I had to learn to guard my thoughts, and soon, because something told me that was a promise he wouldn't be keeping. My suspicions were confirmed when he turned at the threshold of the door, looking back at me with a grin. *Damn you, Callix!* I screamed in my head for good measure.

I REMEMBER Drake had mentioned sleep wasn't necessary for him, but that must not have been the same for every immortal because I felt exhausted despite having slept for days. However, Callix promised to show me how the mind reading worked, and I wasn't about to pass on the opportunity.

Slowly, I shuffled to the edge of the bed and gripped the

bedpost for support. I stood, and this time, I felt steady. Strong. Even my eyes seemed sharper. I took a hesitant step and then another until I found myself before the long mirror.

I cringed at my reflection. My skin was so pale I barely recognized myself, and I was almost skin and bones. No wonder I could hardly stand or talk. Whatever immortality had offered, it hadn't altered my appearance in any remarkable way. I stared at the thin white top, cropped just below my breasts, and the billowy white skirts hanging low on my hips, flowing to the floor.

I poured myself a glass of water and drank from it as I took in the room for the first time.

The walls and the floors appeared to be crafted of frosted glass or ice, adding an airy feel to the room. The large bed was grand, with four marble posts and a canopy adorned with seashells. The most magnificent was the large window that peered out across a breathtaking view of the underwater world.

Unlike Druleska, Serfier wasn't stuck in the past. It was evident in every detail and surface, and in the sleek shower, tub, and toilet located in the adjoining room. *Thank the Fates...*

I wriggled out of my skirt which pooled around my feet, and my top followed as I closed the glass door behind me, stepping beneath the hot spray of the shower. The water cascaded down my back, and I recalled my imprisonment by Dagasti; I would have given anything to have this then. I washed my hair and body until I felt reborn.

I wrapped a towel around myself and shrieked as I reentered my room.

"Damn you, Callix! Don't you knock?" I pressed the towel

tighter around my chest as his eyes traveled the length of my legs.

"I did. I promise," he said. He hesitated before turning around. "You can find something to wear there." He pointed to a small door at the other side of the room.

When I opened it, I froze. The closet was bigger than my entire room back home. I stepped inside and locked the door behind me.

Whereas Druleska favored the dark colors, Serfier was the opposite. The entire wardrobe comprised of pastel colors: light blues and whites—lots of white, in fact. I smiled, remembering my assumption that Callix wasn't from Druleska by how he dressed. He probably could hear everything I was thinking, but I didn't care. I tried to recall the ridiculous names I had conjured up while locked in the dungeons, but I couldn't remember them. If I did, I would be shouting them at him in my head...

I glanced through the mirror at the sky-blue dress that hung around my shoulders and framed my waist, pooling gently down my legs. The one thing I did not find were shoes.

When I came out of the closet, Callix stood in the same spot I had left him.

"That color suits you," he said, and I couldn't help the blush that crept across my cheeks.

"You seemed to have misplaced all the shoes, though," I said, and he smiled.

"I assure you it was on purpose. You will feel better if you are grounded. Besides, you won't need shoes here, and you won't feel out of place. The nymphs prefer not to wear them either."

"Nymphs?"

"Yes. They serve the castle and me." He smiled. "You didn't think I lived here alone, did you?"

"No. I just thought it strange that I hadn't seen anyone."

"They've been curious, of course, but I forbade them to intrude. Besides, something tells me you're used to fending for yourself." Perceptive, I thought. Or not. He had likely read my thoughts, probably before my ascension... ever since we met back at Druleska. I cringed at the idea, refusing to think about everything he might have heard. He smiled. *Damn you, Callix.*

"I'm ready," I said, marching past him, but as I stepped into the open crystal corridors, I realized I had no idea where I was going.

"How about breakfast first?" he asked, moving behind me.

"Lead the way." I smiled, falling in step with him as he turned in the opposite direction down the bright corridor.

NEVER IN A MILLION years could I have imagined Serfier, not the castle made of ice buried in the deepest part of the ocean.

Grand halls and vaulted ceilings with chandeliers of crystalized tears that reflected all light. The most unbelievable views were at the edge of almost every corridor and balcony. The world beyond was a dream.

I stood on an open balcony, watching the ocean form an orb that stretched above and before me like a waving wall of water. Through it, I saw the ocean world come to life. Reaching, I plunged my fingers into the wall of water, and shivered at the cold. When I brought my fingers back, the water droplets flew back toward the wall of water like a magnet, and my fingers dried instantly.

I gaped at Callix, who smiled beside me.

"How?"

"It's all part of the magic that keeps the castle submerged, and the ocean around it contained."

"It's beautiful," I said, lost in the ocean's depths.

"Come. If we keep stopping, we will never make it to breakfast. There is much more to see, but we have time." Callix smiled, and I couldn't help but sense that the thought made him happy.

WHEN I ENTERED the dining hall, the smell of bacon hit me, and something sweet: pancakes or muffins. The smell assaulted my senses, and suddenly, I was starving.

Callix pulled a chair for me and then sat on my other side instead of at the head of the table. It was odd, but it felt nice to have the company.

I glanced around the open room. The chairs looked like sculpted glass mermaids, where the tail was the seat, and the borders of the grand marble table were carved with endless strange symbols.

Laughter flowed around us, and Callix smiled at the two young woman that danced into the room. *Nymphs,* I realized.

I remained transfixed by their subtle tan skin, their pixie-like features, and their glowing scales that appeared tattooed to the sides of their faces and down their necks and arms.

"Sire." A nymph placed a tray of food before Callix.

"My lady," said the other, placing a tray before me. I stared at my plate with a frown. *Was this a joke?* It had to be. I could hear their melodious giggles from wherever they had disappeared to.

I glanced at Callix's tray filled with bacon, eggs, toast, and pancakes, then back at mine. Raw snails, oysters, and clams.

"Are you kidding me?" I whispered, and Callix smiled.

"I promised I would let them have their fun," he whispered in their defense. "We don't get many visitors around here."

I switched Callix's tray with mine and speared a piece of bacon into my mouth. He leaned back in his chair with a grin on his face.

"What?" I asked, and he shook his head, amused, before bringing an oyster to his lips. He swallowed the slimy thing in one draw and looked at me with challenge.

I stabbed a pancake and took a large bite. His laughter filled the room.

When the nymphs returned, my plate was almost empty, and Callix's was too. But the terror on their faces upon seeing their lord had been the one to pay the price for their prank was priceless.

"Sire, we're sorry." The girls fretted at his side, but he paid them no mind.

"Belynda, meet Syllis and Phial." The nymphs giggled behind their master. "I know it might not seem like it, but they are loyal, and if you ever need anything, and I'm not around, they are your girls." My brows furrowed in doubt. "Trust me on this," he added, his eyes piercing mine. Despite my reservations, I did trust him.

"Very well." I glanced at the girls as they curtseyed before disappearing from the dining hall.

"Don't pay them any mind. You will find that lightness of spirit is a quality most nymphs share." I wasn't sure it was a likeable quality, but I didn't know enough about Callix's world to form an opinion yet. "Shall we?" He pushed back from the table, and I was up in a second, eager to begin.

We strode through the endless halls in comfortable silence, though I knew he could hear every one of my thoughts.

"Come. There is something I want to show you." He broke the silence and turned up a grand staircase that veered into two upper wings. I followed him, running my hands over the smooth, crystal-clear handrails, fascinated by the sea vines encapsulated inside the surface.

"This place is magical," I muttered, and Callix paused at the top of the stairs, glancing down at me.

"I'm glad you like it here."

"Who wouldn't?"

He smiled.

"You'd be surprised. The sea is not for everyone." I gaped as if he was insane, and we continued down the corridor.

"Here." Callix pushed open the double doors, and the words caught in my throat. "This is in case you get bored." He winked and moved aside so I could inspect the infinite world of books stretched before me.

"Wow." I walked past him, staring at the floor-to-ceiling windows flanking an entire side of the library. Outside those windows were the endless blues of the ocean. Peaceful. Beautiful. "I thought you said you didn't lie."

He turned to me; he was trying to read my thoughts, I realized, to understand what I meant. "I knew you were lying to Dagasti when you said you had remained in Druleska for his vast book collection," I offered him the answer he sought in my mind, and his laughter echoed throughout the library.

"I said I have never lied to you—truthfully, I'm not accustomed to it—but that time was for your benefit."

Yes, I remembered well enough. After all, it was he who saved me from the monster. Callix's brow furrowed, and I realized that particular thought didn't please him, either.

"You have got to stop doing that." I chided, but he merely smiled. "And enough about trying to distract me with pretty things. You promised you would teach me." His smile vanished.

"Yes. I did, didn't I?" There it was again, that prominent dip in his brow at the idea of not being able to read my thoughts. "Bring me that book now," he commanded.

I glanced behind me at the large volume and then back at him, raising a brow in question.

"Did you forget your manners? I am grateful to you, but that doesn't mean I'll let you order me about."

He didn't respond, but I noticed the hard lines of his jaw became pronounced, and for a moment, I lost myself in the depths of his blue eyes.

I turned around, picked up the heavy volume, and placed it in his hands. I blinked as the oddest sensation abandoned me, and then I noticed he held the book. I spun and saw it was the book that had been on the table.

"Who...?"

"You did," he said, confirming my fear.

"How?" Callix's eyes searched mine, and I found the ocean within them.

Hesitantly, I reached for him, trailing my fingers along the sharp angle of his jaw. I held my breath and leaned in, lost in his scent, and the calling of his lips. Callix took a step back, and as he did, the room spun, and that strange sensation returned.

"What the hell was that?" I snapped.

"How do you think I was able to get past the guards without ever being seen?" He smirked, and finally, I understood.

"It was you! You made them bring water every day, didn't you?" The way his eyes smoldered was my confirmation. "You don't just read thoughts... you can manipulate someone into doing what you ask!"

Why didn't I realize that before? It was one of the things I had learned back home while studying the water realm. '*They could slip into your head and make you do their bidding.*'

"How many times have you done that to me?" I asked, my intrigue suddenly replace with suspicion and fear.

"Never!" said Callix, affronted.

"I don't believe you," I pressed, recalling what he had made me do just now and remembering the first time he saved me in the market. There was a moment when I found myself mesmerized by him, wanting to do what I had just done, running my fingers down his face. His laughter pulled me from my muddled thoughts.

"No. I assure you. That was all you."

I shot him a look, but his amusement only grew. *Get out of my head!* I screamed.

"If you ever make me do anything like that, I will kill you," I said, but he laughed.

"You don't know how." He was right, but I didn't care.

"I'll find a way."

"Don't worry. There's no need for such threats. I would never force you to do anything against your will," He said, and strangely enough, I believed him.

"I don't understand. If you can do this, why don't you just slip into the minds of Dagasti's army and call for a ceasefire?"

Callix shook his head.

"If that were an option, I would have done it long ago. But I cannot enter a mind that is taken. Dagasti already manipulates them through the Nightshade."

"Teach me then. Please."

"What am I thinking?" he asked.

I shifted my stance and stared into his eyes, but I only heard my own thoughts.

"Nothing. I don't think it's working."

"You're trying too hard. Relax your mind and look for the connection. I'm thinking of a color." He winked, and I rolled my eyes.

Glancing over his face, I tried to do as he asked. *Slow my thoughts. Relax.* Staring into his eyes again, I was instantly lost in the depths of blue.

"Blue!" I blurted. He grinned.

"You didn't think I would pick something so obvious, did you?" he teased. "Try again."

Relax my mind... find the connection. I looked into his eyes, losing myself in the depths of the ocean. I stirred the waters and reached deeper. I felt like my mind was floating. *Green...* the soft echo made me blink.

"Holy cow. It's green, isn't it?" I searched his face, but his smile was validation enough.

"Try again. This time let's not limit it to the color spectrum. I'm thinking of a word."

"What sort of word?"

"Any word."

"That will be harder," I argued.

"That's the point." He challenged with a grin.

"Fine…" A word, any word.

The silence from before returned, but there were no whispers. I urged my mind deeper into the silence and the calmness, but there was nothing.

"I got nothing."

He smiled, and I narrowed my eyes.

"Nothing? That was the word? NOTHING?" He burst out laughing. "Very clever." This was going to take forever…

"Despite what you might think, getting past my mind barriers is no easy feat. You're doing fine. Trust me." He had promised he wouldn't lie to me, so his commendation made me feel slightly better.

"Continue," I urged him.

He had the nymphs bring dinner into the library while I spent hours trying to slip past his mind barriers. By the time the clear oceans darkened, and the crystal chandeliers illuminated the library, I was already picking up small phrases from Callix's mind—whenever he wasn't trying to trick me, of course.

"Why don't you teach me how to block my thoughts instead?" I asked, and he abruptly stood from the sofa.

"Tomorrow. I have given you my day, and now I have things to attend to."

I narrowed my eyes suspiciously at him. It wasn't just his duty preventing him from teaching me; there was something else. He was delaying it as much as possible.

"Fine. Tomorrow then," I conceded. He paused at the doors.

"I take it you can find your way back to your room?"

"I'll manage." I rolled my eyes, and he smiled. He appeared to want to say something, but he didn't. I reached, searching his mind, and then I heard it.

Goodnight. His voice echoed, and I smiled as the doors closed.

Goodnight. I offered in return, knowing he was listening.

Now that I was alone, without my mind being intruded upon, I thought about the Fates and the possibilities they had presented me with. I didn't care what it took; I would do everything to change what was written. Even now, I was tempted to ask Callix to deliver me to Drake's side, but the Water Lord was right. I didn't want to be a burden. Not anymore. The next time I saw Drake, I would be his equal. The realms were not the only thing depending on me; Drake's life was, too. I owed it to them to be ready when the time came. When I faced the threads of possibilities, I would have the strength and wisdom to navigate them. I had to. Any other alternative was not an option.

3
NIGHTSHADE

THE ROOM WAS CHARGED WITH TENSION SO *THICK* that one could cut through it with a knife. Herod sat at the head of the table with the three warriors standing before him. Leiwen and my mother offered a sense of amiable balance to the rigidity creeping around the chamber.

"Why would Dagasti need ships when half of his army can cross the Fjord like you did?" asked Herod.

"We've studied Dagasti's army long enough to know those taken by the darkness have only one disadvantage," said Euros. Everyone turned to him for the answer, but we already knew. The only weakness the Darklings had was their inability to use their host's powers. "The Darklings can't fly or shift or use any gifts their hosts possess."

Herod stood and paced the war room.

"That explains why our borders have kept quiet." Herod

looked at me, and I knew what he was thinking. "If it wasn't for your mate, they would have never gotten through."

It was my mother who spoke up in Belynda's defense.

"Pointing fingers will not stop Dagasti from advancing. One way or another, he would have found a way."

"She's right. Dagasti's fleet is what's important. We must find a way to stop him." Leiwen said, and Herod paced slowly to her side.

"Dagasti will never reach our shores. I will make sure of that." Grasping Leiwen's hand, he brought it to his lips.

While I wanted to believe Herod's words, it was easier said than done. Dagasti had proven himself to be a formidable foe, and his army had already inflicted immense destruction in Upherya.

"How will you stop him, your Majesty?" I asked, hoping for a practical solution.

Herod faced me again, his brows furrowed.

"We will fortify our shores, increase our naval defenses, and deploy our elite warriors to keep a watchful eye on the Fjord. If Dagasti tries to cross, we will be ready to repel his army."

I nodded, but the plan seemed too simplistic. Dagasti was not someone who could be so easily trounced.

"I know your men are needed for your own land's defense, but I have a suggestion. We have a chance to end this war before it reaches your borders. But only with the help of your men." The warriors would likely disagree with me later, but I didn't care. "The rest of Dagasti's army is marching towards Phoenix's lands as we speak. If we can put a strong front there, we can drive the Darklings out of the East clan's territory, wipe out the remaining forces nesting in the outer lands, and level his fleet. But we cannot achieve this alone. We have tried. But you have the numbers, and your magic barriers could help us win this once and for all. We need this alliance now more than ever."

Euros glared at me, while Herod released Leiwen's hand.

"Your tactics are sensible, but as a King, I cannot put the fate of my people above theirs... I'm sure you understand." Herod said. I didn't. I wanted to say he was a coward.

"You have nothing to lose. Abryas is safe from Dagasti's army. It is Upherya that is suffering under the darkness. Think of the women and children. You could make a difference if we stood and fought together as one," I pleaded.

"My answer is still no," Herod declared with finality. "I am sorry. It is not my battle to win."

"Oh, Herod," Leiwen whispered, the disappointment clear in her voice. "It might not be our battle, but it is everyone's war." I motioned with my head toward Leiwen in gratitude. I always knew she was a sensible woman.

"Your women and children are welcome here. That, I can offer. But my men, I cannot." Herod glanced between the warriors before settling his gaze on me. "As a ruler with a kingdom to answer to, I thought you would understand my position best?"

"You're wrong. I have no kingdom. Dagasti took that away from me; he took my mate, and he sunk his claws into Upherya, and believe me, he will come for you and rip apart everything you hold dear as well. I only pray to the gods that when he does, you have allies as loyal as these men beside you to confront the darkness."

Silence ensued, but I had said all that was needed and more. The stillness stretched, enveloping us. I knew men like Herod, and he would not change his mind. No... he would only do so once chaos knocked at his doors. Once destruction was inevitable.

"Excuse me." I walked from the meeting, but not before catching the look of despair on Leiwen and my mother's faces. The warriors didn't hesitate to follow. There was no point in remaining here.

"I told you this was a waste of time," said Phoenix, somewhere in the distance, and for the first time, I realized he was right.

Leiwen and my mother bid us farewell. Leiwen had insisted that my mother stay with her after apologizing to the warriors for the King's decision. She promised to speak with him and to try and change his mind.

"Are you certain you don't wish to stay the night? You can ride at first light," Leiwen insisted. "There is no need for you to depart in such haste."

"I think it is best if we take our leave," Euros said with an apologetic smile. "My lady, thank you again for your kindness and hospitality."

"I only wish I could have done more." Leiwen's face crumpled.

Beside her, my mother tried to lift her spirits. "I'm sure if anyone can change his mind, it is you."

Although Leiwen held significant influence over Herod, this was a matter he would not compromise on.

"Thank you again for allowing my mother to remain." I offered, taking Leiwen's tiny hand.

"It is my pleasure. It gets quite lonely here."

I nodded. "I hope when we meet again, it is under more pleasant circumstances."

"May the fates and the spirits travel with you," she offered.

We mounted the horses, trotting at full gallop through the castle gates beneath the blanket of stars and the invisible dome of poisonous mist.

LEIWEN

From the gallery, the city below settled into quiet darkness. Despite knowing Herod to be a good man, his duty and the opinions of the Council of Elders often clouded his judgment. The man in that hall today was not the same man whom I had pledged my eternal devotion.

I refused to turn as the doors sounded behind me, and Herod's presence filled the space. I felt our energies aligning.

"Will you not speak to me?" he asked, his tenor voice echoing into my soul. I remained silent; he would not like what I had to say.

"Your silence is even more lethal to me than the darkness itself, Lei," he continued, moving closer to my side. "Will you not release me from this torment?"

Taking a deep breath, I turned to face him. He was but a breath away from me, the silver details on his armor glinting under the chandelier.

"I'm afraid you would not like what I have to say, my King," I answered. His eyes narrowed at the formalities.

"Lei, please," he implored. "I do this for you. For our *people*." Herod's eyes searched every detail of my face, but I was too angry to succumb to his allure.

"I know you mean well, Herod, I do. But do you have to be so inflexible?" I asked, echoing Drake's earlier sentiment. "We have an opportunity to stop Dagasti before he reaches our shores, yet you refuse to see sense."

Herod whirled away from me and gripped the hilt of his sword. "Leiwen, this is not something I can concede on," he said. I knew him well enough to sense when I could influence him, but this time... he had decided.

"I will take in their women and children and offer any help I can, but I will not send my men to fight a battle that is not theirs to fight!" He drew closer once more, searching my eyes. "Please tell me you understand."

Looking into his haunted gaze, the tension was palpable. "I don't agree with your decision and never will," I granted, though I reached for his face, tracing his cheek, and watching the tension visibly leave his body. "But you are my husband and my King, and I stand by your decisions, even if I believe there is another way."

"Not this time, Lei. Not this time." He cupped my face, tucked the silver strands of hair behind my ears, and leaned in, brushing his lips against mine. He was testing my resolve. But Herod was my weakness, just as I was his.

My fingers trailed over the steel of his armor and up to the exposed skin on his neck. Running through the long locks of his hair, I braided my fingers through them at the nape of his neck. I reached up and kissed the hard line of his jaw while his hands fanned across the exposed skin of my back, pulling me flush against him.

I unclipped the shield plates on his shoulders, and they fell to the floor by our feet. His gaze traveled over my face like a forsaken man searching for redemption, and I kissed his lips, offering the solace he so desperately craved.

He lifted me effortlessly, trapping my body against the wall.

"Herod..." I hesitated, knowing someone could walk in at any minute.

"I need this, Lei. I need you," he pleaded, and his words were my downfall.

I bound my legs around him, feeling the expanding hardness of his desire. He pressed into me, and I ached for him.

Anchoring my hands around his shoulders, I reached between us and released him, his breath fanning my neck.

"Avo bedo 'sevin i dhâf, a garo! Just do it...." His lips grazed the skin of my neck while his fingers teased, parting me for his taking.

"I 'ell nîn," he whispered. His tone was dominant—demanding—as he pressed against my entrance. One drive from his hips, and he tore through my defenses, filling me as I molded around him.

The King was now just a man, lost to his desires.

"This is my sanctuary," he said. His smoldering eyes glowed as he watched our bodies fuse. I savored the feeling, watching as his hard length disappeared inside me.

His hands braced against the wall beside me, and his assault became savage, unbreakable, and unrelenting. He drove into me, branding my skin against the coarse stone wall with the weight of his thrusts. Like Nightshade, he swept me off my senses and took control of my body. I could never deny him. My body and soul belonged to the Earth, belonged to him. We were bound to each other for all eternity.

"Damn it, Lei. Take it. Take it all." His savage grunt came with his liberation and he stilled deep inside me. I felt his warmth trickling down my thighs as he lowered my legs, steadying me against his body. His lips brushed my neck, and he smiled as his nose skimmed against my skin.

"We're not done," he whispered, and the pressure between my legs pulsed. After kissing my lips and cheeks, he pushed back from the wall, running his hands through his hair. He bit his lip as if he had yet to satiate his desire. "I will worship you later in the privacy of our chamber. *That* is a promise." He bent and picked up his armor plates from the floor, and with a smile full of wicked promises, he disappeared.

DRAKE

As expected, Euros was angry about my interference, while Link and Phoenix had no qualms with my suggestions. They agreed that getting Herod to offer his men was a sensible plan. Euros knew it, too, but he would have never asked.

"Phoenix and I will run the night watch," Euros announced as we touched the rocky ground at the edge of the hills.

"Very well." I didn't object. He was clearly still angry with me, but I cared little about what Euros thought. I'd had enough of them all for one day. The monster sought retribution.

· · ·

THE TRAINING FORGE was unusually quiet, and I found solace in its silence. Amirth, who was typically the first to arrive and last to leave, was absent. However, I didn't mind being alone; it allowed me to release all the fury and desperation that had formed inside of me.

I visualized my target with visceral rage and annihilated it. The training planks burned under my fists, but I couldn't stop, even as the fire reached the upper beams of the Forge. All I saw was his face melting.

"Easy there, or you will bring this entire place down."

I whirled to face Link, and slowly, I came to my senses. The fire, burned before us, spreading like a hypnotic dance. "Should I fetch some water?"

I glared at the young warrior.

"There is no need." I opened my hand, and as I closed my fingers in a tight fist, the flames extinguished. Link sighed, relieved I had contained it.

"Is something on your mind?"

"There is a lot on all of our minds," I bit back before shaking my head. Link was not my enemy, nor was he to blame for my all-consuming desperation.

"Does your wrath have a name?" he pressed, and once again, I pictured Callix's face instead of the burnt wooden spikes. When I didn't offer a response, Link didn't press. "If you still feel like letting off some steam, I have some time. I sure as hell could use it myself."

I raised my fists and assumed a combative stance.

"Very well. But I must warn you, you do this at your own peril."

Link grinned. The kid never backed down from a challenge.

"Do your worst," he goaded, unaware the monster could chew him up and spit him out. However, as his fist connected with my chin, the darkness ebbed. I had to hand it to the young warrior.

He was brave.

THE SPARRING DID nothing to tame the monster, but to my surprise, the kid held his ground against the unyielding darkness.

"Very few people surprise me," I said, smirking.

"I don't know if I should take that as a compliment or be offended that you thought I couldn't beat you."

"Oh, you still cannot." I grinned, and he swung his sparring staff, catching me off guard. Blurring before him, I dodged his strike and snatched the stick from his hand. I swiped it behind his legs, and he fell to the ground with a thud. "Take it as a compliment. Trust me," I said, offering him my hand.

"Same time tomorrow?" he asked, and I knew he sought retribution. I smiled.

"Of course, if Amirth is not in the way," I recalled the dangers of sparring with Amirth, whose tenacity, for the most part, was admirable, but it sometimes became a nuisance. She would never have accepted defeat like Link had. Instead, she would have driven the sparring match until she passed out or until I called it off and allowed her to win to end such madness.

"Don't worry if she is. I'll bring Euros along. He can handle her." Link winked.

"If I could sleep, I'm certain those two would give me

nightmares." Link laughed and then patted my shoulder.

"Then I guess it's a good thing you don't need sleep." His laughter echoed across the sleeping buildings as he disappeared down one of the paths.

Restless, I walked through the city, hoping to clear my thoughts. However, peering up at the rising mountainside before me, I realized I had left the city limits some time ago, and no peace had been found. The darkness dissipated from my skin. I knew precisely what the monster required.

THE CURRENTS of the Fjord had shifted, which was the first sign of Callix since their departure. Still, there was no news of her. Gliding above the water's surface, I followed the currents to the bay, far from Upherya's coast and Dagasti's army. The Hereter Isles rose in the distance. The arches connecting the islands symbolized that Callix's kingdom lay beyond. As I flew past the god-made archways, I dreaded the obstacle awaiting me.

Just like I had attempted countless times before, I dove at a steep angle, cutting through the surface of the raging waves into the depths of the Sea of Varenver. The darkness fought against the element, but I willed it forward.

Through the black waters, I felt its presence long before I caught sight of it. *Zodrox.* Callix's Titan. It lurked in the depths and was the reason Callix's kingdom remained impenetrable.

Nothing moved within the depths of Serfier without Callix knowing.

Zodrox lurked in the shadows, and I saw it, but not fast

enough. One of its tails lashed out and narrowly missed my chest. My wing took the hit, and the monster inside me grunted, pleading for air, but I pressed forward.

The Titan wasted no time—it never did. The tails lashed out again with greater determination. One pierced through my other wing, while the other wrapped securely around my neck.

"Go back!" A voice echoed in warning, and I knew he could hear me. Callix knew I was there, reaching for her—for something—but he refused to call off his sentinel. *"Damn you, Callix... I will kill you."* I thought until consciousness slipped away and I sunk deeper into the sea. It was the most peaceful I had felt in a while, so I didn't fight it.

WHEN I AWOKE on the shores of Hereter, the waves lapped against my feet. My fury rose at Callix's cowardice. The mortal scar on my shoulder throbbed, but the rest had healed. Shifting wouldn't be a problem. Trembling with ire, I stared out across the endless ocean, allowing the darkness to consume me. Sand exploded beneath the monster's talons as I launched from the shoreline. Callix thought his Titan would stop me from trying, but he underestimated me. Once again, he had won, but it wouldn't always be like this. I would reach his icy castle, and when I did, his head would be my prize.

Plummeting towards the banks of Tirsia, the sun reached its zenith, and I knew the warriors waited for me. Within minutes, I strode into the meeting room, my armor plates still adjusting to my human movements.

"Looks like someone's been hard at work," Link quipped,

but I shot him a warning glare.

Euros made no remarks; he knew exactly where I'd been. He'd seen the haunted look on my face too many times to count. Instead, they took their seats at the round table while I remained standing, and he cut straight to the point.

"The army moves quicker than we estimated." He marked a path across the eastern territory, bordering the mountain range on the map. "We build our defenses here." He glanced at me, and I offered a firm nod of agreement. "We have the advantage of the mountains. Drake was right. I say we concentrate all our defenses there and end this once and for all."

"Two assaults, one from the north and another from the east." Phoenix appeared to play with the idea as his gaze fell over his clan's territory. "It just might work," he said, with a hint of optimism.

"I will help Phoenix with the magic barriers. They won't hold the Darklings long, but it will grant us a few more days," Link offered.

"Take Amirth," added Euros, and before Phoenix and Link could protest, he cut them off. "She's an earth elemental. Utilize her. She can help with the trenches." They nodded, and their protests died in their throats.

"Drake and I will start on tactics and prepare the men. Phoenix and I will lead the attack from the east, and Drake and Link will guide the counterattack from the mountains." Euros continued, glancing between me and the warriors once more. It was a sound strategy, and we all agreed.

Link and Phoenix leaped from the open sky terrace, and switched before us, gliding toward the blue skies.

"Childish," Euros muttered as we stared at the city far below.

Euros' home. The North clan or, as many called it, the City of Wind. It bore no resemblance to my home. The City of Wind was an architectural masterpiece designed to harness the power of the air elementals residing in the north clan. Buildings were crafted from a mix of stone and wood, their designs incorporating intricate patterns representing the winds and the currents of the air.

Druleska had once been as thriving and as vibrant as Upherya. Dagasti hadn't just taken my father's life to occupy the throne; he had pillaged the beauty of my home.

"I gather you weren't successful?" asked Euros.

"Not this time," I said, staring into nothingness.

"For what it's worth." Euros paced to the edge of the Abyss. "I've never met anyone as relentless as you, so if anyone can breach Serfier... you can."

CALLIX

It had been a while since I last sensed Drake in my domain. I had hoped he had given up, yet there he was again. Relentless as always. Despite what he believed, I was not his enemy, but his stubbornness clouded his judgment, especially now Belynda was here. Of course, I couldn't blame him. I understood now how difficult it was to let her go.

I felt torn, struggling between my honor and the desire to follow my heart and destiny, even though her heart belonged to another. The moment she crossed that threshold into my world, I lost my reason, but I was no monster. Despite what he thought—or what anyone believed—I was here to do as I'd always done. Guide and protect her.

"Go back," I urged, but he wouldn't yield. The Dragon fought against the Titan's grasp in vain, and I knew his fight was lost when my thoughts touched into his despair before darkness swallowed him.

Zodrox delivered Drake's human body to the surface atop a drifting wave, and I guided his unconscious form to shore. Hopefully, he would see sense this time, but deep down, I knew he wouldn't give up.

I veered across the raging waters, and as I slipped through the magic shields guarding the sea from my home, I saw her. Belynda's eyes widened, then narrowed. For a moment, I wondered if she knew how close he had come to finding her, or if she had somehow picked up his thoughts or mine. But as I delved into her erratic thoughts, my worries eased.

"I know. I promised," I offered, and she crossed her arms. Even though I wanted nothing more than to please her, a part of me was hesitant, knowing Drake was so close to the surface. But I hated the look of disappointment on her face. "Fine. If you go change, I will take you now," I conceded. Watching Belynda's face light up was my consolation. As long as she knew the real me, no one and nothing else mattered.

Her imagination ran with her as she disappeared to her chambers, yet I found that knowing her thoughts was as equally rewarding as it was frustrating. Every time her attention drifted to memories of him, a tempest formed in the depths of my soul. But on seldom occasions, I caught a stray thought about me. Although it wasn't often, I had learned to hold on for those briefest moments, and they made the silent suffering endurable.

Her smile brightened the entryway when she returned, but I was distracted by the length of her shapely legs and how the skintight suit hugged her delicate curves.

She shifted on her bare feet, and I smiled.

"Ready?" she asked, while her thoughts jolted in all directions, something I soon must teach her to control. A quiet mind listened more and shared less. She was scared and excited, and a million questions shot at me at once, *Why do I have to wear a water suit when he gets to wear regular clothes? What if I get bitten by a shark? What if I can't breathe?*

"You will be safe. I promise. That's all that matters." Her heart slowed to a steady beat as she walked to my side. "Here. Take this." I placed a delicate crystal bottle in her hands, and her eyebrows furrowed, eyes glinting with curiosity. "The Waters of Isilium," I said, and she grinned up at me. "It will allow you to breathe underwater."

"Where is Isilium?" she asked. "Is that why you were gone?" The tides turned inside me; I hated keeping the truth from her.

"No. I had other business to tend to. I can't tell you all my secrets now, can I?" I smiled, hoping it would quell any further inquiry. She blinked a few times before returning her gaze to the bottle.

"Why must I drink this if I'm now immortal?"

"Because immortal or not, you still need to breathe. You can hold your breath for longer periods, but trust me, eventually, you will need it." The dip on her forehead became more pronounced as countless other questions sprung to life. "Don't worry, you wouldn't die. You would just lose consciousness." I clarified. "But you won't have to worry about it if you drink that. Trust me." The indecision in her thoughts was amusing, but one thought warmed my immortal soul. She trusted me.

"What happens when I drink this? Am I going to grow a tail or fins or something?"

My laughter echoed down the halls, and her lips quirked into a smile.

"If you want a tail and fins, I can arrange that. However, the waters won't change your physical appearance." I clarified.

She looked at the ocean wall before us and uncorked the bottle, glugging the purple liquid in one draw. Her lips puckered.

"Tastes like salt water," she winced, and I relished the knowledge. I had never tasted it myself.

"Shall we?" I offered my hand, and she peered at it briefly, then with a sigh, she placed her trembling fingers in mine. The sensation sent jolts through my skin, and I slowed my breathing to keep my mood from shifting the tides.

I stepped through the magic barrier. Immediately, my body floated, surrounded by the deep ocean and the silence of its depths. My hand remained through the threshold; microscopic bubbles stuck to Belynda's flesh as her hand moved with mine into the water, then her arm and her leg, until I pulled on her hand, and her body followed me through the barrier, floating before me. It was as if I was cradling her in my arms at last as my element supported her. Belynda's golden hair fanned across her face, and with a wave of my hand, a small current made it flow behind her like a halo. Her eyes remained closed, and her hand tightened around mine.

"You're safe." I urged my thoughts to drift freely into her mind. She had progressed enough in a few days to pick up on them. *"Open your eyes."*

Belynda's emerald orbs fluttered open, and the ocean breathed—*I* breathed. Her smile illuminated her face, and small bubbles danced across her lips, tempting me to lean in closer. *What was I doing to myself?* It would only hurt more in the end. I was only fooling myself. *It would always be him.*

"Callix, your hair..." Her thought reached me with a hint of wonder and surprise. I watched the tendrils of hair falling over my eyes turn a frosty white. I realized it was her first time seeing me in my element.

"It changes under the ocean," I explained, and the corners of my mouth twitched as her brows creased. *"You prefer dark hair, I know."* My thoughts slipped out, and I couldn't conceal my sarcasm.

"You don't know anything." The subtle irritation in her voice took me by surprise.

"I'm sorry," I said, smiling apologetically.

"It suits you." She tugged on my hand to show me the wonders of the sea, but I saw only her. I tried to not care, to not want or desire her... but I was lost.

Belynda's thoughts were bright like a child's, before her world became dark and dangerous.

"What are you doing?" Her thoughts poured into mine, tethering me to the moment. The golden strands of her hair danced around her face.

I released her hand, and panic glinted in her eyes, but I advanced, breaking through the water with my hands and feet. She followed.

Although it was darker in the depths of Serfier, her new immortality had gifted her striking vision, allowing her to enjoy every color and detail as if the brightest rays of the sun could reach the depths of Varenver.

The reefs, however, were void of their usually vibrancy. Because of her. No one had visited Serfier in thousands of years, and Belynda's presence here enraged most, who feared what they did not know.

"Stay here." My thoughts drifted into her mind, and she regarded me with uncertainty. *"You'll see."*

Her hair danced around her face as she nodded in understanding.

Drawing on the force of the currents, I propelled myself into a spinning vortex toward the ocean's surface. My kingdom could hide from her, but never from me. Not when their Lord summoned them. I broke through the current and a storm stretched across the water's surface. I felt the life force of every creature vibrating at my fingertips. Closing my eyes, I channeled energy into those strings—pulling, beckoning, summoning their presence, until I felt them give.

Once again, I descended beneath the blanket of the waves into the depths of my kingdom, and finally, to her side. Belynda's face was one of delight and I marvelled with pleasure as she turned in every direction, fascinated by every creature and color.

Her smile added warmth to my soul, and I felt the currents dissolve as my kingdom came alive for her.

"Come," I beckoned, offering my hand. *"There is something I want to show you."* She didn't hesitate. She slipped her fingers

into mine and smiled, eager to discover the secrets of my home, a thought exciting me beyond measure.

She had asked about the Waters of Isilium—a question I had eluded. I had claimed the unique waters were a secret I wasn't ready to share, but I was afraid—scared she would use its power to leave before she was ready. However, I had promised her I wouldn't lie and neglecting to mention Drake's visit already weighed on my conscience. If she chose to remain here, it would be because she wished to, not because of my impulses.

WE SWAM through the cavities of the underwater grottos as the blues and purples glowed and contrasted around us.

"Why does it glow?" she asked, her thoughts flowing through our connection as we broke the water's surface. As we entered the cave, I turned my attention to her, awe-struck at the intrigue in her eyes as she gazed at the ageless tree.

"The Waters of Isilium," I revealed, and her eyes widened, taking in the flowing vines of sparkling blues and purple cascading from the tree. They brushed over the water, tainting its surface.

"It's beautiful," she whispered, her eyes glued to the tree's radiance. "I've never seen anything like it before."

I was glad to be the one to give her this moment. While the realms offered wondrous sights, none would outshine the beauty of this place, and I was the one she experienced it with.

Her face glowed against the dancing reflection of the water, and her lips parted. I wanted to slowly lean in, trace my thumb across her bottom lip, and allow myself a taste. Her eyes flashed to me, and for a moment, I wondered if she read my thoughts... sensed my longing.

"Can I touch it?" she asked, and I released a sigh of relief.

"Go ahead."

The water threaded past her waist as she stepped closer to the tendrils floating on the water's surface. I stayed where I was, watching her from afar. I used the short distance to reign in my impulses and my thoughts. She beamed, glancing at me as her fingers grazed the flowing wisps.

"It's strange." She closed her hand around it and giggled. "It feels like electricity."

"You're sensing the tree's energy. Everything is connected."

She dropped her hand and whispered a thank you so low I wasn't sure if she intended it for me or the tree itself, but I smiled. Perhaps she sensed Isabel's connection to it.

How had I ever doubted if she would be worthy of Isabel's sacrifice? How had I ever despised such a beautiful thing? Perhaps I was destined to love her in silence for my mistakes, and to never have her look at me the way she looks at him.

4
SERFIER

IT FELT PECULIAR, *STEPPING THROUGH THE* threshold of magic, keeping the ocean from penetrating the castle walls. My feet were like jelly the moment they touched solid ground. Without warning, I dove, but Callix was stealthy. He snaked his hand around my waist and steadied me against his body.

Callix's face was smooth, and I watched the magic barrier suck the water droplets falling from his skin and hair. In a few seconds, his hair returned to its usual darkness. I wasn't sure how I had missed that earlier when he first stepped through the barrier. His locks were dry, as were his clothes, except for where I touched his chest. That part remained moist, the water trapped under my touch.

His cerulean eyes regarded me, and for a moment, I was lost within them. His skin was smooth like glistening granite; his firm jaw chiseled by the gods themselves. My stomach fluttered, and as my thoughts muddled, he smiled. Something inside my mind snapped me back into reality. He could hear…

Lalalalalalalalala! I flooded my mind with incessant rambling and ran before he could hear any more of my traitorous thoughts, but I was too late. His laughter reached me down the corridor. Callix was dangerous; I couldn't allow myself to swim in muddied waters with him—*literally!* Except our incredible underwater adventure wasn't as lethal as his presence. I had to get away from him and from Serfier if I had any hope of surviving.

I SPENT the next few days mulling over my precarious situation. I wasn't sure how I could face Callix. The last thing I wanted was to give him the wrong impression. I loved Drake; destiny had bound us together. There would be no one else for me.

And somehow, the thought saddened me. No part of me wished to hurt Callix. I had grown to care for him, but anything beyond friendship was impossible.

Who was I kidding? I couldn't hide in this room forever. We needed to carry on with training. The faster I learned everything the Fates required of me, the sooner I could return to Drake before any further damage was done.

Callix had been nothing but sensible with me. We were both adults, and I would have to be blind—or dead—not to appreciate his God-given beauty. I was acting foolish. I had nothing to be ashamed of. Just because I recognized how handsome he was didn't mean I had feelings for him.

Arming myself with divine resolution, I marched in search of the Sea God.

I strode the empty halls of the castle. What sort of life must he have lived all alone down here? It was no wonder he visited the other realms. It made me curious about his parents and his family, for in the short time I had been here, I saw no other creature except for the nymphs. Nor did Callix seem attached to the merfolk living in the reef city beneath the castle, which had me wondering if he was even one of them. I knew nothing of the Sea God.

LAUGHTER ECHOED THE QUIET HALLS, and I stepped out of my room and followed it.

The nymph's voices trickled through a barely open door, and I paused outside when I picked up the tenor of Callix's voice, followed by melodious laughter. I frowned, unsure whether to leave or knock, but I found myself unable to walk away.

I knocked softly against the door. It parted slightly, and I glimpsed a burning fire and the corner of a desk.

"Come in." Callix's voice was smooth, and I took in a breath before entering.

I froze. The energy of the room sizzled with lust. I wanted to turn and run, but my legs betrayed me.

Callix sat behind the desk, his white shirt unbuttoned as Syllis leaned over him, trailing her hand down his shoulder. I followed the path of her fingers as they brushed the skin at the side of his neck. The other nymph, Phial, sat comfortably on his armrest, staring up at me.

"You finally decided to come up for air…" Callix's eyes pinned me in place. "Did you want something?" His voice was drawn, void of emotion, and for the first time, I struggled to find words in his presence.

I glanced between the nymphs, but neither moved.

"I was wondering if you were ready to resume our training." I almost choked on my words as his fingers trailed mindlessly down Syllis's arm.

"And you're ready now?" His eyes met mine, and I felt the blush creep on my face.

"I—I'm up to it if you're not busy." I paused. "I would hate to intrude."

I glanced between the two girls cemented to Callix's side. I found a subtle pleasure in disrupting whatever plans he had, and I realized it was my immediate dislike of the nymphs that brought out such sentiments. Perhaps it was retribution for the prank they pulled at breakfast.

"There is plenty of time for play later," Callix promised, the corner of his lips quirking into a half smile. The nymphs erupted in giggles, their melodic voices like nails against a chalkboard. Luckily, Callix offered mercy. He pointed to the door, and that was all it took for the nymphs to pull away and leave the room.

The second they were gone, I felt like I could breathe. Callix made no remarks, though I knew he could sense my thoughts. Rising from his chair, he rolled his shirt sleeves up to his elbows and walked around the desk. He closed the door behind us.

"Should we continue where we left off?" His voice startled me; he was standing much closer than I anticipated.

"Yes. I think so."

He motioned for me to take a seat while he paced to the

other side of the desk. He propped himself up on his forearms and leaned forward, the corner of his lips tilting into a grin.

"What am I thinking now?" If the tone of his voice wasn't indicative enough of his thoughts, the storm behind his eyes voiced the unspoken. But I dove in anyway.

I reached with my mind, and when the strobing images, voices, and whispers reached me, I pulled back to catch my breath.

"I... I don't know," I whispered, and his eyebrows rose.

"Try again." Leaning across the table with his fingers intertwined, Callix's eyes became glowing pools of blue. I ignored the warning that chimed inside of me and swam towards it. I sensed the depths of his thoughts, and when the soft whispers and pants of pleasure reached me, I froze, for it was my voice I heard. My mind recoiled, and I stood, knocking the chair behind me.

"I... I'm sorry. I can't." I strode to the door, but his voice made me halt.

"You can't, or you won't?" he challenged. I didn't dare turn around. Why was he doing this to me?

"Callix. I know what you must think, I just..." I found the courage to turn and find his eyes. "Whatever that was... it doesn't exist. There isn't a part of me that could ever feel that way about you."

Callix didn't shift or blink. It was almost as if he was hearing a song he'd heard countless times, and somehow, the thought made my chest ache. For him. "I'm sorry."

It was best to call it a night. I wasn't sure if it was desire or alcohol numbing his senses, but I didn't give him a chance to say anything else he might regret.

Callix didn't follow, and I was thankful for that small mercy. Contemplating my options, I strolled aimlessly down the halls until I reached the door to my chamber, but my restlessness wouldn't be stowed in the confines of my bedroom. With resolve, I turned around and returned to the only place that would give me solace.

I pushed against the white marble doors of the library and, once more, became overwhelmed by its grandeur. I moved along the shelves, inspecting the mountain of books placed neatly on one of the reading desks; they hadn't been there the last time we were here.

I reached for the top book and inspected the back cover. I grinned. *A romance novel...*

I picked up the next one and the next, though it was more of the same. One book in particular made my smile widen. An alchemy book. The joke wasn't lost on me.

This had Callix written all over it. I glanced at the three levels of the library. It was probably his indirect way of ensuring I didn't break my neck this time, which made me question a vital thing about my newfound immortality. What was my weakness? Could I peril under blue fire like Drake? Could Callix? I frowned at the thought.

I took to one of the couches, lying across it with a book. Flipping through the pages, I lost myself in the story, and when I reached the end, I realized I had read the entire volume in record time. Another perk of immortality. Glancing at the world of books surrounding me, I thought of the endless possibilities and the knowledge one could acquire with such skill.

There was so much I had to learn. Yet, as the realization of my potential settled in, I knew there was no point in running. No other realm was as close to the Fates; no other could help me reach my potential like Callix could. Though I understood the risks, this was where I had to remain until I was ready to face the darkness. I closed my eyes briefly, sensing myself slip in and out of consciousness.

"I'm sorry…" The echo of his voice pierced through my quiet mind, and I opened my eyes, startled. I searched the empty library, but there was no sign of him. I pulled open the library doors, but the hallways were empty, and Callix was nowhere in sight. Again, I closed my eyes, focusing on the sounds echoing around the castle. My skills weren't as developed to recognize the distinct sounds. Had I imagined his apology to set things right between us? Unlikely. I knew the extent of his powers, and the echo of his voice pulled at a distant memory until I was suddenly back in Druleska at the water fountain, and then I knew… the voice in the whispering wind had been no other than Callix.

I listened for any sign of him or the nymphs on returning to my chambers, but I was met by silence, except for the subtle sounds of the ocean outside. I frowned, wondering if they had continued their interlude. Slamming the chamber doors more forcefully than intended, I slumped on the bed. I missed Drake. I missed my family and even Tolly's company despite my aversion to being waited on.

Sleep claimed me after a while, but it was not a peaceful slumber.

The blue and purple waters of the caves engulfed my waist, and

I was back there, surrounded by the Waters of Isilium. Callix's curious eyes beheld me.

His white shirt stuck to his skin, and I stared, lost into the depths of his blue eyes. Droplets of water trailed the lines of his chiseled jaw as I reached a hand, running my fingertips over his skin, watching his eyes become a dark storm. His lips parted.

"What am I thinking now?" His voice echoed, and suddenly, we were no longer surrounded by water. I sat before a burning fireplace while Callix sat across from me behind his desk. His eyes were fixed to mine, urging me to explore the depths of his mind. I lost myself to soft whispers and pants of pleasure; flashes of Callix appeared. Callix urging my legs apart. His breath fanning my face. Pressed over me and trapping my body against the bed, he rocked with the sway of the ocean waves.

"Why are you fighting this?" His nose skimmed my cheeks, and I knew he was smiling. "Sometimes what is meant to be is not what comes to be, and other times, what comes to be is not what is meant to be." I pulled back to look at him, but the weight of his body over mine was replaced by the look of the three Fates perched atop their pillars.

"Fight for us..." I glanced around to find Drake's dark, pleading eyes. A piercing sharp pain stabbed through my middle and I glanced at Dagasti's smug face in front of me.

"You cannot stop me," he taunted. He touched the Nightshade necklace around his neck, and the darkness came for me. The shadows slithered like tendrils, but I couldn't move. I was once again in shackles, forgotten in the silence of the dungeons, overcome by despair as the darkness closed in, and it was all I could see.

. . .

I sprung from bed, fighting to regain control of my reality. Tears streamed down my cheeks and sweat coated my sheets. No one lived through what I had and survived without scars, I reminded myself. Shaking off the remnants of the nightmares, I slipped into the bath chamber.

I donned a white skirt and a matching top from my closet, leaving my room in search for food.

The moment I stepped into the dining hall, I froze. Callix was already seated, his eyes closed and head resting against the chair. He looked exhausted. When he opened his eyes, they locked on me, moving over my body with a hunger-filled gaze. A blush crept onto my cheeks, and for a moment, the images of the dream returned to my mind, with Callix's body over mine. *Don't think about it; don't think about it; don't think about it.* I tried to drown out the memory, but as Callix's laughter filled the room, I knew it was pointless.

I turned to leave, but he was at my side instantly, his face humorless.

"I'm sorry," he said, searching my eyes. "I'm not playing fair, I know. Forgive me. I promise I'll behave." He pressed, though the corner of his mouth lifted into a smile. I couldn't help myself.

"Today, you teach me how to block my thoughts."

He pursed his lips, his mouth forming a thin line. Then he smiled.

"Fine," he conceded. I beamed up at him and took my place at the table.

"What's for breakfast?" I asked. Callix strolled back to his place with a bemused expression. "What?" I questioned. His grin merely widened.

"Just so you know, the more you tell yourself not to think about something, the more your subconscious manifests it..." I rolled my eyes, but nonetheless, I appreciated the tip.

"What's a more effective way then?"

"After breakfast," he said, clearly stalling. "Sleep well?" he asked, and I immediately knew his intentions. I narrowed my eyes at him, which only made his smile widen. Before I could question him, the nymphs interrupted us.

Syllis placed the tray before Callix and Phial brought mine. I looked suspiciously at the giggling women, who hovered behind Callix. The food looked delicious, but he must have noticed my irritation. With a wave of his hand, they were gone.

"They really aren't so bad once you get to know them," he remarked, bringing a piece of pancake to his mouth. I rolled my eyes and took a bite of my toast to keep from commenting, not like that would deter him from reaching into my mind.

He smiled and took another bite. I glared at him. He was the devil incarnate...

"Do you make it a habit of invading people's thoughts without permission?"

He chewed with premeditated slowness before resting his knife and fork on the table, finding my eyes. He braced his forearms on the table as he had done the night before, and leaned in.

"Often, but not as much as I enjoy invading yours," he declared, all traces of amusement gone. I swallowed and took another bite, but he didn't continue. His eyes traced my every move.

"Why is that? What's so interesting about me?" I asked,

taking a sip from my cup. His brows shot up and I was suddenly questioning if I really wanted to know the answer. But I did. I wanted to know everything.

"Apart from your colorful imagination?" He paused, and I sensed the indecision in his eyes, wondering whether to say more. "For many years, I imagined what it would be like. The tone and color that your thoughts would take, and now I get to experience it…" He paused and shook his head as if dispelling a thought. He picked up his knife and fork again. "Now I can't stop myself." He confessed before bringing a piece of fruit to his mouth. It was as if his confession was nothing out of the ordinary.

I swallowed and placed the fork down.

"Years?" I repeated. He looked up to meet my eyes. "Why?" So many questions swam in my mind. "Not even Drake knew who I was. The doors to the Realms had been closed. So, please, tell me how you knew of me." I searched his face as Callix leaned back in his chair.

"It's all part of the Fates' grand plan. It was her fault, you know." He ran his fingers mindlessly around the rim of the cup. "Isabel. She was special, just like you."

"You knew her too?"

He did. He must have, because suddenly, everything he said in my last moments in Druleska made sense… *'You're making the same mistake she did. Choosing him will always be your downfall.'*

"I knew her well. Better than most and perhaps even better than Drake himself." His admission left me stunned, but it offered a new insight into the strained dynamics of Drake and Callix. Were their differences because of her?

"Did she tell you about me?" He smiled and nodded.

"She did. She spoke often of you, filling my head with endless notions. I followed along, thinking I could change her plan and her path... but in the end, I couldn't change her mind." The sorrow behind his glazed blue eyes confirmed my worst fears. The decision to sacrifice herself... I would be a fool not to realize how much Isabel had meant to Callix, too. This was much more complicated than I had anticipated.

"You knew," I whispered but I couldn't bring myself to finish the sentence.

"I did, and even though her promise of re-birth came true..." His eyes found mine. "I hated you for it. I hated that you were the cause of her sacrifice, even though she was a part of you."

I couldn't hate him for his admission. Not long ago, before Dagasti claimed my life in Druleska, he had admitted his hesitation to save me. It was the reason why I never saw him in my vision.

"That's why you hesitated to save me..."

"I'm sorry."

I owed Callix my life, and I was eternally thankful for it.

"For what it's worth." I paused, and he watched me from across the table. "I'm glad you changed your mind about me." He smiled, and I was glad for that, too. I hated a brooding Callix.

"Can I ask you a question?"

"Do you have to? Can't you just rummage through my mind, like you're used to doing?"

Callix smiled but shook his head.

"Not unless you're thinking of it. I could coerce you to tell me anything, but I promised I wouldn't do that, and I meant what I said."

That was comforting, at least.

"Ask away then." I took a sip from my cup, and he leaned closer.

"Why didn't you come with me when I asked you to? Why did you choose death?" His question surprised me, yet more surprising was the need behind his eyes to understand. The need to know. I thought back to that moment.

"Isabel's letter said that only in death would I discover my true self. I admit, some part of me was scared, but I was tired of fighting. I figured if that's what the Fates wanted, then who was I to go against it?" Callix stared. "It turns out I was right. If I had come with you, I wouldn't have ascended. I wouldn't be enjoying the perks of immortality." I sipped from my cup and smiled to ease the shift in conversation, yet he remained serious.

"You're wrong." His words sobered me.

"What do you mean?"

His eyes bore into mine. "I mean, you could have become immortal without suffering a mortal death. All that pain and suffering could have been avoided if you would have just chosen to come with me." I stared at him, speechless. "Visions are not set in stone, you know... It is all about the choices we make. Nothing is ever a straight line." The information was a heavy weight on my mind.

"Why didn't you tell me?"

"I tried, but like Isabel, your mind was made up." I swallowed as the blue depths of his eyes pinned me to my seat.

"Did you steal the Sacred Book and find the relics for her?"

"Yes. They were all part of her last requests," he admitted, and I noted the clench of his jaw and the tightening of his fists on the table. The food before us was long forgotten.

"Callix?" I said, and his eyes met mine. "What made you change your mind about me?" His lips parted, then closed, though his eyes never left mine.

"I don't know," he admitted. His change of heart was a mystery to him, too.

"Whatever the reason, I'm glad for it. Thank you," I offered with sincerity. "For saving me countless times back in Druleska. For visiting me when my world was dark and lonely in those cells."

"For bringing you water," he added, smiling. I returned it.

"You know, it would have made everything so much easier for the both of us if you had told me the truth from the beginning." I chided. He laughed, and it warmed my heart.

"We both know it wouldn't have..."

Perhaps he was right. I had misconceptions about the Merpeople, and my view of the Water Lord was already tainted by other people's opinions, especially Drake's. Yes, perhaps he was right, but I would never admit to it... not out loud. Callix laughed wholeheartedly, having surely sensed my thoughts.

"Will you stop stalling?" I fought the urge to stomp on the floor as he delayed our training by showing me the grand ballroom.

"You will have to work on your patience, especially now you're immortal," he said, pacing beside me.

"Seriously, Callix."

He turned to look at me.

"Think about the dream," he demanded, and my eyes widened, unsure if I had heard him correctly.

"What dream?" I feigned ignorance, attempting to lock my mind from the memory. But he was right. All it took was that one command for my mind to conjure up the images I so desperately wanted to block. To my relief—or horror—he didn't smile. Instead, he hesitantly reached to me, tucking a loose strand of hair behind my ear. I noticed he took extra care not to touch my skin.

"You wanted to learn," he said, "then show me, and I will show you."

My mouth opened and closed.

"Is payment a requirement for my training now?" I asked, and he smiled.

"That's not a bad idea. After all the times I've saved your pretty neck..." His eyes found my lips, and a blush tinged my cheeks. "But, no, just this once. I want to know what you desperately want to hide from me."

I narrowed my eyes. "Like you don't already know?" The corner of his mouth turned up into a smile.

"I would rather enjoy the scene without interruptions," he said, and it took me a moment to understand what he meant. "Show me," he urged, and his eyes drew me in.

"It means nothing. It was only a dream."

"Humor me," he said. I wanted to roll my eyes, but I was lost in the depths of his.

I saw him again, back at the caves; my hand reached out, stroking his face, and he was above me, pinning me to the bed as his body moved achingly slow over mine.

Callix sucked in a breath and stepped away from me.

"Yes. I think you should keep those thoughts to yourself," he said through gritted teeth, his expression pained.

"Then show me," I pressed, and my determination made him smile.

"Every thought has a color," he explained. The confusion must have been clear on my face as he added, "When you think about that image of my body flushed above yours? What color comes to mind?" I didn't realize he had closed the distance until I felt his breath fan my face. I shivered. *Colors... he was talking about colors?*

"Red," I blurted and watched the corner of his lips turn up.

"Think of red then. Paint your thoughts. Choose an element. Build a red wall; cover your thoughts in red smoke, red liquid. You choose."

I blinked up at him, allowing my mind to fill with waves of red. My thoughts were submerged, muffled by the depths of a red ocean. He laughed, and the walls crumpled.

"What?" I questioned, staring up at him. His face was so close I felt the warmth of his body brush against mine.

"I didn't think you would pick water, that's all." He noted in surprise.

"Why not?" I replied. "It's my strongest element," I said, and his head tilted.

"Is it?"

"Somehow, it is," I confirmed. "It's always been the easiest to connect with. Water always remained even when I couldn't sense the other elements."

His face was a mix of surprise and curiosity.

"I wonder why that is." He glanced over my face, as if trying to understand.

"If the Lord of the Water doesn't know, how am I supposed to?" I teased, and he smiled.

"I don't know everything," he declared as we walked side by side through the ballroom. "But I intend to figure that one out."

THE TRAINING WAS COLORFUL—LITERALLY. I took great pleasure as Callix and I delved into the complexity of thoughts and their tones and shades. After a few days of playful teasing and friendly banter, I had a loose grasp of how to keep him out of my head. Well, for the most part, at least. Even though he insisted he couldn't see through my walls, something told me it wasn't true. I doubted he could so quickly lose access to my thoughts, but I hung on to his promise that he wouldn't lie to me.

"Is that how you block your thoughts as well?" I asked, aware that each time I attempted to reach into his mind, no waves of colors or walls met me. Only silence.

"I prefer my barriers simpler. Cleaner."

I rolled my eyes; he was such a control freak. If the crystal-clean, polished castle wasn't enough indication of his tastes, his very being was. Callix was always sharply dressed in crisp white shirts and black or midnight slacks, forever perfectly groomed. He always smelled clean and fresh like the ocean tinged with sunlight. I didn't bother blocking my thoughts; he could live with my opinion of his maniacal ways.

His laughter boomed as we paused outside my chambers.

"Maniacal?" he probed.

"What?" I challenged, smiling. "That's what happens

when you snoop into people's minds. You tend to hear things you don't want to," I mocked the Sea God, and his eyes darkened. It was so easy to tease Callix that I often forgot the dangers of it.

"I like order." His eyes scanned my face and paused over my lips. I held my breath as he moved in slowly. "But do not be fooled…" His warm breath brushed the skin of my cheek, and I froze as his voice vibrated close to my ear in warning. "I welcome chaos just the same."

I blinked and took a step back. He was so overwhelming at times that he made me forget everything else. My breath, my mind—*Drake.* I frowned.

I noted Callix's brows furrow, but he chose not to comment. He donned a smile, like a mask, and opened the door to my room.

"I will see you at dinner," he said, hovering at the door's threshold, peering down at me.

"Are you trying to fatten me up? I'm still full from lunch."

His lips quirked into a half smile as his eyes scanned my body.

"You need to eat and regain your strength before we move on to more physical training."

"Physical training?"

"You didn't think it was all mind games, did you?" He winked and turned away, disappearing down the hall.

I was scared. I had never been very coordinated, so I tended to avoid all physical pursuits. I never thought developing my abilities would require physical training, but if a war was coming, perhaps it was time I learned to defend myself. Had I possessed the skill back in Druleska, I would have probably faired differently against Dagasti. At the very least, I could have given those guards a proper fight. Instead, I attempted to drown them in a water bubble. *Pathetic.* I frowned; I had no clue how to use my powers to attack, but that would have to change. If my mind were to become as sharp as a knife, I would make sure my body was just as lethal.

GLANCING at myself in the long mirror, I noticed my body looked fuller, healthier, and alive. I was no longer skin and bones. A pink blush tainted my cheeks in contrast to the pale, deathly complexion when I first awoke here. Running my hand over my lips, I thought of Drake and I wondered how he was. Something inside of me ached to see his face, to run to him and bury myself in his arms.

The thought of him suffering tormented me, questioning if I was alive or dead. He wouldn't understand my reasons for choosing to stay here. He had too many differences with Callix —too much mistrust. Drake's need to keep me safe would never allow him to see things my way. He would never understand my need to remain here until I was ready to fulfill my purpose.

My choices were for the best. I had to endure the guilt of his absence and repel the need to reach out and tell Drake I was okay and that I loved and ached to be with him.

Tears brimmed my eyes, but I fought the crushing feelings. If I allowed myself to think or to feel, I wouldn't be able to follow through with my decision, and I was stronger than that. I had to be. For the realms and Drake. If, as the Fates had revealed, I could change his destiny, I would give the threads of possibilities all my might. I would devastate the balance of life itself to keep him alive. I knew Drake was hurting, but it wouldn't be for long. Soon, I would be with him, and all the pain and suffering would have been worth it. I would finally be worthy of someone like him.

I stiffened as I slipped out of the bathroom and entered the room. I glanced around suspiciously, but there was no sign of Callix or the nymphs, though someone had been in here. A box rested on my bed with a note.

Don't be long... I'm starving.

It had to be Callix's handwriting. I didn't think the nymphs would be this playful or bold to cross me again. I studied the long, clean strokes of his pen and smiled.

I lifted the box lid and beamed at a pair of faded blue jeans. *He knew.* Of course he did. I frowned as I reached inside the box, pulling out a white crop top—that was almost see-through—and a lacy white bra with matching underwear, if one could call it that. I picked up the tiny string piece and shook my head.

My relationship with the Sea God was easy, and, for the most part, friendly. Yet, I often found myself locked within his sea tentacles, especially when he unleashed the full force of his charm. The teasing and the banter made my days go by that much faster, yet not a moment passed when Drake didn't slip into my mind. Guilt often consumed me, knowing how much he despised Callix, and yet I couldn't bring myself to agree with his sentiments.

I could never hate Callix. Even though he was exasperating

at times, I recognized the loneliness behind his eyes. He deserved someone who could love him, and while that person wasn't me, I had sometimes found myself lost to Callix's allure. A mirage of the moment, I realized. Of my desperation and loneliness and my yearning to be with Drake. The unspent desires of immortality.

Peering at myself in the mirror, I smiled. Despite the audacity of his gift, he had good taste. The jeans hugged my body like a second skin, and the long-sleeved top rested inches above my navel. The white mesh left nothing to the imagination. I could see the lacy white bra underneath and the swell of my breasts. I contemplated changing, but the clothes were too comfortable, and besides, judging from the nymphs' usual attire, the lack of clothing was common among the water people. And shoes. I grimaced, glancing at my bare feet on the cold marble floors.

I REACHED the dining hall and found the room and table empty. Frowning, I narrowed my eyes. The nymphs were irritable women, and I closed my eyes, listening for them. After a moment, I heard their laughter. I stamped through the open corridors and followed their irritating giggles. I didn't care what Callix said; I would wring their necks.

Their voices sounded from an open terrace. The contained ocean surrounding the space was like stepping into an underwater snow globe. I swallowed my protests when I saw the dinner table on the open balcony where Callix was sitting. I wasn't sure how it was possible he could look even more impeccable than usual, but somehow, he did. This evening, his dark blue trousers matched a perfectly pressed suit jacket; intricate gold thread crossed the lapels and shoulders, and his signature crisp white shirt peeked from underneath. I glanced down at my own attire, feeling severely underdressed. I didn't miss how his eyes crept slowly over my body. Crossing my arms, I suddenly felt self-conscious.

Callix's eyes locked with mine as he dismissed the nymphs, and holding my gaze, he rose from his chair and took measured steps towards me. The corner of his lips twitched into a half-smile, and my eyes narrowed in his direction.

"What's this all about?" I asked, and he moved to the side, extending his hand towards the table.

"Just dinner. Come, join me."

I attempted to slip into his mind, but I was met with only darkness and silence. He knew what I had done; I could tell by the defiant rise of his eyebrow as he pulled the chair for me to sit. Suspiciously, I took my seat. The table looked so intimate that I couldn't help but feel unsettled.

"What's wrong with the dining hall?" I inquired, picking up my napkin. He brought the glass to his lips.

"Nothing," he said, resting the glass on the table. "I thought you might enjoy the change of scenery." He replied with uncalculated ease, and I stared into his eyes, searching for an ulterior motive. I found nothing. Only blue, calm ocean. He was being truthful, I realized.

"Thank you for the jeans." I watched him in my periphery while I stared at the ocean wall before us. "You could have warned me it was a formal occasion," I added, still sensing his eyes on me. I turned to look at him and found the blue in his eyes had shifted, darkening. Slowly, they perused me, trailing from my face, the swell of my breasts, and stopping over the skin around my waist. Bracing his forearm against the table's edge, he leaned in without a trace of humor.

"I didn't think you would wear it, but you look..." His gaze fell on mine, and the wicked sheen in his eyes made me freeze. "Mouthwatering." For a moment, my heart thumped in my chest, and I felt my cheeks heat.

"Will you stop trying to seduce me!" I warned, feeling trapped in my own body; he stared back at me with brows raised. All traces of his smile vanished as he leaned closer.

"Trust me, darling... if I were trying to seduce you, you would be bent over this table." His voice darkened like the navy depths of his eyes, and for a moment, I felt his mind probing into mine as he ran his thumb over his bottom lip. *"Or perhaps on your knees. I would make sure my cock was so deep in your sweet little mouth that you wouldn't be able to speak."*

My mouth opened and closed, and my heart pounded. What was the matter with him? He looked possessed, like that night in his office. I stood, the chair scraping behind me. His face transformed with confusion, but I didn't allow him the chance to speak. I ran. I only managed a few corridors before my legs gave out, and I collapsed in a heaping mess against the marble floors, fighting to catch my breath as tears blurred my vision.

Why was he doing this to me? Especially now, when I desperately needed someone I could trust. I was so lost in my confusion I didn't hear him come up behind me.

"Please forgive me. You weren't meant to hear or see that. I got caught up in the moment." Callix's voice sliced through the silence of the hall and I glanced behind me. Callix reached for me, but I recoiled. He froze, his face suddenly haunted. "I would never hurt you," he whispered. "Belynda. Please!" His eyes reached for mine, pleading, but I glanced away, staring at my hands. I wiped the tears from my face.

"Why are you doing this to me? What was that?" I waited for an answer, and when none came, I pushed myself to stand, ignoring his outstretched hand.

"I'm trying..." His words gave me pause, his eyes desperately scanning my face. "I'm trying to fight this *madness*—this consuming desire to have you." He paused but didn't move from his spot. "I can't explain this irrational need to drown myself in you. I can't stand to see you pull away every time, fighting against the tide. Wanting to be with him..." He closed his eyes and ran his hands over his jaw. "I'm trying to stow the storm, believe me, but I am desperately fighting not to drown in the process." His eyes looked savage, lost, adrift...

Callix. My heart sank, fracturing into millions of pieces.

I had a feeling this would be hard; I just never imagined how difficult it might be for him. His confession only complicated things further for me—for us.

A part of me ached to close the space and ease his suffering. To offer him comfort. Seeing this side of him pained me, but I couldn't move. Callix was no longer dangerous; he was poison to my heart. He had slowly woven himself into my soul, and it would only hurt to extricate myself from him.

"I'm sorry." I attempted to pull him from the storm, my uncertain eyes finding his. "I didn't know. I think I should leave..."

"NO!" He took a step toward me then caught himself. "It

won't happen again. I promise." While he could try, that promise was a stretch.

"Callix, I hate seeing you like this. I hate that I'm the cause, and I wish…" I glanced at the crystal ceilings for divine intervention. "I wish things were different, but they aren't, and I—"

"You love him. You choose him." His eyes remained locked on mine. "I know." His eyes briefly fell to my feet before returning to my gaze. "Stay," he pleaded, yet there was so much more behind that simple request, so much to consider, and so much at stake. If I stayed, I would have to accept the risks, all the while knowing that one of us was bound to get hurt—perhaps both. I knew the answer before even considering it. I had to remain here. It was the only way to be ready to face the darkness. To save Drake. To change whatever path the Fates had marked for him.

"I will stay," I conceded, though he likely knew my decision already. My thoughts weren't contained from his prying mind, and as I probed his, I found the usually serene and silent thoughts of the Sea God had turned wild, unhinged, and stormy. I didn't probe.

"Tomorrow after breakfast, meet me in the pits at the lower chambers." He glanced over my face once. "Wear something comfortable," he added before turning away.

"Wait… where are the pits?" I called after him. But he didn't turn. I felt him slip into my mind in answer.

"You'll find your way, you always do." His somber voice echoed.

What was I getting myself into? And what was I going to do with Callix?

5
CALM BEFORE THE STORM

WE PREPARED TO FACE THE DARKNESS. Despite the mounting pressure, Phoenix's spirit burned with fierce resolve, a reminder that true leaders were forged in times of adversity. The warrior drew strength from his people's unwavering loyalty and spirit; he knew that, together, they stood a better chance against the coming darkness. I used to think of Phoenix as a spirited fool, but in the last few days I'd glimpsed a different side of the young warrior. He seemed to possess an ability I lost with each passing day. The fire of hope—the beacon to guide me through the darkness looming in my thoughts at every waking moment.

Each passing day without word from Callix intensified my anguish. The flames within me burned with a mix of longing, frustration, jealousy, and something I had never dared to admit. *Fear.* My bond with Belynda had been forged through many trials and triumphs, and the thought of losing her ignited something fierce within me. Questions constantly plagued my mind yet no answers came, fueling the sense of helplessness and a burning desire to not exist.

My thoughts often drifted to memories of our time together, and I recalled each memory with a bittersweet ache. I yearned for her presence, the sound of her laughter, and the warmth of her touch. But no communication had suspended me in a permanent state of agony. Uncertainty weighed heavy on my immortal soul, and day by day, her absence dimmed my fire which once burned bright. I constantly battled the vestiges of hope and the overwhelming despair. I tried to cling desperately to the belief that she was alive, but on days like today when I watched the sun rise in the horizon, I feared the worst.

"No sleep, I take it?" Euros plopped himself beside me while I studied Link and Phoenix's moves, their swords clashing and echoing in the silence of the training forge.

"I can't remember the last time I closed my eyes," I admitted.

"You sure as hell look like you could use a week-long doze."

I snorted. If only I could shut off my mind, then perhaps my eyes would follow.

"How's Phoenix?" he asked, voice tinged with concern. The days to come could shape the future of the Euresian Clan.

"People don't often surprise me," I admitted, "but he has the resilience of a bullheaded beast, making me believe we might actually stand a chance against Dagasti."

"I agree. He is a hardheaded fool." Euros grinned. "Even I have dared to hope that this is the break we need to push back and take back Upherya from Dagasti's claws."

"Honestly, boys. It's quite early to be brooding." Amirth's voice boomed within the Forge's walls, and Euros stiffened at my side. He hated when she called us 'boys,' and while I had learned to ignore her provocations, Euros had not.

"Drake…" Amirth stalled, placing her hands on her hips. "You look like you could use a worthy opponent to pounce on. Want to spar?"

Not if my life depended on it…

"I'm running morning patrol soon, but I'm sure Euros won't mind taking my place." Euros stamped my foot, but I paid him no mind. Her eyes narrowed in his direction.

"Well?" she said, twirling the small blade in her hand. Euros straightened. I pitied the poor fool, for he looked like he was about to accept her challenge.

"I don't know. I don't see a worthy opponent before me." Her eyes narrowed into slits, yet her smile issued the warning. Something Euros foolishly unheeded. I wasn't sure if leaving them was the best idea.

"Well then, you won't mind showing me a thing or two," she challenged. Euros grinned and marched to the dirt-paved ring, falling face-first into her trap. He never learned.

Phoenix and Link hung their swords and vacated the small arena, claiming Euros' seat.

"Doesn't he know that the woman is possessed?" Phoenix smirked. "My money is on the demon girl."

"I'm not betting against you," Link quipped.

"Don't look at me," I said before he even asked.

Amirth and Euros circled, each measuring the other. Amirth's weapons of choice were her lethal twin blades, the perfect weight and size for her frame. She was smart. Euros chose the sword, and while it wasn't a bad decision—for it was his mastered weapon—it was much more useful in battle, not close combat. She would make him eat his words.

Amirth took her time, but Euros seemed impatient, ready to pounce.

Amirth's eyes flashed with determination, her muscles coiled and ready for action. Her controlled power was her greatest weapon, and Euros seemed to realize the same, controlling his impulses. He circled her, calculating, assessing her strengths and weaknesses.

The clash of steel rang out, and Amirth and Euros moved in balance, skill, and strategy. Amirth's agility allowed her to dodge Euros' swift strikes with a combination of evasive moves and well-timed parries. Her earth powers enhanced her movements, allowing her to maintain a solid footing, surprising Euros with her sudden burst of strength.

Euros might have let his impulse blind him, but he was a master of tactics. He took every miss to analyze Amirth's style, seeking to exploit any opening he could find. He utilized his strength and precision, launching calculated attacks to test Amirth's defenses. Euros intended to push her limits and force her into making a mistake he could exploit.

"Are you sure you won't take bets?" Phoenix grinned. "It looks like a pretty close match; I might be wrong about the demon girl after all."

Link chose to ignore him. As did I.

They tired each other out. Amirth's earth powers added an unpredictable element to the fight as she summoned rocks and dirt to shield herself from Euros' onslaught.

"Hey, not fair!" Euros ground out, shielding his eyes. Yet

Amirth didn't yield. Her strike was delivered with a mix of grace and lethal force, proving her mastery over her chosen weapons.

"No rules, remember?" She flashed a deadly smile, and, undeterred, Euros intensified his efforts. He employed feints and swift footwork to outmaneuver her, exploiting any weakness he could find. However, Amirth met his every move with unwavering focus and determination, countering his attacks with precision and tenacity.

As the battle climaxed, it became evident that Amirth had gained the upper hand. Her unwavering resolve and solid skill proved too much for Euros to overcome. She disarmed him with a final, decisive strike, leaving him momentarily stunned and breathless.

Euros tasted the bitterness of defeat, yet I recognized something else in his eyes—respect. However, the moment he straightened and summoned two wind vortices, I realized the fight wasn't over. He was even more hardheaded than Phoenix.

"He's a fool," I said under my breath, rising to my feet.

"You're leaving?" asked Phoenix, amused. "But it's about to get even better."

"I know how it ends, and I have more important things to do. As do you." At my stern words, his smile vanished.

"He's right," added Link. "Let them get it out of their system. We have barriers to re-enforce."

Reluctantly, Phoenix followed, but not before a final smirking glance at the sparring duo.

"Try not to kill each other!" he called, but the warriors paid him no mind.

The last thing I saw was Amirth breaking the earth beneath Euros' feet, throwing him off balance. Link followed me out of the Forge with an annoyed Phoenix in his wake.

EUROS

I smiled, measuring her up. Yes, Amirth was a worthy opponent, but I would rather die than admit defeat.

"Let's see how skilled you are without your weapons," I teased, forcing her back with the swirling wind. If her smile was any indication, she accepted the challenge, and as the earth shook beneath my feet, neither one of us would back down.

"Hiding behind your powers won't help you, little boy," she taunted. I clenched my fists, but I was more than willing to accept her challenge. She wouldn't stand against me in hand-to-hand combat.

The vortices dissipated at my command, just as the ground healed itself beneath me at hers. I raised my fists, and she was ready. *Too ready.*

Amirth surprised me with a change of tactics. This time, she didn't wait to attack. She launched into the air and landed a kick to my side. I stared into her burning eyes and grinned. If it was a war she wanted, it was a war she would get.

At her merciless assault, I retaliated. The full force of my fist connected with her stomach, and she stumbled back, catching her breath. I thought she was ready to end it until she smirked and charged again.

I blocked and diverted her relentless kicks and punches, not wishing to hurt her.

"What's the matter?" she taunted. "You don't think I can handle you?"

I sneered. She was trying to bait me; I continued blocking and evading. She would tire eventually, and while she might be an elemental, she was still mortal. I could keep this up forever.

"Are you ready to give up?" I called, but her brows rose in defiance.

"I'm just starting." She bit back. "Is this what you call a worthy opponent? You don't seem much of a fighter to me. Is this how you get your women? By dancing around them? Putting them to sleep?"

I exploited her momentary distraction, tackling her to the ground. Amirth stared up at me, eyes full of surprise and something else... *anger*. Her chest rose and fell as I pressed the full weight of my body against hers, pinning her wrists above her head. She wrestled beneath my weight, but it was useless.

"Now, are you ready to give up?" I smiled, knowing it would only infuriate her more. Amirth writhed, but her body stirring urged me to press more into her.

"Get off me, you jerk!" she sneered, the fire raging in her eyes. I was enjoying myself too much to comply. Leaning down, I pressed my chest against hers, and her eyes grew wild.

"I'm not so sure you want me to," I said, my voice darkening. As the curves of her body stirred beneath me, I felt myself hardening, straining against the fabric of my pants. No one had ever made me this mad, or this infuriatingly possessed.

"Move," she retorted, breathless, but she wasn't fighting anymore, and I wasn't moving.

"Are you sure you want me to?" I pressed myself into her, and when she felt my hardness, her legs wrapped around me.

"I said get off me," she whispered, but her body and her eyes said otherwise. I leaned down, running my nose along her neck and her heaving breasts.

"Why do you defy me?" I said. "Why do you like to push me so?" I peered into her face, now a mask of confusion, and for the first time, the demon girl had nothing clever to say.

"Do you want to know how I like my women?" I jabbed, hoping for some reaction. I knew I had it when her eyes narrowed. "I like them wild and untamed. The more they fight, the harder I get." I pressed against her, and her body relaxed beneath me. I softened my hold as I felt her give in. With lethal skill, she snaked her leg around mine, and I was beneath her in a second. She pressed her small dagger against the base of my neck, and I laughed. I no longer cared to fight her. I wanted to fuck her senseless, but the demon girl stared down at me with a victorious grin.

"Fine. You win," I said, dropping my head to the ground.

When I looked into Amirth's eyes again, she wasn't laughing, smirking, or moving.

I took her wrist, forcing the weapon away from my neck, and she reacted at the contact. Jumping to her feet, she fled from the Forge, leaving me in a daze. *Fuck!* I didn't need this complication but my cock seemed to think otherwise.

DRAKE

The eastern borders were quiet. Dagasti's army had slowed, bordering the lower part of the hills. The rest of the legion at the outer lands made no move into the Euresian southern region or the bay. But their ships were well on the way. It wouldn't be long before they had a fleet strong and large enough to cross the Fjord and carry his army. But that would be Herod's problem to deal with.

I circled back to the eastern side of the bay, suddenly tempted to turn around. It wouldn't take me long to reach Hereter Isles and retake my chance against the tides, but the warriors waited for me, and with my faith hanging by a thread, another failure would only devastate me further. Reluctantly, I veered toward the North. Back to my duties—back to what I could control.

Before landing at the base of the hills, I turned to inspect the barriers. Amirth had done an excellent job with the trenches. Link and Phoenix stood with a group of warriors, and I descended.

My wings broke through the thick foliage of the tree line, and as I touched the forest ground, my inner fire and darkness raged as I slipped on my clothes.

"How much longer?" asked Phoenix, though I was sure he had patrolled the borders himself before dawn.

"They remain on course. The legion at the Outer Lands is making a quick process on the fleet, but that's not our concern."

"Damn right it isn't!" growled Phoenix, storming off to instruct the man mounting the ground traps.

"I think his patience is thinning as the days approach, and I don't blame him. If I could do it all again..." Link said with a faraway look. I knew what he was remembering. The loss of his Clan, his men—his failure.

"I don't think anyone could have done anything different-ly," I said, though his gaze remained fixed on the horizon. "I don't even know that it will be enough this time, but we will give them a hell of a fight. For the South, the West, and the East. You get another chance to fight back." The young warrior nodded his agreement.

"Are you going to stand around, or are you going to help in the trenches?" Phoenix called out from the trenches. Link and I exchanged a look and marched to the ditches.

When the sun had almost set, my muscles burned as if I had battled an army of Darklings.

We had managed to handle most of the eastern borders outside the magic barriers, and erased our tracks by covering the trenches.

It was the quietest my mind had been. I felt soft furs brush against my back and imagined it was Belynda's touch instead. I rolled onto the bed, pulling the furs over my chest. Reeling in the softness, my eyes closed and my mind drifted, conjuring up images of her.

EUROS

Never in my immortal life had I shirked my responsibilities to my Clan, but today, my mind was elsewhere. All sense had abandoned me to follow her instead.

I watched from afar. Amirth couldn't see me. I should have run after her this morning, or maybe I had done the right thing by staying in my place. However, the more I watched the demon girl, the more convinced I became that something was wrong. She looked distracted, evasive even, and that was unlike her.

Had I pushed her too far? I must have... Perhaps she didn't welcome my advance, and if that was the reason for her odd behavior, then I had to speak with her. Apologize. I didn't want her to think I was a brute who disrespected her boundaries.

I plunged from the round meeting hall, wings splayed behind me as I dove towards the fields where Amirth dried grains with women from the village.

I landed softly behind her, but she turned as I pulled my wings back, her eyes narrowed with suspicion.

"You... What are you doing here?" She avoided my eyes, further proof that I was right. She was uncomfortable.

"I wanted to speak with you." She glanced around at the curious eyes before clocking her gaze to me.

"I'm busy now."

"Fine. Later then," I said, leaving no room for refusal. She frowned.

While I likely should have offered some space after our earlier encounter, I wouldn't be content until we cleared the air.

Flying towards the eastern borders was the sensible thing to do. Joining my brothers would occupy my mind, yet I found I couldn't leave.

So, I continued following her from afar. She breached every opportunity to have a conversation with me, and the second she watched me step into the communal hall for lunch, she stiffened. Her eyes avoided me like before, and it didn't take her long to flee, leaving her food untouched.

I wasn't sure how to feel. For months, I had rebuked Amirth's snake tongue and her exasperating attitude, yet now she was being cold and elusive. I wasn't sure which version I preferred. Who was I kidding? I knew precisely which. I loved the vicious side of her. Her bite. Her fight. I despised seeing her like this, and I hated being the cause.

For the rest of the afternoon, I didn't follow her. Instead, I forced myself to do my duties.

Drumbeats and whistling flutes branded themselves in the wind. My people were celebrating the Autumn Solstice. Despite the darkness and chaos, our spirit would never be dampened.

I pushed away the maps and stood from the table. The night slowly fell, sinking into the last vestiges of light over the horizon.

Fire pits burned throughout the village, but the music thumped from the city's heart.

I plunged from the sky hall, soaring above the city. Once I spotted Link and Phoenix, I began my descent. Drake was nowhere in sight.

"Look who decided to join us," As I touched the ground behind Link, Phoenix jerked his head in my direction.

"I apologize. I couldn't get away." Phin's eyes narrowed.

"You had me worried," Phin teased, patting me on the shoulder. "I shouldn't have bet on her. I'm sorry. Tell us, how bad was it?" He grinned, and I finally understood. He thought I had lost the match and wounded my ego, choosing to spend the day alone to lick my wounds.

I laughed at the absurdity of losing and that he expected me to resort to such pathetic displays.

"Oh, brother. You should know better than to bet against me."

"That's what I said." Link jumped to my defense, taking another swig of his ale.

"I say you should have let her have her victory." Phoenix pushed. "It would have been better than having her glare at us for the rest of our lives, like she's ready to kill us. Well, mostly *you*." He smirked, his gaze disappearing past my shoulder.

I turned, scanning the crowd until finding Amirth. Phoenix was right. She looked furious, and I couldn't suppress my grin.

"I'll be right back," I said.

"Are you sure that's wise?" Link warned, but I was already walking away. My muscles strung taut as if ready for battle.

I made my way through the throng of people in the court, and her eyes narrowed as I drew close. She didn't run. Not this time.

"Can we speak now?" I smiled, and she glared in response.

"You can speak, but whether I choose to listen is a different story." My lips thinned as I fought to contain myself. She was just reacting; I wouldn't let her deter me from my purpose. However, as I glanced at her long legs, clad in those tight leather pants, my whole reason for being here eluded me. "I'm waiting..." She pressed, and my eyes returned to hers.

"I wanted to apologize," I said without pause, suddenly unsure of my words. Clearly, Amirth was stunned, too. "I didn't mean to make you uncomfortable, and I wanted you to know that it won't happen again."

Crossing her arms, she narrowed her eyes, and her forehead creased. There was a subtle tilt to the corner of her lips. She was amused, and, for a moment, she made me question whether I had correctly read the situation. I wasn't even sure my apology was necessary.

"Euros, really? Do you think me so delicate and sensitive?" The bulge in my pants stirred at the sound of my name on her lips. I could do war—those tactics I understood. I offered her a smile.

"I don't know. You seemed quite put out when you stormed out of the Forge this morning. I would even go out on a limb to say you've been avoiding me all day."

"Is that how it seemed to you?"

I took a step closer to where Amirth casually leaned.

"I'm rarely wrong," I teased. "And I never lose." Laughter sprung from her lips, and I grinned, for there was no death threat this time.

"Never? Really? If I recall, I had a knife to your throat just this morning." Amirth paused, stepping closer to me with lifted brows. "You win... those were *your* words." She challenged me to deny it, but I wasn't going to, even if I had allowed her that victory in a moment of weakness.

"A good warrior never accepts defeat," I said, peering down at her face, which was way too close to mine. I stared at her full lips.

"So, you deny it?" She pushed.

"I'll say nothing else on the matter," I whispered.

"I thought you wanted to speak." She challenged with a breathless sigh. Was she just as affected as me? Did she, too, feel the sizzling need buzzing between our bodies?

"You said you might not listen..." I reached a hand,

brushing my fingers along her cheek. "So, why bother?" She froze, traveling her gaze over my face. Once again, all sense abandoned me.

Without thinking, I pressed my lips to hers to test the waters, and when I pulled back, her eyes fluttered open, consumed with too many emotions I couldn't pinpoint one. Fear? Desire? She took a step back, but I held her arm, making her pause.

"Why are you running again?" I asked, but she didn't answer. "Are you afraid?" The corners of my mouth lifted, pleased I could get under her skin.

"I'm not scared of anyone!" she rebuked, shaking free from my hold. However, she couldn't refuse a challenge.

"Prove it then," I defied, placing a hand on her back, and pulling her body to mine. Her hands shot up to my chest, and her eyes widened. "Kiss me. Kiss me like you kiss those fortunate enough to earn your favor instead of your sharp tongue."

Amirth's chest rose and fell, her wild eyes searching my face, pausing at my lips.

With deliberate slowness, she leaned in, allowing her soft lips to touch mine. I held her, feeling the tremble that broke through her body. My hands rested at her hips, pulling her closer and lifting her body slightly so she could feel what she provoked in me.

"There." She pushed against me for release, so I let her go. "Is that proof enough for you?"

"I'm rather disappointed. You call that a kiss? I thought you had more bite." I grinned, countering the anger reflected in her eyes. But there was something else there—something I couldn't grasp.

"I hate you," she spat before disappearing through the throng of people.

"Amirth, come back!" I called, laughing in her trail as I attempted to follow. Link cut me off with a smirking Phoenix at his side.

"You keep sinking further and further, brother." I ignored Phoenix.

"Here. Have a drink and cool off. I don't think you'll get anywhere if you scare her off," offered Link, handing me a pint.

"I thought I understood women, but this one... I'm not so sure," I confessed, succumbing to the bitter taste of ale.

"You really are a fool. Everyone can see the demon girl has a thing for you."

"I'm not so sure about that." Perhaps I was the only blind one.

"I have to agree with Phin on this one." I glanced at Link with genuine intrigue. I knew better than to trust Phoenix, but Link... I felt inclined to listen.

"I must be doing something wrong or losing my touch."

"Or perhaps you're not used to dealing with humans. They're a lot more complicated from what I've gathered. Amirth, in particular. She's not like the kind of woman that usually warms your bed."

"No. She's better. She's a fighter."

"You forget she's also young, mortal, and likely inexperienced."

I stared at Phoenix, allowing his words to sink in. For once, he had offered some helpful insight.

"Phin, that might be the wisest thing you've ever said.

Why didn't I think of it before?" I chugged the rest of the ale down and grinned. "Wish me luck, boys."

"May the winds of the North blow in your favor," Phoenix called from behind, and I laughed at his crudeness.

I SEARCHED THE FORGE, but there was no sign of her. When the music turned to silence, and the warm spring air descended under the cover of night—and not a soul remained—I knew where to find her.

I slipped into her tent, closing the trellis behind me, careful not to make a sound. Amirth sat on her bed, combing through her hair. I had never seen her with her hair down, and it was long, cascading past her shoulders; by the gods, she looked even more alluring. Gentle even.

"Hello."

She jumped from the bed, clutching her mouth to stifle her scream.

"What the hell do you think you're doing?" she demanded, standing at once. I was momentarily distracted by the short camisole which barely covered her thighs. The plunge between her breasts was vast and low. "Get out!" she hissed, crossing her arms.

"I'm not going anywhere," I said, sauntering to her. "Not until you admit that I make you nervous."

"You are out of your mind. Get the hell out before I scream." She threatened, but we both knew she wasn't going to. It really wasn't her style.

"Go right ahead." I closed the distance, stopping behind her and leaning in. "I'm waiting for you to scream,"

I whispered, allowing my breath to fan across her ear. She shivered but didn't move. My nose glided against the raised skin at the back of her neck, and she sucked in a breath.

"Please leave," she whispered, turning around while shadows from the lantern danced in her eyes.

"What are you afraid of?" I asked, cupping her face. "Is it me?"

"No," she said quickly. "I..." Her eyes searched mine. "I just... I don't know *how*." She sighed. Phoenix was right. She was inexperienced and viewed her lack of experience as a weakness—something she wasn't used to showing. I brought her hand to my lips and kissed it, smiling. How far was she from the truth?

"Inexperience is nothing to be ashamed of," I said.

"I'm not ashamed." She resisted; it was her nature to protect herself.

"What I meant to say is that I don't see it as a weakness." I placed a hand on the small of her back, nudging her closer. "On the contrary, your inexperience makes you even more desirable," I admitted, gliding my fingers over the skin of her arms.

"Euros, do not assume that because I am inexperienced, I am a fool."

"I presume no such thing. What I do know is that every time you say my name, I get the urge to do vile things to your mouth," I whispered, moving my hands to her behind. I pushed her against my hardness. "If you want this. If you want me, then I can show you."

My eyes begged for her to accept my offer. The dark and

twisted part of me wasn't so sure I could respect her boundaries if she denied us this.

"Okay." Her voice was no more than a whisper, but it rang loud in my ears, like bells announcing the coming battle. In an instant, my body sprang to alert.

I grabbed her behind and lifted her from the floor; she wrapped her legs around my middle, closing her arms around my shoulders for support. I moved us to the edge of the bed and laid her down, peeling myself back to look at her, eyes wide before me—scared. Expectant.

I unstrapped the shields and the belt holding my weapons and pulled the shirt over my head. The North wind blew, cooling my skin, as I moved gently over her.

"Hi." I grinned.

"Hi," she whispered, too tense to smile. I claimed her lips.

I probed and teased with my tongue, and she responded. She froze but, after a moment, she relaxed. Her hands moved over the skin of my shoulders and down my back, exploring.

I moved against her, grinding my hips into hers, allowing her to feel my taut length. She sucked in a breath.

"Euros, no."

I smiled against her lips.

"Don't worry, little minx. Not tonight. I'm going to take my time with you." I said, and at my words, her body relaxed beneath me once more.

Though we weren't planning to win the battle tonight, it didn't mean we had to stop training. I pressed against her core, moving gently over her, and a soft moan escaped her lips.

"Just feel…" I eased my lips down her neck, crooning against her skin. "Don't hold back."

Her back arched in offering.

I pushed down the front of her camisole, kissing over the swell of her full breasts. Her eyes met mine as I pulled the fabric further down, exposing the rosy peak of her nipples. Her lips parted as I brought my tongue over them, though her eyes never left mine.

Amirth's fingers dug into my skin, her head moving back against the bed, overcome with sensation. I pushed back to my knees and peeled the camisole from her body, exposing her perfect breasts. I was curiously frozen, staring at the sparkling gem on her belly.

"What is this?" My finger pulled on it gently, and she smiled.

"A belly piercing. Haven't you seen one before?" she teased, surprisingly at ease.

"No. I can't say that I have."

"I'm glad I can still surprise you," she said, propping up on her elbows. As I studied her body, I realized how perfect she was. Her scant underwear was unequivocally another surprise from the human world, and I found I was equally pleased. I flipped her around in one fluid move, and she squealed, then laughed.

"What are you doing?" she questioned, peering back over her shoulder.

As I suspected, her underwear was made to torture the male species. Just a tiny strip, exposing her perfect ass. Had I known before this was what she wore, I wouldn't have lasted long in a fight against her.

I leaned over her, trailing the back of her neck and shoulders with kisses, pressing my hardness against her behind. I smiled against her skin when she pushed back, enjoying the pressure.

"Had you mentioned you wore something as indecent as this when we sparred, I would have thrown down my sword and pleaded for mercy."

She giggled, and the sound traveled directly to my cock. *Fates have mercy.*

I bit and kissed my way down her back, eliciting soft sounds of pleasure from her lips. When my teeth grazed over her cheeks, she gasped, and I flipped her again, pulling down the string from her hips and down her legs.

She pressed her thighs together with wild eyes, but I took her knees, prying them apart.

"Euros…"

"Trust me." I settled between her thighs, kissing and nibbling her soft skin.

My cock stirred as my fingers traced her wet folds. I burned to peel my pants off and bury myself in her, but I had promised to take my time. In the end, the wait would be equally rewarding for me.

When my tongue brushed her sleekness, she wriggled away, but I brought a hand over her stomach to hold her in place, teasing her breasts with my fingers.

My mouth closed around her lips. A little tongue and gentle nibbling, and she was undone.

"Euros, please." She gasped, breathlessly wrestling beneath me. I held her in place, grinning against her wetness and continuing my assault.

She stirred and twisted beneath me, but my mouth didn't relent from its onslaught, not until I felt the waves of pleasure rippling over her body. After a few breathless gasps, followed by a sated stillness, I knew she had reached her precipice.

She took one of the furs to cover her body, but I pulled it away.

"What's the point of hiding now?" I teased, claiming her lips. By the gods, I burned to take her. My cock also agreed, but allowing it to command my senses was never a smart move. I peeled myself from her and reached for the furs to cover her body.

"Where are you going?" she asked, watching me strap my weapons. "What about you?" She glanced at the strain in my pants, and I smiled, pleased that she cared.

"Don't worry about me. Another lesson for another day." I grinned like an idiot, knowing I would likely pound myself to sleep or find someone else to release my frustration. Somehow, the latter seemed wrong, considering what she had given me today—her trust, her innocence.

"See you tomorrow at the Forge?" she asked, and the thought of fighting her again made my cock jerk.

"I'll see you at the Forge. But whatever you do, don't wear that." I pointed to the tiny black string on the carpeted ground, and she smiled wickedly.

"Fine. I'll wear nothing then."

I groaned silently.

"Goodnight, minx."

I abandoned her tent before I gave in to my senselessness. Enveloped in the night breeze, my chest felt lighter. I plopped down on one of the sacks, staring at the curtain of stars. I felt luckier than I had felt in a very long time.

DRAKE

I awoke under the eeriness of quiet darkness. Glancing around the tent, I realized I had managed to sleep for the first time in over six months. While it was only a few hours, it was enough to feel the sizzling power of my fire coursing through my blood. Untamed immortality. I would be damned if I didn't take advantage of it. I didn't bother with the armor; it wasn't practical where I was going.

Silence stretched through the sleeping streets, but I was wide awake, wound with lethal force and ready for battle.

"Going somewhere?" I scanned the shadows, startled by Euros' presence. "You missed the celebration."

He sat up from the swinging sack, his expression one of amusement.

"I finally managed to get some sleep," I said, though I wasn't in the mood to attend, either.

"You needed it. You didn't miss much anyway." His grin widened, and I questioned whether it was as uneventful as he claimed. I closed my eyes, taking in the scents in the air. Instantly, I sensed Amirth. The corners of my mouth lifted in amusement.

"I'm surprised you're still alive," I teased, and his laughter boomed in the silence of the night. It was the lightest I had seen the warrior, and somehow, despite their torrid relationship, the elemental was the cause of such happiness.

"I think it's my lucky night." He grinned like a fool. "Can I join you? It would do me good to release some of this energy," he added, springing to his feet.

"I'm not so sure you want to follow me where I'm headed." He drew closer, patting me on the shoulder.

"You're going to try your fortune again, and like I said, I'm feeling lucky tonight."

"Are you certain you wish to go against Callix?" I watched the warrior closely. "After what he did for your people, you risk getting on his bad side."

"Callix will get over it." He dismissed me. "Besides, I'm only offering myself as a decoy; I won't be setting foot in Serfier." With a tilt of his head, Euros smiled. "That battle is all yours, my friend. All yours."

He marched a few feet ahead of me before turning back. "Well, come on. We don't have all night. Let's go pound on this Titan and get your girl back."

I couldn't stop him from coming, and perhaps this was the advantage I needed. With Euros' help, I had a much better chance to reach Serfier and get Belynda back. Maybe I would even get to kill Callix if luck was on my side.

6
TEMPTING THE ODDS

THE SEA WAS ANGRY. CALLIX MUST BE IN A MOOD, and he was yet to realize I was coming for him. Euros and I braced ourselves to face the stormy waters. The beast roared, pleased, as we crossed the Fjord bordering Abryas and reached the bay.

Aiming to surprise, I agreed to Euros' plan to come at it from a different vantage point. So, we journeyed farther instead of choosing the fastest and more direct path across the Hereter Isles. Bordering over the shores of Galnora, we reached the Ruins of the Lost before veering over the rough waters of Varenver.

We took to the thundering skies with a clear objective. Glacier Peaks.

The monster released a piercing shriek upon spotting the towering icy summits in the distance. This signaled to Euros it was time to dive into our plan.

The warrior broke altitude without hesitation until the

rough waves splashed against him. With a final glance at me, I watched as Euros plunged from above, disappearing under the obscurity of the Varenver sea.

It didn't take long for Callix to unleash the Titan. From the skies, I watched the ocean tides move as tentacles brushed the surface. As the decoy, Euros would have his hands full with Zodrox. It was my turn to dive.

As I neared the icy peaks, I descended. The ocean sprayed against my wings, and I quelled the fire as my body took human form. Then, I dove.

I would be undoubtedly slower in human form, but my Dragon's thoughts were louder and more susceptible to Callix's gifts. If I had any chance of reaching Serfier, it was in my human form.

Without looking back, I pushed my lungs and swam deeper. This was the closest I had ever come to Belynda, and my heart thumped in my chest as the castle appeared in the distance. A crystalized beacon of light beneath a blanket of darkness. Like a moth to a flame, I lurched towards the light. Darkness threatened to close in around me as the last of my breath left my lungs, but I was already here, reaching...

"I'm here now, love." I thought, reaching the magic barrier that kept the sea from plunging into the castle of Serfier.

As I pushed through the magic shield, I met the void of water, crashing onto the solid floor on the other side. I felt the stones beneath my fingers and I coughed, fighting to catch my breath.

"No."

I didn't have a chance to recover. Callix waved his hand, and the water barrier protecting Serfier moved at his command, swallowing me into its darkness. I held my breath, feeling the force of the water pushing against me, pulling me deeper into the bottomless pits of the sea. I released my fire, and the beast took over, fighting against the tides with one objective in mind.

We didn't have much time, but it was enough. I reached and the dragon's talons slashed through the skin of its target.

"Tell me she's alive," I pleaded as the last of my breath abandoned me. *"Tell me, Callix. Tell me, and I promise not to return."*

A shadow moved through the water, and right before I lost consciousness, I felt Callix's hand reach for me.

"She lives, but you won't have her. Not until she is ready. She will return when the time comes. You have my word."

His voice pierced through my thoughts, easing my soul. I accepted my defeat with a sense of peace and resignation as the sea claimed me. She was alive...

THE WIND LASHED against my face as I opened my eyes to the filtering rays of sunlight.

"About time," muttered Euros impatiently from somewhere nearby. I turned in the sand to find the warrior's armor shredded. His wounds had almost healed, but he wasn't happy.

"Not as lucky as you hoped, I see," I teased, slightly entertained that he imagined a fight with the Titan would be easy while knowing I'd failed so many times. "Had a nice little chat with Zodrox, I see."

Euros's lips thinned, and I rolled onto my back, still regaining my strength.

"If we had that beast fighting with us, Dagasti wouldn't stand a chance," commented Euros.

"I wouldn't dare put that monster anywhere near a Darkling. If Dagasti ever managed to turn him to the dark, we would all be lost." The warrior's silence told me the alternative wasn't something he had thought about or wished to visualize.

"What happened?" he asked, sitting on the sand beside me. "It took you long enough to resurface; I was certain you had made it this time." I ran my sandy hands through my hair.

"I did, but not for long." I paused, staring at the skies above. "But now I can breathe..." I peered at Euros. "She is alive," I said, and for the first time since Dagasti claimed her life, I felt peace, liberated despite my failure to save her or to end Dagasti's life and get her back.

"Then, we can count this as a victory. Now, you can finally stop brooding," teased Euros, and I smiled, somewhat content.

I felt the whooshing of wings beside me as Euros took to the skies. I drew deep breaths, allowing the fire to swim around me. For a final time, the beast glanced at the rough waves reaching the shores before thrusting from the coastline. Belynda was alive, and although Callix was the last person I trusted, something told me he wasn't lying. I would wait; I would be patient... but not forever.

BELYNDA

Callix was right. Finding my way to the pits was easy. All I had to do was concentrate and curiosity did the rest. The incessant clashing guided me towards the lower chambers of the castle, where I found him, but he wasn't alone.

For a moment, I was lost in the resplendence of the bioluminescent crystals and ethereal light filling the pits. All reflected against the floating wall of the ocean, which fell around the open space. My gaze fixed to Callix, watching him poised with a spear in hand, set to attack Syllis.

To my dismay and surprise, the petite nymph stood her ground against the Water Lord's assault, but his skill was unmatched. With a wave of his hand, the glowing water moved through the air like flying raindrops, transforming into icy knives midair.

My eyes flicked to Syllis. The nymph screeched, and the icy shards fragmented, sending water particles flying. The pale skin on my arm glistened with the droplets of liquid magic, and when I glanced up, Callix's gaze fell on me. Instantly, the air thickened with undeniable tension from the conversation the previous night. That tension wove its way through the space separating us.

"You're late." The cutting edge of his voice stunned me, and I glared at the nymph, whose mouth shifted with amusement.

"My apologies. It won't happen again." My eyes narrowed, though my mind screamed, *jerk!* If he heard it, he showed no reaction. His face was unreadable.

"Your first order of training is to create your weapon," he instructed, balancing the spear in one hand and moving it in skillful circles. "Start with a water spear."

"A spear made of water?" I said, questioning the solidity of such a weapon. Callix didn't speak, and I didn't see his intention until it was too late.

In one skillful move, he swept the spear under my feet, knocking me on my ass to prove his point.

"There is your answer," he replied sternly, offering me his hand. I stared at it for several moments, until eventually grasping it. "Now, the spear," he commanded.

I stared into his eyes, trying to understand why he was suddenly acting so mean.

"Why are you being such a jerk!" My thoughts drifted openly, and I waited for him to reach back and tell me what the hell was the matter with him.

"Syllis. You may leave. I won't be needing you today, after all." He dismissed the nymph without taking his eyes off me. The minute she disappeared from the pits, he took slow steps to close the distance.

"I'm attempting to set boundaries. I'm glad you decided to stay, but for this to work..." His brows creased, his eyes dancing over my face. "I can't be your friend," he concluded with a pained expression, likely mirroring my own. I wanted to protest, to voice all the thoughts he likely read in my mind. I detested this. I just wanted him to be himself. But I knew how much of an effort it was for him, and asking for anything else was selfish of me. I had nothing in return to offer.

"Okay." The soft whisper left my lips, and his eyes beheld me for a moment. Then he took a step back and allowed the spear in his hand to turn to water.

"To control water, you must remember its nature—its ebb and flow. It is a weapon as much as a force of life." Callix's voice resonated like crashing waves against a rocky shore. Emotionless.

I nodded, unsure of what he meant, but my heart pounded with anticipation. I felt the weight of his gaze with a mixture of expectation and impatience. His confession made it harder to ignore the tension; even if he fought and attempted to conceal it, I felt the pull he exerted, calling me. Against my better judgment, I became keenly aware of the energy moving between us, an undercurrent that was sure to add another layer of complexity to our training.

"Focus your energy," Callix commanded after my many failed attempts. Frustration tinged his voice. "Channel your emotions into the water. Feel its power—its wrath. Control and bend it to your will."

The air crackled with anticipation. I closed my eyes, once again delving deep into my core, allowing the energy to surge within me as I drew from the well of my emotions. With a flick of my wrist, a swirling torrent of water rose from the pool beside me, coalescing into a shimmering spear that hovered midair.

As I attempted to direct the weapon, my control faltered, and the water spear dissipated into a spray of droplets. Frustration welled in me and fueled my determination. Not only as a response to my failure but because of the look on his face.

"Again!" Callix's voice boomed, narrowing his eyes with intensity. "You are overthinking this. Control your emotions!"

I wanted to scream at him but held my tongue. Instead, I squared my shoulders and summoned another water spear. Focusing on the rhythmic movement of the waves, I used the power of the ocean currents, channeling its energy into my creation. With what felt like a graceful sweep of my arm, the spear shot forth, slicing through the air with deadly precision.

A mixture of triumph and relief washed through me as the weapon hit its mark, embedding itself in the coral. I turned back to Callix, our eyes meeting briefly in a shared moment of success. He looked away, but not before I felt it again—that palpable tension between us.

"Good," he praised. "Try again." It took various attempts until I could confidently materialize a weapon out of water, holding its form long enough to project it as a defense.

"That was the easy part. Now, you must try to hold its form while engaged in battle."

"But I can't fight." I stared up at him doubtfully.

"Well, that's why we're here, isn't it?" He formed a spear with a graceful sweep of his wrist. "Choose your weapon," he said, devoid of all humor. I watched the spear crystalize in his hands.

My heart pounded as I prepared to face Callix's assault. This training pushed my limits, and I steeled myself for his wrath.

AFTER TWO DAYS at the pits, I was ready to call it quits. Every morning, I reminded myself why I couldn't give up. Drake wouldn't, and that thought alone was enough to push me through another day of training. My immortal ability to heal and regenerate was much slower than those older than me. Callix insisted I remained barefooted while I still gained my strength, mentioning something about grounding and absorbing energies. For the past few nights, I went to bed exhausted, beaten, and bruised, but thankfully, I woke up the following day healed with renewed energy and determination to do it all over again.

After our exchange in the hallway a few nights ago, Callix kept his promise. His boundaries, as he called them, had firmly remained. He didn't tease or flirt, but I watched those walls shake, and I exploited every chance I had to break his resolve. I was being selfish, but I missed the old Callix. The days had become tedious and long ever since his determination shifted.

To make matters worse, he wasn't holding back, though, at times, I wasn't sure if the ire behind his strikes was directed at me or himself. He fought with water spears and his skill was unmatched.

I wasn't sure what he expected; I could never beat him. Callix's whole being was imposing, and the way he regarded me with a mixture of intensity and frustration did little to aid my concentration. He had devoted centuries to honing his skills and now he possessed the daunting task of molding me—my raw, unrefined potential—into something powerful. His azure eyes glimmered with premeditation, and for a moment, I was distracted by his dark hair tumbling over his forehead. He opened a water portal, and in a second, he was behind me, a regal glow in his eyes acting as a constant reminder of his dominion over water.

"That wasn't a fair move," I protested, and his brows shot up in challenge.

"Do you think you will receive gallantries in the middle of a battle?" Circling me, he shifted the grip on his spear, readying to strike without warning. I blocked his attack and dodged the rebound. He didn't hold back.

"That was good." He grinned. Twisting midair, he drove the spear at an angle to hit my side. "But you need to be faster." I held my ribs and winced, melting the spear to water at my feet. His brows furrowed, but he didn't apologize. He cared, even though he said nothing.

"You are no longer mortal. Pain is only an illusion. Focus, and your body will do the rest."

I glared at him.

"That's easy for you to say. You heal quicker." The muscles in his jaw tightened.

"Stop whining and make your weapon." He wouldn't take it easy on me after my retort, but if he was going to be an ass, I'd play his game. Instead of forming a spear, I willed the water to form two swords.

His brows shot up, and his lips twitched.

"Impressive," he said, amused. "Are you sure you can handle those?"

I took the bait.

"Come and find out," I spat with either stupidity or courage. I wasn't sure which was worse.

Callix's spear clashed against the crystalized blade of one of my swords. I twisted simultaneously, swinging the other blade and missing his arm by inches.

His eyes narrowed to slits, and I braced for his merciless assault. As he twisted his spear twice around his hand, I sent a gust of wind before he could strike. He flew backward through the air, crashing against the walls of coral before falling gracefully to the floor. Callix braced himself on one knee, using his free hand to rise.

When his head snapped in my direction, I glimpsed the smirk on his face and sighed, relieved.

"Now, that was impressive." He was right. I was too hung up on my mortal weaknesses, despite having all these gifts at my disposal. "However, your elemental powers won't always be practical in hand-to-hand combat."

"I thought anything was allowed. You said no gallantries, remember?" I repeated his words as he strode towards me.

"I was teaching you a lesson, and I meant what I said. I don't care what tactics you use to stay alive in battle, but your powers shouldn't be your only weapon." Bridging the gap between us, he took the crystalized swords from my hands, maneuvering them before him with skill and precision. "I know you chose these to spite me, but I think they were an excellent choice."

"Does that mean I can call that a win?" A corner of his mouth twisted into a half grin, and I beamed in return.

"Who said we were done?" The smile vanished from my face as he added, "Make your weapons."

I ALLOWED the warm water to cascade over my shoulders, easing the soreness in my muscles, my bruised ribs, and the tiny cuts along my arms and legs. Callix never cut deep, but he always drew blood. It infuriated me, but despite my irritation and slow healing, I awoke every morning to find my body renewed. It allowed me to shift my mindset from what I once had been to accept what I had become. That thought made me hate him less for every win and every cut he branded me with.

But those cuts hurt much less than the ones caused by his indifference.

For the first time in days, I dressed and left my room for dinner. The solitude of the icy castle walls was beginning to get to me. Callix was right. My body was becoming stronger—more resilient. Even my ability to heal was improving.

I bumped into a solid wall of muscle, and a pair of stormy blue eyes pinned me in place. Callix steadied my shoulders, and the moment he touched me, jolts of electricity raced beneath my skin. I wasn't sure if he felt it, too, but he released me just as quick.

"My apologies. I wasn't sure if you would come," he said, and it took me a moment to realize he was apologizing for eating without me. I shook my head, dispelling the haze settling over me. I smiled in an attempt to breach the boundaries.

"It's okay. I didn't expect you to wait. I wasn't even sure if I'd come, either." He shifted on his feet, then turned, allowing me to pass. He hesitated, his back to me. He spun to face me.

"I was headed to the library if you care to join me? I can have something brought up for you. If you'd like."

I studied his eyes, certain that this offer violated his so-called 'boundaries.' The idea made me smile.

"That would be nice."

Side by side, we walked in comfortable silence towards the stairs leading to the upper levels of the castle.

The crystals glowed along the library's walls, and the ocean visible through the clear dome roof brimmed with the sea life surrounding the castle.

I sat on one of the divans, tucking my feet under the folds of my billowy skirt.

Callix disappeared into the upper levels while I watched the sea life through the roof. I realized I had never seen Callix in his elemental form. It made me wonder if he had a tail like the rest of the merfolk. *Was he as ugly as the Earth books portrayed?*

His booming laughter echoed through the silent library, and I craned my neck, searching for him. I couldn't see him, though he was obviously prying inside my mind. It served him right. He probably was just as ugly as they depicted him to be. His laughter roared once again, except this time, it sounded like it came from the lower levels.

"For my own sake, I should rectify any confusion you might have in that regard." His voice startled me as he reappeared in the central aisle with a book. Phial opened the door, carrying a tray in her hands.

"I'll take that." Callix placed the book on the desk to take the tray from the nymph. "Thank you," he offered in dismissal.

Placing the tray on the couch before me, I glanced between Callix and the food, wondering when he had asked for it. He smiled and tapped his temple, amplifying my confusion, yet knowing the reach of his mind and the extent of his abilities, I should have guessed he could communicate from such a distance.

"Eat," he said, rolling his shirt sleeves to his elbows. He returned to collect the book he had abandoned on the table. After flipping through the pages, he returned to claim one of the chairs opposite from me. *Red ocean walls. Red ocean walls.* I barricaded my thoughts before they exposed me, and the corner of his mouth lifted.

"What's so funny?" I demanded, and his grin broadened. He raised the book in a poor attempt to mask his amusement, but his confession surprised me.

"You are," he admitted. His eyes shifted momentarily from the book to me. His posture was graceful; his body leaned against the chair, and one leg crossed the other. Resting the book against his thigh, my attention shifted. *Red ocean walls. Red ocean walls.* His fingers trailed over his mouth, another failed attempt to conceal his grin.

"I'm glad that I amuse you," I said bitterly, grabbing a sandwich and taking a bite.

"You need to work on those walls," he commented. "They shouldn't come up when you're attempting to conceal a random thought. Those guards should always be around your mind like an extension of yourself." I took a sip from the cup, pleased he was no longer laughing.

"How do I do that?" I asked, taking another bite.

"With practice. Just like your body, your mind requires training as well." He shifted in his seat. "Reach into my mind. What do you see?" he urged, and I hesitated. His brows furrowed, noting my indecision. "It's safe, I promise."

With a sigh, I reached with my thoughts, feeling the corners of his mind.

"I see gray, misty clouds." He blinked, and his mind zapped out of my reach just like that.

"My walls are subtle. They give the illusion of calm and control. Anyone who enters can lose themselves within the mist. Your walls are erratic; they're too bright, too obvious, too sudden."

"You said to use the elements and colors."

"Yes, and that was the easiest way to explain the concept. Now you must mold it to your advantage. Make it a part of you." I took a bite of the sandwich and thought about it. Something subtle, calming, a place where one could lose themselves. Such a place came to mind. A lush green forest, bound by the Earth element beneath the curtain of dusk.

I imprinted the images around my mind, surrendering to the silence of the quiet forest. I smiled at Callix as I opened my eyes.

"Give it a try."

Locking his eyes with mine, I watched him falter; he blinked, leaning back.

"You're a fast learner." He smiled, pleased, and I matched it. I had learned to appreciate his compliments now he didn't offer them so lightly.

"Is that what you meant?"

"Yes. It reflects your human side. You will always be bound to the earth, so it was harder to get through this time."

My eyes narrowed.

"This time? You said you couldn't see my thoughts before, so what am I doing wrong?"

"I never said such a thing. However, this is one of those moments where one would say it's not you, it's me."

"What do you mean it's you? What are you talking about?" The ocean dance behind his eyes as he drew closer.

"I'm not so sure you would like to hear it." His voice

lowered with a subtle vibration as he braced his forearms over his knees.

"Oh, I do. Believe me, I do." I pushed the tray away from me, glaring at him impatiently.

Slowly, he shook his head.

"This isn't going to work." He bit his lower lip, and I lost myself so much so that I wasn't sure we were talking about the same thing.

"Callix?"

"We set boundaries, remember? Telling you breaches the terms of our agreement."

"What's the point of boundaries if my mind has no privacy from you?" He raised his brows. "Besides, those were *your* boundaries; I never said I didn't want to be your friend." I didn't miss the muscles on his jaw tensing or the darkening of his eyes.

"You think the boundaries are moot, then? Unnecessary?" He questioned. I was glad to see his walls beginning to crumble, but I understood why he was confused. I was the one who had overreacted before; my outburst had made it perfectly clear I needed boundaries. Boundaries he put in place for the both of us. But I didn't want them. I wanted Callix's friendship. I *needed* it.

"We're grown adults," I said, "We can behave civilly."

He stared at me until dipping his head once in agreement.

"Very well. I will do my best not to cross the line, but I can't promise I won't be tempted." He smiled, and it was like the entire library came alive. In that simple gesture, the old Callix had returned to me. I chose to say nothing. I knew what I was getting myself into, but I had missed him, and as long as

I remained true to my heart, I could deal with the Water Lord and his rough edges. It was a small price to pay for his friendship.

"Don't worry. I'll make sure to remind you when you've crossed it. Now, will you tell me why you're still getting through my mind walls?"

His hesitation worried me, but I had to know. Placing the book beside him, Callix interlaced his fingers, leaning over his knees once again. His eyes searched mine, yet no trace of humor remained on his face, and suddenly, I was concerned. It couldn't be so bad... could it?

"I am obviously much older and skilled," he said, running a hand through his hair.

"But that's not the only reason," I probed.

"No." His gaze strayed to the floor, and his hair fell over his forehead. "Have you ever felt it?" His question took me by surprise as his gaze burned into mine. For a second, I stopped breathing, lost in the storm brewing in his eyes. "That tethered feeling?" When I didn't respond, he shook his head. "Never-mind. All I know is that no walls can stop me from sensing your thoughts. They're like cords, always vibrating, and I seem to be perfectly attuned to their frequency." I dropped my gaze, acutely aware of how difficult this would make things for us.

"This is bad," I blurted, unsure what else to say. It was much worse than I dared to admit.

"I can live with it," he added.

"Obviously, but I've pulled the short straw. How would you feel if it was the other way around?"

"I wouldn't mind it. As a matter of fact, I believe whatever bond exists works both ways. Perhaps your mind requires more experience to sense the pull." He offered, and my eyes narrowed at him.

"It's wrong, and you know it. You're only saying that because I would never pry the way you do. Damn it, Callix!" I said, exasperated.

"Despite what you might think, I don't make it a habit to invade your private thoughts. Most of the time, you're shouting them so loudly that it makes me curious."

"Callix, I'm serious. Do you truly have no idea how to fix it, or are you selfishly refusing to?"

"I don't. I'm not. I promise." I stared at him. He seemed to be speaking the truth, but a strange feeling remained, like there was more he wasn't saying.

"What aren't you telling me? You don't know how to stop it, but you know why it's happening, don't you?"

"Something like that."

Seriously... he could be so infuriating.

"Callix, stop playing games and tell me!"

"There is nothing else to say."

"You promised you wouldn't lie to me," I said as he rose to his feet. It only took two steps before he towered over me. He reached for my chin, and I stilled.

"Nice try." He smiled and dropped his fingers, releasing me. My eyes narrowed at his back as he turned to leave. "Oh, and I left you something. Hopefully, it can clarify some of the questions you have about what I am." I glanced at the book left on his chair. "Make sure you get some rest. You'll need it for tomorrow."

"Callix..." I called after him while my thoughts rushed, pleading for the truth.

"When I figure it out. You'll be the first to know." He winked and closed the door.

What was I going to do with Callix? If my mind wasn't safe from him, I had to find a way to control my runaway thoughts. I pinched the bridge of my nose, sensing what felt like a mortal headache brewing. This was going to be difficult.

Rising from the divan, I moved to his chair; the cushions were still warm as I picked up the book. I read the pages he had left open for me, intrigued.

After living in Serfier for what felt like weeks, I had come to the realization that, despite what the earthly books claimed, it wasn't the merfolk who ruled the water realm. The merfolk lived in the cities deep within the depths beneath the castle; I couldn't shake the deep-rooted feeling that the Water Lord was not one of them.

However, to my surprise—and dismay—I learned Callix was something much worse than I could have imagined.

The Leviathan is renowned for its ability to command the vast oceans and rule over the depths of Serfier. It possesses a captivating and regal appearance. In his humanoid form, he emanates an aura of grace and elegance, with striking features and piercing eyes, flowing hair that cascades like seaweed, and a flawless complexion reminiscent of shimmering pearls. He is adorned in light, iridescent garments that reflect the colors of the sea, and his movements exude a fluidity that mimics the gentle waves.

However, when the ruler of the sea transforms into his true form, his absolute power and magnificence becomes apparent. The Leviathan is ancient and mythical. A colossal aquatic beast possessing serpentine and dragon-like features with immense size and strength. The Leviathan rises to command the vast oceans and rule over the depths of Serfier.

I HADN'T READ MUCH about sea creatures, but Leviathans were depicted well throughout history. They were often associated with legends and folklore from various cultures, possessing different faces and names prevalent enough for me to remember.

In many mythologies, they were considered symbolic embodiments of chaos and the untamed forces of nature. They were believed to embody the raw power of the sea, capable of unleashing devastation. Legends often spoke of their ability to emerge from the ocean's depths, shaking the very foundations of the world with their presence.

It wasn't difficult to imagine Callix as the embodiment of chaos and destruction, for that's exactly who he was. Lethal, raw, and unapologetic. However, I understood how it was necessary to exert authority while protecting and governing the creatures and elements within the Realm.

Callix had allowed me to glimpse another side of him that perhaps not many had a chance to see. A duality of his character: the striking Lord and the mighty Leviathan, encapsulated in a blend of grace, power, and majesty that defined his rule over the Realm.

I had a lot of questions for the mighty Lord, but knowing what he was certainly helped bring his personality into perspective. He was blunt and lethal but greatly misunderstood.

. . .

I woke feeling strong, renewed, and with a fresh perspective.

Callix said nothing could stop him from breaching my mind, but after spending the best part of the night thinking on it, I remembered I was no longer that human girl. I was immortal—an elemental blood witch—and according to the Fates, the potential of my powers was an enigma even to them. If that was true, and I had to count that it was, then perhaps I could protect my mind from the Water Lord. Perhaps I could tilt the balance in Drake's favor.

Callix had said the mind required as much training as the body, and it was about time I started trusting myself. Perched at the edge of my bed, I closed my eyes and took a deep breath.

My trained ears listened patiently to the world surrounding me. At first, the closest sounds reached me, like the last falling drops from the shower head in the adjacent bath chamber, and the subtle cracks from the icicles bordering the castle rooftops.

Quiet voices and laughs came into range, too, and I smiled as I listened to Syllis and Phial.

"Master is smarter than that. He knows better than to fall for a blood witch."

"You forget she's one of us now." Phial's voice, I realized, and knowing she saw me as one of them made me reassess my opinion of her.

"She won't be here for long. Sire can't stand her."

"I'm not so sure about that," Phial responded. I didn't want to hear anymore. Not only did this feel wrong, but I wasn't so sure I was strong enough to accept everyone's thoughts of me, not like Callix could.

However, I would certainly give Syllis a piece of my mind. I had never done anything to her to deserve such hostility.

Reaching with my mind, I chose Phial as my target, hoping she would be less hostile to such intrusion.

"Phial." I knew she heard my call the moment her thoughts shifted from confusion to disbelief.

"Phial," I pressed, and this time, I picked up the hesitant 'yes' of her response . *"Please, have Syllis bring breakfast to my room."*

I sensed her hesitation.

"What is it?" asked Syllis, which meant Phial's expression must have drawn her attention.

Hearing the other nymph's voice while my mind was still linked with Phial's felt strange. It was like the sound had a unique vibration, while the tendrils allowing me access into Phial's mind had a subtle, low-key tune.

"It's her..." Phial's voice shook.

"Thank you, Phial." I offered before extricating from her thoughts.

"She has requested you bring her breakfast." I didn't dare enter either of their minds during the silence that stretched between them. I wasn't sure I wanted to know.

"I only take orders from the Master."

"Syl... she is still a guest. You can't—"

"—Oh, I can, and I will." Syllis cut Phial off. I thought she would be trouble; I just hadn't realized how much so. "If you are so concerned, you can take the food up yourself."

"He won't like your defiance, Syl. You know he has a temper," warned Phial, and for a moment, I wondered what Callix would do if he found out. However, I didn't plan on telling him. I wasn't sure I'd ever acclimate to ordering people about or having them serve me. My intention was to test my skills and, yes—I admit—to mess with the evil nymph. I would never force anyone to serve me, and telling Callix was no better.

"I can deal with the storm. As a matter of fact, I welcome it." I almost detected the smile in her voice, and though her response shouldn't have bothered me, it irked me beyond measure as I knew what they implied.

If my short time in Druleska had taught me one thing, it was that the sexual appetite of immortals went beyond my comprehension. The same was true for Serfier, especially after encountering the intimate way Phial and Syllis cozied up to Callix. I would have to be a fool to think a man like Callix could live such a confined life without taking and possessing what he wanted, when he wanted, as Lord of the Ocean. However, knowing and accepting the truth were two very different things.

I remembered the time when I thought Drake had taken another, and the memory reignited the pain. I shook my head, deciding not to relive it. Abandoning the darkening thoughts, I gave the nymphs their privacy.

Browsing through the clothes in the overly extravagant closet, I smiled when I spotted the jeans Callix had gifted me. Tempting him was begging for chaos; the nature of his beast would never be content with compliance. He could promise to behave, but the more time I spent with the Water Lord, the more I understood him. It wasn't in him to shy away from his truth or desires, which was why he attempted setting such ridiculous boundaries to begin with.

I craved his companionship but also enjoyed his teasing banter, and suddenly, a reckless part of me had the worst idea. I grabbed the jeans from the shelf and pulled them on without thinking.

Checking my reflection in the mirror, I knew that teasing the Water Lord wasn't such a reckless idea after all. In fact, distracting him could serve my plans to beat him at his own game.

A soft rasp sounded at the door.

"Come in."

Phial peaked her head through the opening then stepped in, carrying the breakfast tray. I silently observed her as she placed it on the small table facing the crystalized window.

"Is there anything else you need, my Lady?"

"No, Phial. Thank you." The nymph was obviously uncomfortable. She might not hate me like Syllis did, but she clearly wasn't a friend. "Why did you bring it instead of Syllis?"

The nymph froze at the threshold then turned to me.

"I..." She hesitated, seeming afraid to admit the truth and get her friend in trouble while knowing I could detect any lies. I decided to let her off the hook.

"It's okay. I know she refused to. I can see she doesn't like me much."

"No, my Lady, it's not..."

"You don't have to lie for her, Phial. Don't worry, the feeling is mutual." I admitted. There was no point in hiding my dislike for the nymph.

"Please, my Lady..."

"Don't worry. Callix won't hear of this." Her gaze widened with surprise.

"I'm afraid nothing escapes the Master," she said quietly, then offered a slight bow before disappearing from my room. I frowned. Perhaps she was right. My mind wasn't safe from him, and neither was theirs. It was only a matter of time before he found out, all thanks to his prying.

AFTER EATING LIKE A STARVED HUMAN, I brushed my teeth and peeked at my reflection in the mirror one final time before leaving.

As I walked to the pits, I put my plan in motion. The lush green forest walls under dusk-covered skies filled my mind, and surrounding the lush green, I created a never-ending ocean with storm-covered clouds. I descended the last of the stairs leading to the pits, allowing the last element to fortify my mind. The wind howled around the forest's edge and over the rushing ocean waves. *Let's see you get past that Callix.* I grinned.

His back was to me, and for the first time, he didn't appear to sense my presence, despite me standing a few feet away. Carefully, I closed the distance, and when I was but a mere step away from him, I spoke.

"This..." I didn't get a chance to finish my sentence as Callix held an icy blade to my throat, pinning me against the coral walls, which bit into my back. His eyes were wild, and it took him a second before he blinked with realization, stepping back and dropping the knife.

"I'm sorry," he mumbled, his eyes still wild. I smiled, and slowly, the shock eased from his face.

"Did I just manage to surprise you?" I teased, and the corner of his mouth lifted.

"You did, and only a few have managed that. But if you ever speak of it, I will deny it." He smiled, tilting his head to look at me. "Something is different, though."

I reinforced my walls, and his brows creased. When his smile returned, I felt the silent vibration of his thoughts piercing through my barriers. "Nice try." His voice echoed into my very soul.

"What the hell?" I blinked and stepped away from him. "It really is pointless, isn't it?" I said, with a sinking sense of defeat.

"I must concede that was an impressive attempt. You had me doubting myself for a minute." Callix cautiously circled me, his eyes on mine. "I see you're ready for battle." He declared, his gaze lingering on my jeans-clad legs. "I wonder what brought this on?" He questioned; he didn't wait for an answer. Instead, I felt him slipping against my walls, which I now knew were pointless, but I kept them in place, nonetheless. Just because I couldn't keep the Water Lord out didn't mean they were useless against other people.

"Get out of my head, Callix." I crossed my arms, irritated at his intrusion, but more than anything, my own failure.

"You can't ask that of me, not when I feel like I'm being set up." He narrowed his eyes. "First, you raise the stakes with the mind walls and then come charging in wearing that. Ready to do what? Test my control?"

"Not everyone is as calculating as you are, Callix."

"Liar," he said, but his voice held nothing but humor... and something else.

"Are we training or not?"

"For your sake, I'm not sure that we should," he warned, all traces of amusement fleeing from his face.

"Are you seriously afraid of a girl in jeans?" I laughed, and his eyes darkened.

"Oh no, darling. It's you who should be afraid."

The foolish bravery I felt only seconds before vanished, and I steeled myself with resolve, summoning a water spear. He only laughed.

"That won't be necessary," he said, shaking his head. "Today, we'll partake in some hand-to-hand combat."

Of course, we would. This was bad... so very bad. Callix had warned me, yet I had failed to listen. I glanced at the stairs, wondering if I could make a run for it.

"Don't even think about it. There is nowhere you can run where I wouldn't find you." He stepped closer until he towered over me. "You wanted to do this, remember?" He taunted. "We're doing it."

"I think I liked you better when I thought you were an ugly Merman."

He stood so close that his laughter made my skin vibrate.

"Oh, I can still be ugly, darling."

"No, I think you're just an insensitive prick."

Without warning, he rammed me against the wall, pinning my arms on either side of me. I wasn't sure if it was the look in his eyes or the shock of his closeness that made all breath leave my body.

His face hovered inches from mine, and his hips pressed against me. Quickly, I moved my face to the side.

"What—what are you doing?"

"I'm only living up to your expectations." His lips brushed against my neck, and I trembled. "So, you think I'm insensitive?"

"Don't forget a prick," I whispered foolishly.

"How could I forget...? I'll show you how much of a prick I am." His nose brushed against my cheek, down my ear and to the corner of my lips. He pulled away, leaving me frozen, dazed, and confused.

He poised himself, hands ready for a fight.

"You're serious about this?" He tilted his head, the corner of his mouth lifting.

"Shouldn't you know the answer to that question by now?"

And that was the problem. I knew precisely how unforgiving he could be and how cruel his training methods were. With reluctance, I moved away from the wall, and as we circled one another, my heart hammered in my chest.

"Would you take it easy on me if I admit I'm scared?" Did he not see the terror reflected in my eyes or feel it coming off my body in waves?

He smiled, and his eyes lit up, softening the features on his face.

"What are you scared of exactly?"

"You," I admitted, and his brows rose.

"Doubtful. What are you truly afraid of?" He watched me expectantly.

"I'm terrified that you will hurt me." I declared, and he closed the distance between us until his frame towered before me.

"Every cut I have ever branded you with has hurt me a

thousand times more." His eyes held mine, as the soft stroke of his fingers distracted me. "Surely, you know that." *Did I?* I wasn't too sure I did.

"Then why are you so cruel?" His jaw tensed while his cerulean eyes captured every inch of my face.

"I'm cruel because what is waiting for you out there will not be kind. Because even if the pain I inflict on you eats away at my soul and kills me a little more every time, I would gladly embrace the pain. I would rather you brand me a cruel monster if it means you will be ready. If it means you will win this war. I would accept the chaos, even if the cost is you hating me." I stared at the sea god with a clarity I had never experienced. His expression darkened, and he dropped his hand. "So, if you want someone to take it easy on you, go to him. I will not stand in your way."

I gaped at Callix, unable to reconcile his last words. I was too overcome with a slew of emotions. Anger, contempt, frustration, fear, gratitude, perhaps admiration, and something else—something I couldn't quite describe. I turned, not trusting myself to remain in his presence. He was right. Drake would never hurt me the way Callix did. He would never approve of his methods.

I paused at the top of the stairs, tightening my fingers around the stone railing. I was a coward. If I left, I would always be the damsel in distress. I was tired of being weak. If I could stop the darkness, I must endure blood in the process. Callix was right. Although his words were hurtful, they were the truth. Drake would always love me more; he would always go easy on me. Callix wouldn't, and right now, what I needed was the Water Lord's chaos. I sighed and turned back to him, determined. His face was unreadable, the mask he so often wore when trying to protect himself.

"I could never hate you." The words trickled from my lips as my eyes met his, and his mask crumbled. Without warning, he closed the distance and, pulled me against him. As my arms wrapped around him, the swell of emotions choked me, and I cried without restraint, soaking his white shirt. He didn't seem to mind, and he never pulled away.

"I'm sorry for hurting you." His arms tightened around me.

"It's okay. I needed to hear it." I mumbled against his chest. I turned my head, resting my cheek against him. "The truth is, I keep thinking I will wake up from this nightmare, and everything will be normal. But there's no turning back, is there?" I pulled away to stare into his eyes. "I'm scared, Callix. I'm scared to fail," I whispered, sensing the tears brimming in my eyes once again. He released me, and his hands cupped my face.

"I cannot promise you a happy ending." His thumb caught a traitorous tear. "But I would gladly take my last breath at your side fighting to make one."

My breath caught in my throat at his words. I didn't move. Instead, I stopped breathing as his lips brushed mine, softly at first, like the gentle froth reaching the shores at dawn.

"Callix," I whispered, placing my hands over his. I allowed him that much. *"No..."* My thoughts added, trying to regain control.

"I know." He leaned away. "I know." When he released my face, I could finally breathe.

He paced about the pits, creating space between us, and I

gazed at the luminescent glow of the water reflected in his eyes and where he exposed his skin with the loosened buttons of his shirt. Trailing his hands through his hair, he glanced at me.

"Are you sure you want to do this?" I nodded, not trusting myself to speak. "Very well. Let's see your blocking moves," he said with calculated control. I felt the complete opposite. I felt almost as if every wall I had attempted to build between us was crumbling .

"What should I do?"

"Just try to block my strikes. I want to see your natural reactions, and then we can build your technique." I sucked in a breath, mirroring Callix's attack stance. I braced myself.

His fist flew. I moved out of the way, narrowly missing his other fist, which connected with my stomach.

"Keep both hands up. Remember, one fist always follows the other." I nodded as he circled around me.

Once again, he struck, and even though my arm took the blow, I didn't protest. I was done crying—or whining—as he had told me once before.

I wasn't sure which was worse, the cuts or the bruises. Callix narrowed his eyes at the skin around my ribs, now purpling.

"I think that's enough for today."

"No, I'm okay. Continue," I said, but he wasn't listening. He was already ascending the stairs.

"Come with me."

I didn't argue. The truth was, I wasn't sure I could take much more.

"Where are you taking me?" I asked, clutching my ribs as I fell into step beside him.

"You'll see." I followed him to a part of the castle I had never visited, yet somehow, it felt familiar, as if I had dreamed of it. The grotto walls glowed like those in the pits, and a natural pool rested in the middle of the chamber. Pausing at the edge, Callix faced me.

"Get in." I glanced between him and the glowing water.

"Now?"

"Yes, now. Get in."

"But what about my clothes?"

"Oh, for the love of the gods!" I shrieked as Callix picked me up and marched us both into its depths, disregarding my protests to be released. He only did so when I was completely submerged, like a drowned cat.

"Was that really necessary?"

Callix crossed to sit on one of the underwater stones placed along the poolside; he leaned back against the edge and closed his eyes, ignoring me.

"Fine." I sat on the opposite side and followed his lead. I relished the warm water that reached my neck as I leaned back, resting my head, too.

"How are your bruises?" he asked. I was too content to notice the pain was gone.

I stood up until the water lowered to my waist. I inspected my ribs. The bruise had almost faded. My eyes narrowed in Callix's direction.

"You knew I could come here and heal right away, and you never bothered to mention it!"

"I wasn't your friend then, remember? We had boundaries."

"I'm going to kill you, Callix. I swear I'm going to kill you!"

My threat only made him laugh.

"No, you won't."

"You know I would if I knew how one kills the mighty Leviathan." His laughter vanished, so I added, "That was a joke, by the way."

"Oh, I know."

"Then why the grim face?"

"Just glad to see I have sorted your misconceptions. That's all."

"You don't seem glad. If anything, you look troubled." I said, sitting up. "Were you worried about me finding out what you were?"

"Don't be absurd."

"I'm right, aren't I?" I pushed, and although he didn't open his eyes, his lips shifted, failing to suppress his smile. He wasn't going to admit it. "Don't you want to know what I think?"

"You've already said your piece. I'm an insensitive prick, remember?"

I laughed, and he lifted his head, his lazy gaze finding me.

"We both know you can be sometimes, but no." I studied my hands under the glow of the water, unable to match his stare. "I think you're incredible. No need to deny that."

His eyes darkened despite the reflective glow of the waters. I didn't move as he treaded through the water until only his head bobbed above the surface. I stared at the water droplets cascading down his face as he drew closer. Squeezing my hands into fists, I fought the impulse to trail my fingers after them.

He stopped a breath from me, and I focused on the water dripping beneath the curve of his lower lip.

"Desire is dangerous," he whispered. His mouth disappeared beneath the water. *"But there is no one here to judge you."* He was in my head, but I wasn't sure I was lucid enough to fight him.

His hand reached for mine beneath the water, and slowly, he uncurled my fingers from their tight fists. Bringing my fingers to his face, he splayed my hand against his skin. I didn't move; I wasn't sure I should. Slowly, I did what I had craved to do for so long. I traced the water droplets falling from his hair, and he closed his eyes. I moved my fingers over his brows, his perfect nose, the strong line of his jaw, until pausing at the edge of his lips. His eyes opened, locked on me.

"Go on," he urged, and my fingers trembled over his skin. His hands moved beneath the water, anchoring around my waist. His eyes begged me to continue.

My thumb traced his upper lip, then the bottom. I felt his breath against my skin as he parted his lips.

"This is how you kill me." His hand grazed my cheek and he weaved his fingers through my hair, pulling me closer.

His lips closed over mine—warm, soft, and unyielding. They moved against my frozen lips, and I felt myself cave, responding to his strokes. Lost to the magic of him. His hands grabbed my hips, pulling me out of the water as he stood. The water reached beneath his waist as he held my body flush against his. Hitching my legs around his lower back, he pressed me closer.

"No, Callix. No." My mind shouted, but this time, he didn't care to listen. His lips left a trail of electricity along my cheek while I clutched his wet shirt.

"No," I whispered, finding an invisible speck of sanity. I pressed a hand against his chest.

"You want this. I know you do." I fought to keep afloat, refusing to drown in the depths of his eyes.

"Desire is dangerous," I said, unwrapping my legs from around him and steadying myself. I allowed the water to separate us. "You said so yourself."

Before I lost all control, I stepped out of the pool, watching as every drop of water on my body and clothes returned to the well, like the vortex of magic shrouding the castle. "Thank you," I said before leaving the caves. It wasn't just Callix's fault. If anything, it was mine. All mine for allowing it—encouraging it.

How could I live with myself? Not long ago, I had judged Drake, heartbroken when I thought he had taken another woman. I wasn't any better. No, I was worse. I despised myself for allowing my needs to overthrow my emotions and cloud my judgment.

Throwing myself into bed, I was overcome with a torrent of emotions. Damn the stupid Fates, the realms, and my life. I wanted to reach into my chest and rip my heart out. I wanted to stop feeling, to stop caring and wanting. But mostly, I wanted to squash the guilt slowly eating at my insides.

7

STOWING CHAOS

RAKE ONCE SAID THAT SELF-CONTROL WAS NOT ONE of the abilities he possessed as an immortal, but I was beginning to think it might be mine. The days blurred into nights, though not a day went by where I wasn't hurting. Although my body had fought and won to regain control, my mind reminded me of what it felt like every second I spent in Callix's presence.

He didn't make it any easier for me. With my thoughts open like a field ready for his picking, I had nowhere to hide from his prying mind.

Every night, I cried myself to sleep. I was no longer sure what brought on the sadness. Perhaps a mixture of longing, loneliness, and despair that lodged in my throat as I took to the solitude of my rooms every night.

The one thought of consolation I held to was knowing I was getting stronger—faster. My mind was sharper, too, and my ears had become so sensitive I could pick up sounds from the world outside the ocean. Sea birds, rolling waves along the shore. Even my taste buds had sharpened. I attuned to certain flavors my mortal life had never experienced. Everything was more vibrant and alive, which was ironic, given that I felt like I was drowning.

My body wasn't the only thing changing. My fighting skills improved each day, too. It had taken a lot of effort to impress Callix. He was brutal and, if I was being honest, the best trainer I could have asked for. His cruel tactics had begun to shape me into the skilled warrior the realms and Fates needed me to become.

"Your weapons of choice?" he asked, twirling the spear. I shook my head, smiling.

"Not today."

He raised his brows but didn't drop his spear.

"Very well." As usual, his attack was skilled, swift, and precise. I was no longer a novice to his moves. I jumped out of the way as the tip of the spear nicked the stone floor where I had stood seconds before. Callix smirked, twisting his entire body to strike my side. I jumped—higher than my human body could have—and landed on his spear, which fractured under the force of my fall. His eyes narrowed as the spear turned to water at his feet.

"I was taking it easy on you," he said, and I laughed. He would never admit defeat.

"We both know that isn't true. But if it makes you feel less emasculated, then by all means."

His eyes glowed as he said, "Not many people surprise me. But you do. Often."

"I'll take that as a compliment and your indirect admission to defeat." His laughter boomed.

"Two out of three?" he asked. I rolled my eyes.

"Who's being childish now?" Summoning two swords from the water, I watched them crystalize as I pointed them in his direction. This time, he chose no weapons. He motioned with his hand for me to attack, and I did without hesitation.

Ducking below my arm, he evaded my sword. He grabbed my wrist but failed to predict my move until it was too late. I used my free arm to elbow him in the stomach, and he briefly buckled, offering me enough time to strike back with the hilts of my swords. Without allowing him a reprieve, I thrust my knee into his face, and he staggered back, cupping his nose. His bemused expression turned to one of shock. I wasn't as skilled as Callix, nor did I ever expect to be, but what I did possess was an uncanny ability to observe and predict his movements. He was right. It was like an electric pulsing string. He disappeared through a water portal before me, but my instincts didn't fail. When he swept through the air, I was waiting. I twisted and kicked him square in the chest.

He landed on the stone floor with a deafening thud. I landed above him a second later. Swords raised, and pointed against his neck.

My chest heaved.

"Don't move," I warned, pressing the blades closer to his skin. His eyes danced with emotions: admiration, amusement, defiance.

"I wouldn't dare," he said, but regardless of my warning, his hands trailed my thighs, which currently held his torso in a vise.

"Is that two out of three?" I mocked, and he smirked.

"I pity the poor fool who crosses your path," he said with genuine appreciation.

I smiled, content. I allowed the swords to dissipate into droplets which fell over his chest. I stood and offered my hand. But he had other plans. I should have known. He would never be content unless he had the last laugh. Twisting me with force, he pushed his towering body over mine and secured my hands above my head. He dug his hips into me, and I struggled beneath him, unable to escape.

"You should never trust your opponent's willingness to surrender. They will always have an ulterior motive."

"Lesson learned. Now get off me." I wrestled against his hands.

"I would if you really wanted me to," he teased.

"I'm telling you to move!" But his grin only widened, a storm brewing in his eyes.

"Your lips say one thing, but your mind screams the contrary." He rocked his hips into mine, and I sucked in a breath.

"Callix, please."

"You're pleading to me?" A rumble of laughter rippled from his chest, and his face was one of pain and chaos. "I should be the one begging you to quit fighting this. To end the suffering you're submitting yourself to."

With a sneer, Callix was on his feet. He vanished through a water portal, leaving me stunned and confused.

Sitting up on the stone floors, I listened for him, but as the strange sounds of the ocean filled my ears, I heard it.

"I'm here now, love..." It was the softest resemblance to his

voice, or perhaps his thoughts, though I couldn't be sure. What I knew for certain was who that voice belonged to.

Drake...

I bolted. Dashing up the stairs, I ran through the castle, listening to the surrounding sounds.

"No..." His voice rang out again—clearer and closer this time. *Drake's here—he's here!* I ran to the open balcony, following the last vestiges of his voice, and arrived in time to see the back of Callix's shirt disappear as he dove headfirst through the ocean wall.

"Callix!" I screamed, knowing he could hear me. The passing seconds felt like an eternity. "Callix, please!" I begged. "Please don't hurt him!" I fell to my knees before the ocean wall.

What was I doing? I was immortal now. I couldn't hold my breath forever, but I could for long enough to follow him. As I rose, a swell of water burst through the wall, landing in a heap against the stone at my feet.

Callix clutched the gashing wound slashed across his right shoulder to his hip. His shirt was in tatters as the magic vortex sucked back the blood-tainted water from his open wound.

"Callix!" I shrieked. "What happened?"

"The pool." With a flick of his hand, a water portal opened before us. "Help me to the pool," he said, his blood pooling around us.

I linked one of his arms around my shoulder to help him stand. As we moved through the portal, the edge of the pool awaited us on the other side. Callix didn't wait for me to help him. He tumbled forward with a splash, and I stared in horror as the glowing water turned crimson.

I jumped after him and turned him in my arms. I willed his head to rest against my chest as the rest of his body sank to the bottom. Eyes closed, I sensed his breathing finally ease. I didn't dare speak. He was hurt. I didn't want to think how, but after seeing his gashes, I concluded nothing else. I was right... I had heard Drake's voice. Fear, sadness, and anger consumed me, though I wasn't sure who I was angrier at, Callix or Drake.

"It's not his fault," whispered Callix. I laughed and cried all at once. I kissed his forehead. Stupid idiot.

"You scared me," I said, hysterical.

"Just give me a few minutes and I'll be as good as new." His body floated to the surface, and slowly, the crimson red began to vanish from the water, its luminescent glow returning.

Callix plunged beneath the surface to clean his face. When he resurfaced, he sat before me. The once horrible cuts were no more than light pink streaks along his skin.

"I—I thought you were going to die," I whispered. His brows creased.

"I'm immortal, remember?"

"There was so much blood, Callix—"

"It wouldn't have killed me," he added. "I would have probably passed out and healed much slower, but I wouldn't have died." At his admission, I felt my soul return to my body. Once I knew he was out of danger, I narrowed my eyes at him.

"What the hell is going on. I'm not crazy, am I? That was Drake's voice I heard?" Callix's gaze pierced mine.

"No. You're not crazy." My shoulders sagged. I glanced around the pool, unable to meet his eyes. "He was trying to get to you."

"How many times has he tried to reach me?"

Callix hesitated before answering. "A few." My eyes shot towards him in question.

"A few?"

"He's worried."

"I understand, but it's only been a few weeks." Callix's lips tightened. "Callix?"

"It's been much longer, actually," he admitted, and the temperature of the water chilled around me.

"How? How much longer?"

I steeled myself for Callix's answer as he ran his hands across his face.

"Months. Over three seasons, perhaps close to a year," he admitted. "I've learned not to keep track of the time."

I stared at him, unable to find my voice.

Months? A year... how was it possible? I knew my days had begun to blend, but I wasn't so lost not to have noticed so much missing time.

"How?" I said the only word I could as my mind struggled to find any reasonable explanations.

"Time flows differently here in Serfier. We're connected to the Fates, divinity, and rebirth. It can be a blessing, but it's also a curse." I covered my face with my hands. "I never expected your transformation would take as long, but you floated in this pool for weeks in my perspective, but months to the outside world."

"And days to me," I said. That's how long it had felt when I awoke in my immortal body. "You said Drake didn't know I was alive."

"He didn't know. Not until today."

"How could you? You lied to me."

"I have never…"

"Saying nothing constitutes a lie, Callix! You stayed silent. You allowed all this time to pass and kept Drake in the dark."

"It was for the best! You weren't ready, and you still aren't!"

"I didn't know it had been so damn long, Callix!" I splashed water into his face, exasperated. "Do you know what it must have been like for him, not knowing if I lived or died? What must he think? That I forgot about him?"

"That's the last thing on his mind, I assure you."

"I'm not sure I trust anything you say."

"I know what you think, but I never lied. Perhaps I should have explained the time lapse in my world, but it would have only made you more desperate to leave and return to him, but at what cost?" His hands moved over the calm surface of the water. "Hate me if you want, but I swear to you, my reasons were not selfish. I only did it for you!"

I stared at him. A part of me ached to hurt him for what he'd done, but I could never bring myself to hate him.

"What am I going to do with you?" I muttered. He rested his head on the edge of the pool.

"I have a few ideas," he added suggestively, and when I didn't laugh, the smirk vanished from his face.

"I need to speak with him. I need to explain," I said, determined. The silence stretched between us until Callix finally rose to his feet, all traces of his wound now gone.

"You know he will never understand. He will never allow you to stay," he warned.

"You don't know that!" I argued. "It's my decision."

But by the expression on his face, he wasn't convinced that was enough.

"There is a way," he said eventually, stepping out of the pool and offering me his hand. "Come." He pulled me out of the water effortlessly, and I followed him down the halls toward a corner of the castle I had yet to explore.

"My patience is wearing thin, Callix. Where are you taking me now?"

"My chambers," he replied without breaking his strides. I stopped.

"Why?" I inquired, and he halted his pace and turned to me.

"You wanted to speak with him. Now, come." He marched down the hall, and though I was hesitant, I followed, nonetheless.

Callix's chambers were nothing like mine. An expansive balcony peered across the ocean. The high vaulted columns were supported by crystalized statues of seahorses and intricate pastel corals framing the doors and archways.

"Just a moment." He removed the remaining shreds of his shirt, and his back muscles moved with each of his strides as he disappeared into what I imagined was his closet. I was too mad at him to dwell on the thought. A minute later, he reappeared, buttoning a new crisp white shirt.

"Come." He gestured to a small basin resting over the purest white marble pillar. The large stone bowl was filled to the rim with clear water.

Noting my curiosity, he said, "This works like a two-way

mirror. You can communicate with whoever's reflection you find on the other side."

I had read of such a thing, but I never imagined this to be his solution.

"Is this how you spoke to me once at the fountain?"

"You knew it was me?" His face was a mix of surprise and confusion.

"No, not at first, but once I found out who you really were... I knew it could be no one else." He smiled, pleased. "How does this work?"

"We wait until he passes an object that can catch his reflection, and then I open the link."

"Will he be able to see me?"

"If you want him to, yes."

I debated. How would he react after not seeing me for so long? Though I knew there could be no other way.

"I want him to."

"Very well." Callix moved his fingers over the water, and ripples broke over the surface. "Drake..." His voice echoed in the silence of the chamber.

Anxiety overcomes me, then. What would I say? How would he react after so long? Callix's hand rested on mine, over the edge of the basin.

"It's ok. He will just be happy to see you," he said, and I frowned, staring at the water.

"You don't know that."

"You're right. I don't. But he would be a fool to waste the precious time doing anything but worship you." I glanced at the Sea God and rolled my eyes. "Trust me. I'm right."

"How long do we wait?"

"Like I said, until we catch his reflection."

"But that could take days..."

He smiled.

"Not for us, but maybe a few hours."

I forgot the stupid time lapse.

"What if we miss it?"

"We won't. Once he catches his reflection, it will call out to him, and the basin will vibrate. Like crystal bells." I dropped my hands from the basin's edge and moved to the open balcony, where the ocean surrounded us like a snow globe.

"It's beautiful out here." From his view, one could see the reaches of his kingdom. The Mer city was alive today.

Callix walked to my side, resting his hands on the frozen rails.

"I am sorry," he said.

"What are you apologizing for?"

"For upsetting you. I'm sorry for not telling you sooner. I'm sorry for everything, really." I stared into the ocean. I couldn't stay mad at him. Not for long.

"Perhaps you should be apologizing to him, not me." Callix stiffened.

"If that's what it will take for you to forgive me..." His eyes traced my face. "I will."

I shook my head. Although he was sincere, I would never ask that of him. Not when I was to blame, too. Instead, I changed the subject.

"What happened out there today?" I forced my eyes to meet his, but it was Callix who looked away this time.

"This is the second time he has attempted to breach Serfier since you woke."

"When was the first?"

"The day I took you to Isilium."

"You said you had business to take care of."

His eyes narrowed. Drake must have been the 'business' he referred to.

"I'm sorry."

I glanced at him.

"I don't want your apologies, Callix. I want you to grow the fuck up."

Despite seeming stunned by my outburst, he grinned. He never took anything serious.

"How can I take you seriously when you use language like that?"

"Why didn't you just let him in? Why fight him?"

"I will not apologize for protecting my kingdom. No one enters my realm without my permission. No one. And you're wrong about your assumption. I never touched him!"

"Clearly, you did. Why else would he have hurt you the way he did?"

The muscles in his jaw tightened.

"He was angry. He reached the castle this time after failing every time before."

"How many times exactly are we talking about?"

"Six. Maybe more."

"But you said this was the second time."

"Since you've been awake."

I closed my eyes, struggling to contain my anger.

"I can see now why he would want to hurt you."

"He could try." I spun to face him as if he were insane.

"He clearly did, Callix. Bleeding out in my arms was proof enough."

"That's because you begged me not to hurt him." I paused then. *He did hear...*

"I'm sorry."

"No, you're not." He turned away from me. "It wouldn't be the first time you chose him."

I stared after him as he collapsed on his bed, tucking his hands behind his head. *What the hell is wrong with me?*

No matter what I did, I would always end up hurting one of them.

I GLANCED behind me at Callix's unmoving form in the middle of the massive bed. What was I supposed to do with myself, stuck in his chambers while he slept—or pretended to? I didn't want to miss my chance to see Drake. Callix shifted, freeing the space beside him. He patted the empty side without bothering to open his eyes. Reluctantly, I walked to the edge and rolled my eyes when I noticed his smirk. Plopping down onto the bed, I turned my back to him and closed my eyes. There was no way I would get any sleep with his body so close to mine. I focused on his steady breathing and felt the strings of electricity sizzle in the space separating us. I refused to move a muscle.

"Just get out of my head, Callix. Please. I haven't forgiven you yet."

He didn't say a word, but after a minute, I felt the bed shift. From the corner of my eye, I watched him disappear into the other room.

I closed my eyes, and a minute later, my ears picked up the water in the shower. I concentrated on the soft flow of droplets falling against the stone floor, and after a few minutes, my mind drifted.

DRAKE

Somehow, since my failed attempt at breaching Serfier two nights ago, I had managed to sleep, though I knew it was due to the peace I'd regained after learning Belynda was alive. However, no one in Upherya would sleep tonight. The warriors assumed their posts by nightfall as we waited patiently for the cloud of darkness to arrive. With the outer barriers being breached, we had nothing else to do but stay and fight. I prepared to face our losses. Even with Dagasti's divided army, the odds of saving the Euresian clan were not in our favor.

I marched through the mountain borders, where Link and I awaited signals from Phoenix and Euros to lead the surprise attack. The strategy was solid, but that did little to ease the tension. Everyone knew what we were up against. I paused above the anvil, watching the ironsmith forge another batch of arrowheads. Spotting the barrel with water, I dipped my hands into it, splashing cold water on my face.

"Drake..."

I lowered my hands and stared at the rippling water's surface.

"Drake..." The voice called again. The fire in me burned. Bracing my hands against the barrel's edge, I stared at my unmoving reflection, and slowly, it shifted, morphing into something beautiful. Dream-like. The lovely shape of her face.

"Drake..." Her voice sang, and it trembled in my mind, moving in sync with the tilt of her lips.

"Is it really you?" I knew it was possible, but I had dreamed of seeing her for so long that I couldn't trust my senses.

"It's me. I'm okay," she whispered, and everything in me ached to reach through the magic and pull her closer.

"By the Fates. How is it possible that you could be even more beautiful than I remember?"

"The perks of immortality." She smiled—a smile that sealed the gaping hole in my chest. There was no other way she could have survived.

"I've been to hell and back trying to reach you. Why has he kept you?"

"I have missed you, too. But I can't return. Not yet."

"You don't belong there. You don't owe him anything. Whatever reason he's fabricated to keep you, they are nothing but lies."

I paused, certain my expression was one of desperation.

"You're wrong, Drake. He's not keeping me. I chose to stay. I can't fulfill my destiny or help the realms fight against the darkness unless I'm ready."

I gripped the barrel's rim, and it cracked beneath the pressure of my fingers. The blacksmith and other passing soldiers watched me from a distance. I ignored them. They likely questioned my sanity when all they saw was a madman talking to his reflection.

"I've told you this before. You don't need to fight. Belynda, I can keep you safe. I don't care if I die in the process; I don't care how many promises I must break."

"Drake, my fate is not in your hands. You can't go against what is destined."

"I will kill anything and anyone who stands in our way. That is my promise. That much is in my hands."

"I know you would. But I need to do this. The Fates spoke to me, and they have said this is the only way."

"Damn the Fates! They've taken enough from us already. Callix, I know you're listening. By the gods, if you don't release her, I will kill you."

"Stop. Please! Just listen. He has nothing to do with this. I'm begging you to listen, Drake. I need you to understand, please."

"I can't. I will never trust him. You belong with me." I roared as tendrils of fire broke across my skin.

"Drake..." Belynda's pleading voice disappeared with her reflection. I stared back at myself through the ripples of water. Fire moved across my skin as the wood around the barrel snapped, sending water flying.

"Drake." Link's voice tethered me back to reality. "Are you alright?"

"I'm fine."

"Are you sure you can fight? If your head is not in the game, you could sit this out."

I glanced at the young warrior as the fire singed in my veins.

"If I don't kill someone right now, I'm going to lose my mind."

The warrior nodded as we waited for our signal.

BELYNDA

Disoriented, I opened my eyes to a darkened room, my face pressed against cool skin. I had no idea how I ended up dozing on his bare chest as if it were the softest pillow. Lifting my head, I turned to find Callix sleeping, his face peaceful. I rested my chin against the coolness of his skin and silently observed the Sea God. His fingers grazed the skin of my waist, and I tensed. A second later, his lips moved, and I knew he was awake. I punched him in the chest and rolled away from him.

"Good morning to you too, darling." I glanced at the darkness from the window and rolled my eyes.

"It's not even morning, Callix."

"I know, but I've always wanted to say that."

"Will you put some clothes on, at least?" No longer did I feel the blazing anger from before, and I wasn't sure I could keep my eyes from betraying me this time.

"Why? Does my body offend you?" I glared.

"No, but I'm tempted to punch you again." *Or touch you,* my traitorous mind whispered. He laughed, and I wanted to strike myself instead.

"I know exactly what you meant. Don't worry. See, I'm easing your suffering." He strolled through the darkness, lighting the lamps around the room, replacing the shadows with a soft glow. He slipped on his shirt while regarding me from the far side of the room. That strange electricity coursed through the space between us until a strange buzzing stole my focus. I shifted my awareness to the basin in the distance, sensing its vibration.

"Is it him?" I jumped from the bed, staring at Callix.

"Go ahead." Callix kept his distance as I neared the edge of the marble basin.

"Drake..." I called out, unsure if he could hear me. "Drake..." I called again, and at first, the ripples moved with the vibration of my voice. As the stillness returned to the water's surface, I saw his face, and a knot of emotions clogged my throat. "Drake..." I choked, fighting the need to cry or reach out and touch him.

"Is it really you?" I touched my face, realizing how long it had been since he last saw me. I wondered if the subtle changes were noticeable and wondered what he thought of me now.

"It's me. I'm okay."

"By the Fates. How is it possible that you could be even more beautiful than I remember?" His words stole away my fear, and I found myself grinning.

"The perks of immortality." His eyes traced the contours of my face.

"I've been to hell and back trying to reach you. Why has he kept you?"

My eyes didn't shift from Drake, but I felt Callix draw closer.

"I have missed you too. But I can't return. Not yet."

"You don't belong there. You don't owe him anything. Whatever reason he's fabricated to keep you, they are nothing but lies." I frowned. Convincing Drake wouldn't be easy, especially with the feud existing between them.

"You're wrong, Drake. He's not keeping me. I chose to stay. I can't fulfill my destiny or help the realms fight against the darkness unless I'm ready."

I longed to say I needed to save him, too, but I swallowed the words as the darkness shifted in Drake's eyes. He would never agree.

"I've told you this before. You don't need to fight. Belynda, I can keep you safe. I don't care if I die in the process; I don't care how many promises I must break." Had he learned nothing at all after everything we had been through?

"Drake, my fate is not in your hands. You can't go against what is destined."

"I will kill anything and anyone who stands in our way. That is my promise. That much is in my hands."

He was furious, but how could I make him see?

"I know you would. But I need to do this. The Fates spoke to me, and they have said this is the only way."

"Damn the Fates! They've taken enough from us already. Callix, I know you're listening. By the gods, if you don't release her, I will kill you. I felt Callix's presence beside me, but he didn't interfere.

"Stop. Please! Just listen. He has nothing to do with this. I'm begging you to listen, Drake. I need you to understand, please."

I watched the ripples of black sand unfurl around him. Callix was right. He would never accept it.

"I can't. I will never trust him. You belong with me." Drake thundered, and I swallowed my tears.

"Drake..." I pleaded, but Callix's fist struck the water. I moved from the basin, startled by the splash, and as I stared waiting for the water to settle, I knew Drake was gone.

"Why did you do that?"

"There was nothing else to be said." Callix moved away

from me and stepped out onto the balcony. I stared at his stiff back, not daring to speak. I wanted to tell him he was right, but I wasn't sure if he deserved to hear it. He had done wrong, too.

I turned and left his chambers, wiping the tears sliding down my cheeks. I was doing the right thing. Drake didn't see it now, but he would. Callix wasn't our enemy. He was my friend. Now, if I could just keep them from killing each other...

8

BATTLE OF THE EURESIANS

THE WINDS SHIFTED FROM NORTH TO EAST TO WEST. A sign. Each of the standing leaders of Upherya was restless. Silently, Phoenix stood beside me with a haunted expression.

"Are you alright?" I touched his shoulder, but his eyes didn't move, his line of sight disappearing towards the horizon. Their torches flickered as they approached, the Army of Darkness descending over the Euresian territory.

"How does one feel, Euros? When your land and people are in danger? When you watch the darkness approach, and despair clutches your insides?"

I didn't respond. I couldn't find the words to comfort my brother. Soon, the darkness would meet the last of the barriers, but it wouldn't slow them. We knew the barriers were useless, given the ease with which they brought down the magic of the outer walls. Their darkness was growing, becoming something visceral, and tonight, it had a purpose.

To claim yet another piece of our Realm. To pillage our lands and our people.

NIGHT FELL, casting long shadows across the desolate battlefield, soon to be filled by the howls and cries of war. Swords clashed and hooves thundered as the steeds charged. A quiet song of death followed the descension of the Army of Darkness, meeting the first line of Euresian warriors. Our men charged with purpose. This was a battle they would remember for the decades to come. They fought for their land, their families, and their Realm.

Phoenix's long mane flowed behind him as he rallied the second line of warriors with a deep cry, determination burning in his eyes. He looked my way before he spurred his wings forward, his sword gleaming beneath the wavering lights of the fires. This was it. The moment that would determine the fate of the Euresian clan. If we failed tonight, the North would be next. I touched the horn nesting at my side, waiting for the right moment to signal Link and Drake.

Phoenix disappeared, sweeping through the Darkling's front lines. The clash between the two forces was earth-shattering. The ground trembled beneath my feet as I extended my wings, gearing my muscles—ready to fight. Swords clashed against shields, and arrows swooshed through the night sky. Fire and lightning crackled amidst the chaos. The Darklings were wild, but skilled fighters remained within the madness, too. I recognized many of our own brothers plucked by the darkness—first from the Southern clan and then the West, Link's territory. Tonight, we would be forced to slay familiar faces or face the darkness ourselves.

The Euresians fought with unrivaled skill and unwavering determination, matching the ferocity of the Darklings with their agility and speed.

But it wasn't enough. I raised my sword, calling my warriors to action.

"My brothers! Tonight, we face the darkness. Do not hesitate; do not waver. The dark will show no remorse. For our families, for our lost brothers, for Upherya."

Weapons raised to the skies, the line of men yelled their agreement, offering their weapons to the gods of the wind.

I weaved through the battlefield, peeling a line of Darklings from my path with the force of the North wind. Phoenix still fought for our side, unclaimed by the dark. A pit of darkling corpses surrounded him, claimed by his sword. He fended off three more.

"About time!" he barked as I landed behind the Darklings, taking their heads with a move of skilled precision.

A seething horde of Darklings surrounded us. Clinging to our swords, we exchanged a brief nod—a wordless promise of the unspoken bond forged between us over countless hours of training.

As the Darklings advanced, their sinister forms swayed like shadows. I took the lead, my heavy broadsword gleaming in the shadows cast by the fires. With a powerful forward thrust, I lunged at a Darkling, cleaving it in half with a single swift stroke. The impact reverberated through my arm, but I pushed the discomfort aside. Phoenix was at my back, ready to cover me.

As the Darklings closed in, I executed a wide arc with my sword, creating a perimeter of defense around us. Meanwhile, Phoenix's anger and determination raged as he darted between the creatures, his twin blades a blur of motion. His strikes were swift, precise, and deadly, leaving a trail of fallen Darklings in his wake.

We matched our attacks and left a path of fallen enemies behind. Together, we formed an unstoppable force, inspiring courage in the hearts of our warriors. However, it was Phoenix's wrath that blazed like a beacon, guiding the Euresians through the darkness, allowing us to move with fluidity. When I found myself surrounded, Phoenix leaped over my shoulder, slicing through the Darklings without hesitation. He was a madman. Possessed.

Time seemed to blur amid battle, and my focus narrowed to the immediate threats before me. Every clash of steel, parry, and riposte was a symphony of controlled chaos.

Our battle-hardened bodies were weary, but we fought on, fueled by the knowledge that together, we were stronger than any foe.

Feathers of crimson and gold sailed through the air as Phoenix dove, slicing through the lines of our enemies. But they kept coming; the darkness was never-ending. Even though Dagasti's army was divided, we had underestimated the volume of their forces.

"Sound the horn!" Phoenix called as he took to the air.

Falling behind the protection of our warriors, I sounded the horn. The booming rose above the chaos, and we fought on, waiting for Link and Drake to bring their counterattack from the North.

DRAKE

I willed my sharp sight to pierce through the distance while Link stood at my flank, waiting beneath the shadows of the mountainside. From here, I could see Euros charge forward, his battle cry mingling with the fierce wind as he tore through the lines of Dagasti's army. Amirth shifted beside me, and I sensed the change in her posture.

"I know you are eager like me to tear through their flanks but be sensible," I said to her. "For once. If not for your common sense, do it for his sake." And for the first time, I earned no resistance from the Elemental.

We aimed to flank the Darklings and encircle them to cut off any chance of retreat. Link and Amirth were restless, but the monster inside eagerly awaited. The call would soon come, and it would finally be free to devastate, conquer, and annihilate. We would spread fire over our enemies. Darkness fighting darkness.

It felt strangely ironic to have survived the dark Realm and the forces that served to charge the Nightshade amulet—the same darkness once donned by the monster inside of me, like armor against my human side and against the pain. A darkness I had come to rule and understand during all those years in Xelraa. Tonight, however, the monster fought against it. If we failed, the North would soon follow. If we didn't figure out a way to stop Dagasti from spreading his poison, all the

Realms would soon be consumed by the same force that spurred my monster. My silent companion.

Fire slithered beneath my skin, but as the horn sounded through the cries of war, dark tendrils exploded from my pores, igniting around my body.

My scales glistened an iridescent shimmer as I finally allowed the beast the freedom it sought.

Link swooped into the night skies, wings spread, and Amirth descended with the warriors from the mountainside like a tidal wave over the unsuspecting Darklings.

The beast ascended into the night, and after circling the battlefield, it sloped like a shadow over the enemy. Flames erupted from the Dragon's maw, engulfing their ranks in searing heat, while Link's sword cut through armor and flesh with unmatched precision. The beast flew, missing the spears and arrows aimed to bring us down. The monster was too absorbed in the madness and the chaos to care, spewing fire and wreaking havoc upon its enemy.

Our surprise attack threw the Darklings into disorder, but the shadow of evil fueling their black souls was not easily overcome.

We had witnessed the Darklings in battle before. We understood the greatest threat was the insatiable thirst of their blind command. They fought with a fervor that defied all reason. They spread like a plague, and though they fell, they stole our men. With every soul taken, they managed to pillage in their call to the dark. No matter how many Darklings we claimed, the black magic binding them grew more assertive. A twisted dance of death and despair.

Amirth moved without mercy, killing anything that crossed her path. She cleared the pathways. I took a sharp dive, scorching a Darkling that charged behind her. I helped her reach Euros and Phoenix. She would be safest if they covered each other.

EUROS

Amidst the clash of steel and the roar of battle, Amirth stood fierce alongside Phoenix and me. Her eyes blazed as she commanded the ground beneath her feet, shaping the earth to fight against the horde of dark creatures moving like an avalanche toward us. She manipulated the terrain, creating jagged rock formations and summoning earthen spikes to deter their approach. However, I saw her control slip. I felt the adrenaline rush through her veins with every devastating attack. She was reckless and eager for more.

I moved around her. My strikes prevented Darklings from drawing too close.

"Euros!" Phoenix roared. I shifted in a wide circle, just in time to cut through another Darkling.

The three of us opened our circle, but concern gripped my chest as I watched Amirth move with lethal strength, power, and impulsiveness. I couldn't concentrate. Her headstrong nature could get her killed.

"Amirth!" I called above the howls and sounds of metal against metal. "Amirth. *Control.* Don't let it cloud your judgment!"

She glanced at me, her smile defiant.

"Fight your own battle, Euros!" she bellowed over the uproar, but that second of distraction cost her.

A Darkling twice the size of a man lunged, its claws a breath from her face.

"NOO!" My roar caused her to shift just in time. Amirth dodged the Darkling and countered with a powerful stroke infused with earth magic. The ground trembled as her fist connected, sending shockwaves through the enemy's body. But the creature was relentless, and I was in the air when he charged for her again.

I landed on her side, deflecting the incoming blow, and slaying the giant.

"We fight as a team!" I commanded, my voice resolute and unwavering. Amirth nodded. She wasn't fighting me on this.

The three of us moved with synergy as the battle raged. Slowly, we pressed through the enemy ranks. However, even with our combined strength and unity, it wasn't enough to turn the tide.

DRAKE

Though the warriors fought fearlessly, the relentless onslaught of the Darklings was overwhelming. The sky singed as storm clouds gathered, crackling with lightning. The ground trembled beneath the weight of their advance, and their unholy forces seemed endless. Spewing fire, I circled the perimeter, tightening their boundaries, but the warriors grew weary and battered. They appeared to be slowly retreating as their hope dwindled.

Euros' armor was dented and bloodied, but his voice rose above the din of battle, rallying the warriors for one last stand.

Phoenix's arm bled, but it didn't stop him from advancing with Amirth beside them.

I rose over the field, blazing the Darklings below. The warriors fought with unwavering loyalty to their clan leaders and indomitable spirit; every sacrifice was a testament to the power these warriors possessed. But it was clear. We could not withstand the sheer force of the Army of Darkness, even with our combined strength.

"Phoenix! Pull back!" Euros' roar floated above the chaos, but the warrior did not listen. "Link! Amirth! Cover me." The young warrior landed before the clashing swords, and Amirth broke the earth, providing a reprieve for Euros as he charged for Phoenix.

"This is suicide, Phin. Call your men."

"Never." Phoenix sliced through the nearest Darklings, and his rigid stance relayed his refusal to put down his weapon. If his territory fell, he would fall with it, which was foolish. Our losses only allowed the darkness to grow in power. He wasn't thinking straight.

"Drake!" Euros roared as I hovered above them. Wings splayed, I willed ashes to surround them. Phoenix pushed against Euros.

"You will not bring me out of my battle unconscious like you did with Link!"

"I will if you leave me no choice. Would you rather offer your body and sword to the darkness, to later return and fight us instead? Don't be stupid, Phoenix. Call your men back."

Euros pleaded with him as I reached with my claw, removing the head of yet another Darkling that charged toward them. "Be reasonable, Phoenix. This battle might be lost, but the war is far from over. We need you."

Phoenix's bellowing howl was blood-curling.

"Retreat!" he commanded, and the Euresian warriors began to pull back at his order.

"Drake. Amirth." Euros called. We knew what he required.

Circling the throng of Darklings that moved like a demonic mass, I unleashed a line of fire. The warriors that could fly took to the skies while my fire broke over the earth, forming a chasm to slow the Darkling's advance. The warriors retreated until they reached the mountains, where we knew our enemy would not cross.

As the last of the warriors reached the cover of the hills, I watched, fascinated, as the Darklings paused at the foot of the mountain as if an invisible wall impeded their passage. The first line of raging force attempted to bring down the wall like they had done with our barriers, but they were met with a force they had yet to understand.

Euros was right. Whatever magic those mountains harvested could be used to protect their Realm, if only they could wield it for their purpose. Understand it.

I circled again, searching for the person who would not be foolish enough to show. Dagasti. The man was too clever—too calculating—and too much of a coward to show himself here with only half his army to hide behind.

However, Euros was right. This was just a battle. The monster would get its chance at revenge.

. . .

THE DARKNESS MOVED over the eastern territory like a plague while I watched from above, like a hungry vulture as they set up their camps right over the stretch of the battleground. Over the bodies of our men and theirs alike. Without a care and without a thought. These creatures were nothing like me. Yes, we had both tasted darkness, but these men had lost their minds to Nightshade.

My shadow cast over the mountains as I peered at what remained of the Euresian forces marching back towards the North. Defeat could be tasted as the once-proud army was reduced to ashes. However, even though I wasn't a child of the wind, I felt the quivering force against my wings, like a murmur. The air shifted with magic, and hope came in a quiet whisper. A foresight, foretelling the rise of a star that would bring an end to the reign of darkness.

Another clan had fallen, but hope was not extinguished from Upherya. The North still stood, and they would fight, and I along their side.

9
DARKNESS ASCENDING

Like a shield, Nightshade rested against my chest. Lightning streaked across the skies of Druleska as thunder made the kingdom tremble below. The East had fallen under my command, and the North would soon follow. There was one crown to rule The Four Realms, and I would be the one holding it.

I could almost taste the euphoric weight of power, but first, the walls of Abryas had to fall. Serfier was my greatest challenge, but Callix wouldn't be a problem for much longer, not if my plans went as expected.

"Sir, the people are gathering outside the gates again."

Did I have to do everything myself? I whirled, glaring at the Dravoni guard. "Then break it up, you incompetent fool."

With a bow, he disappeared from the skybridge, and I glared at his back.

An army required men—men which I had been happy to pluck from our enemy's ranks, but it wasn't enough. Not when

Drake and those damned warriors refused to see they were no match against my army. Their relentlessness only served to dwindle my numbers, forcing me to delay my advance. Without a fleet, my only option was to allocate some of the Darklings to the task. It also forced me to increase my numbers by pillaging souls from my own home.

After the losses against the West Clan, the Nightshade summoned every man in Druleska to serve the darkness. Disorder and chaos ran rampant through the city. Many fled before the call claimed them. Those who remained, mostly women, children, and elders, eroded through the city, plagued by starvation.

Now, like savages, they stalked the castle doors instead of showing gratitude for my benevolence. Sparing their miserable lives was a mercy they didn't deserve. The famished kingdom stretched before me. The war had repercussions, and I knew there would be costs, but still, none outweighed the prize: the Realms, my crown, and the blood-witch. She would remain at my side; if not by choice, then by force.

CRIES AND HOWLS cut through the night as the Dravonis forced the throng back from the castle gates. I grinned. Now all I required was patience and a fleet. Yet the second was taking longer than expected, hence my need for patience. Soon, I would sail my army across the Fjord and shatter Herod's barriers. Their magic was nothing against Nightshade. Their walls would come tumbling down.

Silence stretched through the fortress. Since my call beckoned the men to the darkness, the servants were reduced to women. However, many had fled into the mountains. The ones who remained were loyal to me or too afraid to consider betrayal.

I yanked the service cord in the dining hall.

"My Lord?"

"Why the delay!" I bashed my fist against the table.

"My apologies, my Lord. With the reduced staff…" I stared at the woman, daring her to continue. "It won't happen again. I will have supper served right away." She curtsied before disappearing. Waiting was a small price to pay, I reminded myself as I contemplated my victories.

A few minutes later, the woman returned to place a silver tray before me.

"Is there anything else I can get you, my Lord?"

I picked up my fork and dug in.

"Kore." I speared a piece of meat into my mouth. "Have her come to my chambers tonight."

"Yes, my Lord," mumbled the woman before leaving me with the company of my meal and wine.

When I entered my chambers, I was met by the glorious sight of Kore's breasts—a delicacy I was suddenly starving to taste.

"Are you hungry, my Lord?" she purred, sauntering to my side. The curves of her body swayed with her measured strides.

"Starving!" I roared, fisting her hair and pressing her luscious mouth with mine. I pulled away, and her hands clung to my chest.

Her mesmerized eyes beheld the Nightshade amulet at my throat.

"Is that..." Her fingers inched towards the stone, and I seized her wrist. Darkness crawled over my skin.

"You're not here for that. Kneel." She obeyed without complaint. Her willingness was something Drake had not learned to appreciate. Kore could handle fire; she could take the pain. Yet I understood his fascination with the blood witch, too, as her innocence made her even more enticing than the power she possessed. Most enticing, however, was knowing she belonged to him. Claiming her for myself would be the ultimate reward.

I released Kore's wrist and fisted her hair as her skilled fingers worked to release me.

"My Lord, you are so ready for me," she cooed, but I braced my hands on her head.

"Shut up." I shoved my pulsing cock into her mouth, and she cried out in surprise. I buried myself in the back of her throat while her hands pushed against my thighs. She knew better than to fight me. I backed her against the wall and pinned her hands up against the wall.

"My Lord." Her protests died as I plunged my wet cock into her mouth. The back of her head hit the stone as I rammed into her with unrelenting fury. I braced my other hand around her throat, and I felt my ramrod hardness fill the inside walls of her throat. She whimpered, so I moved harder. Faster. Deeper.

"You whore! You cock sucking whore!"

On her knees, she whimpered before me, and the sounds of

her futility made me burst down her throat. I smiled, sated, releasing the last of my warmth into her mouth.

"Leave," I finally ordered, resting my head against the wall. I released her wrists.

As the door slammed behind her, I collapsed onto the bed, clutching the Nightshade, sensing its darkness-like tentacles wrapping around my throat. Taking a deep breath, I allowed it to course through me.

Invincible. Unstoppable. Darkness and devastation were under my command, and nothing would stand in my way.

IO

INTO THE DEEP

ALLIX WAS CHAOS. NO OTHER WORD COULD describe the mighty Leviathan: the Lord of the Water Realm. In the days that followed my exchange with Drake, my relationship with the Sea God grew strained. It wasn't merely his lies—or 'omissions', as he called them—it was the constant internal battle I fought to resist his allures.

When I closed my eyes at night, I recalled Drake's touch, his body, and those lips, until they would morph and transform into something else—someone else. *Callix.* I hated him for making me feel things, but mostly, I hated myself for feeling them in the first place.

What bothered me most was knowing he could read my thoughts, and I knew he often did. He could never hide the pleasure from his face whenever an errant thought crossed my mind.

I tried to focus all my energy on training. The sooner I was ready, the faster I could leave and return to Drake. Be safe from the temptation. From Callix. From those eyes now piercing into my soul.

"Focus!" He barked, tossing his icy knives toward me. I dodged in time to avoid serious injury, but not before a sharp edge nicked the skin on my right shoulder.

"Damn it!" I hissed, though I no longer felt as bound to the pain as I used to. I raised my twin blades, ignoring the blood trailing down my arm. I rushed towards the Sea God.

He charged, and I blocked, but the force of his spear shattered the blades of my swords. The remains dissolved into water, but before I could summon another weapon, he punched my face, the power knocking me back. I braced against the moist floor of the pits, grinning up at him. If he wanted war, then war he would get.

I flew across the chamber towards him as he opened a water portal and disappeared into it. A second later, the portal opened behind me, and I rolled on the floor, pushing myself up into a crouch.

"Nice try," I teased, and he grinned. Once again, he disappeared through a water portal, but it took him longer to reappear this time. I knew what he was doing; he was building anticipation, trying to bait and rattle me.

This time, however, he succeeded. I never saw him. One second, there was only silence, and the next, he was behind me. He held me tight against him, circling his arm over my shoulder to secure my neck.

I fought against his chokehold, but Callix possessed brutal

strength. I summoned a gust of wind, and we flew into the wall, his body cushioning the impact. As he loosened his hold on my neck, I scrambled to create distance, but he grabbed my braid and yanked me back. He twisted in one fluid move and then pressed me up against the stone wall, trapping me beneath the full weight of his body. I tried to elbow him, but he took both my arms and pinned them at my sides. My chest heaved against the stone wall as I fought to catch my breath. His hands were tainted with my blood.

"You know better than to challenge me." I didn't need to see his face to know he was smiling. I sensed his satisfaction in his voice's vibration as his breath traced the nape of my neck. "Are you ready to give up?" he challenged, as if I would ever admit defeat. That was something else I had learned from him.

I struggled against his hold, but his body pressed deeper; one of his thighs pried my legs apart, and I felt him thicken against my behind.

"Callix. Get off me." I huffed, though he gave a melodic laugh. The soft warmth of his lips brushed my ear.

"I don't think I will... unless you're ready to admit defeat."

I sucked in a breath.

"Not a chance," I growled, attempting to fight against his hold. It only made things worse. Every time I struggled, I felt him hardening behind me.

"I could die happily right now." While his words unsettled me, it was the longing in his voice that made me shudder. His nose skimmed the side of my neck, and my traitorous body eased into him. "Darling... let me. Give up." His request incited endless possibilities to race through my mind, and I was no longer sure which surrender he sought. His hips pressed into me, and my breath left my lips.

"Callix..." I turned, feeling the soft touch of his lips against my cheek. "You're not playing fair."

I sighed and felt his smile warm the skin of my ear.

"Nothing's fair in love and war, remember?" I took a deep breath, desperate to clear my mind. He was right. I could never win this fight against him. If I didn't surrender now, I wouldn't just lose the battle... I would forfeit the war.

"Fine. You win." I declared. His body stiffened, as if fearing that this was a trick to lure him into a false sense of security. His mind probed into my thoughts, but then his hold on my arms loosened, and reluctantly, he pulled away, freeing my body.

When I turned around, he was stoic. Detached.

"I think I'm done for the day," I said, and he didn't bother to stop me. However, I felt his eyes following me as I left the pits.

By the time I stepped out of the shower, my cut had already healed. It had been superficial enough not to merit a visit to the pool.

The plan was to avoid Callix—at least for the evening—in the hope he would cool off. Though I realized I wasn't as concerned over his lack of propriety or the ease with which he often lost control... no. My greatest fear was my inability to act reasonably in the presence of his chaos.

"Phial, I'll have supper in my room tonight. Please." I pushed my silent request into the nymph's mind.

"Yes, my Lady."

I stared at the underwater city, or at least the part visible through the glass window. I wondered how the other sea creatures lived. The mermaids, in particular, were a colorful horde, with their scaly tails from shimmering crimsons to bright greens and blues, and their constant travel in clusters; their long flowing manes, elongated arms, bony faces, sunken eyes, and their teeth as sharp as knives. What did Callix truly look like in his elemental form? From experience, I knew with Drake that books were not always an accurate source.

A soft knock came from the door, and I turned from the window in time to see the nymph.

I gestured to the small table. "Just over there, please. Thank you, Phial."

She bowed her head in subtle acknowledgment.

"If there is anything else you need, my Lady..."

"I'm good. Thank you." Bending at the knee slightly, she clutched the empty tray to her chest. "Phial," I called. She paused at the door. "Is Callix dining in the hall?"

I had attempted to detect any sound as an indicator of his whereabouts, given that his thoughts were so well guarded, but his movements seemed just as stealthy.

"No. Master is in his study."

"Alone?" I wanted to bite my tongue, but when the nymph hesitated, I realized I no longer cared what she thought. I needed to know.

"No, my Lady... Syllis keeps him company." A sudden rush of anger swept over me, and my immortal blood rushed to my face. I was certain the nymph could see it, too.

"Thank you, Phial. Have a good evening." As she disappeared, closing the door in her wake, I put down my food. I was no longer hungry. No, I was angry, and the sudden urge to march into his study overpowered every other thought. *Get a hold of yourself!* I chastised myself.

I picked up an apple and took a bite as I settled before the window. What was wrong with me? I had no right to feel this way. I didn't care what the Sea God did. I *shouldn't* care. It was none of my business who he chose for his pleasures. A distinct piercing feeling settled in the middle of my chest, and suddenly, I couldn't breathe. Despite the air flowing around me, it felt like icy walls were tightening around my heart. I fought against the suffocation, and then I ran from my room.

I clutched at my chest as I rushed down the corridors. I spotted the stone steps descending into the ocean wall surrounding the castle. I didn't slow. I plunged through the magic barrier without thinking, embraced by the dark sea. Holding my breath, I propelled my legs and arms against the current, fighting to reach the surface.

Yet, as I counted the stammering of my heart, I knew I wouldn't make it. I was foolish to think I could when Drake had failed so many times. The truth was, I hadn't thought this through. I didn't want to run away, but I desperately needed to see the skies, to breathe in the fresh air—not the stale magic allowing us to breathe inside the castle. I needed to escape the icy walls. I needed to *not* think.

But most importantly, I needed to be far away to keep from doing something I'd regret. Pressure began to set in my lungs. Nevertheless, losing consciousness was far more tolerable than surrendering to my irrational needs.

The only thought that kept me going was knowing I wouldn't die, but as dark spots swarmed my vision and the last reserve of air left my body, that idea wasn't enough to ease my fear. My legs gave out first, and the rest of my body followed. Weightlessness consumed me.

Peace and silence. This must have been how Isabel felt, and that sad realization was the last thing that crossed my mind before darkness claimed me.

CALLIX

The moment Belynda walked out of the pits, I regained some self-control, which seemed to be impossible in her presence, especially as of late. I wanted to behave and be good for her. I wanted her trust and admiration; I wanted to *deserve* her. But I found myself drowning in her presence, fighting against the need to possess her, to claim her body and drown my sinful immortal soul in her.

I passed outside her chambers and picked up the soft droplets of water coming from her shower. For a moment, I imagined slipping in behind her beneath the water's spray—tasting her and trailing my fingers against her soft skin. The strain in my slacks grew unbearable. *What the hell was I doing to myself?* I walked from her chambers and disappeared into the study, where I could hide my pent-up frustration.

"Syllis, my study!" I called into the nymph's mind. A few minutes later, I felt her presence outside the door.

"Come in," I called before she had a chance to knock.

"Master." She grinned, closing the door behind her.

I motioned for her to approach, and she did without hesitation. Syllis had always been a willing participant when it came to satisfying my needs. Rounding the desk, she sat comfortably on the armrest of my chair, trailing her fingers down my shoulders.

"I've missed you, Master," she cooed. I didn't reply. The notions she often pictured of us were always the same yet too far-reaching and delusional. Syllis often forgot her place, but that was perhaps my fault. I had been too allowing; I had indulged in her fantasies.

Her other hand rubbed the strain in my pants, and at the friction, I sighed, leaning my head back against the chair. She brushed her lips along my neck, and although the action had once stirred me, it felt strange. Shoving my rational thoughts aside, I tried to focus on the sensation of her fingers as they touched the fabric of my pants—teasing and squeezing. I fixed Belynda's image in my mind: her face, her body, and the way my hardness pressed against her behind. For a moment, I pretended it was her touch.

"Master, you feel wonderful," murmured Syllis, and her voice broke the mental image I fought to retain. That odd feeling consumed me once again.

"Don't speak," I ordered, closing my eyes, except this time, instead of picturing the blood witch, I listened for her. I needed to slip into her mind and hear her thoughts. Lose myself in her, though not in the way I desired.

A surge of erratic thoughts came from outside the castle walls, and I bolted out of my chair at once. Syllis fell from the armrest, but I didn't stop. I slipped through a water portal without turning back.

Belynda's slumped body floated in the darkness, embraced

by my element. I reached her side and cradled her to me. I debated returning her to the castle. However, in her last moments of lucidity, her thoughts were not of escaping. She wanted to see the skies. She also wanted to get away from me. I watched her closed eyes and pale face. I swam towards the surface.

Perched atop an ocean wave, I held her, admiring her porcelain skin beneath the last remnants of dusk. Slowly, her eyes fluttered open, and when they fell on my face, she smiled. My dark, frozen soul came alive.

"What the hell were you thinking?" My voice boomed with unnecessary fury, but as her eyes regarded me, I felt the anger dissipate. "If you wanted out..." I hesitated, unsure if I was ready to say the words. "If you wanted to leave, to get away from me, all you had to do was ask," I whispered. I buried my disappointment. It was the truth. I would never hold her back. Not against her will.

"I wasn't leaving. I only wanted to see the sky..." Her eyes shifted to the horizon, and I felt the walls fortify around her mind. I didn't push. "I wanted to get away for a little while," she admitted, returning her gaze to me. The sizzling currents eased beneath the surface. Belynda wasn't escaping; she wasn't leaving me. The chaos strummed the strings of the tides, and the tempest began to settle.

"Are you doing that?" Her head tilted, and her curious eyes held mine. I wondered if she felt my mood shift.

"Doing what?"

"The storm. Did you do that?" I smiled at the wonder in her eyes. So perceptive.

"I'm afraid so. More often than not, I lose control. I have a way of letting my temper get the best of me." I admitted, and as a wave rocked us, her grip tightened around my neck.

"Thank you for not taking me back," she whispered, tilting her head to the skies as if speaking directly to the dark clouds. "I miss seeing the sun."

Her admission troubled me as realization dawned. She had not enjoyed its warmth since leaving the human world.

I raised my hand and hesitantly caressed her cheek.

"I promise I will bring you to land when it's morning." She locked her eyes to mine, beaming with excitement.

"Tomorrow?"

"Tomorrow. I promise."

Belynda briefly closed her eyes, taking in a deep, filling breath as if it were the last she would ever take.

"Callix..." Her voice trailed as she peered curiously up at me. "Drowning... dying like that." A shudder broke through her body. "Is that what Isabel felt?" Her question made something tighten inside my chest.

"She didn't suffer," I responded. "I made sure of it."

Belynda nodded and bit her lip.

The images of Belynda's sinking body brought back the pain of the past at full force. Seeing her like that was like watching Isabel's life slip away all over again.

"Why didn't you use your elemental magic to stay conscious?" Her confused face solidified my suspicions. She didn't know the extent of her powers.

"How?"

"You control water and air. What else do you need?" Her face lit up with understanding. "An air bubble would have sufficed to get you to the surface."

"Will you teach me?" she asked.

"Tomorrow." I conceded with a slight grin.

"But you said tomorrow…" I placed a finger over her lips.

"At the island tomorrow. I will teach you." Reluctantly, I removed my finger from her mouth, despite wishing to trace my fingers over them, and to lean a few inches and—

"Are you ready to go back?" I asked.

Though her brows furrowed, she nodded. The water portal appeared before us, but Belynda pushed against my chest, making me pause.

"Can we swim back? I never get to leave the castle. I always see the ocean through the window. Please."

How could she ever think I would deny such a request? She loved my world, my kingdom. With the wave of my hand, the water portal vanished.

"We can, but I have no waters of Isilium." I took her hand, allowing the wave keeping my body upright to support hers, too. "Do you trust me?" I asked, and the corners of her mouth lifted. "What?"

"Nothing. It's not an easy answer, that's all."

"You don't trust me…"

"No. I do. Or at least, I trust the sensible Callix. Then there is your nonsensical side… that one, the dangerous Callix—the one who always breaks the rules. That's the one I'm not sure I can trust."

I wasn't expecting her explanation, but I could live with it.

"I promise to stay sensible." I grinned, and though her eyes narrowed, she didn't object.

Holding her hand, we plunged into the ocean and swam down towards Serfier. We took our time, and Belynda was happy beside me. Content to experience what ocean life had to offer. When her fingers tightened around mine, I knew her lungs burned.

I pulled her to me, firmly holding her waist. Her eyes widened as I brought my lips to hers, offering her a mouthful of air. Pulling away, her eyes regarded me as her thoughts reached my mind.

"You're incorrigible."

I smirked, and she pulled out of my hold.

As we stepped through the barriers and into the castle, Syllis greeted us.

"My Lord, are you alright?" Syllis rushed to my side, but I lifted a hand, breaking her stride. "Your leave was so hasty. I was worried." The nymph made a point to ignore Belynda. Clearly, she felt no concern for her, and had no manners in the presence of a guest.

"Leave us," I said curtly.

"But Master..."

"Was I not clear? I said leave us!" My voice thundered, and this time, Syllis did as I asked.

"I'm glad she's finally being put in her place." Belynda's bitter thought spiked my curiosity.

"Has she been unpleasant to you?" I asked, and Belynda's gaze shifted away from me. By her expression, I knew she wished to say more on the matter. She didn't. I thought about prying, but something told me I wouldn't like what I would see. I wasn't in the mood to deal with Syllis right now.

"I don't like her, that's all. You know that's no secret," said Belynda, turning away. I reached and took her arm. She paused.

"Are you going to tell me what really made you so desperate to leave earlier?" While I wanted to respect her privacy and her thoughts, my need to uncover the truth was greater. The way Belynda averted her eyes and changed her stance told me the words to leave her mouth wouldn't be the whole truth.

"I told you, I needed to breathe. I wanted to see the skies."

I was proud to see how strong her mental walls had become since she arrived. It took me longer than usual to navigate the elements fortifying her thoughts, but when I finally breached her walls, I smiled at the shards of truth she failed to conceal. Thoughts and feelings she wasn't ready to admit—not to herself, and definitely not to me.

The idea of Syllis and I alone in my study bothered her. Belynda did not run from me. No, she was trying to escape her own thoughts and the feelings she kept fighting. All because of him.

"I don't believe you." I tilted my head with a subtle smile. She narrowed her eyes and snatched her arm from my grasp.

"Damn you, Callix! Stop. Just stop!" She stormed away, but I followed. Getting under her skin had become one of my favorite pastimes, but the truth was I craved these moments where I saw how hard she fought to hide the way I made her feel.

"I've done nothing. All I want is the truth." I fell into step beside her, but she didn't slow. She didn't even turn to defy or fight me. She was running again, trying to escape my prying mind. I stepped in front of her, cutting her off.

Her angry emerald eyes stared up at me.

"Callix, I just want to go to bed. I literally drowned, I'm tired, and you're being an idiot! Not to mention, you're in my way."

My laughter rippled through the quiet halls.

"I'll let you pass if you tell me why the thought of Syllis and I upset you." Her eyes were wild then as they shifted over my face. She parted her lips slightly, then closed them, her gaze falling to my feet. After a few seconds, they returned to my face with a glint of anger.

"I couldn't care less what you and your servants do. Now, let me pass." She attempted to move past me, but I reached for her arm, pulling her back. I took a step forward, trapping her against the ice-covered column.

"Darling. You might lie to everyone else. You could even lie to yourself, but you can't hide the truth. Not from me."

"Why are you doing this?" Her pleading eyes pierced through my chaos, and I hated upsetting her, but right now... I *needed* her. I wanted to satiate the burning need to peel the clothes from her body and bury myself inside her. But for now, knowing she wanted me was enough. Her admission would offer enough of a reprieve for my tormented soul. Enough hope to know she could be mine. I ignored her pleading gaze.

"Tell me, and I'll let you go. Just admit you were jealous, and I will free you this instant." My lips were a breath from her face as her chest rose and fell against mine.

"Callix, please," she whispered, but I couldn't move.

I needed something—anything to satiate my starving soul.

"You were jealous, weren't you?" I pressed, and she bit the inside of her cheek, shaking her head. "Liar," I whispered, brushing my lips against her ear. Her body stilled, and she closed her eyes as if in pain.

"What I feel doesn't matter, Callix." Her eyes remained closed as if by doing so, she could somehow hide her truth from me and from herself.

"It matters to me," I said, brushing her chin. Her emerald eyes opened.

"It makes no difference what I think or how I feel or what I wanted..." She lowered her gaze to my chest. "It doesn't matter." When her eyes returned to mine, I knew exactly what she hadn't dared to voice. It didn't matter how she felt. It would always be him. Knowing that was her truth didn't make it any easier. I dropped her arm and took a step away from the pillar—away from her.

"Goodnight. Get some rest."

"Callix..." The break in her voice made me pause.

"I'll meet you at sunrise in the dining hall."

I turned and left her in the corridor. I didn't want to hear an apology, not when we both knew she was lying to herself. She might have loved him first. She might love him still, but I wasn't indifferent to her. No. I didn't want her apologies, not when she refused to see or accept that she wanted me too.

BELYNDA

Immortal or not, I felt exhausted. Not all immortals were created equal, and that I learned the hard way. For instance, Dragons didn't require sleep, but one sleepless night for me was enough to make me feel all too human, and I hadn't been immortal long enough to forget the feeling.

Undoubtedly, thoughts of Callix kept me awake. Knowing I was hurting him made my heart ache, but so did the thought of betraying Drake. I struggled to discern between right and wrong. I loved Drake, but a part of me ached for the Sea God. Perhaps it was loneliness that clouded my judgment, though it was becoming harder to fight my body and mind. Even now, as I made my way down the corridor toward the dining hall, a nervousness settled deep in my stomach.

I felt the tugging of the strange invisible strings before I reached the dining hall, and I knew, without a doubt, that he was already there. He sat at the head of the table today, and his gaze shifted from his breakfast to me the second I crossed the threshold.

"Good morning." He assessed my face, focused on my every move.

"Good morning." I took the chair to his right, and Phial appeared a second later, placing a dish before me.

"Thank you," I said, and she lowered her head in acknowledgment.

"My Lord. Is there anything else I can get you?"

Callix placed down his fork and looked at the nymph.

"No, Phial. Thank you." With a hasty bow, she left us.

Callix turned to me, strumming his fingers against the marble tabletop. "You look tired."

I raised my gaze to meet his, swallowing the knot in my throat.

"Yeah. I didn't get much sleep. I thought immortals didn't require sleep, so perhaps my ascension was flawed. I'm demanding a refund." I tried to alleviate the tension in the room. The corner of his mouth lifted.

"While sleep is not necessary, it doesn't mean we can function optimally without it. Most can go longer without it than others, but eventually, everyone will surrender. The body and the mind will demand it."

"Mhmm. When Drake said sleep was not required for him, I assumed it was the same for everyone." The second Drake's name left my lips, Callix's fingers froze against the table. Nonetheless, he responded.

"The fire element makes his kind more resilient, but he is no exception."

I picked up my fork, focusing on my plate instead of his powerful gaze.

We ate silently for a few minutes, but the usual ease of our relationship felt strained. Heavily charged. I felt the need to clear the air, to apologize.

"Callix..."

"I'm sorry," he said at the same time. Our eyes locked. "I promised I wouldn't cross the line, but I keep breaking that promise." He finished, and I shook my head. It wasn't fair for him to take all the blame.

"It's my fault, too, for allowing it. I shouldn't feel this way or allow my actions to give you hope..." I broke eye contact, pausing to collect my thoughts. "I don't want to hurt you," I whispered, locking my gaze on the table. His fingers brushed my hand, prompting my eyes to return to his.

"Never apologize for your feelings." He looked into my eyes, and I lost myself in the storm. "If the roles were reversed, and I was in his place, I would be content with your happiness, in whichever form and with whomever you choose. If choosing him would make you happy, I promise, I would remove myself from your existence, but I know..." His fingers gently brushed the back of my hand. "And you know... that while you might have been happy loving only him not long ago, that is no longer true." I blinked, surprised at his words.

Did I love Callix? No, I didn't. I couldn't... However, I cared for him more than I dared to admit, and as I stared into his eyes, I could not lie. Not to him or myself. Not anymore.

"Even if you're right about how I feel... it's not enough." Tears clouded my eyes, and his fingers shifted. The tears flowed then, but the droplets sailed in twirling circles between us, crystallizing in the air and falling into the palm of his hand, which rested open on the table. He closed his fist around the icy droplets, which appeared like tiny glistening diamonds. Intrigued, I watched as he placed them inside his shirt pocket.

"You're right. It's not enough," he whispered. "So, I will pretend that nothing has changed between us. Nothing will ever change, and I will take you as I can. I will pretend." His eyes pierced into mine, but I saw only myself reflected in the bottomless abyss. *Oh, Callix...*

"I wish... I could change." I searched his face, trying to convey the depths of my sorrow. "I wish things didn't have to be this way. I wish you didn't have to hurt. I wish you didn't have to pretend, but mostly, I wish I didn't feel as torn as I do." His quiet laugh shifted my attention back to him.

"It's a good thing you're immortal now. You have eternity to sort things out." Was he implying I might change my mind about him in the future? He furrowed his brows, and I knew he was listening, prying into my thoughts. He didn't hesitate to make his intentions known.

"I've waited a thousand years. I can wait another lifetime, but since I'm pretending, I'll settle with making you smile for now." The chair scraped against the floor as he stood. "Are you ready to bathe in the sun?"

His smile lit up the room, and the blue in his eyes danced as he extended his hand towards me. I laced my fingers with his, ignoring the shots of electricity burning under my skin. I smiled in return.

I knew he longed to say more, but his mind was impenetrable. So, as we walked hand in hand through the water portal, I decided to pretend. Forgetting my doubts and reservations, I chose to enjoy the day.

NOTHING COULD HAVE PREPARED me for what awaited on the other side. Even in the human world, it had been so long since I last visited the coast and felt the sand under my toes. I dropped Callix's hand and walked across the shore as the white spray of the waves curled around my ankles. The pearly white sand sunk beneath my feet, and I closed my eyes, welcoming the clean and purest air into my lungs. For the first time in a long time, I felt the warmth of the sun.

This world was reminiscent of the human realm, yet

fantastically different. The sun centered on the horizon, flanked by two large moons—an ethereal touch to the realm's masterpiece. Soft pastels blended seamlessly in the sky with shades of blue, purple, green, orange, and yellow. A breathtaking montage that filled my senses with awe.

"Come. I want to show you something," said Callix. His voice broke through the stillness. A water portal shimmered into existence at his call.

"I don't want to leave. Not yet," I said.

Callix shook his head and offered me his hand.

"I know. Trust me. Come." I took it and followed him through the portal.

The sight that unfolded left me speechless. Temple ruins rose from the edge of the cliffs, their high columns weathered by time. Vines and seashells adorned it, and below the dome of the temple, cracks in its surface revealed countless stone statues—a testament to the passage of time. The statues depicted beautiful humans and fantastical creatures alike, their forms frozen in eternal poses. It was a sight of grandeur and magnificence.

"What is this place?" I breathed in awe. My immortal eyes drunk in the breathtaking view from the precipice as Callix moved closer, his presence a comforting anchor beside me as we peered out towards the crashing ocean below.

"These are the Ruins of the Lost." His voice carried a weight of melancholy, and I tore my gaze from the statues to look at him.

"What does that mean?"

"Long ago, when Serfier reigned over the ocean's surface, this was a temple. Before the first war against the dark. Eventually, my parents were forced to sink the city to protect my people, and it stands as a reminder of what we once had and lost." I listened, enraptured. Callix had never spoken of his parents or the history of his realm with such openness before. The Ruins of the Lost was a testament to the sacrifices and memories preserved in the stone, and I felt a pang of empathy for him, realizing that the mighty Sea God carried his own share of pain and loss, too.

"Drake mentioned his people wrote songs about the first war, but he never said how it came about or how they stopped the darkness."

"The stories say that darkness came from the dark dimension," Callix confirmed, a somber weight to his words.

"Xelraa?" I asked, and he nodded. "How was it stopped?"

His gaze shifted, a hint of distant memory in his eyes. "Drake was younger than I, and not even I remember much. All I know is that the realms united, and light swallowed the darkness. The fire realm swore to protect the Nightshade, yet here we stand again, ready to fight the same war my father lost long ago."

"Callix… what happened to your parents?" My voice wavered in the wind, carried by the breeze that rustled through the ruins. Callix adjusted his shirt collar, a small gesture seeming to mask a need for control. He moved a few paces ahead of me and it almost felt deliberate, as if he wanted to shield the emotions etched on his face. "You don't have to tell me," I added, understanding the weight of his history and the pain within it. Opening up wasn't something he did easily or often.

"It doesn't matter. Not anymore. It was a long time ago." His tone possessed an air of finality, and he stood tall and composed, a portrait of strength. A part of me sensed the cracks beneath the surface. Callix was a master of masking his emotions, but I could see through his façade—at least to some extent.

In the time I had spent with him, I had come to realize the pain and suffering he carried beneath his regal demeanor. His words echoed in my mind. He would pretend; he would pretend that nothing mattered, pretend to be happy and whole, and to need no one. Was his entire existence built on such pretense? A carefully crafted façade to shield himself from the world?

He began to speak of his past, recounting a raw and distant story. "I was a young boy when my father plunged the Realm into the ocean. He did it for our people, but mostly to protect me. But he didn't hide from the dark. He fought and lost. My mother... she couldn't bear it. Not for long, anyhow, so she followed him." Callix didn't falter as he shared the memories, his strength prevailing through his painful recollections. It was a glimpse into a chapter of his life I had never known—a chapter shaping him into the man he was today. As I gazed at his back, I felt a profound sadness for the little boy he had once been.

I wanted to comfort him, to ease the weight he carried, but he had learned to shield his emotions and bear his burdens in silence. So, I held back, allowing the silence to linger between us.

"Your mother. You said she followed your father, but how?" I was learning more about the intricacies of immortality, and my thirst for knowledge was insatiable, though I tread on sensitive ground. I knew immortals could perish under blue fire and certain spells, but I wondered if there was more.

Callix's gaze shifted, a distant reflection in his eyes as he answered. "Ultimately, immortality is in our hands. We can choose to age at any time, but some find eternity unbearable. Aside from blue fire and cradling spells—which are forbidden in all the Realms—the only other option is simply to age. Age until our bodies become stone." His words hung in the air, and it took me a moment to grasp their meaning. He shifted his gaze to the marble statues scattered among the ruins and motioned toward them. "The Ruins of the Lost."

Realization dawned on me then as I stared at the stone figures. Each represented an immortal who had chosen to age, embracing the finality of mortality. It was a choice that carried its own kind of courage.

"These were actual immortals?" I whispered, tentatively reaching out to touch the smooth surface of one. Callix's nod settled my doubts, and I felt a mixture of awe and melancholy settle inside me.

He paused before one, and I knew it was his mother the second I saw her. The resemblance was remarkable, and her presence was majestic amongst the rest. The Queen of Serfier. Her white, pearly stone body glimmered against the sun, unlike the rest of the statues, which, like the pillars, were covered in seashells and moss. Callix must come here often, and despite his denial, he did care. The loss of his parents mattered, even if he pretended it didn't.

"She was beautiful," I whispered, a small attempt to

acknowledge the memories and emotions lingering in this place.

Callix was silent. We stood together, immersed in that silence for a moment. Then, with a subtle shift, he withdrew into himself, returning his gaze to the horizon. It was as if he had put up his defenses once again, a reminder of the mask he wore to conceal his turmoil.

"Are you ready to return to the shore?" he asked with feigned composure. I held his gaze, searching his eyes for the truth that lay beyond the mask, but I could not reach him. With a quiet affirmation, I nodded, and the water portal sprang to life.

Callix moved forward purposefully, his steps measured and controlled while I followed in his wake. As I emerged on the other side, Callix paused, slipping off his shoes . He turned to me, a smile playing at the corners of his mouth as he stepped onto the sand. The water embraced his toes and receded with each tide. I smiled at the sight, at the simple joy of seeing him barefoot on the shore.

"What?" he asked, his amusement evident in the arch of his eyebrow.

I shook my head with a gentle laugh. "Nothing. I've never seen you without shoes, that's all."

His grin widened. It felt as if a glimpse of his true self had broken through the façade—a rare and precious sight allowing me to appreciate the depth of the person behind the godly exterior.

"There's always a first time for everything." A devious glint sparkled in his eyes, a hint that mischief was afoot. Before I understood his intentions, he moved with lightning speed and swept me over his shoulder in a sudden blur of motion.

"Callix! Put me down!" I protested, but my laughter mixed with my futile attempts to escape him. His grip was unyielding as he strode purposefully towards the crashing waves.

"Not a chance," he replied, smirking. My struggles only fueled his determination. With a triumphant laugh, he pitched me into the crystal blue waters. The initial shock of the cool water was followed by the sight of the smirking Sea God. I beamed, caught up in the contagious joy radiating from him. A moment of freedom and letting go—a feeling I had missed.

"You're going to pay for that," I teased, determined. I lunged towards him, but, of course, my efforts were in vain. He was the Lord of the Water, and while I had my own command over the element, it was clear who reigned.

I found myself sprawled on the shore, panting, and covered in sand. My attempts to capture the agile Sea God had failed spectacularly.

"Tired already?" he taunted, his body momentarily blocking the sun. He cast a shadow over me.

"Are you kidding?" I huffed, struggling to catch my breath. "Have you seen the way you move through the water? You're unstoppable!" My hands clutched at my chest as I tried to regain my composure.

"Do you honestly think I would still have the advantage if you used your water element as I do?"

Was he joking?

"We both know I stand no chance."

He didn't smile.

"Maybe, but you won't know if you don't try." He challenged, extending his hand towards me. "Come on. Get up."

"No! No lessons today, please. You promised to teach me how to use my powers, but I'm having so much fun. Really, Callix. No training. Not today." The playful atmosphere shifted as I recognized the stubborn determination in his stance.

"Have you not learned a single thing about me?"

Oh, I knew *precisely* how stern and unyielding he could be when it came to training. I understood he could not compromise on it.

"But you promised to make me smile," I countered the words to incite a reaction, and the subtle shift in his expression told me it worked. I immediately regretted using his words against him.

"I believe I already did, but it can't all be fun and games, can it?" His tone shifted, as did the atmosphere. The mercurial, unpredictable side of Callix had emerged—unbending and relentless. A part of me feared this side of the Sea God, and I found myself reluctantly standing, ignoring his offered hand. This was the Callix of chaos, whom I wasn't sure how to navigate.

He strode against the waves, effortlessly parting them with his presence. Conceding, I followed in his wake.

"You wanted to know how to use your powers to breathe underwater." His head disappeared under the surface, and I followed.

"Let all the air out of your lungs." His command echoed in my mind, and I obeyed, exhaling until I felt the familiar burn in my chest as the sensation of drowning tugged at the edges of my consciousness. Instinctively, I swam upward to break

the surface, to invite precious air into my lungs, but his grip held firm, preventing my escape.

"Relax. You still have time. Now, call on Air. Pull a shield around yourself."

The urgency in his words, and the tug in my chest, spurred me into action. I summoned my control over Air, visualizing a protective barrier forming around me—a bubble of breathable space. With each heartbeat, the darkness at the edges of my vision threatened to engulf me, but I pressed on. My determination overrode all panic.

When the darkness danced before my eyes, I inhaled the water until, suddenly, I was breathing. I had done it. I had created a bubble of air and felt it fill my lungs—a lifeline within the watery depths. I was breathing underwater, an act that defied all laws of nature. The air bubble shifted as I did, expanding and contracting with my every breath.

"Good. Now, you don't need me anymore." He praised but wasn't smiling. He valued my safety above all else, and my mastery over my powers was a crucial step in that journey. Yet I couldn't help but sense a tinge of regret in his demeanor, a subtle longing for the closeness we had shared in those fleeting moments. The brush of his lips had been a necessity and, therefore, acceptable, or so I convinced myself to excuse the action. Now, no justification existed.

I pushed through the water's surface, breaking free. Callix emerged beside me, and the surface tethered me to reality after the exhilarating rush of magic beneath the waves.

"Now, try to catch me, but use your powers this time." He plunged once again under the waves. I took a moment to catch my breath before following him beneath the surface, determined to rise to the challenge.

The water was a realm of its own, and my powers manifested differently here. Callix moved with a speed that defied comprehension, a fluid grace that left me struggling to keep pace. Despite my best efforts, I fell short, my attempts hindered by the watery environment that favored his dominion.

I called upon my control over water and used its currents to propel me. I combined it with the wind, creating a hybrid force that surged me forward. Yet Callix remained elusive, a phantom figure who stayed just beyond my reach.

My attempts grew more desperate as I willed a vortex of wind and water to slow his movements, though even this tactic proved insufficient as his form slipped through the elements like a wraith.

"I give up!" I declared, my voice mingling with my panting breaths as I surfaced. Letting the current guide me, I moved toward the shore, welcoming the comforting sand between my toes.

I sat on the sand, wrapping my arms around my knees while I waited for Callix to reemerge. My gaze never wavered, captivated by the sight of him gliding through the waves while his white shirt clung to his skin. His movements were a blend of power and grace, a mesmerizing sight to behold. He was beautiful, a force of nature, and I couldn't tear my eyes from him. It looked as if he were gliding over the waves.

"You didn't try nearly hard enough," he said, prompting an

eye roll from me. Callix shook his head, sending water droplets in all directions.

The white strands transformed into darker hues as the water was displaced; however, unlike the seamless change in his hair, his clothes remained wet, not responding to the magic that typically dried them once he crossed into the castle's boundaries.

"Does your magic not work here?" His puzzled gaze shifted toward me, until he grasped the nature of my inquiry with a subtle glance at my thoughts.

"It could if I wanted it to," he explained, his gaze holding mine. "But the protective spell that shields the castle from the ocean doesn't make exceptions unless commanded." His command over magic was as intricate as it was powerful, then.

"Could you command it then..." I glanced at the sand-covered dress clinging to my skin, which left nothing to the imagination. The translucent white fabric molded against my curves like a second skin against my breasts, stomach, and thighs, while my hair probably looked a hot mess. I felt sand in places where sand shouldn't be.

Callix laughed, a sound that seemed to dance on the ocean breeze. His eyes regained their cerulean sheen. "I could, but I'm not so sure I want to," he teased, a mischievous gleam in his eyes.

"Are you seriously denying me comfort?" I asked, my voice tinged with annoyance.

"Are you seriously denying me my pleasure?" His eyes locked onto mine, sparking a rush of warmth to my cheeks.

"You can be so infuriating sometimes."

"So can you," he countered, a smirk playing at the corner of his lips.

"Fine!"

"Fine."

"Can we go back now?" I stood, brushing off the sand caked to my behind.

"No. I'm not ready to leave. Not yet," he replied, his smirk growing more pronounced. irritating me on purpose, I realized.

"Suit yourself then. I will swim back on my own." I declared, determined. I pushed against the waves.

"You'll never find your way without me! You don't know which direction to go," he called, his tone one of amusement and warning. He was right, and reluctantly, I splashed back to the shore.

Callix failed to conceal his amusement as he crouched close to the water's edge. His gaze locked on me as he rested his elbows on his knees. The water and sand moved over the hem of his dark blue pants. A picture of casual ease and an embodiment of the sea's capricious nature. He was so absorbed in his own amusement that he never saw me approach until it was too late.

I launched, sending us both tumbling to the sand. His body was a solid wall of muscle that shook with his laughter as he closed his arms around me, shifting to secure me under his hold.

"Really, you only have yourself to blame for this," he teased.

"No, I think this is all on you for being such a prick."

"Do you think calling me names will help your case? Why

don't you try asking nicely? Or perhaps offering something in exchange." A devilish glint filled his eyes. *Damn him!*

"Get off me," I demanded, but he didn't move.

"You're still not being very nice." His lips curved into a smile. I summoned a vortex of wind to push him away, but his brutal strength pressed my body deeper into the sand.

"Now, you want to use your powers?" He mused. His closeness sent my heart racing, and feeling his weight atop me was both exhilarating and disconcerting. "Give me something in exchange, and I promise, I'll do as you please," he proposed, his gaze unwavering as he held me captive with his eyes, which were wild like the ocean behind us.

"You're the devil." My pulse quickened at the intensity of his gaze.

"Oh no, darling... I'm much worse." His words were a tantalizing promise, sending shivers down my spine. My stomach tightened, though I was unsure if it was the weight of his words or his body.

"What do you want?" The question escaped me before I could fully consider its implications, and when his smile brightened, my suspicions were confirmed.

"One kiss," he said without vacillation. His voice was low and lust filled. I felt conflicted, caught between the anticipation of the moment and the lingering doubts in my mind.

"Fine," I conceded.

"There's one condition," he added, and I narrowed my eyes at him.

"Conditions?" I asked. "I'm already offering you enough, and you dare to ask for conditions?"

"I have sand in places you couldn't imagine, but unlike

you, I'm comfortable remaining like this. The sand and the water do not bother me. My conditions... your choice." He was enjoying himself way too much, but I was the one pinned against the coarse sand. The water traveled higher every time a wave rolled in, and I knew he was responsible for it. I had sand in my neck, my face, everywhere...

"A kiss... what are your conditions?" I asked through gritted teeth. He smirked.

"Just one. I get to end it, not you."

This was a bad idea. I knew it the second he asked. I knew it the moment I decided to tackle him. Heck, I knew it since I woke up this morning. Callix was bad for me, yet I sank deeper under his tide.

"Fine. But if you're thinking of dragging this on forever..." His lips crashed against mine, silencing my protests.

My body stilled beneath him as I willed my senses to remain non-reactive. He didn't push, didn't demand—not this time. If anything, he took his time. His lips moved against mine like gentle droplets of water. *I was strong. I was in control...* I repeated, but who was I kidding? I was adrift. I wanted to turn to stone like the immortal souls in the Ruins of the Lost, to forever be unfeeling. But the second he nipped gently at my lower lip, the last of my control vanished. I was alive. Resurrected by the Sea God's touch.

My hands trailed over his sand-covered skin, and I moved my mouth against him, relishing the saltiness on his lips. The world around us faded as his body pressed into mine, his lips moving achingly slow and unhurried, as if savoring the moment. My heart raced, and my fingers instinctively found their way to the nape of Callix's neck, pulling him closer. The taste of the salt air and the warmth of his kiss created a sensation that electrified my entire being.

His hand traced the curve of my jaw, leaving a trail of fire in its wake. My fingers moved from his neck, exploring the contours of his chest, feeling the raw strength beneath his skin.

Everything bloomed around us. The sound of the crashing waves fell in sync with our breathing. Time stood still, encapsulating us in a bubble, as sand molded to our bodies, cradling us while we lost ourselves in each other.

Our lips briefly parted as our breaths mingled for a moment, and then he leaned in again. My fingers tangled in his hair, pulling him closer, desperate to erase any distance between us. The taste of his lips ignited a fire within me that burned me alive.

How could a stolen kiss weigh so heavily on my heart? Deepen our connection? This was not an affirmation of the desire building between us—no. It was a collision of two souls. A dance of longing.

His fingertips moved over my wet dress, closing his hand around my breast, and squeezing gently. My lips parted at the soft stroke of his tongue.

He would never stop. He would hold this kiss until he drove me mad, until I gave my body willingly and there was nothing else for him to claim. Yet even knowing this, I could not bring myself to stop. Sense had abandoned me long ago.

I buried my fingers in his hair. Opening my eyes, I stared at the blue skies above, and a slip of clarity returned.

"Callix..." I whispered, shocked by the desire in my voice.

"You broke the condition... this is not a kiss," I whispered as his lips burned a trail over the swell of my breasts.

"Still a kiss." His sensual voice vibrated against my skin, and my body arched to him in offering while my mind fought for control.

"No," I pulled at his hair and his head snapped up from my chest, meeting my eyes. "No, I beg you."

Resting his forehead against my chest, his warm breath stroked my breasts.

"You want me to be the stronger one?" He laughed.

"I want you to not make this harder for me than it already is." His eyes roamed my face as he rested his chin on my chest. "I know you might hate Drake, but we both know he doesn't deserve this."

His brows creased, and his face moved to hover above mine.

"I never said I hated him. I called him my friend once, my brother, but he forgot that long ago when he blamed me for his mistakes. He might not deserve it, but I don't owe him anything." Callix pushed himself up, extending his hand to me. I took it but didn't dare question him. I was just glad we stopped before any further damage was done.

"Thank you," I murmured. "Will you fix me up?" He shifted his eyes over my sand-covered body and smiled.

"Close your eyes," he said, bemused. "Now, call on your earth power. Feel every grain of sand and will it to return to the shore." I opened my eyes, squinting at him. But I still did as he said.

I called on the element and visualized the particles of sand leaving my body; instantly, the prickly sensation rushed over my skin as the specks fell away.

"You couldn't tell me this sooner?"

"I'm telling you now." I wanted to erase the smirk from his face. "Now, summon water." He was trying to make a point, but really, I was to blame for not trusting myself and for always forgetting the power I possessed over three elements. I was angry—furious, even.

I summoned water. I sensed it all around me, sizzling, and I knew it was because of his presence. At my command, the droplets flew from my hair and clothes until the fabric of my dress dislodged from my skin, flowing freely against the wind.

"Now you're all fixed." He grinned. "Can you do me now?" he asked, and I rolled my eyes.

"Clean your own damn self!" I sat on the rock beside his discarded shoes.

"Yeah, that's sort of a problem." He smirked, walking closer to where I sat. "You see, I can command water, but sand... those prickly little things are a whole different story, and I can literally feel them deep between my—"

"STOP!" I cut off whatever he was about to say, refusing to envision it.

"I could always take my clothes off and go for a swim." I wasn't sure if that image was any better... Ugh. *Damn him.*

So, I summoned water and earth, and watched as the sand and water separated from his body simultaneously.

Smiling, he fixed the collar of his now pristine shirt.

"Take me back," I demanded, jumping from the rock.

"Are you really that upset?" he mocked, but I learned it was best not to react.

"Honestly, I'm over it, Callix. I don't have the strength to stay mad anymore. You're too intense. You're too exhausting to fight against. Now, open the damn portal and take us back." His face shifted, as if pleased he could earn my forgiveness no matter what he did. "Don't push your luck," I warned. The wicked glint in his eyes told me he had no intention to heed it.

The water portal imploded behind me as we reached the castle. I marched past him, hoping to escape to my chamber without any further incidents.

"Dinner?" he asked quietly after me, but I knew any further contact tonight would be asking for trouble.

"Good night, Callix," I said. I made my escape before the cerulean force of his eyes changed my mind.

II

RISE OF THE TIDES

MY DRAGON'S SHADOW FELL OVER THE TIRSIA HILLS AS the peaks reappeared with the sunrise. Almost three weeks had passed since we lost the East to the darkness, and still, metal echoed around the Forge day and night. The warriors were restless. Link and Phoenix were plagued by defeat and resignation, and Euros was overcome by madness.

The warrior didn't sleep; he hardly spoke or ate. He lived inside the Forge as if training harder would offer a different outcome for the North.

After losing Phoenix's territory, we marched back to the North. Hope was rekindled by the echoes of magic we encountered. The trees whispered about the rise of a star to bring an end to the reign of darkness. Not even I had witnessed anything like it before in my long immortal years, and the possibility served to rekindle not just the warrior's faith, but my own as well.

Belynda said the Fates had a plan and that she would play a role in assisting the Realms with their fight against the darkness. After the message delivered through the whispering trees, I couldn't help but wonder if she was the rising star. The one destined to bring an end to the shadows. She was immortal now, and despite the Fates' twisted ways, I couldn't imagine they would allow the Realms to perish, to be consumed by darkness.

The Air people felt inspired by such a prophecy, yet as the days passed, they faced the prospect of an imminent defeat. The possibility of that rising star arriving to help save the North seemed farther and farther away.

Fear creeped back into their hearts and minds, and to be truthful, that doubt plagued me, too. I feared there was no one who could stop Dagasti—no force strong enough to end the darkness. We had the men, the will, and the strength to fight, but it wasn't enough, and every breathing soul in Upherya knew it.

The warriors were already gathered when I entered the round chamber. Silence and tension stretched between the three men before me. While we had assembled to strategize, the spirit of defeat dampened our plans for the Northern region. I knew it wasn't my place. I could not truly understand what they had lost, but someone had to be sensible, and I was willing to play the part if it meant they would stop licking their wounds, and, instead, sharpen their weapons for what was to come.

"Do you think Dagasti is staring at his maps now? Do you think he feels remorse for what he has taken from you? Do you believe he will slow his advance because you refuse to speak, eat, or sleep? If you believe we are already defeated, pack up your men and prepare to leave for Abryas. Herod has granted you passage."

"We will not leave!" The round table shook beneath the force of Euros' fists.

"Then stop looking pitiful. Will you continue feeling sorry for yourselves until his army marches through your city, or will you do something about it?" My voice resounded around the chamber. "Rally your men. If this is to be the end of Upherya, give Dagasti a battle he will never forget."

Link's back straightened as he stood, bracing his hands on the table's edge.

"Drake is right." He glanced between Phoenix and Euros. "We owe it to everyone we've lost."

"No one is giving up." Euros roared.

"Then prove it! Pull yourself together and turn despair and loss into the most powerful tool you can wield. Turn the blade of your anger against the enemy—not yourself." Silence followed, and the energy shifted.

"You're right," Euros conceded. "We've never feared anyone, not even defeat itself. We will face the darkness again because we still have a Realm to fight for, and by the Fates, I will give them *hell*."

Phoenix had remained quiet, but Euros' uprising served to stir the warrior.

"A few moons ago, we sat at this very table with a perfect plan. Yet here we are. Our people have faced three battles and lost. How much more can we ask of them?"

"We can give them a choice, but do you honestly think

they will walk away? Will you hide in Abryas while the North still stands?" challenged Euros. Phoenix shook his head.

"You know I'm with you until the end. There's no question."

"I might not have high hopes that we can defeat Dagasti, but I have faith in our people, Phin. This will be our last stand for Upherya. Let's make it count."

"Who knows, miracles could happen," added Link. "Perhaps the foretelling of the falling star will come to pass."

"No!" Euros snapped. "I will not inspire my people with false promises. We must lead only with the truth. Our victory is uncertain, but our purpose remains the same. We were not raised to abandon our land, and as long as Upherya stands, that is enough reason to fight."

"Then we fight," I offered.

"We fight," said Link .

"You couldn't keep me away," Phoenix confirmed.

"Then, let's get to work. We have a battle to prepare for." Euros rose from the table, and I followed in the warriors' wake, pleased to see the fire reignited in them once again.

The North was all that remained of Upherya, yet the warriors would fight no matter what until they bled or lost their souls to the dark.

CALLIX

I watched the realm sleep under a blanket of tranquility, a reflection of my thoughts. But, even surrounded by stillness, my body felt restless. The silence only served to mask my desires. The remnants of that kiss felt like a punishment when every fiber of my immortal being ached to touch her again. To rekindle that moment, which was not ours to have.

At my command, Zodrox's shadow moved through the darkness towards the Western coast. Dagasti's army was too close to the Bay. Now more than ever, I needed to protect my realm. All creatures inhabiting the waters closest to the shores had been ordered to retreat to the depths of Varenver. The sea witches and Mer sentries had no incidents to report, but I would be damned if I allowed Dagasti to claim any part of my kingdom.

It pained me to see Upherya's losses. After everything I had done to help the warriors, I detested not being there to fight beside them. However, staying with her was vital. She was the key to stopping Dagasti—the key to ending the war. The Fates had entrusted me with her, and I would be lying to myself if I said I didn't hate them for it, at least at the beginning. After the Moirai chose me to carry Isabel's sacrifice through the power of my element, I had detested them. They chose me to bind her soul to the next pure blood. To Belynda.

The Fates gave everyone a purpose, and mine was to remain on the sidelines. Watching and protecting. Loving her was not part of the plan. Yet the second her gaze fell on me that first day in Druleska, I knew all hope was lost. I loved Isabel then, but this—whatever this was—it was different. I had kept my distance from Isabel, choosing to respect her relationship with Drake after she chose him. Friendship was all she could offer, and I accepted that. I was a good friend to her until the end. But Belynda... she was something else. She was placed into this world with the sole purpose of devouring my heart, and one look from her served like a magnet beneath my skin, begging to keep her close.

I pushed from the balcony railing and discarded my shirt on the bed. I listened for her, but there was only silence. She must have gone to bed already.

I loved her; I knew that now. Every pulsing fiber of my immortal being ached to be with her, to have her want me as much as I wanted her. But here I was. Unrequited love was my burden, but I was no longer sure of the path the Fates had weaved for me. Something had shifted.

The cold shower poured over my head and down my back, and as the water trailed my skin, the memories of this afternoon made me burn.

AFTER DONNING FRESH CLOTHES, I felt less savage. Her scent had swum around me all afternoon, and it was a bittersweet ache. I was torturing myself, I realized. I retreated to the comfort of the library— the only other place inside the castle where her scent still lingered. Perhaps in a sick, masochistic way, I craved the burning ache it triggered.

Determined to understand the reason for our strange connection, I spent the next hours studying the original scripts from the days of creation. I paid close attention to the hymns about the first wars, but none spoke of how to stop the darkness, nor did they explain the strange bond Belynda and I shared. I had my theories—foolish, but not impossible theories, yet I had no proof.

"I'm sorry." Her soft voice caught me entirely off guard. Belynda stood at the door. My heart accelerated, and my cock stirred instantly at the sight of her. My gaze moved over the sheer sleeping gown she wore, where I could make out the smooth skin of her breasts and the peaks pushing against the fabric. *Did she do this on purpose?* She crossed her arms self-consciously, and my eyes moved lower at her long, shapely legs. She shifted on her feet, a blush warming her cheeks. "I didn't know you were here. I'm sorry to interrupt." She made to leave, but I was already out of my seat and towering over her.

"Stay," I whispered, moving closer.

"N-No," she faltered. "We both know that's a terrible idea."

I leaned in, cornering her against the door frame.

"I disagree." I reached for her hands, which remained crossed like a shield over her breasts. "I was quite bored, actually."

I unclasped her hands, and she didn't fight me. Pinning her arms to her sides, I brought my lips close to her ear. "You and I are not a bad idea. Can't you feel our bodies singe every time we're near each other?" I whispered, trailing my fingers from her shoulders to her arms. "Will you deny the electricity? The one I know you're feeling right now as my fingers move across your skin?"

Belynda trembled in my hands.

"Callix..." Pulling from my reach, she made to leave but paused in the hall outside the library. I braced my hands against the door frame, attempting to control the impulse to follow. "You said before that I could kill you." I stilled at her words. "I think you have that the other way around." Her sad eyes burned into my soul. "It is you who is lethal to me."

She wanted me. I didn't have to read her mind to know.

Her response to my touch voiced the unspoken truth of her desires, but she was the most stubborn woman to have ever existed. She grasped onto those absurd human morals—a rule we immortals were never bound to follow. How else could I make her see? Our time alone was running out. Soon, she would return to him, and I feared his presence would erase all doubts from her mind. I feared she would forget how good it felt to be in my arms, too.

The only way to incite a reaction from her was to force her to feel until the emotions burst out of her. I hated the idea that crept into my mind, but as I considered it, I knew it was the only way.

She had to face the notion that I was free to belong to anyone, to confront the reality that I could satisfy myself with whomever I pleased. She'd admitted she was jealous of Syllis and me, while making it abundantly clear her heart and body belonged to another. I held no claim to her. But tonight, I would make her burn. She might hate me for it afterward, but by the gods, I would make her feel how she made me feel every waking hour. Helpless. Frustrated. Mad with jealousy.

I had nothing else to lose. I wasn't hers; she wasn't mine. Tonight, she would either crumble or hate me forever.

BELYNDA

My body trembled beneath the cold sheets' embrace, the chill seeping through my skin and into my bones. The weight of self-loathing pressed heavily on my chest, a burden I had never known could be so suffocating. At that moment, the intensity of my self-hatred was an all-encompassing darkness that left no room for mercy or forgiveness.

The weight of my actions, mistakes, and transgressions bore down on me like an unrelenting storm. I deserved the punishment that surely awaited, to be condemned to whatever torment awaited immortals in the afterlife.

The walls around me closed in as guilt tightened its grip. I was trapped in a cycle of self-condemnation; the echoes of my deeds resonated through my thoughts like a torment I couldn't escape—a prison of my own making.

The idea of enduring this anguish for any longer felt unbearable; it was as if the very depths of the sea, that had once offered me solace, had transformed into a merciless abyss that sought to devour my body and mind. If I lingered here, if I allowed myself to remain in this emotional whirlpool, I risked losing all semblance of who I once was.

My tears dried against my flushed cheeks and a weariness —both physical and mental—settled over me. The exhaustion from battling my inner demons wore me down, and left me yearning for escape, and so, with a silent plea for respite, I allowed my eyes to close. Sleep was my only refuge.

Soft sighs reverberated through the corridors of my mind, reigniting memories that clawed their way back with a vengeance. Behind my closed eyelids, flashes of intense blue eyes and hands, firm and demanding, pinned me against a wall. Callix's voice, both commanding and unsettling, cut through the fog of my half-conscious state.

"Tell me you want this," his words echoed, stirring me from my slumber. Clutching the sheets to my chest, I blinked, my heart pounding like a drum. The room slowly came into focus.

I was alone. The tension in my body ebbed as I absorbed my surroundings, realizing that the vivid scenes jolting me awake were mere remnants of my fractured thoughts.

Still, I shivered and settled back against the pillows, my senses on high alert. My trained ears, attuned to even the faintest sounds, picked up something unsettling—a symphony of low whimpers and moans, distant yet unmistakable. With each lustful sound that reached my ears, an ache gnawed at my chest: frustration, longing, and something darker.

I closed my eyes, hoping to shut out the sensations unleashed, but my other senses amplified with it. Callix's heavy breaths filled the room, his presence an illusion that danced beyond my grasp. And then, his sighs melded with another's—a feminine voice I didn't need to see to recognize. The combination was maddening, and an inferno of jealousy and longing engulfed me.

My patience shattered, and with a swift motion, I threw the sheets aside and launched to my feet. The compulsion to act was overwhelming, driven by a force that felt beyond my control. My hand reached for the doorknob, and I hesitated, albeit briefly, before my resolve shattered.

Determined, I paced in my chamber. My steps did little to curb the chaos inside me as the storm of my emotions churned like a tempest. Anger surged within me, a volatile wildfire burning away the remnants of reason. It blazed within the recesses of my mind, fueled by an insatiable longing. Tears welled as my frustration boiled over, and at last, I screamed into the pillow, a futile attempt to muffle my cries of rage.

Instead, I pressed the pillow to my ears, desperate to block out the tormenting sounds, but they persisted. Unyielding. I couldn't escape the breathless cadence of Callix's sighs, the intoxicating rhythm entwining itself with my thoughts, refusing to be silenced.

Driven to the brink, I pulled the door open and followed the path that promised my downfall.

I STOOD mere inches from the threshold of Callix's chamber. The air was heavy with the sounds of their passion, and neither seemed concerned to conceal it behind closed doors. *What was I doing here?* I stepped back, as if my instincts pulled me from a precipice.

But then Callix's voice drifted through the small opening in the door. "What are you afraid of?" His words froze me in place, and his question danced on the edge of provocation. An invitation. It was as if he dared me to retreat, or perhaps he was aware of his magnetic pull that tugged at my resolve. I had no right to be here or to intrude on their private space. I told myself I didn't care. I shouldn't. Yet, my very being resonated with a different truth.

Beneath my rational thoughts, a tempest of emotions churned. Anger, longing, and something almost feral that simmered beneath my skin. Despite my attempt to retreat, my feet moved of their own accord. Through the narrow gap in the door, a sight seared itself into my consciousness. Callix, his bare skin illuminated by the dim light, stood at the edge of the bed, gripping the nymph's hips as he moved with a rhythm that sent shockwaves through me. I couldn't see her face, but I heard her cries—the embodiment of pleasure—which punctuated the air like shards of glass.

My heart was lodged in my throat, and my breath caught in my chest. Callix's body carved a brutal silhouette against my senses; his form, his every muscle, drew me in like a siren's call, the force of his presence a gravitational pull that defied all reason.

I held my breath when our eyes locked, a connection so intimate that it sent shivers down my spine. For a brief, terrifying moment, it was as though he was claiming me with that gaze, as if it were our souls intertwined during this act of raw passion. A knot tightened at the base of my throat, and against my will, tears welled in my eyes, blurring the lines of reality.

"Look at me." His command pierced through the chaos of my thoughts, and as much as I wanted to turn away, I couldn't deny the power of his words. My tears fell freely, and in that moment of vulnerability, my vision cleared. I couldn't bear to watch any longer or to be consumed by the intensity of his presence.

With a quivering breath, I turned from his door, clutching the nightgown tightly against my chest. I retreated. Each step was a painful reminder of the emotions that he had stirred to life. I pressed my palm to my chest to steady the erratic rhythm of my heart, to find some semblance of composure.

The feeling was all too familiar. A sweeping ache of betrayal and jealousy threatened to engulf me. As I walked away, the sounds of their passion echoed in my memory. I was teetering on the precipice of a realization that could alter everything.

"Where do you think you're going?" His voice rocked me

on my heels, and I turned to find him approaching: shirtless, disheveled, and buttoning his slacks. His presence snatched the air from my lungs. I stood, speechless, trapped in a moment where words failed me. What could I say when I had no right to question or demand or feel?

"Why are you running away?" he pressed, searching my eyes. He closed the distance between us. The weight of his gaze was almost suffocating, a mirror to the emotions swirling within me.

"This is wrong. I can't do this," I stammered, taking a step back, as if the distance could somehow shield me. But before I could retreat, he was upon me, his arms encircling my waist, drawing me against his chest.

"Stop. Just stop," he pleaded, his chin resting on my shoulder. He brushed my hair with his fingers, a tender gesture unfamiliar to the surrounding chaos. His lips ignited a trail of fire from my ear to my neck, and the sensation sent shivers coursing through me. Tears welled in my eyes, and their saltiness mingled with the emotions that threatened to crush me. I leaned into his touch, seeking solace amidst the chaos of my thoughts.

"Are you ready to admit you're jealous?"

His words—his breath—caressed my skin and cut through the silence. The dam broke, and sobs racked my body, each tear a testament to the pain I held at bay. I clung to his presence, and his arms cocooned me. "Please don't cry. Why are you fighting this?" he murmured, his voice a gentle plea. I shook my head, my hands finding their place atop his.

"What do you want me to say?" I struggled against his embrace, but his hold only tightened, an unyielding anchor refusing to let me drift. "Would you be satisfied knowing I want this as much as you do? That I ache for your touch, that you suffocate me and upset me and drive me mad, and yet I want you all the same? That I hate you for what you've done. That it took every ounce of my self-control not to kill Syllis in that room while you—while you..." My voice cracked, yet the words tumbled out, a torrent of emotions I struggled to contain.

"Yes. It does," he whispered his confession against my ear, brushing his lips across my skin with a tenderness that made my stomach tighten. "Would it make you feel better to know that it was you I saw, you who I imagined, and your body which I craved instead of hers?"

His admission struck me like a tidal wave, and the impact left me breathless. I struggled to navigate the Sea God's tempestuous ocean of emotions.

"No, Callix, it doesn't. Because it doesn't matter," I whispered, my voice cracking. "Nothing matters. What I want—what you want—this all-consuming pain and guilt. It's all wrong, and I hate myself for it. I don't know what to do anymore. You've managed to slip into the depths of my soul, and I want to run away, but a part of me is fighting. I'm lost, Callix." The admission hung in the air like a heavy fog as I finally spoke my truth.

Silence stretched around us, a sanctuary amidst the storm.

"I think it's time to go back." His voice cut through the turbulence of our emotions, a blend of fear and clarity piercing through me. His words were like a splash of cold water, quickly snapping me out of the whirlpool of conflicting feelings that consumed me.

"I thought I could do this. I thought that having you accept that you wanted me would be enough, but I was wrong. I don't want you to question this. I don't want you to hesitate. The day you come to me; I want you to do so without doubts. I deserve nothing less, and neither do you." His lips brushed against my cheek in a fleeting gesture that held a world of meaning. His hands slipped away from my waist, and for a moment, I held onto his fingers, unwilling to let go of the connection that seemed so fragile yet unbreakable.

"How will I do this?" I asked, my voice tinged with fear. With a hesitant touch, I traced the contours of his face, feeling the roughness of his jaw beneath my touch. "How can I go back to the surface and pretend that nothing has changed?"

He wrapped his hand around mine, his grip warm and reassuring. He pressed my fingers against his lips before guiding them to rest over his heart.

"Don't worry, darling," he murmured, his voice a soothing melody. "The second you return to him, you will find clarity. Soon, all your fears will disappear. All doubts forgotten."

The storm within his eyes mirrored my emotions as he tenderly caressed my face. Tears welled in my eyes, crystallizing like diamonds against my skin. Each droplet froze as his gaze shifted, as if searching for something beyond me. His next words were like a bittersweet song that seeped into my soul.

"Once you're with him, you won't have to pretend," he whispered. It was both a reassurance and a farewell—a glimpse into a future that I yearned for and a reminder of the pain that lay ahead. "Get some rest," he urged. His fingertips lingered against my cheek before he pulled away. "Tomorrow, we return to the surface. I will take you to Abryas. I will take you to him."

As Callix walked away, each step felt like a crack in my heart. This wasn't a mere goodnight; this felt like an eternal goodbye. The realization hit me, a devastating truth I had been trying to avoid. It was as if I was losing him despite never having him in the first place. The ache in my chest was both familiar and foreign, a sensation that haunted me since the beginning of this journey.

As he disappeared from view, the echoes of his words lingered in the air, a bitter reminder of the choices ahead. I pressed a hand to my chest as if trying to mend the fractures within me. The night closed in, heavy with uncertainty, while I grappled with the weight of my own emotions.

I WRESTLED with my thoughts throughout the night, trying to find some semblance of peace. Closing my eyes felt like an admission of defeat, a surrender to the chaos within me.

Callix's actions replayed in my mind like a broken record. How could he have thought such a reckless stunt would be his solution?

But beyond Callix's actions, the impending return to the surface was what truly gnawed at me. A place where I would once again be with Drake, yet the mere thought of seeing him again sent nerves skittering throughout my body.

I clung to Callix's words like a lifeline. Everything would be better once I was back with Drake. I prayed that the doubts and uncertainties would dissolve into oblivion as soon as we were reunited.

In the depths of my heart, I longed to feel that sense of completeness once more, the feeling of contentment that evaporated the moment I met Callix. Could Drake and I truly go back to the way things were? Could we bridge the gap that had formed, the unspoken emotions that had taken residence between us?

The Sea God's presence would be a problem for Drake, and to be honest, I was scared to bring them together. Callix had once confessed that the bond we shared was worth preserving in whatever form, and so, I clung to the hope that he would— at least for a while—pretend that my friendship was sufficient. I hoped he would avoid any conflict with Drake, for my sake.

I LINGERED beneath the soothing spray of Serfier's water, indulging in one of the many luxuries the realm offered. The sensation of warmth against my skin was both a comfort and a reminder of the mundane pleasures I will soon leave behind. As the water cascaded over my body, I allowed my thoughts to drift, contemplating the uncertainties of the future.

Yet, a part of me knew that my lingering was also a delay tactic, a way to postpone the inevitable confrontation with Callix. The weight of our recent interactions had left a tangled mess of emotions within me, and facing him this morning felt like walking onto the battlefield without a shield.

I finally turned off the shower, wrapping a towel around myself. When I stepped into the chamber, my eyes landed on the clothes meticulously laid out across the bed. The sight of them infused me with a newfound strength, as if each piece of the ensemble held a promise of empowerment.

The clothes were unlike anything I would have chosen, yet I recognized the intricate details: the golden accents adorning the garments, like the armor Callix had worn before. The pieces glinted as I traced the sharp lines and golden touches, the cold metal sending shivers up my spine. The woman in the mirror was a stark contrast to the reflection I had grown accustomed to. I looked every bit the warrior: sleek, lethal, and ready for battle. A smile tugged at my lips, a mixture of appreciation and acknowledgment of Callix's intentions.

With purpose, I descended the chambers, each step resonating with a newfound confidence. There was something about the way the clothes clung to me like a second skin that imbued me with power I hadn't felt before. I didn't need to search long to find him. Callix stood on the open terrace, overlooking the expanse of his ocean world.

He was dressed impeccably in a crisp suit, matching the one he wore on the night he first revealed his feelings to me. The deep blue trousers were complemented by the jacket, also adorned in intricate gold, a hint of opulence that accentuated his regal nature. He fixed his gaze on the horizon, the weight of his emotions almost palpable in the air.

The designs on my own clothing mirrored his, as if he had woven a connection between us through the subtle touches of our armor, a silent reminder we were bound by more than words. A complex mix of emotions stirred within me: appreciation, uncertainty, and the lingering yearning for his presence.

I stood beside him, my heart racing. Unspoken words filled the space between us, weighed heavy by our shared history and the tangled emotions we had yet to unravel. As the ocean came alive, I took a deep breath.

"I'm curious about these symbols." I mused, drawn to the intricate golden accents adorning the cuffs around my wrists. They mirrored the ones gracing his shoulder plates.

I felt the burn of his gaze on me, even though I couldn't muster the courage to meet his eyes.

"Runes of power and protection, passed down by my ancestors. Worn exclusively by the royal family." He spoke as if voicing a long-kept secret. Though we stood a foot apart, his voice sent shivers through me.

I traced the unfamiliar markings of the cuffs. The power was undeniable. I questioned why he entrusted me with something so personal that carried such profound sentimental weight for his lineage and kingdom. I was no one. I felt unde-serving.

I sensed the second his mind seeped into my thoughts. Our connection was growing. His posture shifted beside me, and no longer able to evade his gaze, I looked up.

"You're wrong." His touch was feather-light across my cheek. "Even in this charade, nothing holds more significance than you."

Amidst the sounds of Callix's world, my heartbeat resounded loudest. His face, all angles and edges, held me captive as a smirk tugged at the corner of his lips. "You're an immortal warrior now, and you should look the part, espe-cially if you plan to confront the Elvin King and Queen. Not to mention, it looks great on you." He added with a playful wink. In that small gesture, his intention was clear; he aimed to shift the energy between us, to fortify the emotional barriers we built.

"Thank you." I offered. "What do they say?" I asked,

shifting my gaze to the runes on his shoulder plates. Emotions flickered in his eyes—hesitation, fascination, excitement. Did sharing his history sadden him, or did my curiosity thrill him?

"Not sadness," he confirmed, his intrusion into my thoughts evident. His fingers intertwined with mine, locking his eyes to the golden cuffs on my wrists. "I'm glad I get to share this with you." A smile tugged at my lips. "Ansuz symbolizes wisdom. Laguz represents water—the sea, flow, and rebirth." His gaze held mine, and understanding dawned —the waters of rebirth, which allowed my mortal body to transform. "Algiz is the emblem of protection." His focus returned to tracing the symbols around my hand. "Uruz signifies strength, power, and courage." Those were the two symbols I recognized—the same ones etched into Drake's elaborate tattoo.

"Yes, these are some of the same runes that mark royal Dragons at birth, yet these symbols hold personal meanings— a reflection of their character traits." My attention rested on the familiar symbols.

"Yes. Though he holds little faith in their meaning," I remarked, my eyes lingering on our joined hands.

"He's never believed himself worthy," said Callix unexpectedly.

"What happened between you two?"

His gaze shifted to me.

"A long story, founded mostly on jealousy and mistrust." He released my hand, peering back at the expanse of ocean before us. "Mainly his fault, obviously," he added, feigning seriousness, though a hint of a smile gave him away. I smiled.

"Naturally." I agreed.

A comfortable silence followed, despite our unspoken truths. Callix spoke again.

"Regardless of his beliefs, or sometimes your own... I don't harbor animosity for the fool. His life hasn't been a walk in the park. He's always been blind to his own worth."

"Yes. I gathered that much."

"Always brooding and dark," Callix remarked, and my smile widened.

"Always." I offered, and it felt liberating to talk about Drake without any tension. I envisioned the kind of friends they once were—the friends they could have been—yet how impossible that seemed to be now. *Or perhaps, not entirely impossible*, I added as an afterthought.

Callix snorted, and I knew he was in my head, but I no longer cared. He grinned.

"I'll remind you of that next time you ask me not to pry." As he extended his hand, a portal opened before us. "Are you ready?"

I wiped my clammy palms on my pants and nodded. "As ready as I'll ever be."

THE SHORELINE BORE no resemblance to the Ruins of the Lost. The sandy coast stretched only a few yards before giving way to a dense line of lush trees that vanished along the shore. It was a forest unlike any I had ever seen, a sprawling maze of greenery.

"This is the southern coast of Abryas—the shores of Galnora," explained Callix, allowing the portal to seal behind us.

"Why Abryas?" I questioned. Callix paused as he delved into my thoughts, trying to understand.

"The northern Upheryan clan is preparing for battle. Our presence is more useful in Abryas. We must persuade Herod to help the North. Otherwise, Upherya will be lost." I followed closely, shadowed by his frame. My boots sank into the sand.

"Shouldn't we go to Upherya instead? Join the battle?" Callix shook his head and slowed his pace, waiting for me to reach his side.

"Not yet. First, we need to convince Herod of the Fate's plan. You must make him see that we don't stand a chance unless the Realms unite."

"What makes you think I can persuade him?"

"The Fates chose you for a reason. If you can't sway the Elvin King, I fear no one can." We began hiking the small hills.

"Seriously, Callix. Can't we just portal straight into the castle?"

"I doubt the Elvin king will look kindly on the intrusion."

"But you had no qualms about intruding in Druleska." I pointed out, and he paused, narrowing his eyes at me.

"That was different. I had an open invitation from Dagasti," he said, though that only raised more questions.

"I still don't understand your connection with the man."

"Let's just say that being in the monster's favor allowed me insight into his plans. The wind warriors struggled for years to defend their borders against both Dagasti and Herod. I thought they needed an ally," he said before turning towards the line of trees.

"You know, for someone who feigns being dangerous and unkind, you sure seem to have a good heart."

Callix shook his head, managing a slight smile.

"I can be many things depending on the mood."

"Sure, Callix. You can pretend, but I'm finally beginning to understand you."

He slowed his pace and turned to me, extending his hand to help me over a fallen tree trunk.

"That's all that matters." His eyes bore into mine, and I lost myself in the pools of his cerulean eyes. Silence stretched before us, interrupted only by a golden shimmer that moved through the trees.

Callix raised his hand, halting me in my tracks. Elven soldiers, clad in steel-gold armor, glided through the dense woods. Drake had once warned me that Elves didn't age, yet it was still unsettling to see how youthful they all appeared—some even younger than me.

"Commander." Callix greeted the young man, who seemed to lead the soldiers.

"Lord Callix. The King and the Dragon prince have been awaiting your arrival." I glanced at Callix, and his mind pierced through mine.

"*I sent a whisper ahead of time,*" he explained. And my silent thought was of Drake. *Wasn't he fighting in Upherya?*

"*Yes... but Herod must have sent word to him. He is here now.*" My heart somersaulted. "*It will be ok. I promise.*"

Callix extended his hand to me. "Come."

I took it, and he rubbed circles along my palm to soothe my nerves.

•   •   •

A MAGIC BARRIER appeared before us. "Is that what protects the realm?" I whispered as we advanced.

"Yes," answered Callix, and I furrowed my brows.

"Why is the King allowing Dagasti to sweep through Upherya when he could extend this protection to the wind people?"

"The Elven people aren't as skilled in battle as the wind warriors. The magic maintaining these barriers draws from every Elven soul in the kingdom. Herod is unwilling to weaken his defenses by sending his soldiers away."

"But these barriers won't hold forever." I pointed out, and Callix shook his head.

"Herod refuses to believe or accept that. That's why we're here."

"This King sounds like an ass."

Callix stifled his laughter.

"Let's keep those opinions to ourselves, shall we? We don't want to complicate things further. Besides, Herod is a soft-hearted fool beneath it all."

My doubt must have shown on my face as Callix added, "Trust me."

"We have sent a whisper to the castle. Once we receive a response, you can proceed," informed the young Elvin commander. Callix nodded in acknowledgment.

"What's a whisper?" I asked as soon as the commander left our side.

"That's how they communicate. Through the trees. The same way I use the water," Callix explained. I glanced around us at the giant trees, which seemed older than time itself. A shock of energy rolled beneath my skin.

"I can feel their energy. It's powerful."

"I'm sure it is," said Callix with a faint smile. "Considering your connection to the earth, you can probably hear their whispers." His words intrigued me. I never knew the trees could speak or carry messages.

I closed my eyes, taking in the scents of the forest—the wet dirt, the moss, the smell of tree bark and fresh grass mingled with flowers. As the wind rustled the leaves and branches, a soft voice emerged, barely audible. *"You may enter…"*

My eyes snapped open, and I whirled to face Callix. "I think I just heard it. We can enter."

Moments later, the young Golden soldier approached us.

"You may proceed now."

I exchanged a smile with Callix, who thanked him before turning to me.

"Shall we?" A water portal sprung before us. Taking his hand, I followed him through. To my surprise, the commander followed closely behind. The Elvin people were not very trusting; then again, perhaps that was wise.

There was no time to appreciate my surroundings as we reappeared at the foot of the castle stairs, where a familiar face greeted us. Drake's mother and another woman waited, and judging by her youthful appearance and glimmering dress, I assumed she was none other than Leiwen, the Queen of Abryas herself.

Kylram descended the stairs with grace, surprising me with a tight embrace. "Child. I am happy to see you are well. I knew the Fates would not abandon us," she said, pulling back slightly and acknowledging Callix, who stood stoically beside me. "Callix."

"Kylram... it's good to see you again. Well and alive." Callix's tone was a blend of sarcasm and sincerity that only he could muster.

Leiwen approached, and for a moment, I was uncertain of how to address her.

"Leiwen," Callix said beside me, answering my unspoken question. "You look lovely as always." She responded with a polite smile.

"You are too generous. I am happy to see you. It's been a while." Her shimmering eyes danced between Callix and me. "You must be Belynda," she continued. "I have heard a great deal about you. It is a pleasure to finally be acquainted."

I smiled, feeling slightly out of place in the presence of the Queen of the Elvin people.

"Thank you. I assure you, the pleasure is all mine. I read about you in books back in the human world." I admitted, though I immediately regretted the words as they left my mouth. However, Leiwen's soft laugh put me at ease.

"You shouldn't believe everything they say," she teased. To my surprise, she stepped forward and looped her hand around mine, drawing me away from Callix's side. "Come. Herod is waiting." I stole a quick glance behind me at the Sea God, who encouraged me with his eyes. Hand in hand with the Queen of Abryas, I ascended the steps as if we were the best of friends. Kylram walked by my other side while Callix trailed behind us like a sentinel.

"Is Drake...?" I whispered. Kylram squeezed my hand.

"He has been impatient, even more now that he knows

you're finally here."

"Where is he?" I asked, surprised he had not greeted us.

"He is with the King and the elders now. The prospects of the North are not good, and he thinks he can convince Herod to help."

"Not even I can persuade Herod," added Leiwen, her voice tinged with defeat.

"If the realms don't stand together, everything will be lost. The Moirai were specific on that account. We unite, or we all die. His choice..." I said as my revelation hung heavy in the air. A momentary silence permeated around us.

"Perhaps Herod will listen to you," added Callix, breaking the silence.

"I hope he does. For all of our sakes." Leiwen squeezed my hand and leaned in conspiratorially. "You are so lovely. I can see why he loves you." I blushed, her compliment boosting my wavering confidence.

"Thank you."

THE ELVIN CASTLE was a stark contrast to that of Druleska and Serfier. Warmth radiated from it, making it impossible to feel lonely within its walls. Young and vibrant faces bustled through the halls, and everywhere I looked, the corridors, balusters, and pillars were adorned with intricate flowering vines in various shades of green, blue, and pink. An intoxicating scent of flowers filled the air.

"I'm hurt that you find their kingdom more beautiful than my home." Callix's voice pierced through my thoughts with a hint of humor.

I couldn't help the small smile that tugged at the corners of my mouth. *"Just because I appreciate its beauty doesn't mean I prefer it,"* I teased, knowing that he was likely smiling, too. *"But you must admit it is quite beautiful, and the scent is exquisite..."*

"Wait till you see their gardens," Callix offered.

"I can only imagine."

The woman standing beside me remained utterly unaware of our private exchange.

"Let's wait in the ceremonial hall. Herod and Drake will join us momentarily." Leiwen suggested, guiding us through the threshold of two massive double doors that appeared to have been carved from the forest's trees, branches twisting over the doors like vines.

The room was opulent with stone walls and floors, floor-to-ceiling windows, and an open balcony overlooking the Elvin Golden City. It didn't take me long to realize that gold was a staple amidst all the green.

"Tea will be served shortly," Leiwen announced as she took a seat at one end of the table. "Come, sit by me." She motioned to her right. "Callix?" She turned to the Sea God, who still hovered behind us.

"No, thank you. I prefer to stand." He politely declined, walking toward the large windows instead.

"He's awfully quiet today," Leiwen commented, leaning toward me as if I could shed some light on the Sea God's behavior. I briefly glanced in his direction, yet his back was to me. He seemed lost in thought as he gazed at the view beyond the windows.

"I wouldn't know," I replied. "I haven't known him long enough."

Though perhaps I was the only one in this place who truly knew him. Callix's eyes shifted, meeting mine, as if silently confirming my thoughts.

"I hope he has treated you with kindness and respect," said Kylram from the seat across from mine. I had to remind myself she was Drake's mother, hence her misguided beliefs about him.

"He has been a good friend," I said, realizing my tone was harsher than intended. "Not just to me, but to the Realms too. He is not the monster everyone made him out to be." I realized in my passion to defend Callix, I might have crossed a line. Kylram's eyes regarded me, but she remained silent.

"Yes, Callix has been a friend," noted the Elvin Queen, "but also our enemy. His alliance has long been with Upherya."

"He sided with a Realm being attacked on two fronts. By your King and Dagasti. I would have done the same thing."

Leiwen surprised me by smiling instead of reacting.

"I wish I had your passion and conviction. I have been a champion for the Wind people since the beginning of our conflicts. I have never regarded the Water Lord as an enemy. I rather think he is brave enough to follow his heart, even if Herod thinks differently."

It was liberating to discover where the Queen's opinion rested. She was a good ally and likely a good friend.

"I only hope Drake and Callix can reconcile their differences. I would hate to see them drift further apart." Kylram murmured, and a sinking heaviness filled my chest as the wooden doors burst open.

12
ALLIANCES

TIME STOOD STILL as Drake emerged from the doors. The pounding in my heart slowed, and a strange sensation paralyzed me. There was no doubt—I loved him. His eyes locked onto mine before flitting towards the windows. I knew exactly what he sought.

I stood up, but his strides were a blur as he reached Callix's side, landing a blow to his face. Gasps erupted throughout the room, but Callix remained surprisingly calm. Touching the corner of his lip, he smiled. I watched in slow motion as Drake lifted his fist again, but I couldn't allow him to do this, not because of me. Jumping between them, I spun to face Drake.

"Stop this right now."

"It's alright," said Callix behind me. "I deserved that."

"You deserve worse," growled Drake, his gaze fixed past me.

"Enough!" I gave Callix a pointed look, begging him not to provoke Drake further. He turned away, distancing himself from any further confrontation. I turned to Drake as rage emanated from every pore in his body.

"This wasn't the kind of welcome I expected," I murmured, hoping to defuse the tension. Slowly, I watched his face transform. His eyes softened, and I lost myself in those unforgettable gray hues.

When his hands reached for my waist to pull me close, I knew I was home. My body reacted as though we had never spent time apart, and I melted into his touch. Despite an undeniable sense of belonging in his arms, I felt the pull from the other side of the room.

"Later," I whispered, aware of the eyes on us, one pair in particular. But Drake didn't care. He held me close and claimed my lips. The kiss was branding, consuming, and possessive. I was his; he was mine. He channeled all his pain and longing into this all-consuming kiss.

The sound of an opening door made me pull away, yet I remained pressed against Drake's chest, silently begging him for composure. I was relieved when he straightened. He stepped aside in time for me to see Herod marching in.

I knew the King of Abryas would be young, but it was a revelation to feel that kind of power in such a young man. His eyes appeared to measure me while I studied him. If I had any chance of persuading him, I had to rise to the occasion. He would never believe the Fates' plan if I cowered beneath him or Drake. I wasn't his subject; I was their salvation.

As he approached Drake and me, the energy in the room shifted. I felt the earth's vibration coming from the stones beneath my feet and the walls. It felt like they were closing in. I wouldn't let him intimidate me. I braced my stance and released a calming breath, forcing the earth around me to settle to a quiet whisper.

"Impressive. No doubt you are what they say you are," said the young King with a satisfied smile.

"That was unnecessary, and you shouldn't attempt that again unless you're ready to take me on," I responded, feeling slightly offended by his attack and lack of grace. No one in the room seemed to notice the cause of the hostility except for Leiwen, Herod, and me, of course. The King's expression solidified.

"Careful," Callix warned into my thoughts. I didn't blink. I only stared at the young King.

If he thought I was going to apologize, he was mistaken. I stood my ground, refusing to back down.

"Herod, where are your manners?" interrupted Leiwen as she came to stand beside her husband. His entire demeanor shifted when she was at his side, as if she had brought light into his aura. Linking her arm with his, he kissed her hand with adoration.

"My apologies. I often forget myself." While he looked at me, I knew the apology was for his wife's benefit. "You can understand my reservations when she is the one responsible for unleashing the darkness upon us."

"We have already been over this," said Drake, but I placed my hand on his chest.

"I feel shame for what my decisions have cost the realms, and I am saddened that I couldn't choose differently. However, were I faced with the same choices, I don't know that I wouldn't make them again." I glanced at Drake, remembering his pleading eyes the day in Druleska's dungeon when he begged me not to open the rift to the dark dimension—begged me not to listen to Dagasti. I remembered his blood-covered body and the blue fire dagger. I remembered how it felt to know that my choices were to watch him die before my eyes or to do as Dagasti asked.

"There is always a choice," Herod snarled.

"You will not speak to her like that." Drake's anger was palpable, and I pushed against his arm.

"It's alright. This is my battle to fight. Not yours." Drake's silver eyes regarded me briefly, but I turned back to Herod.

"Choices are nothing but an illusion. Trust me. I have learned that the hard way. You think you can control your life and protect the lives of those you love." I glanced at Leiwen, who still clutched to his arm. "But then you realize you are merely a pawn in the bigger scheme of things. You stand there and lecture me on choices when you continuously make the wrong ones: standing against Upherya, refusing to join the fight, criticizing my decisions when we both know that if it had been Leiwen with the fire blade against her chest, you would have made the same choice."

An uncomfortable silence swallowed the room as waves of dark energy flowed about me. Herod blinked, and Leiwen tugged on his arm.

"You are full of surprises, aren't you?" he said with a hint of amusement.

"I'm not here to entertain you. I am here to warn you that if you do not join forces with Upherya, your kingdom will fall, and Dagasti will not be the one to blame for Leiwen's death... you will be. Your decision will be the dagger that takes her life along with every living soul in this Realm."

"Are you threatening me?" His voice was low.

"Would you ask that of the Moirai if they showed you your future?" I challenged. "I am alive because the Fates have deemed my life essential to stop this war. I did not choose this, yet I am willing to do what is necessary to stop Dagasti. I am not here to intimidate you, young King. I am here to tell you that the fate of all the realms rests in your hands."

I willed the earth's power to fill my body. I had nothing else to lose. Slipping silently into the recesses of Herod's mind, I allowed the images of my encounter with the Moirai to flow into his thoughts. His eyes shifted, confused, but the second he realized what he was seeing and hearing, his face transformed with dread and horror.

His eyes shifted to Drake, and I knew he saw the choice I had to make, the price he could pay. I silently begged him not to reveal as much, and when his gaze shifted to mine once more, I ended our connection.

The young King took a sharp breath.

"Cinnaess Athkaraye," he whispered, and though I didn't understand the words, I felt the power of the ancient tongue pulse like the earth's heartbeat.

"It means peace-bringer, friend of the Elves." Callix' said over the dense silence. With that understanding, I dared to hope this was a small battle won in our favor.

"You have given me much to consider, friend." Herod extended his hand towards me for the first time, and I shook it.

"I only ask..."

"There is no need." He stared at me in a silent agreement. Whatever had been shared between us would not be spoken of. He turned to Leiwen and gave her a gentle kiss.

"Come, love. Let them rest. The elders and I have much to discuss."

Before the young King left, he turned to me once more, and for the first time, his smile was genuine.

"Welcome to Abryas," he said. I felt the unbidden power of the earth consume me, and I nodded in subtle appreciation before he disappeared with Leiwen on his arm.

Callix strolled to my side, and I felt the tension rise. I much preferred to battle the young King than to navigate the dark energy exchanged between the dragon and the Sea God.

"That was terrifyingly intense," Callix teased, standing beside me—too close to Drake for my liking. Callix didn't seem to mind or care, though Drake was seething.

"Trust me, I wasn't intimidated by him," I said, and Callix raised his brows.

"I know. I wasn't referring to the King." He smiled, and Drake stiffened at my side.

"I'm sure you have better things to do," Drake said, but when the Sea God smiled back in challenge, I braced myself.

"Actually, I promised I would show Belynda the gardens."

I narrowed my eyes at Callix, allowing my thoughts to convey my frustration.

"Are you out of your mind? What kind of game are you playing at Callix? Please, I beg you. Go." My plea was desperate, and I hoped he would heed it. Instead, his eyes remained locked on me, and though he had heard me, the look on his face told me he was debating whether to listen or continue with whatever foolish game he was playing. *"Please, Callix. Don't make this any harder than it already is. Please."*

His eyes shifted between Drake and me, and I was certain no one noticed the sadness and pain there. But I did; it twisted something inside me.

"Perhaps another time?" he asked, searching my eyes. "I'm sure you'll be wanting to catch up."

Drake didn't speak, but his hands tightened possessively around my waist, his fingers digging into my skin. He was doing everything in his power not to lose himself to the darkness. I felt his rage stretch like a hazy film around us.

I couldn't bring myself to speak, so I nodded. With measured steps, Callix walked towards the door at my silent agreement. I didn't want to let him go like that. He wasn't a monster. He was my friend. *Liar*, whispered the deepest layers of my conscience.

"Callix!" I called, and he paused at the door before turning towards me. "Thank you," and he knew it wasn't simply for taking a step back. It was for everything—everything he had done for me. With a subtle dip of his head, he disappeared and closed the heavy doors behind him.

The second Callix left the room, the tension dissipated like a stream meeting the ocean. Drake's arms encircled me, shielding my body in his.

"I will leave you both. I'm sure there is much to say. I don't wish to be in your way." Kylram rose from her chair, smiling warmly at us.

"You don't have to leave," I said quickly.

"Nonsense." She dismissed the idea with a wave of her hand, following the path Callix had taken.

The moment the doors closed behind Drake's mother, he turned me to face him. Bringing his hands to my face, his silver eyes—brighter than I had ever seen—searched my face.

"Your eyes are brighter," I said, tracing the sharp edges of his jaw and cheekbones.

"I haven't changed, love." The warmth of his voice caressed my senses, and I closed my eyes, relishing his touch. "But *you* have," he whispered, appreciation glinting in his eyes.

He curled a tendril of my hair around his finger, bringing it close to his nose. "You smell divine like spring. Your eyes have specks of blue that were never there before, and your voice... it's like a siren's call to my soul."

"Is that a good thing?"

"Immortality suits you well, love. You make my heart ache."

I laughed nervously beneath the intensity of his gaze, unsure why.

"Belynda, I... I thought you were gone." His eyes darkened, and his face transformed into shadows. "I fought to get to you. I prayed to anyone who would listen, and not a day goes by where I don't hate myself for allowing Callix to play me like a fool."

"Don't say that." I placed a hand on his chest.

"He doesn't deserve your kindness. You don't owe him anything." Hatred laced his words.

"You don't mean that, Drake. You have every right to be upset, but if it wasn't for Callix, I would be dead."

"No. If it wasn't for me, you would have never been harmed in the first place." Drake pushed me at arm's length and we stepped to the windows. "Belynda, if I hadn't made that promise... if I hadn't kept my word, if I hadn't agreed to bring you with me, you would still be human. You could still be with your family." He trailed his hands through his hair, as he so often did when overcome with frustration. "Yes, I hate Callix for keeping you away from me, but I hate myself more knowing everything I have put you through."

"Stop it." I reached his side and placed a hand on his face. "Look at me." Drake lowered his eyes to mine; dark clouds brewed behind his eyes. "It doesn't matter what you would have done. We never had a choice, Drake. I know that now. This was the Fates' plan. This was my destiny. Isabel knew it, too. Remember her words. 'Only in death...' Keeping me safe was never an option." He braced my hips, pulling me closer.

"I cannot exist without you," he whispered, resting his forehead on mine. "My life begins and ends with you."

"I love you, Drake. My soul is yours. For eternity." But the Fates' words echoed in my mind like the strung string of their spindle. I prayed we had eternity. I would move heaven and earth to keep Drake safe.

He held my chin, rubbing his thumb over my lower lip. Inching closer, he slowly claimed my mouth and, unlike his first kiss, which was filled with uninhibited desperation, this one was measured, gentle and I lost myself in it.

The soft strokes of his lips melded against mine, while his hand stroked the back of my neck. He swiped against my lips with his tongue, demanding entry. I parted my mouth, and our tongues danced. My new immortal senses appreciated the heightened taste of his mouth. His scent swam—a combination of pine, sandalwood, and spice, inhibiting all my thoughts.

"I could happily die in this instant." His words tugged at a not-so-distant memory—no, *Callix's words*. The fleeting thought of him made me freeze.

"What is it?" Drake brushed his hand against my cheek, pulling me out of the memory.

"Nothing. I guess I'm tired, that's all," I said, and before I knew it, he swept me into his arms, cradling me against his chest.

"I burn for you. However, I have waited this long. I think I can wait a while longer. But make no mistake, I plan to devour your body and soul." His lips brushed the corner of mine, and his promise made my core ache.

We strode down the halls of the Elvin castle, the corridors a blur of greens and gold. I lost myself in the details of his face—his eyes. I loved him so much it hurt. I had been a fool to think any amount of time could break our bond.

Drake froze before a set of wooden doors and pushed them open with his foot.

"Your chambers," he said, setting me down at the edge of the bed.

I peered around the chamber, awe-struck. It was breathtaking. Like Druleska and Serfier, a large circular balcony opened at the far end of the opulent room. I walked towards it, resting my hands on the stone rails as I looked at the Elvin kingdom before me: rolling green hills, endless fields of flowers, and lush forests. My senses were entranced by the vibrant colors and the subtle fragrance in the air, and the warming rays of sunlight bathing my face. The temperature was just right—not cold like Druleska, yet not warm like Serfier.

"I thought you wanted to rest," said Drake, trapping me with his body. His hands came to rest beside mine on the stone veranda. I smiled, leaning back against him.

"I am. I will. I'm just taking a moment to appreciate the scenery."

"It is quite beautiful here, isn't it?" he said, resting his chin on my head and bringing his hands around my middle. "I wish you would have had a chance to see my home back in the days when father ruled."

"Me too, but that doesn't mean I can't appreciate the beauty of Druleska. What your ancestors and your father built is still reflected in every stone within that Realm. And the people. Your uncle might have caused destruction, but one day... One day, you will reclaim your throne. You will restore your home and your father's legacy. I know you will." He placed a tender kiss on my head and pressed me tighter against him.

He traced the golden details on my armor, and I knew he recognized the meanings.

"Callix is going to be a problem, isn't he?" Drake murmured.

"He doesn't have to be," I whispered. "I know you have your differences, Drake, but I trust him. He has been kind to me. He is a good friend."

"Is that all he is?" His question caught me off guard, and a tremor ran through me.

"Yes, it is," I affirmed. Indeed, Callix was my friend. Was he more? Perhaps. But I loved Drake, and nothing would change that. Drake and I were destined to walk our paths together.

Callix and I were like the tides. A fleeting moment. Nothing more.

"I'll attempt to keep the peace. For you."

I released a breath, leaning into him.

"Thank you."

"Don't thank me just yet," he added, smiling against my hair. "I said I would try, but I can't promise I won't be tempted to wipe that smirk off his face every time we meet."

"You won't do that again," I protested, stiffening in his arms. Drake held me tighter.

"I'll be on my best behavior, I promise."

"It might help if you stopped seeing him as your enemy."

Drake's humorless laugh rocked my body.

"Love, I might have considered that if he wasn't trying to steal my very reason for living—a piece of my soul."

"You're wrong about him."

"Am I?" He challenged. "He desires you, Belynda. Don't be mistaken. I haven't lived as long as I have without perceiving the intentions of others. A man would have to be blind not to notice how he looks at you. I won't allow it. I was foolish enough to let him near you once; I won't make the same mistake twice."

"Drake, he is your friend."

"Not anymore... A friend doesn't covet what is mine. A friend doesn't lie. A friend doesn't betray."

"He never betrayed you."

"You don't know that."

"Neither do you!" My words came out with more force than intended as I struggled to break free from his embrace. However, he held me tighter.

"The ease with which you believe his words, the passion with which you defend him—it tells me you care for him," Drake murmured, his breath warm against my ear. "Please, tell me that isn't true, for I couldn't bear it."

I turned to meet his gaze, locking my eyes to his.

"I love you, Drake, and no one can ever change that." Drake cupped my chin, skimming his nose against mine until he finally released a breath, a silent acceptance of my words.

"I refuse to let you out of my sight. However, I must find Herod. Upherya needs an answer, and if the King has changed his mind about helping the North... then we have no time to waste." He rested his hands on my waist and brushed his lips slowly with mine. "I will leave you to rest before dinner." His gray eyes shone with wicked intent, and the slow upturn of his lips confirmed my suspicions. "Tonight... nothing will come between us, not even the Water Lord." He bent slowly for a brief kiss. "That is a promise." His smile grew as he pulled away. I laced my fingers through the hair at the nape of his neck and pushed up on my toes to brush my lips against his again.

"I will hold you to that," I said, smiling. He kissed my hand, then dropped it as he turned towards the chamber, leaving me standing on the open balcony.

"By the way," He paused at the doors. "I hope you're not too fond of those clothes." With that, he took his leave.

What was I to do with him? Could he sense the torrent of emotions raging inside me, the subtle changes, and my indecisions? He was correct about Callix coveting me, but he was mistaken about everything else. While Callix was indeed dangerous and chaotic, there was still honor within him. If he had wanted to possess me, all he had to do was command it; I would have surrendered willingly. Yet, he always offered me a choice. If anything, I was to blame for my moments of weakness, for allowing desire to cloud my judgment and override my senses. Callix wasn't the villain in this story—I was. And I had a sinking feeling I would soon pay the price.

I curled up on the bed, closed my eyes, and drifted into a restless sleep.

Golden threads wove around me, and a frozen battlefield stretched before my eyes. To my right stood Callix, and to my left was Drake, frozen in time like the rest of the scene. My hands moved painstakingly slow, nudging the threads, seeking a new possibility, a different outcome. Yet, a sense of desperation threatened to choke me.

I BOLTED UPRIGHT, clutching my throat as though I could stave off the suffocating sensation that overwhelmed me. "Just a dream," I muttered, repeating the words like a mantra.

"Are you alright?" Callix's voice flowed into my thoughts like a gentle caress. I scanned the chamber, but he was nowhere in sight. I sensed his amusement. *"Don't worry, I'm keeping my distance."* There was a pause, but I closed my eyes to listen for him. I heard his breath; he wasn't too far. *"I was just checking in to see how you were. I sensed your distress."*

"I'm fine," I replied, reaching my thoughts to him. For a long moment, silence followed from his end, and I attempted to probe his mental shields. They were stronger than ever. *"Where are you?"* I asked.

"Miss me already?" he teased, and I almost detected the playfulness in his voice. I remained silent. That was better than a lie or the truth. *"It's okay. you don't have to answer that,"* he continued. *"I already know the answer. I'll see you at dinner."*

"Goodbye, Callix," I whispered as his quiet laughter dissipated in my mind.

I glanced down at my clothes; I *was* too attached to them to allow Drake to tear them to shreds. Not to mention, the vest was a gift from Callix, and the symbols carried a sentimental value to him and his kingdom, which he had allowed me to be a part of. I opened the door to a large wooden armoire, and as I expected, I found what I was looking for. I removed the metal cuffs, the vest, and the pants, and folded them neatly at the bottom of the closet.

I stepped into the bath chamber, another example of Elvin's appreciation for nature. Vines adorned the walls, and the shower resembled a waterfall between the stones. It felt like bathing in the heart of a forest. The soap smelled like rose petals, and the floor was paved with various shapes and sizes of river stones. If I hadn't been a guest, or pressed for time, I might have skipped dinner to remain beneath the soothing water. But I was the guest of honor, and I was hungry.

My golden tresses cascaded down my back, and the shimmering silver dress clung to my shoulders, the sleeves stopping short of my elbows. The gown was light and elegant. After going barefoot in Serfier for so long, I hesitated at the choice of slippers or heels. However, I was no longer under the protection of the water, so I slipped on the heels instead.

I found it hard to recognize the human girl I had been not long ago. A soft knock at the door startled me.

"Come in," I called, and as the door opened, my eyes fell on Drake. My breath caught in my chest. Was it possible he could be even more striking than before? The crisp collar of his black suit framed his neck, while silver metal details adorned his shoulders. His posture was impeccable, and his eyes roamed my body.

"You look…" His gaze dropped to my cleavage. "Breathtaking."

I smiled, sauntering to him, the heels made me appear much taller than usual.

"You took the words right out of my mouth," I said, reaching for his chest. I traced the smooth fabric of his suit.

"Mmm." He hummed while his hands found my waist and pulled me closer. "We could skip dinner. I have no objections."

Smiling, I gazed into his eyes; his lips were tantalizingly close.

"I must admit, the thought did cross my mind," I replied, "but it's important."

He took my hand and brought it to his lips.

"Yes, it is," he agreed. Stepping back, he gave me one last appreciative look. "Are you ready?"

"Lead the way."

A shimmering night sky befell the Elven Realm. It was a surreal and beautiful sight. As we strode down the corridors, the glow from the chandeliers and stars bathed Drake's face. I longed to be close to him—to lose myself in him. His thumb traced soothing circles on the back of my hand.

"Remember to breathe," he said as we paused outside the dining hall.

When the doors swung open, blinding light poured forth. At least a dozen crystal chandeliers adorned the ceiling with hanging vines illuminating all four walls. The table was unlike anything I had ever seen, carved from the purest, shimmering white oak. A wisteria tree grew from the center of the table, which I guessed could accommodate at least a hundred guests. The Elvin people clearly knew how to host a grand event.

Yet tonight, it was a small affair, but my nerves betrayed me all the same. At the far edge of the table, Kylram was already seated, as was Leiwen. They looked magnificent. Iridescent. Especially Leiwen, who donned a divine sapphire dress.

"Good evening," I greeted, taking my seat.

"To you as well, my dear," replied Kylram. Leiwen delicately lowered her cup.

"You look well-rested," she continued. "I hope your chambers are to your liking."

"I am. Thank you," I replied. "The room is lovely, and the shower..." I let my voice trail, and Leiwen's melodic laughter filled the air, bringing a smile to my face.

"It pleases me," said Leiwen. "Herod and I don't get to entertain as often these days." So, my earlier assumption was correct—the Elvin people *loved* grand events.

Drake pushed the chair in behind me and took the seat to my right. When the doors opened, I turned to see King Herod marching in, with Callix at his side, the pair engaged in silent conversation.

"I hope we didn't keep you waiting for long," Herod apologized as he took his place at the head of the table. He gently brought Leiwen's hand to his lips.

"We've only just arrived," said Leiwen, beaming at her husband.

My gaze found Callix, who settled into the seat across from me. He appeared as impeccable as ever, donning a white suit with blue accents that made his cerulean eyes glow beneath the light of the chandeliers.

"Ladies, you all look breathtaking," he said, but his eyes lingered on me. I shifted my focus toward the head of the table while Drake's hand found mine. I already had a hunch it would be a lengthy dinner and an even longer night.

The servants bustled around, and I welcomed the distraction as it allowed me to divert my attention from the energy emanating from both sides.

"The elders would like to meet you," said Herod, pulling me from my thoughts.

"Oh, yes." I peered at the young King, who smiled at my apparent distraction.

"We have come to an agreement. Abryas will fight alongside Upherya."

I beamed at the news.

"And Serfier," added Callix from across the table. I met his gaze, which briefly lingered. He smiled.

"However, we cannot offer our magic barriers."

I raised my brows.

"Why not?"

"It's not that simple. Our barriers are enforced by the magic of every single soul in this kingdom. By offering my men, we are already leaving our magic in a deficit. You must understand, if I allow the walls to fall, it won't just be Upherya that is lost to the dark, but my kingdom as well. I cannot allow that." I glanced at Drake, who nodded reluctantly.

"Your walls won't hold forever," I said.

"We hope they will hold long enough for the darkness to be stopped."

"We understand. The help of your men will offer us an advantage. Their magic can still be useful in the battle," said Drake.

"The North has me as well," I offered.

"No," Drake said, and I withdrew my hand from his.

"I wasn't *asking*. This is as much my battle as it is yours and theirs." His eyes darkened, but he said nothing. Instead, he took a sip from his cup with premeditated calmness, attempting to contain his fire.

I took a calming breath and tried to make him understand my reasoning. "How can I deliver the Fates' message? How can I become the instrument that ends this war while watching idly from the sidelines?"

Still, Drake said nothing, but I knew his mind raged. I tried slipping into his thoughts, but I was met by a dense wall of molten sulfur, and I immediately withdrew.

"Don't do that again," Drake growled beside me. I froze, casting a sidelong glance at him, but his eyes were fixed on the person across the table—Callix.

I stared at the Sea God, who merely smiled, completely

unfazed by Drake's warning. "I'm trying to be civil for her, but if you attempt to enter my mind again, I will end you." I braced my hands against my legs. *It was me, not Callix.*

Callix brought the cup to his lips, concealing his amusement.

"I'm sorry." I allowed my thoughts to drift into his mind.

"It's okay, darling. I'm not afraid of the big bad Dragon." His humor seeped through my thoughts.

I reached for Drake's hand and squeezed it in silent apology, even if he didn't know I was responsible for the intrusion. I shouldn't have done it in the first place; he had every right to keep his thoughts to himself.

"There's no need to taint this dinner table with my blood," Callix teased. I wanted to wring his neck. "I was only trying to offer you some insight to ease your worried mind." He paused and rested his arms against the table's edge. "She can defend herself. She's quite lethal with a weapon and without." I felt a surge of gratitude for Callix's faith in me.

Drake's eyes bore into the Water Lord. If he could turn him to ashes, he would.

"I assure you; my mind is perfectly at ease."

"I'm sure it is," Callix mused. I glanced at Leiwen across the table, who smiled brightly at me upon sensing my distress.

"I wish I had the skill to fight," she said.

"It's never too late to learn," I replied, attempting to shift the conversation. "Callix is an excellent teacher." After I uttered the words, I fell silent, knowing that was the last thing Drake likely wanted to hear.

Herod laughed and picked up his cup. "That would be an intriguing sight to see, but not one my old heart could endure." The youthful appearances of the royals often made me forget the ages of everyone around this table.

"It would be my pleasure if you ever decide to try," said Callix.

She glanced at her husband with a raise of her chin.

"I think I might." And though Herod shook his head in amusement, he didn't object.

"I will return to Upherya in four nights. Will your men be ready to join me then?" Drake asked, steering the conversation back to more critical matters.

"Yes, they are gathering as we speak."

"I will portal the soldiers to the North," said Callix.

"Thank you. That will save us time," Drake said, surprising me, and by the subtle arch of Callix's brows, it surprised him, too. Drake's small gesture was all it took to ease the tension in my body. He was making an effort.

"I hope we can count on you as well when the time comes. Dagasti's fleet will soon become a problem for us."

"Those ships will never cross the Fjord," Callix said, and no one questioned him. As long as he controlled the oceans, no ship would dare graze those waters.

"I will be saddened to see you go so soon," said Leiwen, glancing at me.

I smiled. "You could always join us." Though, from the look on Herod's face, he wasn't too pleased with the idea of having Leiwen anywhere near the battle.

"We will see them again, Lei, perhaps with triumphant and lighter spirits."

"May the old Gods hear you," Kylram offered.

"I believe they already have," I said, glancing at the young king. "The Moirai brought me here for a reason. Like your husband said, we will see each other again soon."

"I would ask that you extend my mother's invitation to remain here," Drake requested.

"You don't need to ask," Herod said warmly. "Kylram is welcome to stay for as long as she wishes."

"Thank you for your hospitality," Drake's mother graciously replied.

"Nonsense. It would be tediously leaden without you here," added Leiwen, and Kylram smiled, raising her cup.

"Let's toast," she proposed, and everyone raised their chalices.

"To new alliances," said Drake.

"To the Peace-bringer," added Herod, and a flush warmed my cheeks.

"To endings and new beginnings," Leiwen offered.

"To Destiny," Callix added, and everyone drank.

I wasn't sure if it was my immortality, but the lush, heavy liquid tasted divine, coating my tongue like a satin caress.

"Go easy on that," Callix warned through our mind connection. I ignored him and took another sip. He did the same, hiding his amusement.

"If you will excuse us, I think we will retire for the evening," said Drake, and anticipation ignited my skin.

Herod raised his cup to us and winked in Drake's direction. The gesture was so out of character for the Elvin King, yet smiles broke across the table—with one exception, I was sure, though I didn't feel brave enough to look.

Drake stood.

"Thank you for dinner. Have a good evening," I said as

Drake pulled out my chair. This time, when I braved a glance at Callix, the corner of his mouth lifted subtly, though his eyes darkened.

He was pretending.

The strings tugged at my heart as I turned away from the table.

13

TREADING FIRE

Drake intertwined his fingers with mine and gently kissed my hand as we strolled out of the dining hall.

"The longest meal of my existence," he sighed, guiding me into a shadowy corner. He pressed me against the wall, and time stood still as his lips traced a tantalizing path along my neck. He slid his thigh between mine, and I closed my eyes, tilting my head to grant him access to my neck. His fingers slipped under the fabric of my dress, exposing my shoulder as he teased and nipped, marking my skin.

"Drake..." I whispered, tangling my fingers in his hair. "Not here," I pleaded, my breath uneven. He groaned against my skin, his warm breath sending shivers down my spine.

I laughed as he bent slightly to sweep me off my feet. He carried me over his shoulder.

"Put me down!" I hit his back, and he slapped my behind.

"Behave, love. You're only attracting attention," he chided, as he swiftly navigated the corridors and whisked us into my room.

I squealed as he gently placed me on my feet and closed the door behind us. I started removing my heels, but his dark voice stopped me.

"Leave them," he said. Fire burned behind his eyes.

I closed the small space between us and pushed him against the closed doors. A seductive smile tugged at his lips as I ran my fingers over the firm contours of his chest. Sliding my hands under the soft material of his suit, I pushed it down, revealing the sculpted muscles of his shoulders and arms, and I grinned at the wicked glint in his eyes.

"What's on your mind?" I inquired, coaxing a broader grin from him.

"Nothing coherent, I assure you," he whispered, tracing a path down my cheek with his finger.

"I've missed you," I confessed, resting my hands on the planes of his chest. "I've missed this."

"Not possibly as much as I have." His lips brushed beneath the hollow of my ear.

"Want to bet?"

"Love, you know I am always up for a challenge." He glided his thumb over my bottom lip as his eyes sparkled with mischief. "So long as I don't have to spend another second away from you," he added, his smile broadening.

"That, we can both agree on," I said as my trembling fingers deftly unbuttoned his shirt. My eyes wandered over the smooth skin of his neck, chest, and abs, which tensed beneath my touch. I peeled his shirt away from his shoulders and he gently rested his hands on my hips. When the shirt slipped to the floor, I reached for his belt, but he stopped me, a roguish glint in his eyes.

"My turn." His eyes flashed with desire.

In one swift movement, he spun me, pressing my body tightly against his. He wrapped his strong arm around my waist, and I felt his excitement press against the small of my back. Instinctively, I melted into him.

With a gentle touch, he moved my hair to the side as his mouth found my ear.

"First, I'm going to take you hard and fast," he whispered, and the warmth of his breath sent shivers down my spine. "Then, I'm going to worship every inch of your body for the rest of the night." His lips and nose glided down my neck and shoulder while his skilled fingers undid the corset laces at the back of my dress.

I shivered at the coolness of the evening breeze slipping through the thin layer of my camisole. My dress pooled around my feet. Lifting the hem of my underbodice, Drake exposed my thighs before caressing the sensitive skin between my legs. I inhaled sharply, and he spun me, regarding me with his hunger-filled gaze, which settled on the swell of my breasts.

"Is it my turn now?" I stepped closer, pressing his back against the door.

"On your knees," he commanded, and those three words sent a jolt of anticipation through my body.

"Yes, my Lord," I said with a teasing smile. His eyes narrowed.

When he firmly gripped the back of my neck, I fell to my knees, prepared to worship at his feet.

"You want to play?" His intense gaze burned into mine,

and I nodded with hooded eyes as my hand moved toward his belt buckle.

But once again, his hand halted my movement.

"This time, I don't want you to be a complacent maiden, my love." He paused, searching my face while his fingers firmly secured my chin. "What I crave now is the skilled warrior. Fight me."

I stilled, absorbing his request.

"Fight you?" I repeated. His smile broadened.

"Yes. You wanted to play. If you want this..." He tightened the loosened belt buckle and donned a wicked smile. "Then, fight me." I rose my brows defiantly, recognizing his dark desires craved a release. I smiled. I knew I possessed the strength and skill to meet his challenge.

I gripped his thighs and rose to my full height, keeping my face a few inches from his. A coy smile played on my lips as I threaded my hand through his hair. I planted a sweet kiss at the corner of his lips.

"You should leave," I suggested, stepping away. I retrieved my dress from the floor and walked over to the bed. "I want to get some rest." I peered back at him, noting the mix of emotions flitting across his face—confusion, disbelief, and doubt.

"You can't be serious," he protested, taking deliberate, slow steps toward me.

I tilted my head.

"I did ask you to leave," I reminded him. He froze mid-step, and I detected a flicker of uncertainty in his eyes. He wasn't entirely sure if I was serious or playing the game. I needed to elicit a reaction.

"I'll seek my pleasures elsewhere," I declared, and he was upon me in the blink of an eye, pinning me to the bed. He wrapped his hand firmly around my neck, his desire and strength unmistakable.

"Love, I told you to play, not to taunt the darkness... and awaken the *beast*."

I closed my hand firmly around his wrist, and locked my legs around his torso. A sweet smile graced my lips as I twisted, shifting his body beneath mine. Surprise flickered in his eyes, and he responded with a grin as I pinned his arms above his head, fully aware of my limitations, and Drake's own power. If he desired to break free, he could easily do so. Yet, he made no such attempt.

"I can handle the monster," I teased, and Drake growled.

"You asked for it, and I hate to disappoint." In the blink of an eye, he released his hands from my grasp and seized my waist. He began to rise, but my legs remained securely braced around him. I shifted my weight, deftly landing on the floor, and rolled his body over mine. The moment I was free, I dashed to the other side of the room. However, I had underestimated his speed. He gripped my waist again, but my training with Callix had prepared me for this scenario. I drove my elbow against his ribs, using his arm as leverage, and executed a mid-air twist to land securely on his back, locking my arm around his neck in a vice grip.

"Is that all you've got?" I teased against his ear, but he slammed my back against the wall, and the force was enough to loosen my grip. Taking the opportunity, Drake spun me, pinning my body firmly against the wall with his own. I was trapped, and before I could make a move, his hands gripped the base of my neck.

A savage sound tore through the room as he ripped my camisole in two, exposing my skin to the cool air. His teeth sank into my shoulder, sending shivers down my spine, and he pressed his hips firmly into me.

He unbuckled his pants, and his fingers found my moist spot. I sucked in a sharp breath in anticipation of what would come next, and then, his full length entered me.

I cried out, and the sound echoed through the room. A deep grunt escaped from him. He had warned me he wouldn't be gentle, and at this point, I craved nothing less than his primal passion—his darkness. Moisture pooled between my legs as his hardness pounded me with relentless abandon, a savage and unbound connection. His thrusts were wild and unhinged as he sank into me, each one igniting an inferno within.

He gripped one hand firmly around my neck, while the other cupped one of my breasts, teasing and torturing me further. I surrendered to the wild rhythm of his thrusts, lost in the fire of our lust. The hand at my breast trailed over my stomach, leaving a path of fire in its wake until resting at the apex of my thighs. He cupped me, intensifying the sensations coursing through my body. Nothing but blinded pleasure existed, and his thrusts only served to drive us further into madness.

"You are so tight," he growled against my ear. "Can't you feel how perfectly we fit. You belong to me, love... Don't ever forget that." He rammed hard into me, knocking the breath from my body, and in the next thrust, he spilled his seed into me. Warmth filled my insides as his body rocked with the last tremors of his release. He rested his head between my shoulder blades, and his breath shallowed as the fire in him eased.

"I'm sorry."

"What are you apologizing for?" I asked, my words tinged with playful humor.

"Where do I begin?" He pressed a tender kiss on my neck and slowly shifted his weight off me.

I couldn't resist a playful quip. "Is there a list?"

But when I turned to meet his gaze, there was no amusement in his eyes, only torment. "Drake..." I said, reaching for his face. He gently seized my wrist to stop me.

Instead, he cradled my face, his eyes reflecting a multitude of emotions.

"I don't deserve you," he confessed, and I raised my eyebrows. "I'm ashamed of what I am, and of the suffering I bring upon you."

"Drake, please," I urged.

"No, let me speak," he insisted, tenderly stroking my shoulder. "I am a monster. While a part of me comprehends gentleness, love, and emotions—after all this time apart from you and denying myself your touch for so long—tenderness wasn't what the monster craved." He dropped his gaze briefly before meeting my eyes again. "This moment should have been about us—about you. Instead, I selfishly surrendered to the darkness. I claimed this reunion to satisfy the monster within me." He seemed to question our connection, but I shook my head. I had cherished every moment of it.

"Why are you always so hard on yourself?" I said gently. "Why do you constantly focus on the darkness, the negative?"

"Because I battle it every day. I know what I am, love. There's no denying it."

"You might know what you are," I said softly, "but I know *who* you are, Drake." I traced my fingers down his cheek.

"I am a selfish fool," he admitted, his voice remorseful, "and I will grovel at your feet for the rest of the night—for the rest of my life, if necessary—for not taking your pleasure into consideration. For being such a savage beast." He paused. "I'm sorry, love."

I smiled, shaking my head at his dramatics. "One of these days," I teased, "you're going to make me combust with desire."

His eyebrows shot up in question, and a hint of a smile teased the corners of his mouth.

"Should I keep my distance then?" he asked.

I allowed the remaining shards of my underbodice to cascade to the floor before wrapping my arms around his neck and encircling my legs around his waist. My breasts grazed against the inviting warmth of his chest, and he grunted.

"Not unless you want me to hunt you down," I whispered, and his darkness roared. "You promised me hard and fast, and you delivered," I added, nipping his neck. He inhaled sharply. "Shall we move on to the part where you worship my body for the rest of the night?" With that, he firmly gripped my behind and carried us towards the bed. Tossing me onto the soft sheets, he leaned back to take in the sight of my naked body bared before him.

I raised a foot, and he deftly removed one heel, tossing it

aside with a casual flick. He caressed my leg with fiery kisses, his stare unwavering. He teased my skin with tenderness, and after he removed the other heel, he planted a path of feather-light kisses up my inner leg.

"I'm pleased to know that he was right," he murmured, his lips and tongue igniting a blazing trail up my thighs.

"Who?" I whispered, my mind succumbed to desire.

"Callix." My eyes flew open to meet his. At the mere mention of his name, a chilling wave washed over me. I had no desire to think about the Water Lord, especially not now. "I'm immensely relieved to know that you can put up a fight," he continued, and I forced a smile. However, when his lips resumed their seductive assault up my thighs, my smile faded.

His hands parted my thighs, and his tongue caressed the apex.

"Besides my constant desire to know you were safe, I often found myself yearning for this," he confessed. He traced my moistness with his fingertips, and instinctively, I tried to close my legs, but his firm grasp kept me in place. "Don't move," he whispered. "You would be cruel to deny me this pleasure." His fingers entered me, and I drew in a sharp breath. We locked eyes, and I returned his smile.

"The same pleasure you denied me a few moments ago?" I teased. I made a playful attempt to close my legs again, but he responded with a grunt, forcing them apart.

"We have nothing but time, love. I will savor every moment, and then, you may have your way with me as you please." A mischievous grin tugged at the corner of his mouth before he lowered his head, replacing his fingers with his tongue.

My back arched against the sheets as he sealed his lips to my core, licking and teasing until I writhed with pleasure.

"Drake—please," I begged, overwhelmed by sensations. "I need you inside me..." His teeth gently clamped my most sensitive spot, and I reached between my legs, tangling my fingers in his hair. "I need—Drake..."

"I know what you need, love..." he whispered, and his warm breath caressed my wetness. "Trust me. Let go." His tongue resumed its merciless assault, and he dug his fingers deeper into my behind, anchoring me to his face. I gasped when he lifted me, expertly flipping us over.

His eyes darkened with desire as his hands firmly gripped my hips, guiding my movements. "That's it, love. Ride my face. Don't stop." His words were muffled against my core as his lips and tongue became my anchor. He devoured me like a starving man, and I dug my nails into his chest as waves of pleasure surged up my spine. My body surrendered to a primal, unrestrained rhythm as I continued to grind against his face, giving myself over to him completely.

"Drake." The strangled sound of his name escaped my lips as the universe exploded. Breathlessly, my body rode the last waves of my climax as he greedily savored every drop of my release.

I giggled, feeling slightly embarrassed but utterly satisfied. Drake took his time, but when he finally opened his eyes, they sparkled.

"That was..." I began.

"The best meal I've ever had," he interjected, completing my sentence.

"I was going to say *out of this world*." The corner of his mouth turned up.

"And that, love..." He gripped my hips and moved me over his chest until my backside rested against the firm bulge in his pants. "Is only the beginning."

My core clenched eagerly at his words as I pressed my lips to his. I could still taste the remnants of my release on his tongue.

"Is that what I taste like?" I whispered, brushing my lips over the side of his neck.

"Yes," he said. "Divine."

His expression darkened as he anticipated my intentions. I slid down over his sculpted abs, leaving a trail of feather-light kisses along the soft, barely visible stripe of hair that disappeared beneath his waistband.

My breasts rubbed against his hardness, and I couldn't help but smile at his sharp intake of breath.

"Do you like that?" I asked, locking my gaze with his.

"Yes," he replied, his voice thick with desire.

"Mmm, we'll see what we can do about that." I released the button on his pants before leaning back on my knees. I tugged down at the waistband, exposing his strong, muscular thighs. I stared at his rigid length. It was smooth and glistening and it pulsed as my fingers closed around it.

"Take it, love," he urged, sucking in a breath. He brought his hands behind his head. "Take it all." He thrust in encouragement as my lips closed around the glistening tip of his erection. His body felt unusually warm, hotter than usual, as I welcomed his throbbing hardness into my mouth.

My tongue swirled around him as my hand tightened on

his throbbing length. I enveloped him with my mouth, and his hips surged, driving his hard, thick cock deeper down my throat. I choked, and he momentarily eased, but only briefly before thrusting deeper into my mouth once more.

"Take it all, love... take it all," he pleaded, lost in the sensations. His hands moved to my head, holding me firmly in place as he continued thrusting. My throat burned as his length filled the hollowed space.

"Fuck," he groaned, his head falling back against the pillows as his hands released my hair. "If you keep doing that, it'll be over soon." He reached for my breasts, so they brushed against his arousal. "And I want to play."

The glint in his eyes promised more pleasure.

Cupping my perky breasts, he molded them around his throbbing hardness until he nestled between them. He moved in a teasing rhythm, building moisture at the tip of his cock.

"Do you see what you do to me? He rocked harder between my breasts. "I'm burning for you." His hips quickened their pace, and he closed his eyes as waves of pleasure washed over him.

His warmth erupted, spilling against my chest and coating both of us in his slick seed. He rose to his feet to retrieve the tattered remains of my camisole, and with it, he wiped away the remnants of his release from my breasts and carelessly tossed the ruined undergarment to the floor.

He stood before me, the taut muscles of his body on display as he removed his shoes and pants completely. With his sex sprung taught, he sauntered towards the bed, a devilish smile playing on his lips.

"Are you ready for more?" he inquired, crawling over my body.

Drake had not exaggerated when he vowed to worship my body for the rest of the night. By the time the sun rose, his skilled fingers and mouth were still discovering new and inventive ways to elicit pleasure from my body.

"Are you tired?" I asked. Drake's body lay beneath mine. He smiled.

"Not even a little. I haven't been this rested in a long time."

"That makes one of us," I added, resting my chin on his chest, our contentment palpable in the gentle light of dawn.

"You'll find you're not the only immortal who is required to keep regular sleeping habits," he mused, prompting my curiosity. "The wind people," he added. "They share a similar need."

"Drake..." I whispered against his chest, and he caressed my hair. "I'm sorry for not returning to you sooner."

"You're here now, love. That's what matters."

I asked about the situation in Upherya, aware of the gravity of their circumstances.

"Not good," he admitted. "I fear, even with Herod's help, it might not be enough to stop Dagasti."

I lifted my head to look at him.

"It must be. The Fates said we had to unite, and that's what we are doing." I insisted, but he shook his head.

"You haven't seen what I have. Two clans swept away by the darkness as if they were nothing, leaving a realm completely devastated."

"It will be different this time," I assured him, and his eyes softened. He pulled me in, brushing his lips over mine.

"I pray to the Fates that it is. I don't know if Euros can handle the loss of the North."

"Euros?" I inquired, and Drake smiled.

"You'll have the chance to meet the clan leaders of Upherya soon. I think you'll like Link and Phoenix. They are... light of spirit." Drake said, and a hint of an inside joke glinted in his smile. "Euros, however, is constantly brooding, but there's a lot of responsibility resting on his shoulders."

"Is that why he's your friend? Because you're both equally dark, heavy, and ominous?" I teased. Drake tilted his head.

"No, love. No one will ever be as dark as I am." His words held a solemn truth, and he shifted from underneath me.

"Do you have to leave?"

"I don't have to, love, but I must." He slipped on his shirt and suit. "Herod wants to discuss our strategy plans, and I must oversee the legions." I wrapped a sheet around my body, moving closer to him.

"When do I get to meet the elders?"

"I'll ask Herod. In the meantime, you could spend time with Leiwen. She seems to have taken a liking to you. I'm sure she or my mother can offer you a tour." His lips tightened, conveying what he couldn't put into words—anyone but Callix...

"Don't worry about me. I'll be okay." I reassured him, rising on my toes to plant a kiss on his cheek. He lifted me off the ground and claimed my lips with his own.

"I will see you this evening." He promised, reluctantly peeling himself away. He hesitated by the doors, and I knew what he would say next.

"Don't go to him." His voice wavered between a plea and a command.

"Drake," I said, though his eyes pleaded with me.

"I'm trying..." He paused. "But I will let my soul burn before I ever let him come between us."

"Don't say that. He's my friend," I said, and Drake closed his eyes for a moment, a clear effort to collect himself.

When they reopened, his gaze was somewhere dark and distant. "Very well. I'll see you this evening." He closed the door behind him.

I couldn't begin to fathom what was going on inside his mind, especially as I couldn't access his thoughts without him sensing my intrusion.

THE CASTLE WAS EVEN MORE magnificent in the morning light, yet I couldn't shake the feeling of being out of place. The bustling halls were filled with too many people—Elvin court members in their impeccable garments and servants in more modest but pristine attire.

Drake had warned me to stay away from Callix, and I understood his reasons. To an extent. After all, he wasn't entirely wrong. Callix desired me, but he would never act against my will. Yes, he had been forward; yes, he had taken liberties, but I was equally responsible for allowing it. Encouraging it. I was aware of the strain between us, the unspoken truths, and against my better judgment, I craved the ease of his friendship—his company.

Standing at the top of the staircase leading to the gardens, I closed my eyes and searched for any sign of the Water Lord.

After a few futile minutes, I gave up. The castle was a cacophony of noise, and though my ears were keen, I lacked the skill of navigating the sea of voices and sounds. With resignation, I descended the stairs and followed the soothing sound of cascading water from the fountains.

As I rounded the overgrown hedges, I jumped when I heard a noise.

"Belynda."

Surrounded by flowers, the young Queen stood before a canvas, a paintbrush poised in her grip. She giggled, and I smiled.

"I didn't mean to startle you," said Leiwen. "I'm sorry. Come. Sit right there. You'll be a marvelous addition to my painting."

I raised an eyebrow, unsure if I was the right muse, but I complied, nonetheless. Lifting my flowing dress, I sat on the moss-covered rock at the center of her floral masterpiece.

"Perfect," she said, returning her attention to the canvas. "Where is your shining prince?"

"He had matters to attend to with Herod—the King, I mean." Leiwen's laughter was melodious.

"You can call him Herod, you know. You've made quite an impression on him. Whatever you shared—or didn't share— made all the difference, and I'm glad of it. He's been too stubborn for too long. It was about time someone stood up to him."

"I... I didn't mean to."

"No need to apologize or explain. Truly. You've changed Herod's mind, and not even I have been able to. I knew you and I would be great friends the second I met you." She smiled warmly, and I returned the gesture.

"Thank you for your kindness and your friendship. It can get quite lonely being so far away from my family, my home." As I uttered the words, the truth of how much I missed them dawned. Yet now I had the power to open portals again, I could return home—or at least visit—to reassure them of my well-being. However, exposing the human world might not be the wisest choice, with the war and darkness looming.

"I understand. Even in a castle teeming with life, one can feel lonely," Leiwen empathized. "But you're not alone. You have the God of the Ocean watching over you, and your prince, who seems very protective of you."

I opened my mouth at the mention of Callix but stopped. Leiwen laughed, clearly perceiving my unspoken thoughts.

"I wouldn't be alive if it weren't for Callix's intervention," I admitted, "and I suppose Drake can be a little overprotective. Life hasn't been kind to him. We've faced many trials to be together, so it's understandable."

"Have you told him that you love him, too?" Leiwen's question caught me off guard as she smiled from behind her canvas. Her eyes met mine.

"Drake knows that I love him," I replied, and my confusion must have shown on my face. Leiwen shook her head slowly.

"I was referring to the Water Lord."

I froze, my mind racing, until finally, I found my voice. "No... Callix is a friend."

Leiwen dipped her brush into her colors and met my eyes again.

"Beautiful child, I have walked this world for centuries,

and I recognize the spark of love when I see it." She paused, glancing briefly at me. "But perhaps *you* are not prepared to see it yet."

I stared at Leiwen, and for a moment, I wondered if I could confide in her, and if she was the friend I desperately needed to listen to my fears without judgement.

"The truth is I care for him," I confessed in a whisper. The stroke of her brush paused mid-air, and she shifted her attention to me. "But I love Drake. We are destined to be together, and I cannot live without him."

As I spoke those words, I knew they were the truth.

Leiwen dipped her brush in the colors before meeting my eyes again.

"There is no doubt about your love and devotion for the Fire Prince. In fact, your love story could become the stuff of legends. However, it's not impossible to love two people at once."

"It is for me," I said. "I am bound to Drake by more than just feelings, desire, and words. We are bound by Isabel's sacrifice. I was reborn through her penance—a sacrifice made in the name of love. I will love him until the end of days."

Leiwen's eyes softened, and she smiled gently. "Are you saying that the Water Lord has no place in your heart? Is it entirely impossible for you to love him as well?"

I hesitated, torn by my conflicting emotions. "I would be lying to myself if I said I did not care for him. But love? It doesn't seem possible. Not when my destiny is intertwined with Drake. I love Drake. I choose Drake."

"Wasn't it you who said that choice is but an illusion?" Leiwen questioned, surprising me once again.

"I was referring to our free will. We have no choice when the Fates meddle in our destiny."

"Wouldn't you say the Fates have meddled enough this time?" Leiwen tilted her head, and her gaze was penetrating. "Perhaps putting the Water Lord in your path is all part of their grand plan."

I shook my head, resisting the thought. "That's not how things work. I would never choose to be separated from Drake."

A heavy weight settled in my chest as I contemplated the idea that failing to change the unforeseeable future might lead to his suffering.

"Ahh. There's that word again. *Choice.*" Leiwen's lips curled into a smile. "What if you never had to choose? What if you didn't have to make that decision? It's not uncommon for people to share their affections, you know."

My cheeks flushed at her audacious words.

"That, I'm afraid, is not an option for me," I said, unable to imagine a world where I could love both, not without it ending in conflict.

"All I suggest is that you learn to listen to your heart. Denying your truest feelings rarely leads to happiness," Leiwen advised as she resumed her painting. "And if you ever need someone to talk to, I'm always here to listen."

"Thank you," I said, grateful not only for her offer of friendship but her guidance too. Even if it was advice I couldn't follow.

"That's it. It's perfect now," she said, wiping her hands on the cloth hanging at the waistband of her dress. "Come see for yourself."

I rose after what felt like hours and peered at the canvas, immediately captivated by the sight of the girl in the portrait.

Her face was divine, her beauty immortalized in perfect strokes of paint. Nature swirled around her like a living force. It was me, but Leiwen had captured much more than my features. She had painted my very essence.

"It's... beautiful," I murmured.

"It's yours," she said, gently removing the painting from the easel.

"No, I couldn't."

"You must," she insisted, extending the painting toward me. "It's my gift to you."

I glanced at the beautiful girl in the painting once more and smiled, reaching out to accept it.

"Thank you," I said sincerely. "I've never had anyone paint me a portrait." Such a gesture was untypical in the human world.

"Hopefully, it's the first of many," replied Leiwen as we began strolling through the maze.

"Have you given any thought to the training?" I asked, remembering her interest from last night's dinner. As I was beginning to understand the young Queen, I was surprised she hadn't pursued it sooner.

"Honestly, I'm a little scared to try," she admitted. "I've always been good at diplomacy. The arts come naturally to me, but wars and battles scare me terribly."

I took her hand.

"I was once a mortal human girl in an immortal world who had to face death and be reborn. If I could do it, so can you," I encouraged with a smile. "You are strong. If I could face Callix's wrath, so can you, and believe me, it will be worth it."

"Okay, you've convinced me," said Leiwen. I laughed, knowing I had done little more than support what she already felt inside.

"Will the King approve?" I asked, lacing my arm with hers. She responded with a mischievous smile.

"Herod doesn't have to know," she replied. "And when he does, it will be too late to stop me."

I marveled at Leiwen's spirit. Not only was she strong, but she was also determined.

"Now, where do we find your Water Lord?" I couldn't help but notice the use of *your*, as if Callix belonged to me somehow.

"I'm afraid I can't help you there," I replied as we reached the stairs leading out of the gardens. "He seems to have vanished."

"Who has vanished?" The voice sent a shiver through me. Leiwen and I turned to those cerulean eyes, where Callix regarded us, standing beside the fountain.

I glanced at Leiwen, momentarily lost for words. Our earlier conversation felt like it loomed between us.

"Just the person we had set out to search for," Leiwen said, gracefully breaking our strange re-encounter.

"I see." Callix's eyes moved between the two of us before settling on me. "And how may I be of assistance?"

"I wanted to see if your offer to train me still stands," Leiwen said, and the corner of Callix's mouth twisted into a smile.

"Of course, it does," he replied, his gaze shifting to me. "Will you be joining us?"

My heart pounded in my chest.

"Yes, she will," answered Leiwen, and her eyes met mine. "Won't you?" I glanced between her and Callix, unable to resist the Queen's request.

"I will join you," I said, unable to suppress my excitement. "But we'll need to change, and I'm afraid my wardrobe has nothing suitable for the occasion."

"I have just the thing," Leiwen said, ascending the stairs. She paused midway and then turned back to me. "Stay and enjoy the gardens, seeing as I've kept you all morning. I'll make sure your wardrobe is adjusted, and we'll meet later this afternoon," she declared with unwavering determination. "Unless you're needed elsewhere, my Lord?" she asked Callix, who shook his head.

"This afternoon sounds perfect." He graced us both with a heart-stopping smile.

"I'll see you then." Leiwen disappeared up the steps and through the castle doors, leaving me alone with the Water Lord.

I attempted to keep my distance, but Callix stepped closer, overwhelming like always. Intoxicating my very being.

"What have you got there?" he asked, glancing at the painting, which I had momentarily forgotten was in my hands.

"Oh, it's nothing," I replied, suddenly self-conscious.

"May I see it then?" he asked. He reached for it, and when I glanced briefly into his eyes, Leiwen's words pierced my soul. *Have you told him you love him...?*

I turned the painting towards him as a distraction from my

thoughts, and it seemed to work, for his eyes only focused on the canvas.

"Leiwen painted it," I said, trying to sense his reaction.

"I didn't know the queen was so skilled with a brush."

"Neither did I, honestly."

"You look beautiful," he said, surprising me. Our eyes locked, and neither of us managed to look away. "But the painting does you no justice."

My breath caught in my throat, but when I peered back at the painting, our connection broke. I took a step back.

"I should go and get ready." I stammered, attempting to escape. However, my plan failed. He closed the distance between us, and I looked up at him as his hand rose to stroke my cheek before resting on the canvas.

"May I have it?" he asked, and confusion furrowed my brows.

"Why?"

"I think it's only fair I get to keep this small part of you since he gets to have it all," Callix said, his expression devoid of amusement.

"Callix..."

"Is it much to ask for?" he inquired, tilting his head. His eyes conveyed far more.

"No. It isn't. I just..." I struggled to find the words.

"Giving me this portrait doesn't violate any rules." He assured me.

"I know."

"Then it's settled." He pulled the canvas from my hands and looked at it again with a smile.

I pulled away and made for the stairs before he could stop me. "I'll see you later."

"I'm looking forward to it!" he called. "Oh, and darling! The canvas... it wasn't enough of a distraction."

Heat flooded my cheeks, angry and embarrassed for failing —again—to shield my thoughts from him. I turned, leaving him at the foot of the stairs, though I felt his gaze burning into me.

I was in danger. I had believed that with Drake by my side, any lingering thoughts of Callix would vanished. I was wrong. I was drowning, and I didn't know how to reach the surface.

LEIWEN KEPT HER PROMISE. The wardrobe had been modified to include riding and training clothes, so I slipped into a pair of black leather pants and a matching top. The outfit clung to me like a second skin, but it allowed for easy movement. The wrist cuffs were silver, intricately engraved to match the details on the buttons of the vest.

I pinned my hair up, and after enjoying lunch, served in my chambers at Leiwen's request, a creeping thrill of anxiety dawned on me. I wasn't sure why; I had never experienced anything quite like it before.

Leiwen waited near the stables. As I approached, I couldn't help but stare at her back, surprised that, despite her lack of training, she looked every bit the warrior. With her hair pulled up into a tight ponytail, her pointy ears were visible.

"There you are," she greeted, assessing my attire. "I have a feeling tonight is going to be interesting." I didn't need to read her mind to understand why she said it. As if I needed *more* trouble.

"Are you ladies looking for trouble?" Callix said from behind me. I spun, startled, and narrowed my eyes at him.

"Will you please behave?" I pleaded.

He smiled and winked at Leiwen.

"What will I get in return?" My heart sped up at his audacity, recalling the last time we had struck a bargain.

"You already got the portrait, Callix. What more could you ask of me? Please."

Leiwen appeared entirely unaware of our silent exchange.

"I don't want you to shut me out," he said, surprising me. *"You shouldn't keep your distance just because he asks you to."*

"I wasn't planning on shutting you out. Despite what you and Drake might think, I can make my own decisions." The corner of his mouth shifted.

"I'm happy to learn that you're not easily persuaded." He retorted. *"I'll behave."*

"Will we train today or will the two of you continue to torture me with the silent monologue?" asked Leiwen. My mouth dropped, and I stared at Callix, who grinned.

"You picked up on that?" Callix asked. I didn't dare speak.

"My youth always makes people forget how long I've lived," said Leiwen, a smile in her eyes. "You might fool them all, but not me." She looked at me before briefly glancing at Callix, who seemed to enjoy the Queen's insight far too much for my liking.

"After you," said Callix. We entered a fenced camp, which appeared to be the Elvin-designated training space. The moment I spotted the soldiers, I froze. In the distance, I saw Drake, and it didn't take him long to find me. His demeanor shifted, first upon noticing my attire and then as his gaze moved past me. He straightened and furrowed his brows as he approached.

I longed to delve into his thoughts, to know what he was thinking, but I couldn't bring myself to pry. I wouldn't.

"Drake, I'm glad you're around," said Leiwen, intercepting his approach. His gaze shifted with the realization that I wasn't here alone with Callix. "Are you ready to see me make a fool of myself?" asked Leiwen, using her wit to defuse the tension.

"Leiwen," he said curtly in greeting. "If Belynda's skills are any indication, you're in good hands." His eyes darkened, and I knew he was remembering our evening interlude.

"Please, spare me the details." Callix's voice cut through my thoughts, and his presence suddenly loomed beside me. I attempted to raise my mental walls, and although they were no use against him, I knew he would not intrude this time.

"Would you care to join us?" asked Callix, and for a moment, I froze. Having the two of them training together seemed like a recipe for disaster.

"Later, perhaps," said Drake, stepping closer to me. He slipped a hand to the small of my back and pulled me toward him. He leaned down.

"Could you possibly be any more tempting?" His breath warmed my cheek, and his lips brushed the corner of my mouth. A shudder trickled down my spine as I glanced up at the silver in his eyes. "I'm looking forward to this evening," he added, though it felt like an attempt to stake his claim. He didn't need to. I was already his. Body and soul. Yet, in my short adult years, I had come to understand that men—especially immortal men—were possessive jealous creatures.

Drake returned to the soldiers, while Callix and Leiwen stood a few yards away. Callix demonstrated combat stances. I joined them, taking a seat on one of the barrels by the arena.

I watched the entire time Callix trained Leiwen. His eyes shifted to me often, but he kept his distance. The young Queen was a fast learner, but this was only the beginning. Soon, the Water Lord would unleash his wrath, and that... *that* would mark the beginning of her real training. I smiled, recalling the many times I went to bed hating Callix for his mercilessness. I had often called him cruel back then. His gaze shifted to me, but like the many other times, his face remained devoid of emotion.

"You have a natural talent for blocking," Callix said. "Just shift your weight." He demonstrated the movement. "Like this."

Leiwen mimicked his stance, and I watched, eager to join them.

"Belynda, why don't you take my place?" Callix suggested, and I immediately rose and crossed to their side. I assumed Callix's position before Leiwen.

"Show me simple attack and block moves," he ordered, and I complied. Slowly, I attacked while Leiwen attempted to predict and block my moves.

"Faster," Callix called. By the time the sun set, Leiwen was much lighter on her feet. Callix was right; she showed great aptitude for blocking, more than I ever had when I first started.

"I think that's enough for today," said Callix. "Perhaps Herod might like to join us tomorrow?"

Leiwen glanced at me, then at Callix.

"Perhaps we can keep this between us for the time being?"

Callix glanced between us in understanding.

"Sure."

Leiwen smiled. "I will see you at dinner," she said before leaving us.

"I should probably go, too." But I couldn't move from my spot.

"One match?" Callix asked. "I know you want to."

"I do," I admitted. "But perhaps I shouldn't." I glanced at Drake and the golden regiments in the distance.

"I thought you said you were capable of making your own decisions," taunted Callix, strolling towards me. "What are you afraid of?"

His taunt worked, and I marched to him, positioning myself for combat.

"Weapons?" I asked, and he smiled.

"Your choice, but perhaps it is best, seeming as you want me to behave."

At his response, I summoned two water swords and Callix a spear. He was right; the less contact we had, the safer it was. His attack came without warning, and with one strike, his spear shattered one of my swords.

"You're not concentrating," he noted. I narrowed my eyes at him. "This is your space. Forget everything else."

I regenerated the tip of my sword.

This time, when his assault came, I was ready. Our weapons clashed, and the echo of glass rang like metal bells around the arena. I defended his blows with precision, moving weightlessly through the air as I dodged the lethal ends of his spear. I even managed to nick a button off his shirt, earning a narrowed gaze from the Water Lord. His chaos came at me without reservations, his strikes and blows steady and unyielding. I lost my footing, and he broke both of my swords. Before I knew it, he twisted and pinned my back to him, pressing a small icy dagger against my throat.

Applause erupted behind us, and I turned to find Drake. Callix released me.

"Next time, perhaps you'd like to take on someone your own size," said Drake, his eyes locked firmly on Callix. "It would certainly even the odds."

Callix raised his brows as he smiled. Nothing good would come out of his mouth. "If you're trying to prove something, then I'm up for the challenge," said the Water Lord. "But we both know who the better fighter is."

"I have nothing to prove to you, though perhaps we should settle your disillusions once and for all." Drake stepped into the arena.

"No," I snapped, standing between them. "Will you both stop acting like children?"

They glanced at me like I'd gone insane, but I was done with the pair of them. I wouldn't stand by as they shredded each other to pieces. I stomped from the camp, not daring to look back.

. . .

ON THE BALCONY, I watched the starry night descend over the Elvin kingdom. My crimson-red dress flowed in the breeze. I dreaded to think of how another dinner between Drake and Callix would go, and I felt no desire to move from my spot. However, I understood what my absence would imply, especially when Herod and Leiwen had been so welcoming.

A soft knock sounded at my door. I sighed and strolled back into the chamber, opening the door to find Drake leaning casually against the wall.

"Are you ready?" His smile grew as his eyes roamed my body. "You look... *breathtaking*." He reached for me, but I stopped him.

"I don't want to do this," I said, and his amusement dissipated.

"Refusing the dinner invitation will not look well."

"I don't care. I refuse to be in whatever this pissing contest between you and Callix is."

Drake's roar of laughter filled my chamber.

"You have a way with words, love," he said. However, I found no humor, and my face showed just that. "Nothing happened. I didn't kill him, and I don't intend to do so over dinner, so I think it is safe for us to join them." He still failed to understand my feelings.

"Drake, we have a bigger war coming our way. This petty feud between the two of you must come to an end," I argued.

"You forget, there is plenty of room in a battlefield for the both of us. We will never cross paths."

"You're missing the point."

"We don't have to agree on everything, love," he countered. He could be so exasperating.

"This is important, Drake. We're all on the same side here. It's about time you started acting more like allies and less like enemies."

His brows shot up, and though it looked like he had more to say on the matter, he refrained from doing so.

"I promise to remain civil," he said, "*If* you join me for dinner."

I searched his shadowed expression, and I knew I couldn't remain angry forever. I extended my hand, and he took it, bringing it to his lips.

14

A RISING STAR

NOT LONG AGO, DRAKE HAD KEPT A VITAL PROMISE AT my request. However, a promise to remain civil appeared too much to ask of the dragon prince.

The second we sat at the dinner table, tensions rose.

Drake was displeased about lying to Herod about the queen's secret training, but I managed to convince him it wasn't our secret to tell. He was honor-bound, yet he didn't fight me when I asked him not to speak of it. However, when Herod asked lovely Leiwen how she had spent her day, Drake stiffened beside me. Callix, however, had no qualms about keeping Leiwen's secret from the King.

"I did a little bit of painting," said Leiwen, and I panicked, realizing if she said I was her muse, Drake would demand to see it.

"She is very talented. She captured the gardens to perfection." I glanced at Leiwen, my eyes forming a silent *please*. Surprise flickered in her eyes, but as did understanding.

The Water Lord brought the chalice to his lips to conceal his smile. I hated myself for lying like this; Drake would never understand or approve, even if it meant nothing.

The servants bustled, refilling cups and exchanging trays, allowing the energies to shift.

"Drake said I will get to meet the elders tomorrow?" I asked, looking at the young King.

"Yes. They are eager to meet you." I smiled and brought the fork to my mouth. The truth was I was anxious. I didn't have to be. I already had Herod's support, and that was all that mattered. And yet, I still worried about their interest in meeting me. What could they possibly want to know that Herod had not already conveyed in private?

"*I promise you. The second you meet them; all your worries will disappear.*" Callix's silent words slipped into my thoughts, and I glanced up, startled, finding his eyes directly on me. It was brief, so brief, yet in those seconds, my chest ached. I lowered my gaze, then peered at Drake by my side, who smiled. He covered my hand with his.

"It will be okay. I will be there," said Drake. Even though he couldn't read my thoughts, he knew me well enough to perceive my worry.

"Will you and Herod still host the Winter Solstice ball?" Kylram asked Leiwen from my other side, and I was thankful for the shift in conversation.

"We understand it's terrible timing with the North's eminent battle on the horizon, but Herod and I think keeping traditions in the face of darkness is also important. Especially in times like this. The solstices have always been a time to unite and set aside our differences."

"I agree," said Callix, surprising me. "Win or lose, the people need something other than bloodshed and devastation to look forward to."

"It's settled then," Herod said. He placed his cup on the table. "We will open our gates for the Winter solstice, as is our tradition."

"I would be happy to help with the preparations." Kylram offered, and Leiwen smiled.

"Thank you. I will take you up on that offer."

Everyone enjoyed dessert, but I couldn't quite agree with their decision. What was more, I was surprised Callix had agreed to it. War and destruction were upon us. So many risked facing death.

I strengthened my walls to keep my thoughts to myself, though I couldn't be sure if it worked. Callix's expression remained unchanged. The thought that I disagreed with him didn't bring about any silent remarks.

"If you don't mind, I will leave you. I must return to Serfier," said Callix suddenly. My heart hammered in my chest. *Why was he leaving?* The oddest sensation seized me, as if I were to be parted with a piece of myself.

"And the troops?" asked Drake.

"I will be back in a day to allow them passage."

"I could open the portal as well," I said, and the second the words left my mouth, I hated myself for speaking. Callix's expression hardened, but I couldn't decipher his thoughts. Was he upset with me for suggesting I take his place? It had not been my intention; I only wanted to help.

"Then we will not need you after all." Drake directed his gaze to Callix.

"I said I will be here in one day, and I will be." He stood and wiped his mouth with the napkin before tossing it at the table. "I don't care who opens the portal. I will be joining you in the North, regardless." With a forced smile, he shifted his gaze towards the head of the table. "Thank you for dinner."

He began strolling away.

"Callix. What about Leiwen's training? Why are you leaving?" My mind reached for him before he was gone.

"Training can wait."

"Callix..."

"Darling, I cannot submit myself to another night..." His voice trailed in my mind. *"I need to breathe."*

After that, there was nothing but silence. That strange, tethered feeling I felt when he was near had evaporated. He was far from my reach.

"Is everything alright?" asked Drake from my side, bringing me out of my head.

"Yes. Of course. I'm fine."

The look on his face showed he didn't quite believe me.

"Are you ready to go?" he asked, and I nodded.

His chair scraped against the floor as he stood and offered me his hand. "We will retire as well," said Drake.

"Thank you for dinner." I offered, and Leiwen, Herod, and Kylram bid us good night.

Drake held my hand as we walked the corridors, and though he said nothing, I knew a lot was on his mind.

"What is it?" I asked.

"You tell me," he said, lacing his fingers through mine. "I

know you said nothing has changed, but I can't help sense that they have." He stopped and turned to face me. "What aren't you telling me, love?" Drake's eyes pierced mine, and my heart sped up.

"I... I lied." The words left my lips before I could stop them. His forehead creased, and his eyes narrowed, awaiting my explanation. "Yesterday, at the dinner table. It was me, not Callix, who attempted to slip into your mind." I met his eyes, trying to sense his reaction. His expression gave nothing away.

"I see. So you share Callix's gift?" I said nothing. "Is there anything else I should know?"

I wanted to say no, but my conscience refused. I glanced down at my hand and braced myself.

"When you asked about Callix, when you questioned if something had changed..." My words trailed off. I spared a glance at him, but the fire burning in his eyes made me recoil. "The truth is I care for him."

"Do you love him?" The harshness of his tone made me step back.

"No," I responded quickly, though the hammering of my heart betrayed me. "I don't know."

Yet the fact I even entertained the possibility made the feeling somehow more real.

Drake leaned away from me. Dark clouds stirred around him as he flexed his fingers in a futile attempt to regain control.

"Have you?"

"No. Never." He didn't have to finish his sentence for me to understand him. "I love you, Drake. *You* are my life," I said, desperately trying to reach him. The darkness in his eyes made me pause.

"But that's not enough, is it?" I froze at the bitterness in his voice.

"Yes, it is," I whispered. "I cannot live without you." The swirls of darkness danced around him.

"But you cannot live without him either." Drake's voice lowered, and he stepped closer. For a moment, I was scared. His fingers paused a breath from my skin, his eyes the darkest pools of despair. I could not bring myself to deny his words, for I was sure there was a part of me that would never be able to let go of Callix.

Drake dropped his hand and stepped away from me before striding in the opposite direction down the hall.

"Drake!" I called, but I didn't dare follow.

It wasn't the time. So, I did the only thing that felt right... I let him go.

My bed was cold and empty, and I battled the impulse to go and find Drake, yet every time I remembered his pained expression, I hated myself for causing it. Tomorrow, I would find him. I would make him understand that he was more important, despite whatever Callix meant to me. I would convince him that I would fight for us because I chose him. Always him.

I watched the sunrise from the gardens, ready to face the day and the elders without Drake.

Kylram paused at the top of the garden stairs but descended when spotting me amongst the flowers.

"Couldn't sleep?" she asked, taking the seat beside me on the bench.

"No. Not much, you?"

"I don't rest much these days. I worry too much about the war and our kingdom. My son." At her last admission, my chest tightened.

"I worry about your son too," I admitted. "But also, I fear what is required of me to win this war and what it will mean if I fail. The costs." She cradled my hands in her lap and turned to me.

"You will *not* fail." She spoke with such deliverance that I almost believed her. "My son will never allow you to."

I dropped my gaze.

"I don't think I'm his favorite person at the moment," I admitted. Her son already hated me; I couldn't bear Kylram's indifference, too.

"I find that hard to believe," she said. "I know my son. He loves fiercely. He is loyal. His heart will burn bright for you for as long as you both breathe." I peered up at the woman's words, praying to the gods that he would forgive me so I could prove how much I loved him. My admission was only an attempt to be true to myself —to him, to allow him into my deepest feelings and fears. I knew that Drake learning that I cared for Callix wasn't something he would take lightly, but I wanted nothing but honesty between us.

"I hope you're right because I cannot live without him," I said, and tears clouded my vision. I blinked a couple of times, forcing them down.

"Whatever has come between you two, it will resolve itself. I promise. Just give him time." Her kindness surprised me.

"Thank you."

"Anytime, child. Anytime." She lifted my chin to meet her eyes. "I will never forget that it was you who saved my son. It was you who brought him back."

"Sometimes I question if it was the other way around, if it was him who saved me," I admitted, recalling the days when I was lost in the human world, questioning my life and sanity. Yes, I had freed him, but he had saved me in return.

I rose to my feet, wiping my hands on my pants.

"I should go. I am meeting with the elders."

"You'll be alright."

I forced a smile and nodded.

"Thank you," I said before returning to the castle.

Never in my life had I ridden a horse, but I wasn't about to back down from a challenge. Herod mounted his steed, and I did just the same.

"Have you ridden before?" Herod asked, noting my grimace.

"I would be lying if I said I had." The young King laughed, and it was as if nature itself laughed with him. Contagious.

"Had you said sooner, I would have arranged for the carriage."

"Now you tell me," I said, and his amusement only grew.

"I will keep it in mind for the future." Herod took off in a slow march, and I imitated his movements, but I had never been so frightened. Horses were magnificent beasts, but to be appreciated from afar, not on their backs. As luck would have it, the elder's temple was close; however, I almost collapsed as I dismounted. My legs felt like jello.

"Are you ready?" asked Herod as I followed him into the high dome. Trees surrounded it, resembling carved stone. Vines ran over the floors, like veins under the skin of white marble, and I felt the presence of Earth—its heartbeat.

The second we entered the meeting hall, I froze. Drake stood there, surprising me. After last night, I had not thought he would still come. But there he was, and I relaxed slightly in his presence. I allowed my mind to reach his, and I whispered a silent *"Thank you."*

I prayed my small intrusion would not spark his fire. However, he showed no response, except for the brief shift in his gaze, landing on me for only a second. He returned his attention to the elder before him, who was deep in conversation.

I realized at once what Callix meant when he promised I would no longer worry once I met them. I didn't think it was possible, but somehow, the elders were even younger than the Elvin people. They were *children*. I knew it was an illusion, of course. In reality, they were old—much older than I could ever imagine—but it made all the difference. I was no longer intimidated or frightened by their presence.

"Cinnaess." One of the elders approached me. I fought to recall the meaning of that word. It was what Herod had called me, a word from the old tongue. *Peace-bringer.* "I am Cirdan, and these are my brothers: Calon, Melian, Ardreth, Virion, and Zaos."

The six young faces stared at me. How could I possibly remember their names?

"I'm afraid it will take me a while to remember all of your names," I confessed, and smiles broke around the room.

"We are the ones honored to know your name," said the elder closest to me.

"Thank you for having me," I said, "and for choosing to join Upherya."

"Our King was very convincing but refused to share how you persuaded him," said the elder, who stood by Drake. I glanced at Herod. "Touched by the Fates... yes, we can see that. There is light in you, but how exactly will you stop the darkness?"

This time, the room fell silent.

"The Fates are never direct or open about their plans, but they spoke of the threads of possibilities. They said I would be able to navigate the delicate balance of time. That I would possess what was necessary to end the darkness."

They stared at each other as if I had spoken of a folktale.

"The songs of the first war speak of ending the darkness with light, but never were the threads of possibility mentioned," he responded.

"A short while ago, I was only a human, living in the mortal world."

"A blood witch," one of them corrected.

"A girl in the dark about your world, about magic, and about the endless possibilities. Yet here I stand, chosen by the Fates." I paused and briefly glanced at Drake, who now watched me. "I cannot predict how the future will unfold. All I know is that I am here because the Moirai believes it is my destiny to end the darkness. I was presented with immortality and the knowledge and strength to travel the threads of possibilities. I do not question their wisdom, but I choose to follow their path if it means we will win this war."

"We do not question the validity of your connection to the Moirai and their divine intervention. We merely believe you will need more than your strength to touch the strings of possibilities."

"What more would I need?" I asked, glancing at Herod.

"If, in fact, that is the path to take, you will need the sands of time and our help to find them." The elder at my side explained. I froze. The Fates had failed to mention that. Then again, they offered up very little.

"How do you find it?" They exchanged glances and shook their heads.

"The sands are a precious relic, lost in time and space itself. We would have to start by searching our archives and manuscripts for any sign that could lead us to one of the sacred locations."

"Then you must get to work," I said confidently. If finding the sands was so impossible, I wondered how Callix had managed to get his hands on them back then. Perhaps he could point us in the right direction.

"We will do everything we can to find them," Herod reassured as he took me about the room to show me the relics displayed around the temple.

"Thank you," I said, glancing at Drake. "For keeping what I shared to yourself."

"I gave you my word."

"I know, but your loyalty lies with your people and the

elders. I thank you for keeping your promise." Herod nodded as we left the elders behind in the grand hall. There was more to the young King than met the eye, though perhaps it was easier to judge someone when the weight of all realms didn't rest on their shoulders.

Everything he did was to protect his people, and I saw kindness and honor in him. To me, that was enough to enforce the alliance we so desperately needed. To defeat what was to come.

CALLIX

The halls at the castle felt colder and lonelier without Belynda. I had grown used to my solitude and the silence. But now, I found myself waiting to run into her at every turn. I listened for the sounds of her presence before quickly realizing she was no longer within my reach. She wasn't mine to have.

I needed to get away from the torture of her thoughts, even for a few hours. I chose to inflict such agony upon myself every time I breached the barriers of her mind. I had known from the beginning how our stories would end for I had lived it once with Isabel. However, I never imagined it would be so difficult to remain cold and indifferent. I had hoped that whatever bond forged our unbreakable connection meant something. However, the sea witches and I had yet to decipher that mystery.

The bells chimed in my ears, and I moved from the balcony to the basin and dipped my fingertips into the water. A moment later, I saw her. Her reflection was in a million surfaces as she entered the elder's temple. My fists tightened around the basin; I wanted to be there. I wished I could read her mind, but by the look on her face and the slight fall of her shoulders, I knew she was nervous. There was something else, too. She seemed... sad.

I should never have left her. Standing by her side in Abryas is where I should have been. Instead, I was beneath the surface of Varenver, hiding from the suffocating madness and pain, attempting to drown my desires. Icy shards formed across my body, training my skin not to feel—not to burn at the loss of her touch, but it was useless to think I could ever go back.

Life was cruel and empty, but I relished the days and nights that delivered coldness and silence. Chaos and despair was all I craved. I yearned to forget and exist; even now, I longed for the icy fortress, the prison for my demons, my desires, the one who once protected my heart. I craved the bitterness of the cold, for it had been kinder, safer... However, only fractures of the walls I had built remained. Instead, I was here, feigning indifference. I was more alive than I had ever been in my long, immortal existence.

I smiled at the defiant tilt of Belynda's chin as she urged the Elders to not delay their search for the Sands of Time. She was fearsome yet didn't realize the half of it.

A soft knock sounded at my chamber doors, and I allowed my fingers to run over the water's surface. Her image dissipated.

"Come in," I called. I did not have the mood or the patience to deal with Syllis, but I could smell her from beyond the door and heard the anxious running of her thoughts.

"Master." She allowed her magic to flow in the waves of her voice as if I couldn't perceive it. As if it could ever affect me.

"Syllis," I said, turning away.

"I didn't know you were back?" Her tone was almost accusatory, and it stunned me. Since when must the Lord of the Water Realm announce himself to his servants? I spared one glance in her direction and returned to the balcony, ignoring her.

"We've missed you, Master." She meant Phial had missed my presence too, yet her mind betrayed her. She moved closer.

"It hasn't been long." I said, staring at the city below.

"No, my Lord. I meant you've been absent. Ever since she arrived, it just hasn't been the same." Syllis brushed her fingers over my shoulder and down my arm. "She took all of your time. We've barely had any chance."

I reached for her hand and removed it from my skin. Bitterness screamed in her mind.

"From this moment on, you will remember your place here." I directed the full force of my brewing anger towards her. "And you will treat my guests with the respect they deserve. Do I make myself clear?"

Her pixie features sharpened, and her eyes darkened. She was angry, but she would get over it. I had allowed this to go on for far too long.

I was a good ruler. I provided the protection my kingdom needed, and the nymphs served me by choice, not by my will. She chose to entertain my desires freely, but I had been too forgiving—too allowing—and perhaps, my kindness gave her the wrong impression.

I wasn't cruel; I wasn't despicable. I had given her exactly what she sought, but thinking I could offer her anything beyond those moments was a plain delusion.

Syllis snatched her hand from my tight grasp, and with a tilt of her chin, turned away from me.

"Did you forget your manners? I did not dismiss you." I roared. She stiffened, her back to me.

"Is there anything else you need... my *Lord*?" she asked without turning. It took every ounce of my self-control not to wrap my hand around her neck.

"Have Phial, bring my dinner," I said through gritted teeth. She curtsied without saying another word. "And Syllis? If you no longer wish to serve me, you are free to return to the city. But if you stay. Let this be the last time you disregard my authority. I do not give second chances." I warned before she closed the door behind her.

BELYNDA

Once we completed our circuit around the temple, the elders had mostly dispersed, attending to more pressing duties—except for one, who remained deeply engrossed in a conversation with Drake. Drake's gaze met mine over the elder's head as I stepped into the meeting chamber. In that one look, I sought to express a myriad of emotions.

Herod broke the stillness. "I'll leave you in Drake's capable hands now. I have other matters to attend to."

"Thank you," I murmured, lost in my thoughts.

I exited the temple and sensed his presence without the need to turn. "Can you ever forgive me?" I whispered. My words hung in the air between us, the silence stretching by the moment. The energy shifted, and I glanced at him now beside me. We faced the distant horizon.

"There is nothing to forgive," he said, and his words took me by surprise. "I bear the responsibility for all of this."

Uncertainty gnawed at me. Why would he burden himself with such unfounded guilt?

"Perhaps Callix is right," Drake continued. "I was a coward, just as I was with Isabel. I should have never made that promise. I should have never allowed you to follow me to Druleska. I should have never let you go."

"Stop!" My voice quivered. "Please, *enough*." I turned to face him, and this time, his gaze lowered to meet mine. "No one is at fault for my choices nor Isabel's. Certainly not you."

"Not your choices or hers... but mine. My choices, my weaknesses, my descent into darkness. My failure to do what I should have done—to fight for her, for you." My heart ached, and I reached out to him, overwhelmed by the emotions bottled up since last night. I enveloped him in a tight embrace. A sigh escaped my lips as his arms wrapped around me in response.

"I don't care about what was or what could have been," I whispered, pressing my cheek against his chest. "I only care about us and ending this war. Nothing else matters." He cupped my face, brushing his fingers against my cheek as he gently tucked a loose strand of hair behind my ear.

"And Callix?" His brow furrowed, though there was no anger in his expression, only resignation.

"Please, let's not speak of him," I begged. "I need time to forget, to move forward." *Please.* I willed the silent plea into his mind, but I encountered resistance. His mental barriers held strong, emitting a sulfurous scent.

"Don't attempt it," he warned. He raised my hand to his lips and planted a kiss on my palm and the woven bracelet I wore—the relic crafted by my mother and me. It felt like lifetimes ago since I last saw her. The bracelet was a protective shield against prying minds. "Unless you're willing to share your thoughts in return," he added. He was right. Taking without giving was hypocritical of me, particularly now when I had yet to sort through the labyrinth of my own mind.

"My thoughts are the last place you want to be right now," I admitted, and a wry smile played at the corner of his lips.

"The feeling is mutual, love." As he held me close, I realized his mother was right. Drake loved me with a fervor that matched my own, and nothing could ever sever the bond between us.

He drew back and gently took my hand as we descended the stone steps. Our horses awaited, and I watched with fascination as Drake mounted his steed with remarkable grace and ease. I hesitated, contemplating the idea of walking back to the castle; it wasn't far, after all.

"Out of all the things to fear," he teased, "you're afraid of a horse?"

"Not exactly," I admitted, hesitating to climb the horse's back.

"Come." Drake offered his hand to me. "Trust me."

I was unable to refuse him. Placing my hand in his, he effortlessly hoisted me up and positioned me across his lap. He secured his hands around my waist, then took hold of the reins.

"Please don't run," I begged, terrified by the look on his face.

"I will never let you fall, love," he assured me. His breath grazed the nape of my neck. "Besides, what's the worst that can happen? You're immortal."

He had a point, but I couldn't help myself.

"Fear is still very real," I confessed. "As is the embarrassment of me screaming, even if I trust your riding skills." His laughter rocked my body as he took off into a sprint through the woods.

I closed my eyes and clutched to his arms, forcing my mouth shut.

The wind kissed my face, and strands of hair whipped against my skin as we rode through the Elvin woods.

"Open your eyes," he whispered, and I obeyed.

The sight before us was nothing short of breathtaking. To the left, the Elvin woods appeared to stretch indefinitely, while towering cliffs touched the heavens to our right. Before us lay an expansive sea of emerald grass, as though the world was awash with green.

My body gradually relaxed against Drake's, attuned to the subtle rhythm of the stallion. As I shifted slightly in his lap, the horse slowed its pace, yet quickly resumed its former speed. The position must be uncomfortable for Drake, I realized, so I repositioned myself, aligning my legs astride like his, but in the opposite direction. My hands wound around his neck, and I pressed a tender kiss to the corner of his lips. This time, the horse slowed to a near leisurely stroll.

I adjusted my position across Drake's lap, and his hands relinquished the reins to grip my behind firmly. He pressed my warmth against his growing desire, and the horse's leisurely pace felt like an exquisite torment.

"Of all the days... you chose to wear pants today," he growled. I chuckled, sharing his exasperation. I undulated against him, both equally breathless and aflame with desire.

Leaning against the horse's mane, Drake steadied me. "Just tear them. Right here," I urged. I didn't have to ask twice; his fingers found the seam of my pants and ripped. Soon after, my underwear snapped.

Drake's eyes blazed with longing as I reached between us, unfastening his belt and undoing the button of his pants to unveil his long, rigid arousal.

His fingers tensed around my hips, lifting me enough for a seamless entry. I couldn't be sure whether it was the lingering frustration from our fight or the mounting tension, but every inch of him felt like paradise.

I welcomed his length, and our bodies swayed in sync with the soft gait of the horse's steps.

"Are you still wary of riding?" he teased, his voice warm against my ear. I playfully nipped at his neck for reminding me.

"I much prefer riding you." But in an instant, we were plummeting towards the ground. My cry of terror was cut short as Drake caught me, supporting my weight.

"You can't say that and expect me to maintain control," he growled, pulling me closer and shifting me over his body. He guided his pulsating cock into my core. "Show me," he urged, clinging to my thighs as I sank deeper, claiming all of him. I moved. I rocked slowly at first, but soon, it wasn't enough.

Drake repositioned me onto my knees, his hands at my

behind, followed by the sound of fabric tearing as he exposed more of my skin.

"Drake..." I began to protest, but my words faded as he sank into me.

His fingers dug into my hips as he drove forcefully into me. He wrapped one hand around my neck, drawing my body close against his chest. At this angle, I felt him so deep it hurt—a pleasurable ache that burned my insides.

"That's it," his voice, was seductive and alluring, as he whispered in my ear like a tempting demon. "Take it all."

I cried out as his dominant thrusts shattered my resolve. I came around him in crashing waves, and his release followed shortly after. His warmth trickled between my thighs.

I fell over the blanket of glass, entangled with him. Both sated and replete. After two sleepless nights, I allowed my eyes to close in contented stillness.

I drifted off. Through the exhaustion, I felt Drake's hands as he jostled me in his arms, and my eyes opened briefly as we neared the castle. I was too tired to remain conscious for long.

"We're here, love," he whispered.

"Too tired," I mumbled, my protest barely audible. His laughter vibrated against my neck.

"I know you are, but we must do something about your pants," he said, and his words reignited the memory of our heated encounter and the unfortunate state of my clothing.

"This is all your fault," I grumbled, jabbing him with my elbow, which only made him laugh harder.

"If I remember correctly, you were the one who insisted on it."

"And if I remember correctly, you took it upon yourself to tear it all the way up to leave my backside on display."

"Mhmm, yes. I'm not sorry about that, though," he murmured. He playfully slapped my thigh.

"Your jacket," I said. Drake slipped his arms from out of the sleeves, and I secured the jacket around my waist.

He dismounted and helped me down after him.

"Well?" I inquired as Drake assessed my makeshift attire. He smiled.

"You're very resourceful. No one will be able to tell," he assured me, leaning down to plant a kiss on my cheek.

"Good, let's hurry then." I rushed up the stairs, sensing him close behind as we approached my chambers.

"This is as far as I will accompany you," he said, and I paused, facing him.

"You're not coming in?" I raised an eyebrow and flashed a teasing smile.

"Later." His tone held a solemn vow. "I need to get back to the legions. We will be ready to depart tomorrow morning."

"So soon?"

He nodded. "Dagasti's army is closing in on the North. We have little time to prepare for the upcoming battle."

"I understand."

"You don't have to come," he said.

"I do. I will do everything in my power to slow them down until the elders can uncover the Sands of Time."

"What if they don't?" he mused.

"Then we'll do what we must. We'll fight. We must try," I replied, and he mirrored his agreement with a resolute nod.

"You're exhausted. Rest. I'll return later," Drake kissed my forehead before vanishing down the corridor, and I watched him go, glad to have him back. Though I knew that beneath his facade, my revelation weighed heavy on his soul.

Unlike previous evenings, I managed to unwind during dinner. Callix never returned, leaving me with mixed emotions. While I longed for his company, I felt a sense of relief, free from the tension between him and Drake.

"How long until Dagasti's army reaches the North?" I asked.

"A couple of weeks at best if we're unable to slow their advance," Drake replied.

"That doesn't give us much time," I muttered, my thoughts racing.

"If we can find a way to harness the shields protecting the mountains of Tirse..." Drake's voice trailed. "It would make all the difference."

"What's so special about those mountains?" I inquired.

"The Darklings cannot cross them. The magic that shields those mountains is powerful enough to keep them at bay."

"And I assume the clans have no idea how to use this to their advantage?"

"Exactly."

"I'd like to try. Once we arrive, I want to visit these mountains and see for myself," I said. "Perhaps I can help. Maybe fate has led me here for this very purpose."

"It doesn't hurt to try," he replied, his expression hopeful.

"As soon as we have any leads on a sacred location to find

the Sands, I will send word," offered Herod. "I can only hope we aren't too late."

The evening simmered into a flurry of good wishes and goodbyes. I prayed to the Fates—or anyone who might listen—for the strength and wisdom to defeat the darkness before it devoured what remained of Upherya. Drake's arms tightened around me and pulled me closer. I found solace in them as he slept, sated after our lovemaking.

But when I awoke the following morning, the bed was empty. Drake's restless nature had driven him to return to his duties. He would likely be at the training camp. The warm water of the shower eased my tensions. I dressed in the warrior outfit Callix had provided and adjusted the golden cuffs. I was a warrior, ready for battle. Taking a deep breath, I left the chamber. It might be the last time I'd walk these castle halls.

I descended to the stables and wove through the bustling camp, where lines of Golden soldiers marched. The hush of dawn had been replaced by the clamor of hooves and swords. I moved through the legions of armored men until I spotted Drake... and Callix. I froze but they didn't appear to be fighting. Gathering my resolve, I marched toward them.

"There you are," I said in a light, playful tone. Both men turned to me at once. "I was looking for you." I looked at Drake, who took two steps toward me and kissed my lips. As his eyes scanned my body, Callix's gaze followed suit.

"Prepare to send the first legion through. I will march with them and wait at the other side," Drake instructed Callix.

"Wait." I held Drake's arm. "Can I go with you?" I asked. His gaze shifted to Callix.

"No. We don't have time to waste. Once the legions are through, Callix will take you to the mountains to see what you can find out about the shields," Drake said. I blinked, staring up at him.

"Can't you fly me there yourself once we're there?" I questioned, not comprehending his sudden acceptance of Callix.

"I would like nothing more, love." A shadow passed over his eyes. "But I have work to do at the other side, and if we can deliver Euros some good news about the shields, I'd prefer not to waste any time."

His selflessness and dedication to the people of Upherya deepened my love for him.

"I understand." I rose to my toes to kiss the corner of his lips before he left.

Callix remained silent, a sign that often forebode trouble.

"Took you long enough," I said, and his eyes shifted over my face with amusement.

"Just a few hours for me, remember?"

"I don't think I will ever get used to that," I admitted.

"It's a good thing you no longer have to," Callix said, implying that I was free of him and his realm. Yet the thought saddened me. I loved Serfier.

"What were you and Drake talking about?" I asked. "It didn't seem like you two were fighting, which was surprising." Callix raised his brows and his heart-stopping smile made my heart flip.

"Is that what it seemed to you?" His laughter was drowned out by the soldiers' marching. "Darling, make no mistake. He would have my head if he could. The only thing stopping him now is knowing you care for me. You could imagine my surprise when I learned that you had confessed as much to him—which warms my heart, by the way." A wicked glint shimmered in his eyes.

"Callix, caring for you is one thing..."

"I know. It's not enough; you choose him," he interrupted. My frown mirrored his.

"That's not what I meant. I love him. I care for you. You are my friend, Callix. Nothing else."

"Are you trying to convince me or yourself?" he asked, catching me off guard.

"Get out of my head, Callix!"

"Actually, this time, I wasn't. It's just getting easier to read you."

How was I going to do this if, at every turn, I ended up hurting one or the other? I sighed.

"Hey." Callix turned to me, gripping my chin. "I will never make this a choice. Your decision, always yours. I will stand with you as your friend, as your shield, or as chaos itself."

I stared into the depths of his blue eyes, and my chest constricted. I longed to wrap my arms around him, and without hesitation, I did. For a few moments, I allowed him to shelter me in his arms, finding contentment in the Water Lord's embrace.

After a moment, Callix pulled away and stepped out of my reach. When Drake reappeared a minute later, I knew why he had done it, and I was grateful.

"Ready?" Callix asked.

"Start there, from the legion at the North. I will follow after them. Remember the sequence. One legion a few kilometers apart along the border," Drake ordered.

"I think we've got it covered," Callix said. With a wave of his hand, an immense ring of water blasted in the distance, and Drake's gaze regarded me for a moment.

"See you on the other side," he said before disappearing through the water portal with the throng of marching Elves. There were so many—too many to count—and this was only one legion.

"How many men did Herod volunteer for the North?" I asked Callix, who smiled.

"Three legions. Around six thousand men each."

My mouth dropped.

"Don't make that face, darling. It's a war, after all, and Herod can spare the men."

"I guess this gives us an even better advantage." Callix raised his brows.

"Upherya has lost ten times that number, and they are skilled warriors trained from childhood. The legions might give us an advantage or, at the very least, delay the Darklings' advance, but one hundred Elvin soldiers are no match for a single warrior of Upherya."

The more I heard about the wind warriors, the more intrigued I became to finally meet them, especially Euros, whom I had heard so much about.

When the legion had finally filtered through, Callix closed the portal and waited for the next group to march forward. Callix opened a different portal this time, and the next legion marched through.

"I was waiting to speak with you," I said as we stood, watching the procession of soldiers disappear through the water gate.

"The Sands of Time?" he asked.

"How did you know?"

"I might not have been present, but I didn't miss the elder's meeting," he said, and it made me smile, knowing he hadn't abandoned me. "I know what was said. I know what you will require, but I'm afraid I cannot help. Not this time."

"How were you able to find it then?" I asked.

"Isabel. It was revealed to her in a vision. Her last request." I knew he was telling the truth as he had mentioned her final requests before. One of them was that he sealed her sacrifice with the bond of water, allowing the soul connection between her and me to come to pass.

"I didn't think of it before," he whispered, his gaze lost.

"What is it? Do you know how to find the Sands?" I asked, but he shook his head, his eyes adopting a strange look. "What did you mean?"

"Nothing." He shook his head. "Don't mind me."

I knew him well enough by now to realize that nothing always meant something, but I decided to let it go.

WE WATCHED the line of men from the last legion disappear through the last portal before Callix closed it. By this time, the sun was well over the horizon.

"Are you ready?" asked Callix, offering me his hand. I took it, smiling.

"To the mountains?" I asked, ensuring he wouldn't run away with me to the ends of the Earth. His laughter made me smile. He was very much in my mind.

"Running away with you sounds tempting, but something tells me he wouldn't approve."

"*I* wouldn't approve," I added, and he smiled. Leaning forward, he gently kissed my cheek.

"Still trying to convince yourself, darling?" he whispered. A chill seized me.

"Just open the damn portal, Callix," I said.

"Yes, my Lady," he replied, and a portal opened before us.

15
WHISPERS OF THE PAST

THE PORTAL CLOSED BEHIND US, AND I WAS SUSPENDED IN TIME, surrounded by a maze of trees that whispered the history of the realm.

This place was charged with energy, its magic like tiny prickling insects crawling over my skin.

"Do you feel that?" I asked, facing Callix.

"No, nothing out of the ordinary." He stepped next to me, shifting his head from side to side, trying to detect what I could. "What do you sense?"

"It's strange. I can feel the Earth's energy and the quiet whispers of the trees, much like in the Elvin forests, but there's something else."

"Describe it."

"It's hard to explain. I don't know. It's..." I closed my eyes, attempting to refine the sensation in my mind. "It feels familiar."

When I opened my eyes, I placed my palm flat against a tree.

"What was that?" I glanced at Callix with alarm, who stared back at me, brows furrowed. "Someone just ran through those trees!" I pointed in the direction of the movement, and Callix turned to look.

"I assure you, there is no one but us here." I peered through the bend of the trees where the apparition had been.

"I know what I saw."

But Callix wasn't convinced.

I followed the shadow's path. After walking for a few minutes and straining my ears to listen, I knew there was no one there but us. Perhaps Callix was right, and this place was playing tricks on me.

I braced my hand on a tree and took a deep breath. Closing my eyes, I listened once again to the quiet sounds of the forest. Yet clashing metal interrupted the earth's stillness and howls sounded in the distance. I blinked, stunned.

"Okay. Please tell me you heard that." I said, but Callix shook his head. "This place… did something happen here?" A haunted look flashed across his face.

"Yes. The first war," he said, and I suddenly understood. He had lost his father in these lands. I wondered if that's why he felt so inclined to help the Wind people.

"Is it possible that I can see ghosts?" I asked. Here, I felt overwhelmed and out of my element.

"Or echoes of the past?"

"We don't believe in echoes of the past or ghosts, not in the sense that humans do," he replied. "But magic can carry memories. Potent magic, that is."

Whatever the cause, I needed to know more. I braced against the tree again, and this time, when the cries of war enveloped me, I didn't let go. Instead, I opened my eyes to concentrate on the hazy veil ahead. It moved and thickened through the forest until, slowly, the shadows took form. Soon, those shadows had faces, bodies, armor, and weapons as they charged through the trees. Their deadly howls closed in, and I trembled where I stood.

"Callix... are you seeing this?" My voice trembled.

"I can see it in your mind, but they are not here. Not truly here," he whispered. Stallions with their riders charged past me and clashed through the trees like smoke. Amidst the darkness, I spotted golden armor, but it wasn't the luminosity that caught my attention. It was the details carved on the man's suit.

"Callix," I whispered, unable to believe it, for I could not be certain.

"Father..." Callix's hand tightened on my shoulder, and I stepped away from the tree, severing the connection to whatever memories the forest held.

"Callix." When I turned to him, his eyes were distant, and his face had paled. "We don't have to do this," I said, stroking his face, but even that seemed unable to pull him back.

"No," he said. "This isn't a coincidence. These trees are trying to tell you something, and you must listen."

"Will you be all right?" I asked, and he took my hand, bringing it to his lips.

"Shouldn't I be the one asking you that?" He smiled, but it was forced.

"You don't have to pretend with me," I said, and his brows furrowed.

"I promise you, there is nothing more in this world that can shatter what's already broken."

A sinking feeling settled in my gut at his words, at the implication he was too broken to feel more pain, though that wasn't entirely true. I could see it in his face. He was pretending again.

"I will be okay." He placed my hands against the tree. This time, he stepped behind me, resting his hands over mine against the tree's bark. "I'm okay," he whispered. "Close your eyes."

I did as he said and relaxed into him.

Once again, I was lost in the past of the First War. Waves of Darklings moved through the trees, pushing back the soldiers.

The bodies shifted like bursts of memories and amongst the valiant was Callix's father. The fallen King of Serfier.

Callix's body stiffened behind me, and I knew he could see what I could, watching through my mind instead. Chaos, destruction, and death ensued as the avalanche of shadows fell over the warriors. While they fought with ferocity, the darkness claimed them one by one. Callix's father was one of the last to fall, and the instant he was lost, he became the enemy. He fought against his own, like the rest of the fallen warriors from across the realms. Callix's hands tightened as he leaned his head against my shoulder, but I didn't open my eyes. Suddenly, I was blinded. The bright, bursting light rushed through the trees like a ripple of an atomic bomb. The remaining soldiers froze as the army of darkness exploded into shimmering specs of light. At that precise moment, I knew. I understood what protected these woods. It was the magic force of every freed soul. The tales had been right. The light had defeated the dark, but at what cost... so many lives were lost—souls I could never save.

Callix closed his hands around my waist and pulled me into him. At last, I allowed my hands to fall.

"You can't save everyone," he whispered.

"This is all my fault," I confessed. "I released this monstrosity into your world." Having witnessed the reality of what awaited us, I understood the gravity of what I had done.

"You will end it," he said. He turned me in his arms and stared into my eyes. "I know you will."

I nodded, drawing strength from him.

"I think I have an idea of how to extend the barrier," I said. "Can you portal us to the edge of the mountain? I need to test my theory."

The minute I set foot outside the shadow line of the mountains, the energy shifted, almost like stepping through an invisible wall.

"Right here," I said. I stepped over the pulsing barrier. "Do you feel it?"

Callix shook his head.

"I do," I said. "This is where the barrier ends." Yet the more I concentrated, I couldn't just feel it—I could *see* it. The wall of energy was like a hazy, vibrating film.

"I believe you. The Darklings have not been able to advance beyond this point."

"Stand over there, just a few feet out. I'm going to try and extend the barriers."

"I still won't be able to feel them," he said, and I rolled my eyes.

"But I will. I can see them. The more I concentrate on its magic, the clearer it becomes. Once I attempt this, I want to see how much more it expands, if at all." Callix acquiesced and walked a few paces outside the barrier. With my eyes closed, I rested my hands flat against the ground, sensing the energy crawling through my fingertips. The vibrations coursed through my body and I willed it to expand. The energy moved and slithered until a few minutes later, the ground where Callix stood was shielded beneath the protection of the mountain. I grinned.

"It works."

Callix beamed and his eyes glimmered with something akin to pride and wonder.

"I never doubted you," he said. But like an extended rubber band, the power snapped back and its force sent me flying back against a tree. The barrier collapsed.

I fell to the ground and Callix was at my side at once, offering me his hand.

"It's too strong," I said. "I need to try again."

I dusted off my pants and ignored the look on his face. He wouldn't stop me. That wasn't Callix... and I loved him for that. I paused, glancing at him, but he must have been too preoccupied with his own thoughts to invade mine, for which I was glad.

Callix returned to the spot where he had stood before. Once again, I allowed the magic to surge through me and extended it toward the barrier's edge. It moved underneath Callix's feet, and I willed it into place. It fought back, taking from me in equal measures. I struggled against it and gritted my teeth, but its force brought me to my knees. With a blast, it recoiled again, and I spiraled into the trees.

"I'm all for testing your limits, but you're not doing that again," said Callix, hovering above me. I did not have the strength to stand.

"So much for immortality," I said, fighting to push myself from the ground.

"You're not fighting a mortal entity, Belynda. You're trying to bend powerful magic, and from the looks of it, it's draining you."

"I just need more elemental magic. It's not impossible. I just need enough power to hold it."

"You can't hold it forever. The Darklings have nothing but time. They will wait this out. They will wear you out if the magic of the barriers doesn't do it first," he said, and for the first time, concern—perhaps fear—etched across his features. He braced my arm over his shoulder and pulled me to my feet, supporting my weight.

"We don't have to wait forever. Only until the elders find the Sands of Time. I only intend to hold them back for as long as possible."

"There's no way I can convince you to change your mind, is there?" he said, and I shook my head. His eyes roamed my face in defeat.

"Then perhaps the elementals can help," he offered. I smiled and leaned in, planting a chaste kiss on his cheek.

"What was that for?" he asked with a heart-stopping smile.

"For your brilliant idea, and for allowing me to be who I want to be. For believing in me." Slowly, his smile faded.

He brushed my cheek with his fingers, and his eyes reflected his intentions. I could not bring myself to stop him. Slowly, he leaned in, and his nose trailed a path along my cheek. His finger brushed my lips as he rested his forehead against mine.

"Anytime," he whispered. He dropped his hand from my lips and leaned back. I blinked, pushing the haze of the moment away. An emptiness consumed me. Did I want him to kiss me?

"I can't believe I forgot about the elementals," I said, trying to find my voice. My mind was lost in a haze. "We will need to speak with Drake. He will know what became of them and where to find them."

"They followed him to Upherya," said Callix, surprising me yet again.

"And you know this how?"

Callix smiled.

"There isn't much I don't know, darling. And what I don't know, I make it a point to find out." He winked, and I rolled my eyes. "Come, I'll take you to them." A moment later, he was guiding me through a water portal, where we stepped through to the other side. If this wasn't a sign from the Fates that this would work, I didn't know what was.

HUDDLED before us against the fire were Amirth, Rashe, and Alexia. Never had I been so happy to see them. We had set aside our differences long ago, and it was nice to see some familiar faces from the human world. Amirth was the first one to spot me. She rose to her feet; surprise flashed in her eyes.

"You're back!" She closed the distance and hugged me; I froze, shocked, and then eventually hugged her back. Amirth pulled away, and I smiled. "We weren't expecting Drake for another night." She watched Callix with an odd expression. It didn't take a mind reader to sense her reservations.

"Yes, Drake was eager to return," I said. "I'm glad to see you." I glanced at Alexia and Rashe, who now hovered close to Amirth. "All of you."

"It's good to see you alive and well." Amirth paused, assessing me. "More than well, it seems." I smiled. Although immortality had hardly affected my appearance, the change was noticeable in my physique and presence.

"Where are my manners? This is Callix. The Lord of the Water Realm." I said.

Rashe and Alexia greeted him, but Amirth's eyes narrowed, confirming my suspicions. Her alliance rested with Drake, which was comical considering our beginnings.

"He's a friend," I whispered and clasped her hand. Amirth glanced at him and then at me.

"If he is an enemy of Drake, he is no friend of mine."

"He is a friend to both Drake and me," I said. "Drake is biased. For personal reasons." She glanced at Callix again, but this time, the corner of her mouth shifted.

"Yes. I can see why."

"I never got a chance to thank you back at Druleska for helping Drake. I know you expressed your wish to come with us, but I never expected you to sign up for any of this." I offered as a way to defer Amirth's wrath.

"We are happier here than we have been in our entire lives. We are free, and despite our situation, we are glad to help. To have a purpose," said Rashe, who had matured much since I last saw the boy.

"I feel the same. We have found purpose here amongst these people. We don't get to join the battles like Amirth does, but we feel our duty to remain in the mountains and protect the women and children is equally important," added Alexia.

"It is. But I have yet one more favor to ask of you all." I said, glancing between the three elementals.

"Who do we need to kill?" Amirth asked. Callix's booming laughter made me smile.

"On the contrary. If my plan works, we might be able to stop the Darklings from advancing."

"We're in," said Amirth, speaking for all of them. I looked at Rashe and Alexia, who nodded their agreement.

"Very well. Here is the plan..."

Amirth was skeptical at first. To be honest, I felt as if she resented not having been the one to pick up on the Earth's connection. After all, she was an Earth elemental. But then again, her powers and mine were nowhere near the same.

"I know it will work. It already did for me. Now, if I could just pull from your energies like we did for the Psypher, we might be able to hold the walls in place for longer."

"How much longer?" asked Alexia.

"I don't know," I admitted. "I'm hoping for as long as necessary, or until the elders find what I need."

"We have nothing to lose," said Amirth. "When do we do this?"

I smiled, eager to test the theory again.

"Now."

"Wait—" Callix held my arm. "Your magic was drained only a short while ago. Do you think it's wise to try again so soon?"

"I feel fine," I said. "I promise. I don't want to return to the North without positive news." He shook his head but didn't oppose me.

"We will use the portal to reach the limits of the mountains, just where the energies break," I instructed the elementals. Callix opened the water portal with the gentle sweep of his hand.

I stepped through it first, and Callix followed.

Amirth was the first to appear after Callix, just like I knew she would. She was always a leader to them.

"Right here. This is where the barrier of energy stops. Do you feel it?" I asked Amirth.

She moved around me, extending her hands.

"What does it feel like to you?" she asked.

"Under the barrier, it feels like pins and needles against my skin. If I concentrate long enough, I can even see it. Like a hazy film." She nodded and walked slowly, sensing the Earth's energy.

"I see what you mean, but I wouldn't have noticed the subtle difference unless I was really paying attention. It feels more like a shudder, one that I only sense when I step through the barrier. But you're right. There is definitely energy here."

"I managed to push it out at least two yards to where

Callix stands, but not for long. The energy refuses to be manipulated."

"The fact that you can perceive it with such ease—even glimpse at it—proves how powerful your magic is. How do you know we'll be able to make a difference?"

"I don't, but I'm hoping you can. Just as you said, we have nothing to lose." For a moment, silence crept between us.

"Why are we wasting time then?" Amirth stood behind me, resting her hand on my shoulder.

"We will form a chain, and you will draw from all of us at once. I suggest you keep both hands on the ground; it will give you a better yield."

I nodded. While I might have been more powerful, Amirth was wiser and well-trained regarding elemental magic. I kneeled and placed both hands against the ground. Alexia and Rashe took Amirth's position; Rashe placed his hand over her shoulder and Alexia over Rashe's.

This time, the surge of magic that rushed through me wasn't a current. It was a powerful, relentless wave. I allowed it to swell, and the barrier expanded much faster, easily passing Callix. It extended far beyond the valley, and I took a deep, calming breath to relax my mind. Then the magic pushed against my efforts. Please... *let this work.* Callix's eyes found mine.

As I drew from the elementals, Amirth's grip on my shoulder tightened. They could feel me slowly draining them, but that slight draw was enough to maintain the barrier's expansion. Minutes passed, and for the first time, I sensed it was fully under my control. A few more moments passed, and when the resistance didn't come, I allowed the barrier to return to its natural state.

Amirth, Rashe, and Alexia fell to their knees the moment I removed my hands from the ground. "I'm sorry," I said, well-aware of their discomfort, particularly for half-mortals like them.

"It's tolerable," Rashe assured me, and Alexia nodded.

"Do you think you can hold it without killing us in the process?" teased Amirth, her mouth twisting into a smile.

"I won't let it get to that," I replied. "We will hold for as long as it's safe and not a moment longer."

Rashe and Alexia returned to their watch in the heart of the mountains, but Amirth insisted on accompanying us. I couldn't help but notice her excitement at the prospect of delivering the good news to Euros.

THE INSTANT I passed through the water portal, I fell in love with Upherya. Finally, I understood why it was Celest's favorite realm.

Despite the looming hopelessness, the city teemed with life. Its denizens danced and congregated around fire pits in what seemed to be the heart of the city. The mountain peaks vanished under the blazing orange sun, and in the distance, a towering structure resembled a Roman temple which loomed high above the hill's peak, almost as if one could reach up and touch the sky.

"Where is Drake?" I asked, glancing at Callix as we weaved through the bustling crowd.

"He's probably with Euros. If I had to guess, I'd say at the round table." Amirth chimed in. Her eyes lit upon mentioning the warrior.

"That's precisely where we're heading," Callix confirmed.

"I take it you're quite fond of the warrior?" I asked Amirth. We fell a few steps back.

"Things are complicated," she confessed, shaking her head. "He is complicated, but then again, so am I."

I laughed, and so did she.

"Then I guess you found your match," I mused.

"Perhaps I have," she admitted, and once again, I was glad for the companionship and the strange friendship we had forged.

"What's the deal with you and him?" she asked, equally curious about Callix. I hated myself for speaking, acutely aware that he could hear my every word and aware how much it would hurt him.

"He is a good friend," I said cautiously.

"Does he know that?" Amirth asked boldly, and for a moment, I was at a loss for words.

"*He* is right here." Callix surprised us, turning to respond to Amirth himself. "I can hear you, not to mention I have the exceptional ability to read your mind. To answer your question, Amirth, I am well aware that her affections lie with the dragon prince. No need to worry on my behalf." he added, flashing a sarcastic smile. He marched off then, disappearing into the bustling crowd.

"Can you please take it easy on him?" I asked. "It's not his fault, and the truth is, I wouldn't be alive if it weren't for him."

"I know. I'm sorry. I'll behave. I promise." She smiled reassuringly. "But I can see why Drake would be jealous. The Water Lord is a hunk."

My mouth dropped, but I couldn't help but laugh.

"I'll tell him you said that," I teased. "He would love to know you don't actually hold such a low opinion of him."

"Don't you dare! My opinion has nothing to do with his muscles. Besides, something tells me his ego doesn't need to get any bigger." We both laughed. I would never convey the truth to Callix, but knowing him, he might pick it up from my thoughts—or Amirth's—sooner or later.

"Tell me about the warriors," I asked, feeling slightly nervous to meet them.

"Not much to tell. A bunch of babies." She shrugged, unconcerned. "But with exceptional fighting skills. You'll see soon enough."

The hills appeared less daunting from a distance, but its steepness made our ascent longer than anticipated. Callix sat perched on a rock by the winding road, his patience wavering.

"Took you long enough," he said with his characteristic humor.

Amirth couldn't resist a jab. "Maybe we wouldn't have been so delayed if you had not abandoned us and used your portal." She was playing with chaos, and when Callix smiled in her direction, I knew it was too late. A water portal manifested right before her, and as she took a step, she vanished from my side.

"Callix!" I scolded. "Where is she?"

"Wait until I get my hands on you!" Amirth's voice echoed from the base of the hill.

"Really, Callix, this is childish," I admonished, though I couldn't help but smile. Amirth had pushed him to his limits. "Please bring her back up."

"I don't think I will," he replied, stepping down from the large rock. "Even if you ask nicely." He turned towards the road, and when he noticed I wasn't following, he glanced back at me.

"Aren't you coming? They're waiting for you."

Reluctantly, I moved to his side. "Please," I pleaded. "You'll only anger her further."

Callix remained stubborn. "I've spent my life angering people. I've learned to live with it. She won't rob me of my sleep." He extended his hand, smiling. He was impossible, but if there was one thing I had learned from Callix, it was that when he made up his mind, nothing could sway him. He was indomitable. I glanced back at Amirth, who sighed with resignation.

"Fine. I'll sit here and wait," I conceded.

"You're being difficult," said Callix, and I stared at him as if he had lost his mind.

"I'm difficult?" I questioned, my voice tinged with frustration. "I don't seem to be the one abusing my power here and refusing to admit when I'm wrong."

Callix stepped closer. "*Now* I'm wrong? Even a good friend doesn't deserve to be treated in such a way." His words stung for the painful truth they held. He didn't deserve Amirth's disdain or my own indifference.

I sighed. "I'm sorry. I know it's not your fault." Silence followed as his eyes locked onto mine. Without breaking his gaze, he opened a water portal, and a second later, Amirth stumbled through.

She marched towards him but Callix didn't flinch.

"Can we just move past this, please? There are more important matters at stake here than this ridiculous quarrel." I pleaded.

Amirth paused and reluctantly stepped away. She didn't say much as she walked off, leading ahead of us. Callix walked to my side with a satisfied and bemused expression.

"Thank you," I whispered to him, and he nodded.

The second we broke through the pillars of the temple, the wind was like a soft caress against my skin. A moment later, Drake strode through the doors and pulled me into his arms.

"I was beginning to worry," he whispered.

"Worried I was going to run away?" teased Callix. Drake narrowed his eyes at him, but when I squeezed his hand, I regained his attention.

"Come. The warriors are eager to meet you," he said. "I hope you have good news."

"I do. I most certainly do."

Drake brought my hand to his lips, and we entered the temple together, eager to share the positive developments with the waiting warriors.

My gaze fell first upon the large round table, where three unfamiliar faces sat. The moment they spotted me, they rose to their feet. One of them did so leisurely, and if my assumptions were correct, that had to be Euros.

"I'm Link," one of the warriors said, stepping closer and

offering me his hand. He appeared young, several years younger than the rest of them.

"It's a pleasure to finally meet you, Link," I replied, and the other warrior approached, offering his hand, too.

"This is Phoenix," Link introduced the second clan leader.

"Welcome to Upherya," Phoenix greeted, smiling.

"Thank you," I said, turning my attention to the one who had yet to introduce himself. "You must be Euros, then," I said, breaking the ice. "I've heard much about you." As Euros approached, his forehead creased.

"We are honored to have you and happy to see you alive and well," said Euros, sparing a glance at Drake. I didn't miss the subtle exchange between them. "I wish we could have met under better circumstances, but fate has brought you here now."

"Yes, it has, and in good time, it seems. I have good news." I glanced at Drake, who placed his hand around my waist.

"Apologies for not saying something sooner. I didn't want to raise your hopes if she was unsuccessful," Drake explained.

"For the love of the Gods, woman! Tell us already." Phoenix pressed. The outspoken one of the group, it seemed.

"We have figured out a way to extend the barriers that protect the mountains," I revealed, and the warriors exchanged disbelieving glances before turning back to face me.

"How is it possible?" whispered Euros, his voice disbelieving. "Our people have tried to understand the magic that holds those mountains for centuries. We've attempted to bend the spirits of Air that bind those mountains, but all our efforts have failed."

"That's because the magic upholding those barriers isn't

solely wind magic," I explained. "The force safeguarding those mountains is the collective souls of all those who perished in the first battle, every life claimed by the darkness now turned to light." Silence filled the room for a prolonged moment, and I wondered if they doubted my words.

"She speaks the truth," Callix confirmed.

"I felt it as well," added Amirth. "She's right. We managed to expand the protection of the energy field."

Link was the first to smile, a glimmer of hope in his expression. "If anyone doubted the prophecy of the Lightbringer, they will doubt no more," he declared. I turned to Drake with a questioning glance.

"I'll explain later," he whispered.

"Having the protection of those barriers will certainly tilt the outcome of this battle in our favor," Phoenix conceded.

"But the point is not to hide behind the walls; it's to defeat the darkness. The question is, how do we do that?" Euros asked, his eyes on me. "If you are the Lightbringer, how do we stop this?"

Everyone in the room waited expectantly for an answer that I didn't have. Not yet. The Fates had drawn me into this journey and declared me the salvation against the dark, but I didn't know how. Their assertion that I could navigate the threads of possibility was my only lead. Thanks to the Elders, I knew we required the Sands of Time, but I had a lot of work ahead of me, and this battle was already at our doorstep.

"I will not stand here and lie, pretending that I have all the answers when I do not," I began honestly. "All I am certain of is that the Fates have chosen me as their instrument to end the war. I have yet to decipher their plan and the role I will play in stopping the darkness."

It felt like I had given them hope and snatched it away in a matter of minutes. They deserved to know the truth. "The Fates spoke of the threads of possibilities, yet we lack the necessary elements to access them or the knowledge of how to unlock such powers. We aren't certain if I can."

"We require the Sands of Time," Drake explained.

"So, you're telling us that the outcome of this war hinges on the Elvin people finding a mythical relic?" Phoenix asked, skeptic.

"The sands are not a myth," I clarified. "They were used once by the guardianship." I didn't reveal more, unsure of how much of his time in the human world Drake had disclosed.

"As it stands, *you* are meant to stop the darkness yet we have no idea how. The threads of possibilities might hold the key, but we lack knowledge about how to access that magic, and when we do, we'll need the Sands of Time to do so. Am I correct?" asked Euros, retaking his seat. He braced his arms against the table. No one in the room needed to speak; we understood exactly where we stood, and he was right. The walls were merely a temporary fix, and the odds were daunting.

"When have we ever allowed the odds to defy us?" Drake's voice startled me. "We will fight as we have always done, and if we fail, at least we tried. This is your home, your land, your realm, and after enduring so much loss here, *you* still stand. You will continue to do so whether we win this battle or not." The atmosphere shifted, simmering with determination. "If this is not the final battle against the darkness, you can hope that one day, we'll be glad to see it end. Whether that day is now—or in the future—you must hold in your hearts the belief that Upherya will one day be reclaimed from the clutches of darkness." Euros rose from the table and approached us. He paused before Drake, placing a hand on his shoulder.

"Thank you," said Euros with profound sincerity. "I needed to be reminded that this isn't about our land anymore. My realm might fall, but we are not yet defeated. This war has taken much from us, but it has also brought us together. It has forged friendships, turned lifelong enemies into allies. We are stronger because of the trials we've faced." He paused to look at me. "We believe in you and we are grateful to have you on our side."

He extended his hand to me, and I finally understood why Drake held the warrior in such high regard. Euros could be just as intense, dark, and brooding as my dragon prince. I smiled warmly at him.

Their speeches ignited the spirits of the Wind People. The calls to fight were no longer for the North alone but for all the Realms. Despite the looming threat of defeat, my presence rekindled hope for a more favorable outcome.

As the days passed and the impending battle neared, the tensions rose. My daily battle involved preventing Callix and Drake from tearing each other apart. When I wasn't mediating disputes, I worked with the elementals at the foot of the Tirse mountains, harnessing their energies to extend the barriers and maintain the shields in place.

The wind people celebrated each night as if it were their last. Music, dancing, and blazing fires ignited along the city streets. Days of intense training and preparation ensued, followed by nights of joy and freedom—the spirit of Upheryans.

As night fell, even the warriors seemed in better spirits as they gathered around the firepits. They teased and often fought, but Amirth was right. They were a bunch of babies with lousy attitudes, yet they were incredible fighters with beautiful wings. They often had me questioning why, out of all the possible gifts immortality offered, flying wasn't one of them. But I wasn't complaining. I was happy to be alive, even if death loomed.

THE FLAMES in the pit danced before my eyes as I sat between two boulders of raging masculinity. Drake to my right and Callix to my left. Link and Phoenix arm wrestled over a barrel of beer, while Euros and Amirth were just as she had described. *Complicated.* They were not together per se, but everyone sensed the sexual tension between the pair. I think they thought no one noticed or perhaps they didn't care. However, I was keenly aware that when Amirth often excused herself for the evening, Euros would follow not long after. Just like they did now. It was comical to glance into the minds of those two at times, not that I often did, of course. I wasn't inclined to pry into people's private thoughts like others were.

"I do not pry into your mind all the time," Callix's voice invaded my thoughts. I glanced to my left and shook my head.

"I choose not to fight this battle. In truth, I gave up long ago." His quiet laughter danced in my mind, and at that exact moment, Drake's hand shifted on my thigh; perhaps it was an involuntary reflex or he somehow sensed my private exchange with Callix.

Link forcefully slammed Phoenix's arm against the barrel, and the wooden edges splintered from the sheer force.

"You cheated," Phoenix protested.

"How does one cheat at arm wrestling, exactly?" Link argued, and I couldn't help but smile. With those two, there was never a dull moment.

Euros returned with a sour expression, suggesting his nightly excursion hadn't gone as planned.

"Patrol?" He glanced at Drake, who hesitated before reluctantly standing up from my side.

"I won't be long," Drake assured me. He lifted my chin and placed a gentle kiss on my lips. When he rose to his full height, he glanced at Callix and narrowed his eyes. A clear, silent warning. However, when Drake disappeared with Euros, the Water Lord leaned in closer.

"What do you say to a walk?" He proposed. I shook my head. "A sparring match, perhaps?"

I hesitated, tempted by the idea, but spending time alone with him—in any way—was perhaps unwise.

When I didn't respond, he stayed silent, then I felt his quiet voice in my thoughts.

"I thought you said you wouldn't shut me out?"

He was right, and I hated myself for it. Because every time I chose to indulge in his company, I witnessed the pain in Drake's eyes. And when I didn't, I contended with Callix's quiet despair.

"Do you think this is easy for me?" I pushed desperately back.

Without answering, Callix rose to his feet and extended his hand to me. I glanced at it, but his eyes left no room for refusal. Hand in hand, we weaved through the lighted paths.

"I'm not asking you to make a choice," he murmured. "I'm asking you to be true to yourself. I want you to choose yourself, your passions, your desires—above anything and *anyone* else. Even if it means upsetting me or him. I want you to always do what feels right for you."

"I wish it were that simple," I whispered.

"It can be. You just have to choose to be happy."

"I can't be happy making others miserable."

"Then the alternative is you will be miserable, too."

"A small price to pay," I said. I was responsible for this situation, after all. For causing them pain.

He paused and turned toward me, reaching out to tuck a loose strand of hair behind my ear.

"Darling, you are not a martyr. You are a goddess, and none of this mess is your fault." I smiled. He always had a unique way of comforting me.

"If I were a goddess, I wouldn't be in this mess," I said, and he laughed.

"I disagree. If you were a goddess, you would have altars raised at your feet with a host of men bowing before you, myself included." My laughter rang out, and he smiled, interlacing his fingers with mine. "You said you wouldn't be in this situation if you had the power," he continued, and I sensed where this conversation was headed. "So, how would you rectify it? What would you have done differently?"

I glanced at his face, hoping to find an answer there, but I couldn't think of anything I would change. Meeting Drake and Callix—denying either of them—felt like a betrayal to myself. "Honestly, I don't think even a goddess's power could help me figure that out."

"But your wish would be our command," he teased, and briefly, I envisioned a world where I felt ultimate happiness. A world without war, conflict, disagreement, or resentment between Drake and Callix. A world where it might be possible to equally love them both. The Water Lord's hearty laughter shattered my thoughts, and my eyes narrowed.

"Darling, it would take much more than divine magic to achieve that. You would need to exist in a different dimension and command the power to warp the reality of that hard-headed fool. Even then, he might not yield to see me anywhere near you."

"You forget Drake is not the only one with a dominion problem here. You are equally as bad," I said, and the corner of his mouth quirked.

"I can be possessive, I'll admit." He leaned in so close that I felt his breath fan my neck. "But I'd be willing to compromise. If you desired, I'd have no qualms sharing my bed with him." His hands moved to my waist, pressing me against him. "Sharing your body..." he whispered. "Imagine all the wicked things we could do to you."

I had stopped breathing. He turned me around, bringing

my body flush against his. His hardness pressed against my lower back.

"Callix…" I said in a breathless attempt to—I didn't know what exactly. Ask him to stop? Beg him to continue? Or to demand he tell me more of this imaginary world.

"I would take all options except number one." He breathed into my ear. He was in my head again… always in my head.

"Callix," I said, this time with more clarity. He sighed with resignation, but he didn't move. Stilling behind me, he braced his hands securely around my stomach.

"Why are you denying yourself this?" he asked. A question he had asked many times before. Still, I had the same answer. The one he did not want to hear.

"Because that perfect world doesn't exist," I said, gently removing his hands from my middle. I turned to peer into his eyes. "And because I don't want to keep hurting him or you."

His cerulean eyes took me in, and I lost myself in them until he took my hand.

"Come." He pulled me back through the throng of people. "Visiting the forge for a few hours will do us some good. It will dispel some of this tension." He glanced at the noticeable bulge in his slacks.

I halted, suddenly fearful of his real intentions.

"Relax, darling." His wicked smile reappeared. "Just sparring will suffice. Unless you'd like to bend the knee?"

"Sparring will do. Unless you'd like your head spiked on a pole tonight."

"I much prefer the thought of your mouth wrapped around my spear." The crudeness of his joke was not lost on me.

"Seriously?" I punched him in the chest and shook my

head at his relentless attempts of seduction. I could not change him, even if I wanted to, though a part of me preferred him like this. Rough edges and all.

The forge was quiet as we entered the arena. I formed my swords and the thumping of my heart rang in my ears like beating drums. I had missed this. The pumping of adrenaline. Blood rushing. Callix was right. I wanted this, and I could no longer deny it, even if Drake despised my contact with the Water Lord.

When he materialized his water spear and skillfully circled it before himself, he smiled. I didn't have to read his mind to know exactly what he was thinking.

"Will you stop with the insinuations?" I asked, swinging my twin blades.

"Insinuations?" he quizzed, feigning offence. "I have yet to speak a word."

"You didn't have to. I can see it in your face, and the way you wave that..."

"Spear... say it. Callix's spear," he said, knowing exactly what he was doing. "Perhaps you're just intrigued by it?" I attacked, forcing him to retreat. "Am I right?" He moved out of the way, predicting my next move. "Nice try."

He swung the spear in a wide circle and hit my behind with force, knocking me to my knees.

"On your knees so soon? I knew you couldn't resist me." I braced against the ground and landed a firm kick against his rock-hard abs. The force made him stagger back.

"Less talk and more action," I said, and his brows rose in challenge. The teasing was over.

Even after days without training, I stood my ground. I didn't beat him, but I was close a few times, especially whenever I diverted his attention.

A sheen of sweat coated my forehead, so I wiped it away with my sleeve. Callix's shirt was no longer white and crisp. Sweat and dirt covered it in patches, and loose tendrils of matted wet hair fell over his brow.

In a perfect twist, I soared through the air, slashing his chest with my swords. Once I landed, bracing my swords, Callix's proud and surprised eyes locked with mine.

"That was impressive," he said, ripping his shirt down the middle. He tossed it aside, revealing the light pink line where my sword had cut him. Already, the wound was healing.

"I'm sorry," I apologized, lowering my swords.

"Never apologize for your skills," Drake's voice broke the silence, surprising me. Callix, however, didn't seem surprised. He must have been aware of Drake's presence. I wondered how long Drake had been watching. Drake walked toward the edge of the arena, rolling up his shirt sleeves.

"I have to say he's right. That was impressive," Drake said, flashing a smile. "And you were holding back on me," he added, a reference to our first night in Abryas.

"I had a good teacher," I responded, giving Callix the credit he deserved.

"I can see that." Drake glanced at him.

"Are you ready to go?" I asked, allowing my swords to dissipate. Drake's eyes remained fixed on me. I sensed pride in his gaze, yet an underlying tension, too. Unspoken emotion.

"He hates that I was the one who taught you," Callix revealed,

offering insight into Drake's private thoughts. I panicked, fearing Drake's wrath.

"I warned you not to pry into my thoughts again," Drake thundered, stepping into the arena. He unsheathed his sword. The blade ignited with flames, but Callix remained unfazed. Instead, he smiled.

"Drake, please."

"I think this is overdue," Callix interjected.

"Shut up, Callix," I muttered, stepping between them.

"Drake. Why are you doing this?"

"For fun," he responded, though his eyes remained locked on his opponent. "Don't worry, love. I promise not to kill him."

I jumped out of the way as their weapons clashed. It echoed through the forge, like two boulders colliding.

I dug my nails into the wooden post each time a blow was delivered to either side. They were relentless and equally matched in skill. Every punch delivered was matched, an incessant dueling of force and strength. Neither would yield.

"Enough," I screamed, unable to see an end to this bloody madness. I stepped into the arena.

"Belynda, stay out of this," Drake said. His cuts healed as quickly as new ones appeared. Callix did not look much different. Blood covered their faces and arms, but they refused to give in.

"This is insane," I yelled. "I hate you both!"

"No, darling. You love us both," Callix taunted, but Drake's rage-driven punch silenced him. I stared at them both. This feud would never end. They would never stop hating each other, and I would never stop hating myself for being the cause. Rage coursed through me, and with all the energy sizzling through my veins, I pulled on the force of air and rammed them against opposite walls. They struggled against the force of the wind rendering them immobile.

"This ends now," I stated, looking between them. "I refuse to be caught in the middle of this. We have a war to fight, and you're behaving like children."

"Belynda. Release me," Drake demanded; his dark eyes seethed.

"No. Not until you both promise that you've had enough."

"Darling, what you're asking for lies in the realm of impossibilities. Neither of us will ever have enough," Callix mocked.

"You will do it for me," I claimed. "If you care for me, you will put an end to this now."

"Fine," Callix agreed. I turned to Drake, but his lips remained tightly sealed.

"Release me," he finally said as his eyes regained their normal color. "Let's go to bed."

Once I felt reassured their anger had simmered, I released them both. Callix smiled at me as Drake and I left the forge. This was far from how I had envisioned this night to go, but it might have been exactly what they needed.

At least for a while.

16
THE DARKEST TEMPEST

HE CLOUDS DARKENED AND SWARMED, LIKE AN OMINOUS OMEN, as if the very skies sensed the impending doom. An eerie hush blanketed the North as we braced for nightfall. With hearts pounding and swords raised high, the legions dispersed across the northern borders. I soared beneath the brooding clouds, stretching beyond the clan's boundaries. A ceaseless tide of obsidian shields and armor advanced, accompanied by the billowing banners of Dagasti's army. Death descended the hills, ready to claim more of my friends and family. The dragon roared as it circled back over the Tirsia Mountains, relishing its power. Our silent companion.

The women and children moved through the water portal, leading them safely into Abryas. I spotted Belynda's lovely face and gentle smile as she encouraged them forward. Although the decision to move the women and children from the mountains signaled a prediction of defeat, Euros understood the need to be cautious. If we were forced to retreat, as we had been required to thus far, they would be protected by the mountains, but nonetheless, trapped. There was also the concern that our magic shields could collapse, and with Belynda harnessing the elemental energies to bolster defenses, there was concern of the safeguard faltering, exposing the women and children.

The water portal sealed, enveloping Belynda, Callix, and the elementals.

Euros, Link, and Phoenix resided with the remaining soldiers before the legions. If we had any opportunity to push back, this was our chance. The mountain range flanked us on the left, leaving only a narrow valley as an entry point into the North. With the protective barriers to our left and the cliffs to our right, Dagasti's army had one viable path. We were determined to ensure they advanced no further, and we counted on Belynda's barriers to secure that outcome.

After one final sweep of the perimeter, I descended toward the cover of the mountain, positioning myself close to the border where Belynda, Callix, and the elementals awaited to extend the barriers.

I donned my armor in the hushed surroundings, interrupted by the distant roar of marching legions and the soft approach of footsteps. The dragon and I stilled, recognizing her distinct gait and breath. Her unmistakable essence.

"There you are." Belynda's smile lit up the forest, which slowly surrendered into darkness as evening approached. "Here. Let me help." She fastened the shields to my shoulders, studying my face. Worry reflected within her own. "All set. You look... lethal." Her smile was strained.

I cupped her face in my hands and tenderly kissed her lips. "You have nothing to worry about. I won't allow anything to happen to you."

"Drake," she gently admonished. I knew she could look after herself, but the instinct to protect her was deeply ingrained. It was hard to surrender.

"I know you are a lethal creature." A smile played on my lips, and she responded with a hesitant attempt at her own. "That's how I know we'll come through this unscathed," I said, drawing her close to my chest. I cradled her small frame.

"Please be careful," she whispered, and at her absurd request, the monster's sardonic laughter echoed.

"Have you ever seen me in battle?" I asked, while knowing she never had. She shook her head, her eyes glazed with worry. "I promise. You have no reason to fear." I leaned in and kissed her forehead.

The elementals stood at the foot of the mountain. Amirth wore her armor, except her duties required today meant she would not set foot on the battlefield, a reprieve that Euros welcomed.

Callix gazed at the legions forming in the distance; the magic-infused golden details on his vest matched those on Belynda's arms and shoulders. Part of me resented him for giving her yet another thing I had not, but I couldn't bring myself to resent him completely. After all, I had no kingdom and she had left her family behind. I recognized the honor in those who bore the Serfier runes of protection, and I was pleased he deemed her worthy of them. No one else deserved them more. That small acknowledgment lessened my resentment, somewhat, if only by a fraction.

"It's time," Callix declared, turning to face us. I sensed the fear gripping Belynda and felt her heart quicken. The darkness within me roared; I suppressed it.

"You'll stay with them," I instructed, and Callix defiantly raised his brows.

"They are more than capable of defending themselves. They will have the mountain's protection," he argued.

"Nonetheless." For the first time, I willingly opened my thoughts to the Water Lord. *"Protect her,"* I pleaded before turning away. I stole one final glance in Belynda's direction before vanishing into the ranks of the legions.

CALLIX

Nothing often surprised me, especially with my mind-invasion gifts. But Drake often did. Somehow, the brooding bastard held that power over me. Perhaps I was to blame. I had stopped expecting kindness from him long ago. Of course, his silent request wasn't for my sake, but it was a quiet compromise for hers, and that was enough for me.

"You're not obligated to stay," she offered, coming to stand beside me. I sensed her thoughts churning with worry.

"You heard him," I said. She tilted her head, watching me.

"Since when do you unquestioningly obey Drake's commands?"

I sighed, turning to her. Honesty was paramount, and I had promised that much.

I held her gaze. "Since he silently asked me to protect you," I confessed. Her eyes widened.

"He did? Of course, he did," she corrected herself. "He doesn't trust that I can take care of myself."

"No. I don't believe it was his lack of trust. Not this time." For the first time, I understood why people made selfless sacrifices in the name of love. "When you love someone so deeply, you shield it at any cost."

She rolled her eyes, and I couldn't help but smile.

"Weren't you the one who preached to me about tough love? About not taking the easy route because it's best?"

"I was and still stand by my beliefs," I affirmed. "But those are my methods, darling, not his. And today, I'll choose to selfishly heed his request." I was unwilling to confess to her or even myself, the unsettling unease I felt at the thought of any harm befalling her. Yet, from the curve of her lips, she was clearly unconvinced.

WE WATCHED the legions march forth outside of the expanse, where we planned to extend the protective shields.

"I still find the idea of engaging in battle foolish. If the magic barriers hold, no one has to die."

"You and I both know those barriers won't hold forever," I said, and though I sensed her desire to believe otherwise, deep down, we both understood the amount of energy to sustain them exceeded her abilities.

"I know." She conceded, her voice tinged with sorrow. The weight of the war weighed down upon her, as did her inability to end it.

DAGASTI

The desperate wails from the beleaguered realm penetrated the castle walls. Tonight, Upherya would crumble to its knees. Fire and darkness would quell the winds in their lands, and soon, my army would storm the shores.

"My king, you have an unexpected visitor," informed the servant.

"Who is it?" I demanded.

"They refuse to divulge their name, my lord, but they claim it's a matter of great importance."

"Send them in," I gestured, intrigued. Perhaps the warriors had come to their senses and sought surrender.

However, my suspicion deepened when the hooded visitor revealed their face before me.

"What is your purpose here?" I thundered, vexed by the audacity of a time waster.

"I have something valuable to offer, my Lord." The voice slithered around me like tentacles.

"I possess everything I desire. Soon, all realms will bow to my command."

"But you do not possess the blood-witch," declared the daring visitor. My interest was piqued, and I wondered if I had been too hasty in dismissing their offer.

"Speak," I urged, as the weaving voice detailed a plan to bring me closer to my prize. With the blood-witch on my side, our mission would be swifter. Smooth. She would come to recognize the futility of continuing the slaughter and blood-shed, which, of course, was something I welcomed. I was confident it would be enough to encourage her cooperation.

With the new plan set in motion, my newfound ally departed.

"Dispatch word to the borders and prepare the fleet," I commanded the Dravonis commander.

"Sir?" he questioned.

"Do I need to repeat myself?" I roared. "Get those ships on the water. Now!" The guard obeyed, and I relished the sudden shift of events.

Soon, I would claim my prize.

BELYNDA

We stood on the rugged edges of the towering mountain. I felt the surrounding waves of the elements: earth, air, fire, and water. We watched as the legions of Elvin soldiers united with the Wind warriors, their armor glistening beneath the dappled spell of moonlight. They advanced toward the approaching darkness. Tension charged the air as the impending battle loomed.

The mountain pulsed with a subtle energy, almost as if it remembered the souls bound by light, protecting it in spirit. A gentle winter breeze carried a calming fragrance of pine trees, and the earthy scent of the forest floor. Yet a faint hint of sulfur mingled within it, a grim reminder of the approaching army. The same scent had halted my attempts to breach Drake's mind. As the realization crossed my thoughts, I froze, comprehending the darkness he often spoke of and his years in Xelraa. Xelraa was the dimension from which the darkness emanated —a dimension that once held him captive until, by fate's design, I helped him to escape. Could he carry such darkness within himself? I dismissed the thought as I observed Amirth, Rashe, and Alexia exchanging silent glances.

They heard it, too, even with their human hearing. The first clash of battle echoed through the night as the Elvin legions and wind warriors approached the enemy.

I braced against the forest ground, and the elementals followed. They formed a circle, their hands intertwined like we had practiced. The energy turned grim as the distant sounds of battle served as a reminder of the encroaching darkness.

The elementals' touch sent shivers down my spine. I allowed their energies to flow into me. Amirth's energy was cool and grounding, Alexia's light and airy, and Rashe's scorching hot. Together, their forces melded with my own.

Closing my eyes, I felt the mountain's protective barrier— a shimmering, invisible shield that had guarded it for centuries. With effort, I pushed the power outward, extending the magical wall from the mountain's edge and into a line that spanned across the hills into the Northern territory. The invisible shield materialized, translucent and shimmering.

Even as the barrier reached the edges of the windless cliffs, I felt the strain it imposed on my own powers and that of the elementals. It took a heavy toll. However, I willed it to remain in place, and it acquiesced to my command.

DRAKE

Euros, Link, Phoenix, and I stood at the forefront of the battle-field. Behind us, three legions of Elvin soldiers and wind warriors formed an unbreakable line. Their weapons gleamed against the wavering torches, ready to face the enemy.

I unsheathed my sword. Its blade was forged in Dragonfire, and its edge radiated an otherworldly sheen. As the first wave of Darklings surged forward, I leaped into the fray, and the warriors followed. Darklings fell before me, their savageness unable to withstand the fury of my onslaught.

Soon, we were submerged in a sea of bloodshed and death. A beastly Darkling charged my way, a giant spawned into the darkness. It snarled as it charged, unsheathing its claws like jagged obsidian. With a deft flick of my sword, I parried its attack, locking eyes with the creature, whose gaze was a depthless black. With a forceful, powerful kick, I sent the giant Darkling flying. Its body crashed into the ranks of its companions.

Euros moved alongside me. He weaved through the battle, his twin swords a whirlwind of death. He willed gusts of wind to lift Darklings into the air, vulnerable to his swift and deadly strikes. Link extended his wings and darted through the enemy lines like a force of nature—a harbinger of destruction —as each burst of energy from his wings sent Darklings hurtling back into their ranks. Phoenix was no less lethal. I had seen the warriors fight, but tonight, they were agents of devastation, and their intent was clear: wreak havoc upon the dark army.

A Darkling wielding a war hammer came down against my sword. My muscles strained, and with a well-timed feint, I sidestepped the Darkling's next swing and drove the blade into its chest. Euros moved through the air in a skilled display, severing the Darkling's head with visceral rage and madness.

While less skilled than the warriors, the Elvin allies fought with unyielding resolve as the plains became a battlefield of carnage and chaos. The battle raged as a relentless wave of Darklings surged forth, overwhelming our ranks. The once-orderly formations of the Elvin legions dissolved into a chaotic maelstrom of combat. Soldiers turned on each other as the darkness claimed their souls for its cause.

With obsidian black eyes, the army advanced like a force forged of nightmares. Their movements were eerie, and their numbers were seemingly endless. Guttural cries filled the air, competing with the clash of weapons. It drowned out all other sounds.

Despite our efforts, the Darklings overran us and slowly pushed us back. Link, Euros, and Phoenix pushed on with all their might, but I knew it was time to take to the skies. Embracing the power of fire and darkness, I released my companion to roam and sow devastation once more. The dragon's talons carved a path through the dark forces as the creature soared. With a thunderous growl, I descended on the enemy. Flames erupted from the beast's jaws as fire dispersed the horde, sending Darklings tumbling in a vortex of black smoke and anguished screams, replaced by yet another wave of eager Darklings. Their lines were endless.

Euros issued orders to the remaining Elvin lines, moving fresh troops to the front while those who were fatigued or battered drew back to the rear. We needed renewed strength to hold the line.

Spears and arrows rained towards me, melting beneath my fiery breath. I swung my tail like a battering ram, knocking Darklings off their assault. Another giant took its aim, his body reinforced with heavy armor. It swung a colossal mace, which I dodged with a skilled serpentine twist. I rounded and retaliated with a blast of scorching flames, melting the Darkling's armor and sending the towering giant to its knees.

However, as the fire cleared on the battlefield, more Darklings advanced. It was useless. This would never end. I took to the skies, keeping close to the clouds, and traveled over the expanse of the extending army of shadows. I saw no end. Dagasti had lost his mind. There was so much loss—countless souls...

Veering back, I flanked the coast, and the low burning lights caught the dragon's attention. I had to return to the flanks, but something wasn't right. I descended toward the coast.

It couldn't be... not yet. Dagasti was no fool. We had focused so much on defending the North that we had neglected to anticipate his plans to cross into Abryas. Hundreds of ships stood ready to sail across the bay to the Elvin lands. Yet Dagasti was nowhere to be seen.

I pushed my wings against the roaring currents of the North and found my way back to the frontlines. The beast landed with a clashing rumble, sending a spewing line of fire to hold back the Darklings advance, enough time to allow me to shift back. Skin-clad, I weaved through the lines of the legions.

"Euros!" I roared, and he whirled to face me while another Darkling fell beneath his blade.

"The ships are preparing to cross the bay!" I shouted above the din of battle. Link and Phoenix moved to cover us. "Euros. We can't win this," I said, and he shook his head. "Remember what you said: this is no longer a battle for the North; it's a war for the Realms."

Link and Phoenix turned their gaze toward us. We all searched for a strategy that would allow us to push back the darkness, to maintain the lines, and protect the North from being engulfed by the shadows. But we all knew that this battle was over.

"Retreat!" Euros called with a resounding cry, and the warriors fell back.

CALLIX

As the call for retreat echoed through the chaos, I knew Belynda couldn't hold the barrier much longer. Her brows furrowed, and sweat beads formed along her forehead.

With the walls at risk of falling and the Darklings poised to break through, she would also be in danger.

"I'll be right back," I assured her, though confusion clouded her eyes. I vanished through a water portal and reemerged behind the retreating lines of soldiers who had managed to return safely under the mountain's shield.

With the wave of my hands, I allowed three giant water portals to emerge.

"You, you, and you," I called out to three Elvin commanders. "Guide the men back through the portals to Abryas. Let only those who can cross the shield through and ensure no one is left behind. Understood?"

They nodded and hurried off, instructing the troops to abandon this realm.

The barriers shook as I reached Belynda and the elementals. Their bodies were nearing their limits. I hesitated. Channeling my energy into the barrier would leave me vulnerable, but Belynda needed me. Those walls had to hold until every one of our people was safely through. Until the portals sealed behind them.

Determined, I stood behind Belynda's trembling form and placed my hands on her shoulders. A surge of pure crystalline energy flowed forth, merging with the barrier's magic. The power responded, growing stronger and expanding the shield.

"Just a little longer," I said through gritted teeth. I felt the barrier's power drain my immortal strength.

In the distance, the front lines continued to withdraw past the barriers, and as soon as the darkness clashed against our defenses, we felt it recoil. Belynda screamed.

"I don't know how much longer we can hold," Amirth admitted, breathlessly.

"We will hold," I commanded. "Just until they've all crossed the water gates. And then, we let go."

With a deafening roar, I forced the last of my energy to hold against the darkness pounding at the barriers. The reverberations surged through my body.

"Callix," Belynda gasped. She crumbled, and Alexia and Rashe collapsed, too, with Amirth following suit. The walls trembled, shaking the very foundations of the mountains. As the warriors slipped through the portals, I waited until only dust remained before commanding the portals to close with the last threads of my strength.

The energy of the barriers recoiled, sending us flying into the mountains.

My head rose from the ashen forest as horror seized me. Darklings slipped under the shadows of the mountains. The forcefield had given way. We needed to move but couldn't. I had promised to protect Belynda. My gaze fell to the tree branch impaling my midsection and the crimson blood pooling around my stomach. I would lose consciousness soon.

Nearby, Amirth shifted, and hope flickered within me.

"You need to go. Now," I pleaded. With my waning strength, I summoned a water portal before her.

"Take them, please. Hurry," I implored.

She dragged Alexia through first and a moment later returned for the young boy. A mist clouded my vision as consciousness slipped. Through the haze, I observed the elemental's return as she hauled Belynda through the circle of water before the forest's darkness sealed around me.

BELYNDA

The once-deadly battleground transformed into a serene expanse beneath clear blue skies, a stark contrast to the preceding nightmare of darkness. I took in the scene, reorienting myself amid the hustle of Elvin soldiers and Upheryan warriors.

"Thank the Fates you're awake!" said Kylram, taking my hand. I sat up.

"What happened?" I inquired, disorientated, and then I remembered. "The walls fell…" I whispered, touching the tender part of my temple as I fought to remember.

Not far from me, Alexia, Rashe, and Amirth sat on the ground. I attempted to stand, but my legs trembled beneath me.

"Easy," Kylram urged, offering her support as we weaved through the chaos.

"Belynda!" Amirth stood and enveloped me in a hug.

"What happened?" I asked, hoping for someone to fill in the gaps.

Amirth furrowed her brows, and dread gripped my heart.

"The barrier collapsed. The Water Lord managed to open a portal for me to pull you and the others through, but before I could return for him, the portal closed."

He was fine. I repeated it like a mantra, assuring myself that Callix was safe in the forest. He would open another portal once he'd regained his strength. He was fine, I told myself, but the weight in my chest persisted.

"Has anyone seen Drake?" I asked, my worry growing.

Kylram shook her head, and the elementals remained silent.

"They're okay," I said out loud. "They have to be."

"There is something you should know," Amirth added, her expression somber. "When the barriers collapsed, the mountains lost their protection, too."

"No," I choked. This was not how things were supposed to unfold.

I fell to my knees with a sinking feeling. *Not like this. Not like this!*

"Euros!" Amirth cried, rushing toward the warrior. He took her into his arms and cradled her. For the first time, they didn't seem to care who saw them. I rose to my knees and closed the distance.

Euros' gaze met mine over Amirth's shoulder. Words were unnecessary; he understood what I needed to know.

"He didn't go through the portal. He went back to find you." My heart plummeted. It couldn't be. I couldn't lose them both, not like this.

"Come, child. Let's get you to your room. Your friends will be settled shortly."

I walked alongside Kylram, numb and disconnected. Everything seemed surreal, like scenes from a passing movie.

"How can you stay so calm?" I asked, struggling to accept the uncertainty of not knowing where Drake was or if he was okay.

"Because I know how relentless he is. It's too early to worry." I wished for his mother's strength but was burdened by a knowledge she did not possess. The Fates had warned me he would pay the price for my immortality, and that thought gripped my heart. Drake and Callix were gone. Warm tears stained my cheeks as their absence tore at my soul.

"Kylram," Leiwen called, hurrying down the stairs. The urgency in her voice made Drake's mother tense beside me. Despite her outward composure, I knew she was worried. "We just received a message from the soldiers stationed at the Ishtar border wall. It's Drake." Leiwen glanced at me. "And Callix."

I released a sob, a mixture of relief and hysterical laughter. They were okay... they were okay! I was going to kill them both.

"How did they get there?" asked Kylram, her relief evident.

"Drake flew them across the Fjord. Callix is still unconscious; he's lost a lot of blood. We've granted Drake permission to fly into the city." Leiwen must have noticed the panic on my face. "He'll be fine," she reassured me.

"Where do we meet them?" I asked.

"Come. Drake should be here any minute. The healers are already waiting in the Water Lord's chambers."

Ignoring my usual manners, I rushed past the two women and took the stairs two at a time. I ran through the halls like a madwoman until I reached the wing where his chambers were, and as I reached for the door, somebody pulled it open before I could manage it. I swallowed back sobs as I found Drake, who was still in the process of buttoning his shirt. I crashed into him, and he stilled before encircling me with his arms.

I sobbed into his shirt. "I was so scared," I admitted, pulling away from him. I punched his arm. "They said you went back. Why did you do that?" I hit him again. "Why?" He took my hand and pulled me to him, his lips against my hair.

"It's okay, love. I'm right here."

"Don't ever do that again," I said, glancing up into his gray eyes.

"It's a good thing I did... if I hadn't." He jerked his head behind him, to where Callix lay on the bed while the healers worked over him. His white shirt was now blood-red, laying in shreds on the floor.

"You saved him," I said, shifting my gaze to Drake's.

"I would be lying if I said I didn't hesitate," he admitted, and I didn't doubt it.

"You still did it."

"You wouldn't have forgiven me if I didn't. I did it for you, not for him," he confessed, though something told me that wasn't entirely true.

"Thank you." I glanced past him at Callix.

"You can go in," Drake said, surprising me. "I need to speak with Herod."

He leaned down and kissed me tenderly before taking his leave. I entered, allowing the door to close behind me. I stayed out of the healer's way, but the moment Callix stirred, I moved closer.

"Blasted gods, that hurts," he groaned, his voice breaking the room's silence. I smiled and my heart swelled with relief as I fought back tears.

"He should be as good as new in a few hours," declared one of the healers before leaving the room.

"Who's there?" asked Callix, his voice curious. I moved from my spot behind a dresser, and he smiled as soon as he saw me.

"Like you can't read my mind from a mile away?" I teased, grinning. Though what I truly wanted was to crawl into bed and hug the fool.

"I'm afraid those skills are temporarily out of order. That barrier drained all my energy. My body must have used whatever remained of it to keep me alive."

"It must be a hard life, not knowing what others are thinking," I said, and he grinned.

"I don't need to read your mind to tell you what you want, darling." I froze.

"And what is that?"

"Just come here," he said, and I hesitated. Perhaps he knew me all too well.

I moved slowly around the bed's canopy and sat by his side. His hand held mine while I examined every detail of his long, thick fingers, trying to find any distraction I could.

"How are you feeling?" I asked, forcing myself to meet his eyes. He smiled and mimicked my movements, turning my hand in his.

"Honestly, I've been better. I believe this is the closest thing to feeling like a human," he admitted. I smiled.

"Not bad, is it?"

He furrowed his brows. "You're insane."

"And you're a crybaby?" I teased, but he tugged my hand, pulling me to his chest.

"Callix." His hands held my waist, not allowing me to move. "Your wound!" I said.

"Almost healed," he assured me, but I couldn't be sure. The bandages were still wrapped around his abdomen.

"Be that as it may," I whispered. I attempted to move away, but his hand glided up my back, holding me in place.

"If I had died," he began. "If I had turned to the dark..."

"Don't say that," I interrupted, refusing to entertain the idea.

"Would you have missed me?" he asked, and I gazed into his eyes.

"Of course. Do you even have to ask?" My eyes roamed his face, hoping to capture every detail of it.

"Kiss me," he said. I froze. "Do it because you want to. Do it because if you don't, I will," he threatened, his breath mingling with mine. When I hesitated, he reached up and gently brushed his lips against me. My eyes closed, and a wave of desire surged through me. He was safe; he was alive. I rested my hands on his chest, and when I didn't pull away, he leaned back against the pillow. His cerulean eyes met mine, and he closed the distance again. This time, his kiss was far from passive; his lips molded against me, exploring, teasing, tasting, and taking. For a moment, I forgot how to breathe.

A knock on the door made me bolt upright. I placed a hand against my lips, a warm flush creeping across my cheeks.

"Such bad timing," mused Callix. He propped his hands behind his head, his expression lively. He seemed healthier than moments ago. I was sure of it.

"Come in," I called, and a servant girl entered with a tray of food. The moment she left, Callix grinned mischievously.

"Leaving so soon?" he asked, noticing my hesitation to return to the bed.

"You look much better," I said, placing the tray beside him. "Eat, and I'll check on you in a few hours."

"Will I get another kiss later?" he teased as I reached the door. He knew the answer without me having to face him.

"Don't worry, darling, I won't hold my breath," he laughed, and I knew he would be just fine. He was back to his old, arrogant self, testing me at every opportunity.

THE CASTLE BUSTLED with preparations for the Winter ball and accommodations for the Wind people and Upheryan soldiers. Clan leaders and elementals were offered chambers within the court. The dinner table was more crowded than usual, with Amirth, Rashe, and Alexia on one side and Euros, Link, and Phoenix on the other. I occupied my previous seat, with Drake beside me and an empty chair opposite where Callix should have been.

"I understand that the Winter ball may seem ill-timed,

given our recent losses," remarked Leiwen. "Perhaps we should consider postponing it."

"You don't have to postpone it on our account," Euros voiced. "While we may have suffered a setback, the war is far from over."

Not long ago, I had opposed the celebration myself, but considering all the loss and devastation, I reconsidered the matter.

"Despite the challenges we've faced, we still have reasons to celebrate. We're alive, and we've forged valuable alliances and friendships to be grateful for."

Euros agreed, raising his cup for a toast. "Indeed, we have much to be thankful for. Let us raise our cups to life, friendship, and alliances."

I raised my cup, and everyone around the table followed.

After dinner, I walked the quiet halls alongside Drake, unable to consolidate the recent events. Just last night, we were fighting against the dark, and now here we were, striding the halls of the Elvin kingdom after enduring so much death and carnage.

"How do you do it?" I asked, and Drake slowed his pace to glance at me. "Live through something like that—the killing, the losses," I said. He shook his head.

"I can't speak for the others, but Belynda, you forget that I lived in the world that birthed the darkness. I have seen death and devastation, and I have lived with it, embraced it—and sometimes—craved it." On the rare occasions he spoke of Xelraa, I had never understood what he meant. Until now.

"I see," I said, attempting to grasp the depth of his fight against the darkness.

"Do you?" he asked, and I noted the concern behind his question. The fear that he wasn't good enough for me.

"Yes. I guess I never truly understood the depth of your struggle against the darkness," I admitted. "Is it still difficult? I've not asked, not since Druleska."

He smiled.

"The darkness has been free to roam and devastate. I believe it is happily sated for now." Smiling, Drake brought my hand to his lips. "I, on the other hand…" He trailed off, pulling me against his body.

"You, my Lord, are insatiable." I teased, yet I couldn't succumb to my desires—not now. Guilt would torment me if I abandoned Callix after he had sacrificed himself to save me. "Later?" I asked, smiling up at him. Drake narrowed his eyes as I pulled from his hold.

"Where exactly do you think you're going?" he asked when I started to leave.

"I promised I would check in on him," I confessed, and he tensed. "Will you come with me?" I asked, but he regarded me as if I was insane.

"Belynda, if you must check on him, do so, but do not ask more of me, I beg you," he said, his patience waning. Standing on my toes, I kissed the corner of his lips.

"Thank you," I said. "I'll come to your chambers shortly."

He nodded and disappeared down the hall.

• • •

I raised my hand to knock on the Water Lord's chamber, but his voice stopped me.

"Enter," he called. When I pushed the door open, I found him sitting up on the bed with no bandages in sight.

"Your powers seem to have returned," I noted; he must have heard my approach.

"Somewhat, yes," he replied. "Thank you for coming back."

I nodded, smiling.

"Of course. However, you appear well enough. You could have joined us at dinner."

"I think I'll skip those dinners from now on. If not for my sake, then for yours." His eyes locked onto mine. I didn't argue because he could clearly see how challenging it was whenever the three of us were in close proximity.

"I hate this," I admitted, realizing that a simple 'thank you' didn't suffice when someone had made such sacrifices on your behalf.

"I know. I hate it more." Callix swung his legs over the edge of the bed edge and stood. His dark blue pants rested low on his Adonis belt, revealing the smooth muscles of his chest and stomach as he bridged the distance between us.

He paused before me, raised a hand to cup my chin.

"Callix," I warned, unable to shift my gaze from his.

"I have never..." he began to say but stopped. He shook his head slightly, as if dismissing a thought. Then, he forced a smile. "Goodnight, darling." He leaned in and placed a gentle kiss on one cheek, and then the other, before releasing me. I studied his expressions, but he wore the mask he so often did when trying to hide his feelings. I yearned to know what he was about to say, but if he wasn't ready to share, perhaps it was better left unsaid.

"Get some rest." From the door, I glanced at him. "You might skip the dinners, but I doubt you'll escape the Winter Ball." Though if I was being honest, I wanted him there. I wasn't prepared to navigate such an event on my own. Even though Drake, the elementals, and the warriors would be present, it wouldn't feel complete without Callix.

By the slight lift of his lips, I knew he heard my thoughts.

"I wouldn't miss it for the world," he said. He crossed his arms over his chest and leaned against one of the bed's columns. "I hope you're planning on saving me a dance."

I hadn't thought about the dancing, and suddenly, dread seized me. His laughter boomed around the chamber walls.

"Don't worry. It's all in the leading. You will be perfect." He winked. I stared at the way he bit his lower lip, and I swallowed.

"Goodnight," I said. I almost ran from the room before I lost my senses as I had done this morning.

WATER CASCADED in the bath chamber as I entered Drake's room. A pleased smile touched my lips, and I removed my shoes, carelessly discarding them on the floor; my evening dress followed, pooling around my feet.

The dim light accentuated the shadows dancing around his body beneath the waterfall. His eyes, aflame with desire, locked onto mine. Turning towards me, he covered the distance in three swift strides and pulled me flush against his wet body. His hardness pressed into my stomach, and leaning down, he claimed my lips while his hands slid behind me. Effortlessly, he lifted me and carried us beneath the falling water. My legs instinctively wrapped around him, and I shivered as his throbbing hardness rubbed against my core.

I guided him to my entrance, and with a single thrust, he entered me, connecting with my very soul. I clung to his shoulders as his hands pressed into the curve of my behind, lifting me slightly to drive into me again and again. His mouth found mine and kissed me with insatiable hunger, trailing over every inch of my face and shoulders.

"You are mine," he whispered, grinding his hips. I gasped; the sensation tore me apart.

"Yes," I panted, offering him my neck. I tightened my fingers at the base of his neck as I moved in rhythm with him. Pressing my back against the moss-covered walls, he thrust into me with abandon, and I shattered around him. My body quivered, and in the next soul-shattering surge of pleasure, he released inside of me. His warmth filled all of me like molten heat.

I brushed dark tendrils of his hair away from his forehead, gazing into his eyes of liquid silver.

"You are a goddess," he whispered, a sweet endearment reminding me of Callix's words. *'If you desired, I'd have no qualms sharing my bed with him. Sharing your body... imagine all the wicked things we could do to you.'* I pushed those thoughts aside, my body still trembling with the intensity of our connection.

. . .

MORNING CAME IN A SURREAL HAZE. The Elvin kingdom remained thriving while the Wind realm had succumbed to destruction. Euros and Amirth spent the day secluded in their chambers. Link and Phoenix trained as a distraction from the daunting truth and to forget what was lost.

Callix wasn't in his chambers, and Drake had left early in the morning to sweep the shores, where Dagasti's fleet loomed on the horizon, poised with ominous intent.

Throughout the day, the servants came and went, each busy with various tasks. Intrigued, I followed one of them through the high-vaulted hallways leading to a grand set of doors. I was greeted by a breathtaking sight upon entering. The dancing hall was a vision to behold. Blossoms, vines, and flowers of all colors and sizes adorned it, artfully arranged. Dozens of imposing columns served as natural dividers. Crystal chandeliers hung from the ceiling, adorned with flowing floral vines, and white and silver drapes cascaded elegantly from the floor-to-ceiling glass doors that opened onto an immense terrace.

"There you are," Leiwen's voice brought me back from my daze. She and Kylram were overseeing the final preparations. "What do you think?" she asked, her voice brimming with pride.

"It's magical," I said. There were no other words to describe the enchanting scene before me. However, I couldn't shake the awareness that the celebration was bittersweet, to say the least.

"I only wish we could have celebrated under different

circumstances. Tonight should have been filled with joy and merriment." Kylram said, as if sensing my unspoken thoughts.

"Perhaps a little beauty, magic, and light is exactly what everyone needs after enduring so much darkness."

"You're right..." Leiwen concurred. "We need more light, much more light!" She hurried off to instruct a young servant, determined to infuse the evening with joy.

"No matter how somber our spirits may be tonight, I'm certain Leiwen will find a way to lift them." Kylram said with a warm smile. She was right. Leiwen was a kind soul, at least when she wasn't meddling in my love life. I smiled at the thought.

THE EVENING DESCENDED, marked by the resonating chime of bells throughout the kingdom. Drake stood on the balcony, casually resting his elbows against the stone railings. He gazed out at the realm illuminated below. He was a sight to behold, a prince in his own right. My prince of darkness. His very presence took my breath away.

When his silver eyes found me, my heart skipped. He straightened; his gaze traveled from my face, down the graceful curve of my neck, the swell of my breasts, and the curvature of my hips.

"You tempt me like this... when I promised we wouldn't be late," he murmured, his voice lower, filled with desire. With a soft smile, I turned, allowing him to appreciate the full scope of my attire. The back of my dress plunged as daringly as the front, revealing the smooth expanse of my lower back. The satiny material clung to my body like a second skin and pooled gracefully around my feet.

"Hmm," he purred. He sauntered toward me with a wicked glint in his eye. "I wonder." Drake's hand slipped between my thighs and gently brushed my bare skin. His eyes darkened. "Love, I hate to break my word, but I fear we'll be late for the festivities," he growled, working on the button of his suit's collar. I couldn't help but laugh, batting his hand away.

"Stop it," I chided with a grin, though I found it hard to resist him. "Save it for later." He groaned against my neck, teasingly slipping his hand between my thighs again, drawing a breathless sigh from my lips.

"Are you sure you want to wait?" he teased. "It seems you're more than ready for me, love." I playfully clamped my legs together and stepped out of his reach.

"If you keep doing that, I'm afraid we won't make it to the dance at all," I warned. "But it's my first ever ball. I don't want to miss it."

Drake's eyes softened as the sound of bells traveled through the open balcony.

"We should be going then," he said, stepping back and adjusting the button at his neck.

"What's with the bells?" I asked. His smile widened.

"They announce the arrivals of royals and court members."

"Was it the same in Druleska?" I asked, and I didn't miss the quiet sadness flashing in his eyes.

"I'm afraid so. Royal traditions are alike in all the realms. Or, at least they used to be for Druleska when my father ruled."

"You will sit on that throne again," I assured him. "I know

you will." He brought my hand to his lips, but said nothing in return. Instead, he guided us to the celebrations.

The bells rang out as Drake and I made our entrance. As we stepped inside, my eyes wandered, taking in the rapidly filling space and the multitude of faces. Many were familiar, though most were unknown to me.

"Prince Drake Raden Tyrgar of Druleska and Lady Belynda Hershton, the light bringer," boomed the bellman's voice. Suddenly, all eyes were on us. I clung to Drake's arm, borrowing his confidence as we navigated the sea of curious gazes. Further ahead, I spotted Euros and Link, which brought a smile to my face. Amirth and Alexia stood beside them, both striking and elegant in their gowns. Rashe stood between the two warriors, his short height offering an intriguing visual contrast, but the young elemental didn't seem to mind.

"Where's Phoenix?" asked Drake, noticing his absence.

"Our presence is merely a courtesy," said Euros. "You know Phoenix has never been one for tradition, and this time, I choose not to hold it against him."

Drake nodded.

"How about a drink?" suggested Amirth.

"Allow me," Euros offered.

"Don't go too far," Drake said. He planted a gentle kiss on my hand before heading off with Euros and Link to retrieve some drinks.

I peered around the room for one familiar face, but there was no sign of the Water Lord.

"Walk with me?" I asked Amirth, and together, we

weaved through the elegant gathering of the Elvin court, the young and beautiful; a soft, iridescent glow adorning their skin.

"It's going to take some time getting used to all of this, isn't it?" Amirth admitted. "It's strange. Even though I'm bound to the earth, I should feel more connected here. The truth is, I felt more at home in Upherya than I ever did in my entire life." She confessed.

"Would that have anything to do with a certain complicated warrior?" I teased, nudging her playfully. She smiled.

"No point in denying it." She finally admitted.

CALLIX

Although my wounds were healed, my powers remained depleted, except for one—my connection with her. It was the first thing I sensed. I felt the strings tensing, recognizing she was near.

"Enter," I called, sitting up on the bed. Belynda seemed tired, and it was clear she hadn't had the chance to rest like I had.

"Your powers seem to have returned," she noted, and I responded with a smile. I was relieved that, at the very least, I could hear her thoughts.

"Somewhat, yes," I replied. "Thank you for coming back." I was acutely aware that escaping Drake to visit me couldn't have been easy.

"Of course. However, you appear well enough. You could have joined us at dinner." I shook my head.

"I think I'll skip those dinners from now on. If not for my

sake, then for yours." I held her gaze. There was no need to prolong our suffering when it could be avoided.

"I hate this," she murmured, and I knew what she truly wanted to say. She wanted to thank me for sparing her. For being the one to make the sacrifice, and I watched her with silent understanding.

"I know. I hate it more." Every time she was near, I had to fight the urge to pull her into my arms and devour her mouth. To claim her like the tide. I stood and took deliberate steps towards her. Her eyes fell on my naked torso, and her cheeks flushed with embarrassment. I smiled, fighting the crushing desire to lean in and seal my lips to hers, as she had allowed this morning. Instead, I held her chin between my fingertips and tilted her head.

"Callix," she warned. Indecision danced within her eyes. But I wouldn't push her. I had vowed not to make this any harder than it needed to be.

As I stared into her eyes, I felt the memory of those last moments in the mountains crushing me, suffocating me, as fear gripped me, not knowing if I could save her. I had never felt so powerless in my entire existence.

"I have never..." The words tumbled out without my command, and I paused and shook my head to dispel the thoughts. Instead, I focused on her scent, her velvety skin under my fingertips, and the golden specks in her eyes. I took a steady breath and forced a smile. "Goodnight, darling," I whispered, planting a gentle kiss on one cheek and then the other.

She stared at me for an immeasurable moment, and I discerned her scattered thoughts. She wanted to know what was on my mind yet my thoughts were buried in a dark place and had resurfaced in the span of a single evening. I had vowed to stay away from the dinners for her sake, but a part of me wasn't sure if it was for my own benefit, too—a way to create distance between myself and the overwhelming emotions that made me vulnerable.

"Get some rest," she said, hesitating at the door. "You might skip the dinners, but I doubt you'll escape the Winter Ball." I couldn't help but smile at her inner monologue. The beast wanted to hide behind the mask, yet the man was eager to drown himself in a sea of emotions at her feet.

"I wouldn't miss it for the world," I said, smiling. I leaned against the bedpost, and she followed my every move as I crossed my arms over my chest. "I hope you're planning on saving me a dance," I added, suddenly relishing the idea of having her body close to mine, with my hand at the small of her back...

Her scattered thoughts about uncoordinated dancing interrupted my vivid imagination, and I couldn't help but laugh. Her lips curved at my amusement.

"Don't worry," I reassured her. "It's all in the leading. You'll be perfect." I winked and battled the all-consuming desire to close the distance and press her against the wall. I bit my lower lip, wishing it were hers. I noted the way her eyes darkened as they focused on my mouth.

"Good night," she said. She practically fled from the room. Belynda was clever; she knew if she stayed another minute, I might have found a way to breach the distance coax my way through her defenses, and stolen another kiss.

I collapsed onto the bed and sighed. I needed my powers back.

I spent the rest of the evening under the cascading waters of the shower, hoping to drown out the murmuring echoes of her lovemaking. I rested my fists against the walls, instead focusing on the specks of energy beginning to rush through my body. I flexed my wrist and managed to spark a water portal. Though my powers were returning, I felt no relief.

Her soft pants of pleasure danced in my mind, and for the first time, I wished I could drown. I wished I could somehow stop breathing, even for a little while. Long enough to succumb to darkness and avoid the shattering ache in my chest and my relentless arousal.

Her release provided me with some reprieve, but as her thoughts cleared, the moment of release was scattered with memories of our conversation, about the promises of uninhibited passion. I couldn't help but curse as I closed my hand around my throbbing hardness and surrendered to my desire.

I TOUCHED my fingers against the reflection in the mirror and watched her standing before hers. My breath caught at the dress she wore, a shimmering midnight blue. Her emerald eyes glinted as she studied her reflection.

I longed to confide in her about my suspicions, to ease her mind and my soul, but she would never accept it. She would never believe me.

The ripples in the mirror wavered, and suddenly, I felt the ocean call. The sound of the waves rushed through me like a warning. Something wasn't right.

"Damn it," I cursed the gods for their lousy timing. I had promised to be there.

This shouldn't take long, I convinced myself as I loosened the buttons at my neck. A few minutes in Serfier was a mere few hours up here, and maybe I'd have the chance to claim that dance. I smiled as I slipped through the water portal.

Dagasti's ships crashed headlong against the relentless waves towards the Elvin coast. The darkness wasted no time to knock again, and unless I intervened soon, the Shores of Galnora would be swarming with Darklings.

My magic surged like the roiling currents, resonating with my wrath and power as I unleashed a tempest over the fleet. But it wasn't enough. I growled as the ships fought against the raging storm.

There was no way I could shift, not while my magic still wavered. If I unleashed the beast, it would only weaken me further and leave my kingdom vulnerable.

So, I plunged beneath the churning, frenzied waves, and with a sinking feeling, I released the command.

"Zodrox..." I called as the currents rapidly shifted. I sensed its powerful presence as it swirled around me in circles, its tentacles brushing the water's surface.

"Go," I commanded the Titan, and its mind instantly yielded. He disappeared under the dark waters towards the Fjord. Seeking and destroying.

From a distance, I watched the ships beginning to sink into the ocean's abyss. Darkness devouring darkness.

"I'm sorry," I muttered, for I knew the sacrifice I had to make. But I would do anything to protect my realm, and I knew Zodrox knew that, too, even if he was lost to me, into the darkness. His mind now silenced from my thoughts and my commands.

The ocean floor quaked as an icy fortress emerged from its depths. It stretched high above the surface and extended like a trench along the Varenver Sea, shielding the Glacier Peaks and the Island of the Lost with a protective barrier even Zodrox could not traverse. It was the only way to safeguard my people and kingdom from the Titan—the only way to keep the darkness from spreading.

The kingdom sensed the dramatic shift. Anything left beyond the icy wall was no longer under my dominion. Upon crossing the threshold into the castle, Phial greeted me with a look of terror.

"Master," she exclaimed, rushing to my side.

"It's okay. Everything will be okay. You are safe."

"But Syllis, she's out there," she explained.

"Where is she?" I demanded. Phial hesitated, and I delved into her mind for answers. Syllis had vanished, and there was something else—the sea witches had left a message. My suspicions regarding the bond had been correct.

"The witches message?" I inquired, seeking confirmation from her.

"It was delivered to Syllis, master. She was the one who informed me."

"Where did she go?" I insisted.

"I don't know, Master."

I probed deeper into the nymph's thoughts. She was telling the truth. With a roar, I swiftly returned through the ocean wall.

I willed my heightened senses to trace the residual scent of

Syllis and I followed it to the Island of the Lost, where her trail ended at the icy protective wall. She was beyond it. But why? What in the world could have possessed her to abandon the safety of the castle?

I slipped through a water portal and exited on the Shores of Galnora, closer to the eastern border on the other side of the glacier wall.

Syllis's scent confirmed my suspicions, but I couldn't fathom her purpose for coming to Abryas. Had she sought me out, despite my warning and my orders?

As I neared the Elvin magical barriers, I froze. My own magic tingled in my veins—a pricking, sinking sensation.

The protective walls had been breached, but the golden Elvin guards were not dead. Whoever had done it was claiming bodies for the dark army. The scent was strong, and the intentions were clear. The Winter Ball was about to take a dark turn.

DRAKE

Despite the low spirits, Euros found comfort in the Elvin wine, and Amirth, the pair often eluding my sight. Link spent most of his evening in the company of Alexia while I remained lost in the soft curves of my beloved. I leaned in, pressing Belynda's body against the balcony as the music flared from inside the ballroom.

She had been quiet all night, and I knew why.

"Why are you out here all alone?" I asked her.

"I'm feeling a bit warm, that's all."

"Dance with me?" I murmured, and she sighed.

"How many times do I have to tell you? I can't dance," she protested. This time, however, I disregarded her objection. Clasping her hand, I lead her back into the illuminated ballroom. She regarded me skeptically as I pulled her close, placing one hand against the exposed skin of her lower back and clasping her hand with the other.

"It's all in the leading," I assured her, and she smiled, as if enjoying a private joke.

"I've heard that before," she teased, and her body swayed slowly in time with mine, following the gentle rhythm of the music.

My eyes shifted above her head as the doors hurtled open. Callix stormed through, and my hands tightened around Belynda's arms as his icy spear whizzed past us, grazing my shoulder. For a brief moment, time froze as I realized that Callix's spear had found its mark.

Releasing Belynda, I whirled around, seizing an Elvin soldier by the neck. His eyes were black pools, much like the one pinned to the wall by Callix's spear. A roar of darkness broke through my throat as I tore the soldier's head from his body. So close—they had come so perilously close.

Chaos erupted in the room as the nobility scattered. I saw nothing else but her, though. Belynda was safe; she was breathing. Her clear emerald eyes were wide as she watched the darkness flare around me in waves.

BELYNDA

Amirth and Euros had vanished, and Drake was engaged in deep conversations with Herod. Leiwen and Kylram skillfully kept the nobility entertained, which left me to my own devices. I was certain Callix wouldn't make an appearance. If he had intended to, he would have done so by now. I sighed and reached for a glass of wine.

"Here." A familiar voice danced before me, and I turned to find Syllis.

"What are you doing here?" I asked, taken aback.

"The Master invited me," she said, offering me her cup of wine. She helped herself to another. My heart sank. Why would he extend such an invitation?

"Where is Callix?" I asked, taking a sip to quell my irritation.

"He's around." She flashed a mischievous smile. "He promised me a dance," she added, and her words felt like a dagger in my chest. I downed my wine and set the cup on the table.

"Thank you. Excuse me." I wanted to heave. It felt like a knife was twisting in my chest, wrought with jealousy, and though Callix was free to make his own choices, I couldn't escape this irrational feeling.

I leaned against the balcony's railing, my barely covered dress offering little protection against the evening chill. As the music played inside the ballroom, I stewed in frustration, unable to shake off the maddening sensations flooding my mind. The warming effects of the wine, or the sipping ire, creeped in.

Unexpectedly, Drake's arms enveloped me from behind, drawing me close.

"Why are you out here all alone?" His arms rested either side of me.

"I'm feeling a bit warm, that's all," I responded, attempting to quell my unfounded irritation.

"Dance with me?" he whispered, and I sighed.

"How many times do I have to tell you? I can't dance," I replied, unable to keep the frustration from my tone.

Ignoring my outburst, Drake smiled and gently pulled me into the ballroom. I decided to go along with it, distracting myself from the emotions swirling within me.

Drake pulled me in and the warmth of his hand rested against the skin of my lower back.

He led me through the dance, his hand a gentle reassurance. "It's all in the leading," he assured me, echoing Callix's words. I couldn't help but smile, despite my anger at the Water Lord.

"I've heard that before," I teased, trying to clear my mind. I moved to the rhythm of the music, and slowly, I realized dancing wasn't as dreadful as I had thought. Yet our dance was abruptly interrupted by the thunderous crashing of the ballroom doors.

Drake's grip tightened around me as an icy spear flew past my shoulder, grazing his arm. My heart skipped as Drake swiftly and brutally dispatched an Elvin soldier while another had been impaled to the wall by Callix's deadly spear. Chaos erupted around us as people scattered, but I couldn't tear my gaze from Drake.

Ribbons of black swirled around him as Link, Euros, and Herod closed in.

"You..." The familiar voice pierced through the haze, capturing my attention. I spun to find Callix; his soaked clothes clung to his body, and his hair was disheveled and fell over his brows. He clutched the nymph by the throat until her feet dangled above the ground. Syllis released a pained roar.

"Callix!" I called, trying to reach his senses, but he was lost in a world of chaos. His eyes held nothing but madness. He didn't acknowledge my presence, and with a swift twist of his wrist, a water portal opened behind him.

"I'm sorry, darling. She won't get a second chance," he said before he plunged through the watery gate, taking the struggling nymph with him.

Drake's body simmered in darkness, but his gaze remained locked on me.

"Are you alright?" he asked while fighting his own demons.

"I'm okay," I whispered. I fixed my eyes on him as the darkness gradually receded, merging back with his skin.

"You touched him," Euros muttered, his voice uneasy. "I don't understand."

His confusion mirrored that of everyone in the room.

"It doesn't matter," Drake replied.

"The hell it doesn't!" roared Euros. "How are you not one of them?"

"Xelraa..." I whispered. '*I have lived within the darkness, embraced it, craved it.*' Drake's words danced in my mind, and suddenly, I knew there was no other explanation.

"It is possible," interjected Herod, stepping closer. "I had always wondered, given his history."

"Are you saying that all this time you've been immune to the dark?" Phoenix questioned.

"I think you're a little late to the party, Phin," said Link.

"This isn't the time for jokes or theories." The shadows around Drake's body blazed. "No one is safe. If the castle was breached, we need to move now." He shifted past Herod. "I will sweep the castle grounds. Link, take the east walls. Phoenix and Euros can take the south shores." He said.

"I have already ordered to close the shields around the city limits. No one enters, and no one leaves without me knowing," declared Herod.

"Your immediate problem is not what is outside, but what might have slipped in," pressed Drake, but his face blurred as he spoke, the rest of the room shifting with it.

"Drake!" I cried out. My voice sounded distant and filled with fear, and then, everything plunged into darkness.

17
TIES THAT BIND

A POUNDING IN MY HEAD, ALIKE TO A MORTAL *HEADACHE, STIRRED ME AWAKE.* Leiwen's familiar face greeted me warmly.

"She's awake!" she called, and as my eyes adjusted to my surroundings, I realized I was in bed, still in my ball gown, while the night stars sparkled beyond the balcony.

Kylram sat beside me, clutching my hand.

"Thank the gods," she whispered. The relief was evident in her voice. "You gave us a fright."

"What happened?" I asked, trying to piece the hazy thoughts together. Memories of Drake flashed—the Elvin soldiers turned to darklings, Callix, and Syllis. I couldn't understand how I ended up in my room.

"You were drugged," explained Leiwen, and her revelation shocked me.

"How? Why?" I whispered.

"Syllis. Callix confirmed it," added Kylram. "Their plan was to deliver you to Dagasti."

Syllis. How? Then I remembered. The wine cup. Her words were intended to incite a reaction from me, and she had succeeded. I knew she hated me, but to betray Callix... now I understood his chaos and fury. I shuddered at the thought of ever returning to Dagasti and what could have happened. I touched my head as it pounded.

"It's normal. The healers gave you something. The effects should wear off soon," Leiwen reassured me. I nodded, still hazy and confused.

"Where is Drake?" I asked as the last moments before I lost consciousness resurfaced.

"He is sweeping the castle. The entire realm has been on alert," said Kylram.

"Is he alright?"

"Yes, child. He is more than alright, and he knows you are safe. That's all that matters," Leiwen assured me.

"We will leave you to rest."

The women stepped out of the room, leaving me alone in the quiet night. I stared at the leaves adorning the bed's canopy as the events of the past two days sunk in. I moved my feet over the edge of the bed and walked to the balcony. The soft evening breeze helped to clear my mind and ease the discomfort in my head. In the distance, the torches marched, and light extended through every corner of the kingdom.

How had Callix known? I dreaded Syllis's fate. Callix was kind, but I knew how unforgiving he could be. If the look in his eyes was any indication, I feared she had paid the price.

The Elvin city was chaotic under the blanket of night, and I was restless.

Slipping on my shoes, I left my chambers, searching for something to distract my mind. Despite the late hour, the castle was awake. Servants came and went, and I searched their eyes fearing that any of them could be servants of Dagasti, sent to collect me.

THE THUNDER of voices made me freeze outside the dining hall. With my newfound abilities, I cautiously pressed against the closed doors. On the other side, the echo of Drake's voice boomed, accompanied by another familiar voice. Callix.

"She chose you once," said Callix. His words resonated clearly through the door.

"And she has done so again because she is bound to me!" Drake growled.

"She is bound to me, too! Water bound by Isabel's sacrifice." Callix's voice sliced through the air like a blade. "Do you think it was easy for me?" His tone dripped with rage. "It killed me to watch Isabel sacrifice herself and to bear the weight of her wishes. Never had I anticipated the price I would pay for that binding."

A heavy silence loomed from the other side of the door until all I heard was my racing heart.

"I've remained on the sidelines out of a sense of duty, unwilling to let your baseless accusations distort the truth," Callix thundered. "But I'm tired of denying my feelings. She is as bound to me as she is to you, and I will no longer stand in the shadows. If she desires me—if she chooses me—neither honor nor friendship will stand in my way."

A sudden, violent crash inside the room startled me, and I jumped.

"Do you think me naïve enough not to know?" Drake roared. "Do you think I couldn't sense your pull, the undeniable claim I felt in her human essence?" I couldn't move; my thoughts were scattered. By the Fates...

"Why the pretense then?" demanded Callix.

"Because she is mine!" Drake roared, and his declaration resonated through my body.

"Seems rather possessive, doesn't it?"

"You will not have her," Drake's voice was low and menacing.

"Her choice still remains."

"She has already decided. She chose me."

Every second felt like an eternity as I lingered outside the door. Things began to fall into place. My irrational feelings for the Water Lord, my inability to stay sensible around him... their words sunk in. I was bound to them both through Isabel's sacrifice. How could I ever decide when the decision was beyond my control? Making a choice would shatter me.

"You should leave," demanded Drake, and I felt a surge of anger—anger at the lies, anger at being kept in the dark. While Callix's mental barriers were intact, his control was slipping.

I pushed against the heavy door and it creaked open. Drake's dark, intense eyes found me.

"Don't worry. I don't intend to stick around to watch you break her." Callix's back remained turned to me as he spoke, though I was certain he could feel my presence. He pivoted, and his azure eyes locked with mine. Then, he stormed out of the room.

The instant Callix departed, Drake roared and sent a chalice hurtling against the wall.

"Drake," I whispered. "What is going on?" my voice soft as I reached out in an attempt to ease his darkness.

"Everything," he replied, his voice tinged with frustration, his gray eyes piercing into mine. "This must come to an end. You must make a choice. Me or him." His roar made me step back my brow furrowed in confusion. How could he ask this of me? How could he demand such a decision knowing how difficult it was? Even after he had refused to reveal the truth.

"Drake," I implored, my heart aching. "Please don't ask me that." His expression remained unyielding.

"Then your decision is clear," he said, and his words surprised me.

"No!" I cried, rushing to him in a panic. His face remained impassive, his eyes dark. "You're being unreasonable. This isn't like you."

"Choose. Now."

I opened my mouth, but no words came out. I couldn't bring myself to give him what he wanted. It was an impossible request, and I knew that now.

"Very well," he murmured, pausing before me. His hand hovered a breath from my face, but he stopped himself. Withdrawing his hand, he walked away, leaving me alone and shattered.

As the doors closed, my resolve crumbled. My legs gave way, and tears streamed down my cheeks.

Drake was hurting, but I was too. I felt like I was being torn apart by lies and half-truths. Drake, more than anyone, should have understood. After all, he had loved Isabel just as he loved me, and it was all because of her sacrifice. Why couldn't he see that it was impossible to choose? The aching pain in my chest was worse than death itself. Drake had refused to admit the truth in my presence, but I had to know. There was only one person I could trust to be direct enough to speak the truth.

Rising from the floor, I gathered my dress and strode with purpose through the corridors. The gardens awaited, bathed in the soft, ethereal glow of a million lanterns. Descending the stairs, I made my way to the fountain.

I leaned over the water's surface, the starry night a background canvas to my reflection. I dipped my fingers tracing the still water and whispered his name.

"Callix."

Ripples formed on the fountain's surface, awaiting a response, and to my surprise, a water portal materialized instead.

I hesitated, but after a deep breath, I stepped through it, aware of who was waiting on the other side.

STEPPING into his chamber felt like a distant memory. The portal behind me dissipated as I moved toward him. The soft glow of bioluminescent waters outlined his silhouette as he stood on the balcony, his back turned, facing the vast ocean dome.

"You lied to me," I said, cutting to the heart of the matter. He remained silent, not even turning to acknowledge me. Yet he was unperturbed by my question, meaning he was fully aware I'd overheard their conversation.

"Would you have believed me?" he asked, still refusing to

look. I pondered his words, and I had to admit, he was probably right. I wouldn't have believed him.

"I had a right to know." I insisted, and finally, he faced me. "It would have helped me understand." I added, and his usual composure transformed.

"You mean it would have eased your guilt for the feelings you had but refused to accept, is that it?" he chastised. I paused, staring into his eyes.

"Why are you so angry with me?" I asked, and he turned his gaze toward the ocean wall, running his hands through his hair before fixing his eyes on me again. His voice took on a softer edge, but I had never seen him look so defeated.

"Because you persistently make the wrong choices. Because you frustrate me. Because you *tempt* me. Because I detest that you desire him. But above all, I *loathe* myself for loving you, knowing you love someone else," he admitted. His chest heaved, and his eyes became a tempest. At that moment, all I wanted was him.

I took slow, measured steps to bridge the gap between us, attempting to quell his anger.

"You're wrong," I whispered, pausing before him. I brought my hand to his face, and he froze, much like the ice encasing the castle walls. "I choose you as well."

His eyes roamed my face, and his thoughts unraveled as I closed the gap to press my lips to his.

The world might burn, but tonight, I chose to embrace the flames. I chose to love him. I chose to stop fighting. Tomorrow was a different day, and I would face my decisions then. Yet, for the first time, I was grateful that time was my friend under the tides.

BECOMING CHAOS
BEGINNINGS

OVE HAS MANY FORMS AND MANY FACES. It grows and wanes; it conforms and yields for the weaker. As I gaze at her sleeping form, my resolve wavers. Promising to help and remain reasonable in the face of her request seemed sensible. At the time, knowing that she needed me was enough to agree to anything. Now, I wasn't so sure I could honor that promise.

It was simpler to disregard the Fates' plan before. However, now they haunt my dreams with sparks and remnants of an uncarved future. I do not know what to believe; as I peer down at her once more, something shifts within me and realization dawns. I understand. I will never find the strength to say no to her, regardless of the cost or pain.

"You're doing it again." Her brown eyes capture my attention, and I blink, my thoughts dissipating. "You're overthinking."

"I can't change your mind, can I?" I plead for what feels like the millionth time. She responds with measured silence, though her lips shift, attempting a smile, though we both know it's too hard. The scent of burnt candles and the embrace of humidity grips my heart, a poignant reminder of her home —of her—and the sacrifices ahead.

"It's the only way. I know you can't see that now, but the Fates' plan is bigger than one miserable life."

"Your life is worth everything. You can still find happiness." I frowned and reached for her hand, but she pulled away and sat, her legs covered by the dark and coarse material of her skirts.

"Now *that* is a lie, Callix, and we both know you never lie to me." This time, the corner of her mouth shifts. I stare into her brown eyes, committing every detail of her face to memory. The dark tresses cascading down her delicate shoulders, the dark circles around her eyes, and the pale contours of her lips. I realize with a sinking heart, that this girl bears no resemblance to the lively Isabel I fell in love with, not since him... not since she lost him.

"Will you come back with me? Spend a few days in Serfier?" I plead. She shakes her head, refusing me like she has done time and time again.

"I still have preparations to do," she says, glancing around the small cabin. Her eyes glaze over; I detect the images running through her thoughts: a passing glimpse of a time when she was happy—when *we* were happy—when Drake, her, and I were friends before she chose him. Her gaze shifts back to me, and with it, concern replaces her memories.

"You don't have to stay," she says. "I know it's not easy for you." Suddenly, a heaviness lodges in my throat.

"I want to stay," I say. It's what a friend would do, though, deep down, I don't want to be here, not for this. I don't want to see her go. I need to breathe.

"Go, Callix. Just go," she says, taking my hand. "It's better this way."

I look into her eyes, speechless. What does one say to the person they love when they know it's the last time they'll ever see them alive? The final time they'll hear their voice? The bed creaks as she stands, and I rise, towering over her.

She embraces me. Her small frame feels frail, and I allow my hands to envelop her momentarily as I breathe in her scent, searing it into my memory. After a moment, she pulls away, reaching up to press her lips against mine. I stare back at her in surprise.

"I'm sorry I couldn't give you what you wanted or be what you wanted. I promise things will be as they should," she whispers, pulling me from my trance. I drop my hands and take a step back, trying to breathe despite the scents assaulting me. My insides turn at the finality of this moment.

"I'm sorry. This is harder than I thought it would be," I admit, barely above a whisper.

"Just go," she says, walking around me. "I promise you will hear my calling when the time comes."

It's a promise I desperately wish she wouldn't keep, but I won't abandon her. I won't go back on my word.

With the flick of my hand, a water portal bursts at the foot of her bed, and I step toward it, only pausing to glance back at her.

"It's okay," she whispers, and I turn, stepping through the portal before the storm takes over me.

TIME WAS MY ENEMY, and I felt her calling two days later as I sat at the dining table. Alone. My heart constricted, and I allowed myself the rare release of tears. For the first time since I was a boy, I braced my hands against my head and allowed my cries to fill the empty halls of the castle. The ocean raged around the realm, mirroring the storm within me, and as the tempest passed, I crystallized my tears, preserving them. A keepsake of the pain. That night, I transformed into ice, into stone—unbreakable, unyielding, for I understood there would be no other way to move forward.

The calm waters of the lake shifted. If I didn't know she was gone, I might have mistaken her for a sleeping goddess, suspended above the lake's surface. Starlight bathed her pale face as I lifted her ethereal form into my arms, clasping her to me as I stepped into the water portal.

THE WATERS of Isilium radiated around us as I laid her body at the base of the tree. Luminous wisps swirled, encircling her and claiming her for eternity. As I witnessed her energy and body merged with the forces of Isilium, I felt the icy fortress solidify against my heart.

I took pleasure in robbing the sacred book from the guardianship. I entrusted it to the care of the water elementals in the human world, alongside Isabel's belongings and relics from the realms—an act that granted me a sense of closure, a mere speck of peace. "I've done as you asked," I said to the glowing tree, like I often did. As expected, it offered no response, and I knew it wouldn't. Yet somehow, coming here made me feel closer to her.

FOR A WHILE, I dwelled in misery, disconnected from the rest of the Realms, while ensconced in a semblance of peace. Solitude became my refuge, and after a few years, I felt something akin to contentment. I occupied my existence by drowning out my desires in the flesh, and when that proved insufficient, I embraced other pursuits, forming an alliance with Upherya and the Wind warriors. In my solitary confinement, I became chaos. However, when the Fates returned to haunt my dreams, reminding me of my unfulfilled duties, I began to curse her.

I chose to dismiss the visions, understanding that their persistence signified one thing: the pure blood had been born. With every passing day, I began to harbor a deep disdain for everything the human girl represented. Nevertheless, the Moirai were nothing if not insistent. Soon, it wasn't just my dreams they invaded. Their presence grew relentless, an irritating reminder of my duties and my role in their grand plan.

STANDING before the mirror in my chamber, I observed with a frown as my reflection shifted. In an attempt to appease the Moirai, I guarded the human girl, witnessing the intriguing mundane moments of her life that occasionally intrigued me. Her happiness—which irked me—served as a reminder of the life Isabel never got to experience. She didn't need me, and I was relieved to discover that checking in on the human every few years sufficed to keep the Fates' pestering at bay.

EACH TIME I was summoned to my duties, I marveled at how rapidly the human witch grew and transformed while I remained frozen inside my icy fortress. The human world had never captured my interest, but I learned to appreciate the delicate balance of their mortal lives. Glancing at the mirror, I watched the girl by the shore, her mother in the distance. She seemed happy chasing the waves as they brushed the shoreline, and something shifted within me. The corner of my mouth turned up into a smile as I observed the human witch—something I hadn't done in a long time, not since her... since Isabel. The storm resurfaced at the thought. Like the tide, sweeping away any remnants of emotion, reminding me of what the girl before me represented.

"She doesn't deserve to exist. She doesn't deserve to be happy!" I thundered, and the glass fragmented. With a loud crack, it shattered at my feet.

TIME WOVE its intricate tapestry around me once again as I remained frozen. Before I knew it, the Fates returned with merciless intent. I refused to heed their call until I felt compelled to bend to their will. This time, as the waters shifted in the marble basin, I caught a glimpse of a young woman. The human witch had grown, but she looked conflicted, lost, almost a reflection of me, somehow. Something flickered in my frozen heart.

Despite my refusal to follow my predetermined path, I found myself drawn to observe her mundane life, convincing myself she was mere entertainment in my tedious, unchanging existence. However, I slowly sensed my icy walls begin to shake as the young woman stared at herself in the reflection, her emerald eyes reflecting back at me. Haunting me.

This time, I chose to linger, driven by sheer curiosity, watching her as she held Isabel's cup in her hands. Yet, suddenly, the memory became too unbearable. The stark contrast of seeing Isabel's belongings with her made the young woman's existence all the more real. I strolled out of my chambers and joined the Upheryan warriors for training. It proved insufficient to keep the shifting tides at bay. The storm remained contained, but I sensed it simmering beneath the surface.

I resisted the temptation to reopen the link and probe further into the witch's life, but my resolve crumbled after a mere two days. I was back at the marble basin, staring at my reflection, bracing the white stone. She weaved through the carnival lights, and suddenly, I froze. My grip tightened as a man assaulted her, and at that moment, the energies shifted. I prepared to open a rift into the human world when the sight of him made me freeze. I stared in disbelief at her protector—Drake. Freed from his prison, he was in the human world, saving her from the clutches of the monster. Something within me snapped. Jealousy, anger, and chaos unfurled as I watched Isabel's purpose unfold before my eyes. I stared at the one who once called me a friend finally getting the girl, almost as if history was repeating itself.

I wasn't sure how I truly felt. I should have been content knowing that Isabel's sacrifice wasn't in vain, and that he was freed at last, like her visions predicted. Yet, as I watched Drake and the human witch day and night, witnessing their love story unfold. It almost felt like reliving Isabel and him all over again. The girl bore no resemblance to Isabel yet I couldn't shake the sense that something lurked beneath the surface. This time, however, I would not allow myself to fall. I resolved to protect myself. Whatever my duty once was, it was no longer necessary for me to remain to watch over the blood witch. She was happy, now safe with the one she was destined to love. With one last glance at them, I walked from the room, and the water in the basin turned to ice.

DESPITE MY RESOLVE TO free myself from any obligations to the blood witch, I wrestled with myself day and night, resisting the urge to glimpse again into her life. However, I consistently found the strength to calm the storm, and as days and weeks passed, it gradually became easier to ignore the irrational impulses. I dedicated my time to serving the Wind Warriors. I chose to rise to the unfounded accusations of my deceit, which allowed me to form alliances with Dagasti. The despicable man deserved disloyalty and more; he was a cold-hearted monster. While I considered myself coldhearted, Dagasti knew no bounds. I, on the other hand, felt I was somewhat redeemable.

The voices of the Moirai danced in my mind, and my dreams stirred. Glancing around me, I stared at the glowing waters of the pool of life. The human blood-witch floated before me, her golden tresses like a blanket above the water's surface. I reached for her small waist, pulling her to me, but then her blood pooled around us, turning the flowing waters crimson.

I SHOT UP FROM BED, an ache lodged in my chest, a sensation I hadn't felt since Isabel. A distinct pull overwhelmed me—a tug I couldn't quite explain. I needed to know she was okay, and the sensation was all-consuming. Before I knew it, I was gripping the marble basin and watching the water shift. As the image cleared, I stilled, watching the human girl walking through the gates of Druleska, following none other than the conniving, slithering Dagasti. Suddenly, I was moving— unsure of how or why—but I needed to see her. I wanted to confront the one responsible for Isabel's sacrifice, to release this hate, to quench my ire, or at least that's what I told myself. Although all I could think about was taking her as far away from Dagasti as possible. Fighting against my chaos, I felt the strings pulling, calling me to Druleska. Wondering... Where the hell was Drake?

I pushed away from the basin, and the images faded. I could no longer see her, which meant I could think clearly. It would be irrational for me to show up in Druleska now, though I could conjure a myriad of excuses to visit Dagasti. I could pretend to carry information from the borders, I thought, but the rational side of me cautioned against it. Strolling through the castle halls, the ocean tides shifted while I attempted to quiet my thoughts. However, they often shifted to the human witch. I avoided my chambers for the rest of the afternoon; I would be too tempted to check on her. But as darkness fell around the kingdom, my resolve caved. The waters in the basin shifted, and her reflection was as clear as day. She stood close to the water. I watched the elegant lines of her slender neck and her beautiful blue dress. Her emerald eyes hit me with an intensity I had never felt.

"Beautiful." The words left my lips, and I was unable to stop them. She whirled, shifting her gaze to the water, and it felt as if she stared back at me.

"Hello... is someone there?" Her voice was alike to the soft chime of bells, and for a moment, I held my breath. Could she hear me? The exchange was possible, but I had been careful not to open the connection. Was it possible she could somehow sense me? Intrigued, I watched as she glanced around, a frown etched on her face. Then, she collected her dress and ran.

I dipped my fingers in the water in the basin, and her image dissipated. I sighed, running my hands across my face to clear my muddled thoughts. What the hell was wrong with me?

I discarded my shirt at the foot of the bed and removed my shoes before lying down. I ignored the strange sensation in my chest, which felt like a taut string. I glanced at the marble basin for what felt like the millionth time in the past hour. I brought my legs over the bed's edge and strode to it, reopening the connection. She slept her reflection etched by her chamber mirror and I suppressed the urge to open a portal and breach the distance.

To do what... I did not know. I tried to rekindle my hatred for the human girl, but my feelings were clouded by other emotions. As I watched her shift in her sleep that night, I knew I couldn't stay away. I had to cross this breach and face her. Perhaps it was the only way to find closure.

"Sweet dreams," I found myself whispering, before the water on the basin crystallized.

The Dravonis guards welcomed me as I stepped through the portal.

"I'm here to see your King?" The words sounded bitter on my tongue, for he was no true King. Not in the eyes of his people, nor the rest of the Realms. Nor in mine. But I bid my time and played my part.

"I didn't expect to see you back so soon." Dagasti greeted me, his approach one of surprise and irritation. He stepped into the dining hall, where I awaited him.

"Good morning to you, too," I replied, merely to irk the man. His brows shifted, and I contained my smile.

"You have news from the borders?" He cut straight through business, disregarding the burly maid as she rested the plate of food before him.

"Is there anything else I can get you, Master?" she asked, but he ignored her, waving his hand in a petulant dismissal. Gods, how I longed to punch him in the face.

I offered the monster insight into the troops of the Borean

Clan. I offered what he needed to hear, but only what the warriors were happy with him knowing.

"And how do I know I can trust you?" asked Dagasti. I stared at him as he chewed on his dried meat like a savage.

"You don't. But you've done so in the past. Is there a reason why you should stop now?" I asked. He mulled over my words while the string tugging on my chest tightened, followed by a soft knock on the door. It was her.

The human. The blood witch. The vessel for Isabel's soul...

"Come in." Dagasti's voice resonated, and I collected myself. The second the door shifted, and her bright face appeared at the threshold, it felt like my heart was ripped from my chest and squeezed by an invisible force. Her purple dress bundled around her, but I couldn't peel my eyes from her face.

"Good morning. I apologize for the intrusion. I didn't see Drake this morning and thought he might be with you," she said, frozen at the door. Her gaze shifted to Dagasti, then briefly to me. When her brows creased with curiosity, I allowed my prying mind access into her thoughts. Her mind was loud and her thoughts were wild. She was scared, hesitant, curious.

"You're awfully attached to him, aren't you?" Dagasti asked, and once again, I fought the desire to seize him by the neck.

The girl had spirit. I detected anger simmering in her thoughts, though she wisely kept silent in the presence of the monster.

"I believe he went off early this morning. Why don't you join us? Have some breakfast." Dagasti offered, but I knew him enough to detect his sinister intentions. I shifted my gaze to the table and read the hesitation on her mind, but none-theless, she accepted. My skin prickled the moment she neared me, circling the table. When she pulled the chair to my right, I stood on reflex, and she locked eyes with me. Her gaze was accusatory, but I struggled to reign in the storm.

"You're not staying?" asked Dagasti, and I shook my head curtly.

"I'd rather not," I responded tersely, trying to understand my irrational response to the girl. I stared back at her, grappling with conflicting emotions—resentment, frustration. Her gaze shifted over me, and then her eyes brightened. I wasn't sure if the glossiness were tears, but then a flush reached her cheeks as she jutted out her chin defiantly.

"Actually, if you'll excuse me, I seem to have lost my appetite." She stood abruptly. Before I could react, she stormed past me, and a fleeting thought crossed my mind to follow, apologize, and explain. However, I remained rooted before the table while Dagasti stared after her.

"I thought you were leaving." Dagasti's voice snapped me back to the room. Grateful for the distraction, I strolled toward the door, offering the monster a cold smile.

"If you don't mind, I'll stay for the night." Dagasti's gaze left his plate of food and focused on me. Despite his well-constructed mental walls, I sensed his indecision. "It's getting quite tedious down under," I added with a suggestive wink. I hoped he believed my interests were solely to satisfy my carnal desires with the fiery women of his realm. Though, I had enjoyed doing just that during my other visits. However, this time felt different.

"Very well." He waved his hand dismissively, forgetting I

was his equal. I wasn't interested in lingering, so with an appreciative bow, I removed myself from the dining hall and from the monster's presence.

THE BUSTLING SOUNDS of Druleska assaulted my senses, a sharp contrast to the serene quietude of Serfier. Typically, I limited my awareness when in the fire Realm, but today was an exception. I strained to catch the faintest traces of the human witch's voice, and the moment I heard her voice mingled with Drake's, I recoiled. I couldn't listen any further. A sudden wave of disgust seized me, though it was mostly directed at myself —at my own weakness for lingering here. I stared around the room I normally occupied and shook my head. I had to leave.

I left the guest chambers, and the second I reached the open landing atop the winding stairs, I frowned, watching Drake and her emerge from the small room beneath the staircase. I wanted to turn, but I fought the impulse. They had taken everything from me already and only ice remained. With that thought, I donned the mask of coldness and chaos as I descended the stairs.

"If it isn't the prince of the Fire Realm himself." My voice resonated through the grand hall, and both their eyes shifted to me at once. I spared Drake a quick glance and the second his eyes narrowed, I allowed my smile to broaden before shifting my focus to the girl by his side. My gaze traveled the length of her body, and as expected, his hand tightened around hers. He hadn't changed much—just as possessive as I remembered.

"What are you doing here?" he asked, devoid of all pleasantries. I sensed the witch's curious gaze as she studied me.

"What happened to the realms being at war?" asked Drake, walking closer to meet me at the bottom of the steps.

"Dagasti and I have come to some agreements. But I won't bore you with the details. I see you're busy," I offered, willing my eyes to linger on the girl's blushing cheeks. Drake's gaze pinned me.

"Don't let me keep you then," he said curtly. I smiled; I had finally gotten under his skin after so long. As I walked away, I felt their eyes boring into me.

"Who was that?" Her quiet voice reached my trained ears, and I smiled to myself. Indeed, she was a curious one.

"No one you want to know," Drake interjected with a tone harsher than necessary.

"Where are you going? I thought you said we'd go for a walk?"

I paused outside the castle doors, listening in.

"Belynda, I must speak with my uncle. The walk can wait." His thoughts were elusive, but hers became clearer the longer I listened. She was displeased with him for abandoning her after promising a tour of the city. I smiled at the thought. Shaking my head to dispel whatever enchantment she had cast upon me, I walked out of the castle gates.

As was my habit, I kept a watchful eye on Kylram from a distance. After what Dagasti had done, her safety relied on the belief that she had perished at the King's side. While I owed nothing to Drake, the rumors of Upherya's responsibility for the King's death troubled me. The Wind warriors had advocated for peace, and Drake's father had done the same. Heartbroken yet relieved to learn the Queen was alive, I considered offering her asylum in Serfier. However, my loyalty to my kingdom took precedence, and I couldn't risk bringing war to my people. For now, she was safe, and that's what mattered. With Drake's return, I knew it was only a matter of time before she sought him out, yet the implications of Drake reclaiming his father's throne unsettled me. Going against Dagasti could jeopardize the human witch's safety.

Navigating through the bustling market, I welcomed the slow drizzle of rain against my skin. A peculiar sensation tugged at me before I spotted the human. Without seeing beneath the hood of her cape, I knew it was her. She rushed through the crowd, seeking refuge from the rain. A smile played on my lips, but terror gripped me as her boot caught on the cape, propelling her toward a moving cart. I instantly reacted. Opening a water portal, I jumped through it to stand before her, pulling her into my arms and away from danger. I held my breath, clutching her close, and as her scent enveloped me, I closed my eyes. Relief washed over me.

I could breathe. She rested her hands on my shoulders briefly for support, and as the human regained her composure, she stepped back, lowering her hood.

Surprise flickered in her emerald eyes. She was close—too close. She withdrew from my hold, though my hands were still secured on her waist. Her gaze averted from mine. She wanted to run away, but I couldn't let her go... not yet.

"What? No, thank you?"

I remarked, hoping to sound casual. Her expression shifted between one of surprise and annoyance.

"I was perfectly fine. You didn't have to bother. Good day."

She shielded her face from the rain again and practically ran down the alley. I smiled, choosing to follow from a close distance. After a few turns, she stopped abruptly and spun to me.

"Stop following me!"

I grinned at her, amused by her unfounded anger. I had just saved her. I should have walked away—in fact, I should be leaving now—but I found myself transfixed by the green of her eyes.

"What makes you think I'm following you? Perhaps you're in my way," I teased, knowing it would only fuel her irritation. She sneered and stomped off in the opposite direction. I couldn't remember the last time I laughed, but I chuckled as I watched her. To my relief or horror, my laughter made her pause.

"I thought you were on your way? Or perhaps you're stalking me."

Her words and her delirious notion made me laugh that much harder, drawing attention from passersby.

"That's an interesting assumption. I'm merely trying to assist someone that is clearly lost." I provoked, and her expression mirrored her thoughts.

She thought I was insane.

"I'm not lost. I'm perfectly capable of finding my way back."

"Are you now... point the way then." I challenged knowing she could but I was enjoying our exchange too much to see it end so soon. While I was pushing her buttons, I was pleased to learn she wouldn't back down from a challenge. Glancing around the market, I didn't miss the small frown on her face, which shifted into a smile as she spotted the peak of a tower in the distance. She pointed to it.

My laughter filled the silence, and the sound felt foreign, even to me.

"Let me guess. The tower gave it away?" I mocked, and she crossed my arms.

"You are no gentleman, sir."

I smiled. She was furious now, but perhaps I should dispel any notions she might have about that right away. I was the farthest thing from a gentleman.

"I never claimed to be," I offered with a chilling coolness, allowing the smile to fade from my lips.

I was frozen then. Crystalized in the moment as her pale face regarded me, studying me with her emerald eyes. Her thoughts reached me like a jolt of thunder, fragmenting the cold vestiges of my frozen heart. I felt her desire to reach and touch my face, and I felt my heart melt. At that instant, I knew.

I couldn't stay away.

"You shouldn't be out alone. You're not safe, and he is too trusting," I warned, feeling the need to caution her—against Dagasti, perhaps even myself.

The girl blinked as if pulled from a precipice. She stepped away from me.

"From you. I'm not safe from you!" she whispered, and I couldn't bring myself to deny her words.

Not long ago, I had cursed and churned her existence. Yes, she was smart enough to consider me a villain. The corner of my mouth shifted, and the mask fell into place as I watched her thoughts shifting like a storm—amusingly finding me annoying yet good-looking. The fact that she did stirred something in me.

"I could be dangerous to you, but I think you're safe today," I conceded. Before she asked more questions, I turned and walked away, sensing her gaze burning into my back. Tempted to glance at her one more time, I paused and turned.

"Oh, you were right... just follow the tower." I called out with a wink. Then I disappeared through the market.

I sensed her questions, her curiosity, while my own curiosity intensified. I didn't want to care. I didn't want to stay, but the further my steps took me from her, the tighter the strings pulled, and it was as if I couldn't breathe.

I paused at the edge of the city before the water portal that would take me back to Serfier. I stepped closer to the water and halted. I knew the dangers I was in if I stayed here. But I couldn't walk away.

"You never make anything easy, do you?" I cursed the Fates for their ill plans and allowed the water portal to dissipate behind me. I knew what returning to Druleska's castle would offer me—pain and nothing else. Though despite that sinking realization, I found it impossible to leave. To walk away from her.

Acknowledgments

I would like to extend my deepest gratitude to those whose support, encouragement, and contributions have been invaluable in the creation of this book:

To my husband and children, your unwavering support and understanding throughout this journey have been my rock. Thank you for being my pillar of strength.

I am profoundly grateful to my best friend. His insights and encouragement have been instrumental in shaping my perspective and refining my work.

A heartfelt thank you to those who have taken the time to read my work. Your input has enriched this story beyond measure.

A special thanks to my wonderful editor, Eden, whose expertise and guidance have played a crucial role in shaping and refining this manuscript. To my book cover design team, thank you for your talented creativity and for turning my vision into reality.

Last but not least, to the readers who have been with me from the beginning and to those who will embark on this journey – your curiosity and engagement with this story have brought it to life. Thank you for investing your time in these pages.

Morgan Vela

ABOUT THE AUTHOR

Morgan Vela is a debut author of romantic fantasy novels. Her stories join with shifters, witches, and dragons and explore other realms—while magic fills the pages of her stories, romance guides her imagination.

I have made up stories in my head for as long as I can remember—I have seen dragons and magic-filled worlds since I was young. I have traveled long and far and lived many lives through the pages of books I've read. This freedom of believing in the impossible, even briefly, made me want to share my stories. And so, my journey began as a writer.

My debut novel 'Vanished' is in paperback at Barnes & Noble and Amazon. It is also available as an eBook through Kindle Unlimited. 'Vanished A Guardian Story' is Book One of the Vanished Series. 'Throne of Fire' is the sequel, followed by 'Tides of Destiny,' book three in the series. The fourth book and last of the series, 'Shadows and Light,' is projected to be released summer of 2024.

ALSO BY MORGAN VELA

VANISHED SERIES

A Guardian Story

Throne of Fire

Tides of Destiny

Shadows and Light (Coming Summer 2024)

Book Two
VANISHED
THRONE OF FIRE
MORGAN VELA

Book Three
VANISHED
TIDES OF DESTINY
MORGAN VELA

STAY CONNECTED

Morgan Vela Author

www.morganvelaauthor.com